IRISH HEARTS

JOSIE RIVIERA

5 STAR READER REVIEWS

Oh Danny Boy

"Oh Danny Boy is a book full of emotion and very well written. J. Riviera takes us to Ireland and creates quite a believable setting with her descriptions and voice. I visited Ireland two years ago and enjoyed this armchair trip again. I could hear the Irish locals in their own towns.The story is sweet and touching, with Clara trying to save her brother rand keep a family life. Danny is a great hero, strong and tender, who will sweep you off your feet. A recommended read." -Amazon Reviewer

Maeve

"Impossible to put down. Maeve is the perfect Irish working girl. When she accepts a week's vacation at a perfect island resort, she really isn't expecting to meet the man of her dreams. Her match, Edward, is a wealthy businessman, who is used to the finer things. He looks at this vacation as a working one with maybe a pleasant companion. Then he meets Maeve & the sparks eventually fly. Terrific read!" - Amazon Reviewer

1-800-IRELAND

"I loved, loved this story. It is the third in the Flipping for You series on flipping houses and buildings and finding romance at the same time.

I think 1-800-Ireland is my favorite in this series so far, as it has characters from Oh Danny Boy another book by Josie Riviera and one of my absolute favorites of her stories and characters from the first two books in the Flipping for You series.

Get this book and your favorite beverage and sit in your favorite reading place and read this book that hooks you from beginning to end and you won't be able to put it down." - Amazon Reviewer

A Chocolate-Box Irish Wedding

"This beautifully written romance whisks the reader off to the Irish town of Wexford. High school sweethearts who had gone off to pursue their individual dreams after graduation are there to attend the wedding of her mother to his father. She is divorced and he has never married.

Is there any chance that the old spark between them can be rekindled or will the physical distance between them keep them apart despite their obvious attraction to each other? While Kiera has returned to live in Wexford, Colum teaches dance in another city.

I loved learning about some of the Irish traditions which Josie Riviera intricately weaves into this story.

This novella can easily be read in one sitting, but once again the author has found a way to make the major characters come alive within the limited number of pages.

Remember to check out the included recipe for Irish Soda Bread." - Amazon Reviewer

PRAISE AND AWARDS

USA TODAY bestselling author

Irish Hearts:

#15 Amazon Bestseller Short Story Anthologies
#15 Amazon Bestseller Women's Short Stories
#3 Amazon Bestseller British Literature

INTRODUCTION

To keep up on newly released ebooks, paperbacks, Large Print Paperbacks, audiobooks, as well as exclusive sales, sign up for Josie's Newsletter today.

As a thank you, I'll send you a Free PDF ... The Beauty Of ...

Josie's Newsletter

Did you know that according to a Yale University study, people who read books live longer?

DEAR FRIENDS

Dear Friends,

A heartwarming story is the hallmark of every romance. Savor the magic with three, sweet contemporary Irish romances, plus a bonus romance!

Irish Hearts

Cozy up with your choice beverage, and lose yourself in these joyful romances featuring Irish heroes and heroines.

<u>OH DANNY BOY</u>

A reader favorite! This pot of gold could hold more than they bargained for...

<u>MAEVE</u>

He's all business. She loves to laugh. When business conflicts with pleasure, what could possibly go wrong?

<u>1-800-IRELAND</u>

A strong minded Irishwoman pursuing her dream. A disillusioned businessman ready to retire. Can two determined people separated by years find true love at the end of a rainbow?

A Chocolate-Box Irish Wedding (Bonus Romance)

A woman who wanted more. A man who wanted her. Can they rediscover their love in the seaside town where it all began?

Josie Riviera

Oh Danny Boy

This book is dedicated to all my wonderful readers who have supported me every inch of the way.

THANK YOU!

PRAISE AND AWARDS

USA TODAY bestselling author

Oh Danny Boy is an Amazon Bestseller

#1 Amazon Bestseller in Contemporary British and Irish Literature
#9 Amazon Bestseller in Cultural Heritage Fiction
#2 Amazon Bestseller in Historical Irish Fiction
#7 Amazon Bestseller Women's Fiction

1

———

"Seamus, don't jump!" Clara Donovan heard her own cries, the shouts resounding through the misty night air. She raced across the sidewalk toward Farthing Bridge, her gaze riveted on a horror she didn't want to believe. Her older brother Seamus sat on the edge of a tall bridge with his head slumped in his hands, a bottle of whiskey beside him. The arched stone bridge spanned the River Farthing, connecting the town to a once-popular marketplace.

No. It couldn't be. Her breath burned in her chest as she took in gulps of dampness and drizzle. *Don't stop. Run faster.*

When she reached the bridge, she elbowed through a group of late-night revelers. Several pointed up at Seamus. "He's off the rails!" someone shouted.

Her brother seemed unaware of the gathering crowd. He swung his legs back and forth like an underwound metronome and stared into the ice-cold river below.

She shook off the image of him on her living room floor several days earlier. He'd been passed out drunk. Should she have phoned a treatment center? No. She could fix her brother's problems. He simply needed encouragement, surrounded by his loving, supportive family.

Seamus. Gentle Seamus. Kind and fiery-haired, quick to temper, quicker to make amends. Her heart squeezed at the scruffy, dejected man he'd become since his wife had died.

Clara put her hands on her knees and took in calm, even breaths. Quickly, she assessed the corroded pedestrian catwalk leading to the top of the bridge, the skull and crossbones sign that warned *Danger*.

She stared upward at her sweet brother. "Dear saints in heaven, Seamus," she whispered. "You promised me that you'd never drink again."

She stuffed her wool gloves into her jacket pockets and bent to lace her weatherproof boots tighter. There was no time to dash around the river to the street that crossed the bridge, and she certainly wouldn't ask anyone in the crowd to lend a hand.

She yanked off the "Danger" sign and threw it to the ground. That pressing feeling in her chest, like she was running out of air, slowed her movements. Dragging in another breath, she grasped the slippery wet handrails and stepped onto the bottom rung of the catwalk.

"Missus, are you trained for this?" a man from the crowd inquired.

She glanced around. The man stood a hairsbreadth away. He was tall with piercing blue eyes and carried a guitar case. His dark brown hair had a reddish tinge and his navy wool jacket strained against his athletic form.

"Thanks. I can manage on my own."

Despite her refusal, she hesitated. Was she trained to climb to the top of a rusted bridge when she was crippled with fear and could hardly breathe? Umm, no. But she was desperate, and desperation made people do things they thought they could never do.

"I insist." The man set his guitar case on the grass and stepped forward. "Who's sitting on the top of the bridge?"

"My brother!"

"I'll follow behind you. No worries."

No worries. Dear saints in heaven, her brother was about to jump off a bridge.

She gripped the slick railings with both hands and began climbing, acutely aware of the guitar player's encouraging whispers behind her. She counted each step until she reached the top, scrambled to her feet, and raced to her brother. Seamus's chin was hunkered in his hands, the empty whiskey bottle beside him.

She stopped a foot away from him. "Seamus, come with me."

His legs stopped swinging. He turned to her, his metallic-grey eyes glazed with drink. "What're you doing here?"

"I'm looking out for you, same as always." She attempted to keep her tone light. "The weather's a wee bit fierce up here. The wind and rain are driving my hair sideways."

Inwardly, she shuddered. He was a sight wearing tattered clothes, his flaming red hair caught in a ponytail.

"And who's that dodgy bloke behind you?"

"Someone who's offered to help." She struggled to control her trembling. Her brother's big-boned body was precariously close to the edge.

Seamus's mouth twisted. "It's better if I end my life. I'm on me tod, I'm all alone."

She extended a hand. "You're not alone. I'm here for you."

Despite the chilly night air, Seamus was sweating. "I long for my wife. My beautiful woman ..."

"We all miss Fiona very much."

Seamus's fingers found the empty whiskey bottle and flung it into the river. "I'm warning you. Leave me alone or I'll jump." Slowly, he stretched out his hands.

"Seamus!" Clara hunched over, sick to her stomach, listening to the hoots and jeers of the spectators.

"Shut your gob!" Seamus hollered to the crowd. "Are ya' thick?"

Clara caught her breath. Stay calm. Level-headed and composed.

She straightened. "Those people won't help you, but I will."

What was she supposed to do now? Move slower, speak gentler? On watery knees, she started forward.

"You're managing perfectly," came the whisper behind her.

The guitarist. She'd almost forgotten. His breath was warm and reassuring against her hair.

She extended her hand again. "Please, Seamus, please. Come with me."

Seamus openly sobbed. "I'm no use to anyone."

"Think of Anna and me. We're your sisters and we love you." Clara tried to smile. "What would I do with myself if you weren't sleeping on my couch every night? You know I don't like to be alone."

Seamus squinted at her. Using his worn shirtsleeve, he wiped at the tear-stained bags under his eyes. "I lost all my money on the horse races. Five hundred euros that I'd borrowed from a friend, and one hundred euros of Anna's money, too. The bookies were certain Green Dragon would win the second race, but the ponies double-crossed me."

Clara dug her nails into her palms. "We'll pay the bookies all the money you lost." How, she had no idea. Her income as a factory worker and part-time dance teacher was scarcely enough to pay their current living expenses.

In the distance, insistent sirens blared, angry red lights flashed.

"Keep talking," the guitar player told her.

What to say? The wrong words might send her impulsive brother over the edge. She chanced a peek at the guitarist and lost her footing. Gasping, she held in a scream.

His arms went around her. "I've got you," he said softly.

She steadied herself and shook off his hold. Without making a sound, she ventured another two steps until she stood behind her brother. "We'll return to my flat and I'll light a fire in the hearth. Won't that be grand?" She heard her voice shake, the rale insistent.

"And make me a cuppa tea?" Seamus's copper-red beard showed days of neglect and grew in dirty spikes below his chin.

She placed her hands firmly on his shoulders and gave a reassuring squeeze. "I'll brew the entire pot and fry a proper Irish breakfast in the morning."

Several beats passed. Seamus seemed to be trying desperately to concentrate. He looked up at her. "You don't cook."

"I can manage fried eggs and bacon rashers."

He relaxed beneath her hands.

She licked her lips, her mouth so dry. "Please come home. Please. We're a family. We'll work this out together like we always do."

Seamus rubbed at his eyes, sniffled, and started to stand.

The guitarist stepped around Clara. Carefully, he assisted the wobbling Seamus to his feet.

The crowd applauded. They'd observed every detail of her family's private business. Clara pressed her lips tightly together, willing herself to think of her brother and nothing else.

Her sobbing brother slumped into her arms. She hugged him for a long time, then roughly shook his shoulders and stared into his bleary eyes. "I understand you're in a lot of pain. You'll be independent again, you'll see. It took me a long time, remember? And now I'm fine."

"Yeh." Seamus's lopsided grin showed missing teeth. He nodded so quickly that he stumbled, so unexpected they both cried out. She clung to his beefy hand, his body still so close to the edge of the bridge, as she stared into the frigid waters of the River Farthing far below.

"You'll both be safer away from the bridge." The guitarist's voice came loud and urgent. He guided Clara and Seamus to the side of the road, removed his jacket and placed it on the damp grass.

"Who are you, bloke?" Seamus asked.

"Danny Brady." He wheeled, clear in his intent to walk away.

"What about your jacket?" Clara called out.

Danny half turned and looked upward. The clouds had parted, the sky bathed in moonlight and stars. "No rain and no worries. Keep the jacket."

An emergency vehicle swerved onto the bridge, and Clara squinted into the blinding headlights. Several paramedics sprinted toward her and Seamus. A Channel Four television news van streaked past, reversed, and screeched to a stop. A woman reporter and cameraman leapt from the van and scurried to the guitarist.

Clara recognized the reporter, Maeve Flanagan, an anchorwoman for the local television station. Maeve clutched the microphone, speaking urgently, then held the microphone out for Danny. He spoke lengthily, the bright camera light illuminating his china-blue eyes.

"Where are you from, Brady?" her brother shouted from across the road.

Danny's handsome face showed signs of fatigue. "Dublin." He focused on Clara. "Do you have a name, missus?"

"Clara Donovan." She nodded at her brother. "And this very foolish man is my brother Seamus."

From across the road, the reporter shouted, "May I quote you, Ms. Donovan?"

Clara stretched out a tired arm. "Absolutely not! And please take your slanderous reporting elsewhere!"

Maeve muffled the mouthpiece with her palm. In a loud voice, she asked, "Do I have permission to make a plea to the community on your behalf, Ms. Donovan? There are resources available for poor—"

Clara cut Maeve off with a wave. Heat flushed through her body. "My family fends for themselves, Miss Flanagan! If you want to do something for us, then stay away!"

2

D anny watched as Clara Donovan poured boiling water into a bone-white teapot with shamrocks painted on the sides, moving easily in her tiny kitchen.

He'd rung the Gardaí, the police, as soon as he'd spotted the desperate, drunken man on the bridge. They'd arrived, along with the paramedics, a few minutes afterward, though fortunately they hadn't been needed.

Danny had gone for a short walk along the river's edge to clear his mind from the numerous business decisions plaguing him. His coffee shop's grand opening had brought him to the town of Farthing for a fortnight. He hadn't known the town existed until his planning board had scouted the area and discovered a fresh, natural spring located nearby, ideal because the water was clear and pure for brewing coffee.

When he'd volunteered to help her, Clara Donovan's dark, shining eyes had reflected panic and fear, despite her protests. So, he'd climbed the catwalk behind her, intending to leave as soon as he was certain that she and her brother were safe. Then he'd reversed, reconsidering, rationalizing that he shouldn't leave a helpless woman with a drunken brother at the top of a bridge until help had arrived. He'd pushed off the insistent reminder that he'd vowed never to get involved in other people's problems. He'd only been mindful of the desperate scene playing out before him.

After the Gardaí had filed a report and the paramedics had left, Danny offered to drive Clara and Seamus home. At first she refused, telling him she lived only a few blocks away.

He offered a second time. Surely, Clara and her brother were in no condition to walk any distance, he said. In a gesture of friendliness, or perhaps to thank him, she agreed by inviting him to her flat for tea and scones.

Despite the late hour and tomorrow's long work day, he accepted. After he'd assisted her brother into the backseat of his Mercedes, Clara slid onto the front passenger seat.

She raised a brow. "Quite a posh car. You fancy the metallic silver?"

He wrapped a hand around the steering wheel and started the engine. "I've worked hard for this car," was all he said.

When they arrived at her flat, he supported a tottering Seamus through the downstairs foyer and up the stairs, then persuaded Seamus to drink a glass of water and down some Ibuprofen. After that, he assisted Seamus to the bathroom and then helped Clara guide her brother to the living room couch, where Seamus immediately fell into a deep yet fitful sleep. Apparently, that cuppa tea for Seamus would have to wait until morning, Danny thought with a grin.

Danny had set his guitar in her foyer and removed his damp, grass-stained jacket, insisting he build a fire in the hearth while Clara changed out of her wet clothes.

"Would you put the kettle on when you're done lighting the fire?" she called from the bedroom. "We can keep an eye on my brother from the kitchen."

"Aye." Danny shoveled coal into the fireplace, added a fire lighter and kindling in the middle of the grate, then turf. He waited for the smoky fire to clear, then strode to the bathroom and worked the soap in his hands up to his wrists, rinsing until the black sooty dust was gone.

As he made his way into Clara's kitchen, a lemony scent wafted through the air, a mixture of sweet and tart, and he sniffed appreciatively. Her faux marble countertops and stainless-steel sink and appliances sparkled, the forest-green vinyl swept clean as the finest hotel. The kitchen walls had been painted a luminous green hue, her cabinets a cozy charcoal. Several lush potted ferns added freshness and lightness, giving the intimate space a snug, appealing appearance.

He filled the kettle with water, placed it on the stove to boil, and strode to the window. Why, he wondered, was the window dead bolted shut? The neighborhood seemed a bit run-down, although safe enough, illuminated by a lamppost on the street corner and with a stone wall beyond.

Clara padded into the kitchen wearing thick socks, black leggings, and a clingy long-sleeved T-shirt that accentuated her slender, graceful figure. Danny shifted from the window to watch her. She was a fetching contrast between vulnerability and self-determination.

"Your flat is charming," he said. "Did you decorate it yourself?"

"Yeh, and thanks. I enjoy decorating and painting on a budget. One of my favorite colors is green."

"Duly noted." He grinned. "The color of our emerald isle."

"Green is relaxing and reminds me of nature." She went to her cupboard and brought out cups and saucers. "Thank you. You've done so much for me and my brother tonight."

"No bother." He basked in the respect lighting her chocolate-brown eyes. She'd banded her thick hair back, emphasizing her high cheekbones. Despite her olive complexion, she was still pale, still looked shaken.

"Can I assist?" he asked.

"With setting the table? No bother. I'm extremely self-sufficient." She gestured to a pair of stools. "Brewing tea is my specialty, as it is for most anyone who's lived in Ireland long enough."

"Aye." He perched on one of the stools. "However, coffee is my specialty."

She pulled some napkins from a cupboard drawer. "So you're from Dublin?"

"Aye."

"A Dubliner who drives a fancy car. You're posher by the minute."

He didn't reply.

Now she carried the white teapot to the kitchen table, setting it among gleaming porcelain cups, a sugar and creamer, and the napkins. She set the scones near the butter and raspberry jam, the teapot on a trivet.

"Coffee's too bitter for my taste," she continued.

Not my coffee. My coffee is the best in all Ireland, soon to be the most successful coffee chain in the world.

He answered her smile with one of his own and zeroed in on the scones. "I thought you didn't cook?"

"I bake." She pointed to a garden stool in the corner, piled neatly with bakery cookbooks. She plated a scone and handed it to him. "They're better with butter and jam."

"Plain is best. Then I can taste all the ingredients." He

sampled a bite, the biscuit soft and chewy. He detected a citrus zest, which explained the lemon scent wafting from her kitchen, the same subtle fragrance he'd sniffed on her hair when he climbed behind her on the catwalk.

"Your scone is delicious. Do you use a special recipe from one of your recipe books?" he asked between bites.

He could sell lemon scones in his coffee shop for three euros and make a small profit on each. A quality product sold at a fair price was one of the reasons his coffee shops were so successful.

"No special ingredients—only what's on hand in the kitchen." Her dark-lashed gaze was clear and warm, her cheeks slowly regaining a flush of color.

He set the scone on his plate, his gaze staying on hers. "You're a very brave woman, Clara Donovan."

"For baking scones?"

He smiled. "For climbing to the top of a precariously high bridge to rescue your brother."

She was silent for a moment. "I've become an expert at dealing with disastrous situations."

"You were rushing up the most dangerous flight of stairs I've ever seen."

"Seamus rambled on and on about jumping off that same bridge several weeks ago, and I'd calmed him down. He'd seemed to listen to reason and promised me he'd never think those scary thoughts again. I was frantic when I saw him tonight." She gave a regretful shake of her head. "I should've arrived home earlier. I work on the edge of town, and one of the trains broke down."

"Don't blame yourself for what happened tonight."

"My brother is my responsibility." Her composure seemed to slip a notch. "When I didn't see him in my flat when I got home, I phoned all our friends. Then I prayed that my worst fears ... He'd promised to stay away from those awful gambling places." She wiped quickly at her eyes and focused on a snoring and twitching Seamus. "My dear brother has always loved his whiskey."

"You can't keep a grown man under surveillance twenty-four hours a day," Danny countered. "Though his promises will sound sincere, don't believe him. Assume every word coming out of his mouth is a lie."

Danny had garnered that wisdom from hard-earned experience. No one this side of Scotland had made more excuses and promises to quit the drink than his parents had before they'd committed suicide.

"Harsh advice, Mr. Brady." She added quickly, "My brother is a good man."

"Danny," he corrected. "And don't offer excuses because you'll hurt his chances to get better. A suicide attempt is a serious cry for help, and he should be admitted to a licensed rehab center."

"I'll not commit him to an institution where he'll be alone, doctors evaluating him and filling his veins with drugs so his brain's in a fog. You don't know what Seamus has done for me."

Danny held up a hand. "You're doing him no favors. You only enable when you coddle him."

"Once he's sober, I'll have a serious chat with him again." She sighed, and a slight wheeze sounded. She clasped her hands around the teapot. Danny studied her lovely, expressive face, her valiant attempt to keep her features composed.

"Are you all right?"

Her chin lifted. "Yeh, of course." She tucked an errant strand of hair behind her ear, the blonde ends falling to her shoulders. She poured the tea through a strainer into his teacup. "How do you take your tea?"

"With cream." He poured cream into his cup and stirred. "I'll be in town for a fortnight. I'll give you my business card before I leave. If you need anything—"

"I won't. Thanks."

He sat back, admiring her heart-shaped face. "I've always had a thing for beautiful Irish damsels in distress."

Her grin was dubious. "I'm not Irish. And if I'm ever in distress, I can fend for myself."

She'd needed help tonight, although he didn't think it wise to remind her.

"With a name like Clara Donovan and your Irish brogue, I assumed—"

"I was adopted by my Irish parents. I was born in Italy and lived there with my birth parents, then in an orphanage after they died." She chewed her bottom lip, suddenly quiet, and flicked imaginary crumbs from the table onto her empty plate. She seemed to be silently chastising herself for telling him too much.

He stared into his cup. He wouldn't pry. He'd built a home in Howth, far enough removed from Dublin's city centre to get away from family addictions and heartbreaking memories. He didn't want any additional secrets to carry around, not regarding adoptions, nor alcoholics, nor compulsive gamblers.

Suicide pacts and a dead sister were enough burdens for one lifetime.

He just paid the bills for the evergreen, shrubs, and red and white begonias placed at their graves every morning.

He sipped his tea, grimaced because it was still too hot. He emptied a good deal more cream into his cup and gazed out the kitchen window. A cloudburst had forced the moon and starlight aside, covering the sidewalks in murky, sodden sheets of rain.

Clara's Irish lace window curtains were pristine clean. His filthy, chaotic childhood home had been fraught with ongoing hardships and poverty.

Not anymore, he amended, because wealth kept filth and chaos at arms-length. And coffee had become his pot of gold.

He caught her staring at him and pushed his reflections aside. Grinning, he gestured to the window. "Isn't it lovely weather we're having?"

She poured herself tea, the steam wafting from the pot, casting her face in a rosy veil of heat. "You're not afraid of a few spots of rain, are ya?"

He stretched out his long legs and crossed his arms, enjoying her infectious smile. "At least the rain gets warmer in the summer."

"Yeh." Her smile was stunning, her teeth gleaming white. She tipped her chin toward his guitar case in the hall-way. "You play guitar?"

"Aye. Music is my first love."

"Are you an expert musician?"

"I've played guitar for most of my adult life. I was returning from a gig tonight when I spotted your brother."

"Whereabouts do you play?"

His restive fingers strummed a beat on the table. "A new coffee shop on the other side of Farthing Bridge. Perhaps you've heard about The Ground Café?"

She nodded over the rim of her teacup. "That coffee shop is a very successful chain. I read in the papers that the company's headquarters are in Dublin and the owner is only thirty-five years old. He's opened a shop in Farthing then. My little town must be coming up in the world. That's good, because so many families have moved out, looking for work elsewhere."

"The grand opening is this weekend. The company remodeled the marketplace off Farthing Bridge and added a bookstore and children's playground."

Seamus gave a loud snuffle from the living room. Clara opened her mouth as if she were about to say something, then coughed several times. Her rasp bumped into the tidiness of the kitchen.

Danny reached across the table and took her hand. He studied her face, reddened from coughing. "There's a bad dose of flu going around. Are you sure you're all right?"

She shook off his hand. "I'm grand, thanks."

"Have you been coughing a while?"

She nodded, caught her breath, and took a long sip of tea.

"Do you suffer from asthma?"

She set her cup down and busied her hands with rearranging the sugar and creamer, dabbing a spill of cream off the table with a napkin. "No, and don't be troubling yourself with my ailments. It's late and I'll feel better in the morning."

This was his not-so-subtle cue to leave. "Aye. I'll head on then." He pushed back his stool.

She walked in front of him to the door, both of them silent as they passed her snoring brother.

Danny reached into his pocket and handed her a business card. "I'm at the coffee shop all weekend. I promise good craic, fun, and coffee if you visit."

She arched a slender eyebrow. "Musicians sing in a coffee shop twenty-four hours a day?"

"Usually my gig starts later in the evenings."

"Will you sing to me if I try the coffee?"

"Absolutely. Do you have a song request so I can practice

in advance?" he asked. "How about an Italian song from your heritage?"

"I've lived in Ireland all my life, so any Irish song is dead-on."

"Do you know 'Oh Danny Boy'?"

"Of course." She rubbed at her eyes, smudged with dark circles.

Aye, he was being unfair because she was clearly worn out. Nonetheless, he enjoyed her company. She was unassuming and fearless and down-to-earth.

She began singing softly in a perfectly in-tune soprano voice.

He added his baritone voice. A bit off-key, he acknowledged, blaming it on the late hour.

She regarded the crackling fire burning in the hearth, then gazed at her brother. Tears glittered in her eyes, and she stopped singing.

"There're more verses," Danny prompted.

Her sigh sounded so sad, so poignant. "I don't know what the lyrics mean. However, I'm always moved to tears when I hear 'Oh Danny Boy.'"

"No one knows the true meaning of the words. They seem to signify a loss."

"The loss of a loved one," she finished.

"Aye." And he'd endured enough losses for one lifetime.

He shrugged on his wet jacket, the expensive wool scratching against his neck. With a final "Cheers," he strode out Clara's flat door.

3

———

The following morning dawned with a powder-blue sky, scarcely interrupted by low-hanging clouds. Clara quietly closed her flat door behind her so as not to awaken Seamus. She breathed in, filling her lungs with hope and optimism she couldn't explain. A sunlit breeze carried the promise of spring, and the eighteen-hour winter nights were finally lessening.

Anna, Clara's older sister, pulled up her battered car to Clara's flat.

An hour later, the women deposited their groceries in the boot of Anna's car. They'd both dressed for a shopping day in town. For Clara, that meant dressing in comfortable clothing—a ruffled turquoise blouse with a matching belt, slim ankle jeans, and saddle-brown loafers. Anna preferred to shop in black platform booties, a faded denim blouse, and ripped salmon-colored skinny pants.

Anna zippered her black faux-leather biker jacket and ducked into the driver's seat while Clara slipped into the passenger side. Both women fastened their seat belts.

"Thanks for driving your car today," Clara said. "It's odd that the brakes went on my car with no warning."

"At least you discovered the problem while you were in your driveway and not on the highway." Anna screeched out of the parking lot and made a sharp left, nearly clipping a parked taxi. Clara gripped her seat while the taxi driver sat long and loud on his horn.

"Bunk off!" Anna shouted, then looked at Clara. "I didn't hit him, did I?" Her coal-black penciled eyebrows always seemed lifted in a question, as if she didn't quite believe that a woman as dark-skinned and gorgeous as herself could've landed in Ireland's rainy climate. She was an exotic beauty with flashing amber eyes who had been born in sunny and hot Portugal.

"The taxi driver was waving his hands and swearing, so I'd venture you came close," Clara said. "Since you were forced to enroll in driver education classes after your last accident, you should know there's blind spots you can only see when you turn around."

Anna ran her fingers through her straight black hair, frosted with royal-purple highlights. "I can't because my hair would get mussed."

Clara grinned. "You could've bought an extra can of hair spray if you hadn't spent all your money on Irish cheddar cheese and cream crackers."

"That's all the groceries I can afford. I'd made arrangements to enroll in university this semester before Seamus mooched the little money I'd saved and gambled it away. Another hundred euros that he'll never repay."

"You've been putting off university for years."

Anna pulled into traffic and shrugged. "I'm not smart enough."

"You earned the highest grades in secondary school."

When she was done fixing Seamus, Clara decided, she'd work on Anna's low self-esteem.

Anna sighed. "Seamus's mental condition is more serious than my education. He belongs in The Flyaway Treatment Center."

Sternly, Clara shook her head. "The center relies on donations and we don't have any money. Besides, I know what's best for Seamus."

"Who's with him today while you're out?"

"Liam Lynch."

Anna pumped the gas pedal and merged into the passing lane. "Liam's a bloody bad influence. He used to sit around on his computer all day long. Besides, he steals anything that isn't bolted down."

"Liam's changed. He's working full-time and quit the drink."

"Sometimes you're a bit too optimistic, Clara."

"Life is so full of sadness. I choose to see the good." Clara ran her fingers along the sleeve of her grey jacquard-weave coat. "Liam's living in Donegal now, and he told me he only returns to Farthing from time to time."

"He's full of ..." Anna slapped on the brakes as the traffic light switched to red.

"Didn't you date him for a while?"

"Yeh. He's a good-looking chap, though good looks won't make the kettle boil. Does he still bleach his hair?"

"Bleached and spiked."

Anna adjusted tortoise-framed sunglasses, showing off her perfectly manicured vivid violet fingernails. "I wouldn't be surprised if Liam is off the rails again. Seamus's friends are a bucket of snots who drink and gamble and don't work."

"I was skeptical too, until Liam showed me his pay stubs

to prove he's working. Besides, it's essential to Seamus's well-being that he spends time with his friends because it occupies his mind."

"You're not a social worker."

"I'm his sister and I love him and that's enough." Clara drew in a lungful of air and wheezed, earning her a frown from Anna.

"And then there's Jack Connor," Anna said, "the love of your life, for reasons I could never fathom."

"Jack Connor," Clara repeated, struck by how the mention of his name sent a tremor to her very bones. She resisted the compulsion to glance behind them, forever believing he followed her. He was far away, locked behind bars, she reminded herself. She tried to keep the memories of him at bay, although oftentimes she'd replay the worst memories.

Within a few months of their dating, he'd moved into her flat. Slowly and systematically, he'd rearranged her life, forbidding her from seeing family and friends. She'd quit her shopkeeper's job because Jack had been so jealous of her working outside the home. The isolation had left her depressed and anxious.

Silently, she shook her head. She'd never seen it, the lies, the deception, the control. She'd been spineless and gullible and oh-so-trusting. And irresponsibly dependent.

He'd been an expert at fraud, and she'd been ten times a fool for believing him. Even as she'd endured his physical and mental abuse, he'd also been cheating on her with other women.

She pressed a hand to her throat, recalling Jack's terrible blows. The external bruises had disappeared; the unsettling memories persisted. His final beating had landed her in the hospital and her lungs had never been the same. Fortunately, her condition improved when the weather became warmer.

"Our brother must have professional intervention," Anna was saying, snapping Clara back to the present.

"I know what's best for him," Clara said, and ignored Anna's blatant scowl.

As they passed the River Farthing, Clara scanned the stairs leading to Farthing Bridge. Her heart raced at the chilling recollection of Seamus, his feverish, over-bright eyes staring down into the unforgiving water. Determinedly, she jerked her gaze to the road. "My ex came out from rehab meaner than when he went in."

"Seamus and I warned you a thousand times to leave Jack. He was useless, only fit to find mice at a crossroads. What were you thinking?"

"I was a complete fool." Before she'd finally come to her senses and decided to leave Jack for good, she'd been reduced to going through the motions of life completely numb.

"I hope Jack rots behind those prison bars," Anna said. "Those pale eyes of his and his hulking body always sent me shivering into a near coma. And that awful spider tattoo covering one side of his neck was enough to freeze me in one spot for days."

"He won't be released from prison for several years. And when he is, my restraining order states that he won't be able to come anywhere near me, so I have nothing to fear."

Despite her brave declaration, Clara shivered. While the order guaranteed her safety, she couldn't shake off her uneasy feelings of late, because she swore she'd seen Jack in Farthing only a fortnight ago. She hadn't told anyone, didn't want to set her siblings in a panic. Silly imaginings, she'd told herself, merely old fears conjuring Jack's heavily built image under a flash of moonlight.

"Enough about Jack," Anna said. "Our dear brother is our concern."

"I might be able to get Seamus a job in the factory if RJ Dougal Restaurant Supplies starts hiring," Clara said.

Anna flashed a sardonic grin. "And how will you get him to and from the factory? Drag him when he's hung over and too wrecked to stand? Even if he finds a job, you'll struggle to make ends meet."

"I'm hoping the dance studio will offer me a full-time dance position. I'd like to teach more preschool classes."

"There's not much demand for full-time dance teachers in a depressed town with no jobs."

Perhaps she should try to find a dance teaching job elsewhere, Clara thought. Perhaps Dublin. Mentally, she added the travel time, knowing the public transportation expenses would far outweigh any extra income.

She blew out a sigh. She'd prefer to open her own dancing school. However, she was twenty-nine, with bills and responsibilities, and owning her own business was far beyond her reach. For now, she'd focus on what she did best —getting by on what she earned and taking care of her brother.

Anna flicked on the car's right blinker. "Wanna try the new coffee shop that everyone's talking about? We have a couple hours to spare before Seamus expects you."

Anna didn't wait for a reply. She zipped across the bridge and straight into The Ground Café's busy parking lot. She circled the lot twice, finishing up a string of curses at the lack of spaces before parking on the grass.

Clara adjusted the standup collar of her grey coat as the

women exited the car. "Seamus was still buzzed when he woke at five this morning before dozing off again."

Anna considered that information. "Any thoughts on how he'll survive without you the next few hours?"

Clara managed a smile, although she didn't respond.

They headed for the coffee shop, and Clara felt the hum of excitement before she saw the revitalized marketplace. Three vans with Channel Four News emblazoned on the doors, satellite dishes perched on their roofs, were parked across the street from the coffee shop. While the women took their place at the end of a long queue, Clara admired the spectacular renovations. The old buildings in the shopping plaza had been restored, the round cobblestoned sidewalk fitting together like a giant puzzle. Fresh golden-yellow and orchid flowers adorned the window boxes along a row of upscale boutiques. An art gallery exhibited locally painted Irish landmarks. Nearby, a children's playground painted in bright primary colors featured a wooden fort, pirate ship, and swings. Children played noisily while their parents sat on adjacent park benches and sipped coffee.

The Ground Café's well-known logo of a pot of gold, along with the statement "This coffee house runs on love, life, and laughter," was prominently displayed above the main entrance. The door was partially opened while the unseasonably pleasant weather cooperated. Aromas of freshly brewed coffee, thick cream brownies, and Irish salad wraps enticed customers. Every few seconds, a sharp burst of relaxed hilarity sounded from inside the shop.

As they waited in the queue, Clara opened her purse and withdrew Danny's simple white business card, outlined in gold trim. Embossed in black letters:

Danny Brady

The Ground Café

Beneath was a 1-800 phone number.

Why so fancy? And why wouldn't Danny's personal cell phone number be printed on the card, unless the company moved him from shop to shop? Was he not ambitious enough to become successful on his own, and was dependent on a coffee chain to earn a living? Except that he drove a Mercedes, she considered.

"I met the guitarist who sings here. He said he'd be working this evening," Clara said.

"The guy who helped you with Seamus?"

"Yeh. He suggested I come by tonight." Clara checked her watch and grinned. "We're early."

Anna rooted in her purse for her lipstick and then applied it, a flaming-red shade. "What's his name? Is he good-looking?"

"Danny Brady. He's tall and his hair is dark brown." With a reddish tinge, Clara added to herself as a faint smile touched her mouth. How could she begin to describe his boyish features, the light sprinkle of freckles across the bridge of his nose? Or the way he'd spoken in a quiet, reassuring brogue, reacting promptly and decisively?

Anna fished out her compact and applied coral-colored blush. "Is he single?"

"How would I know?"

"You were with him for several hours. What did you two talk about?"

"We discussed Seamus, and the rain, and ... coffee." *And we sang together.* Clara smiled, remembering Danny's off-key harmony. She shook her head. So much for his musicianship. No wonder he couldn't book his own gig. "He said he'd only be in town a few days."

Anna studied The Ground Café's coffee logo. "Danny

Brady. That name sounds familiar, like I've read it somewhere."

Clara shrugged. "It's a common Irish name."

The name Danny was so masculine, like a strong-shouldered Irish chap who'd grace the cover of any glossy men's fashion magazine. He'd been dressed in a casual black shirt, ripped at the forearms, and wore snug-fitting worn jeans. Laughter had pulled at the corners of his full lips as he'd teased her about the incessant Irish rain. She'd felt her face flush when he'd smiled at her approvingly.

Do you have a song request? His clear blue eyes had reflected both warmth and devilment as he'd asked that.

"Will he recognize you?" Anna was asking.

"He should." Hopefully she wasn't that forgettable. Clara feigned absorption in searching through her purse for lip gloss and didn't meet Anna's gaze.

Clara wouldn't dispute that Danny was good-looking, although there was no room in her life for romance, certainly not with a musician who traveled from town to town. Her abusive ex had cured her of falling for shiftless men who couldn't hold a stable job.

Anna, one hand perched on a curvaceous hip, had decided to flirt with a man ahead of them in the queue. He sported a topknot of wooly grey hair and looked twice Anna's age.

"We'll be inside by noon," the wooly-haired man assured Anna. He went on to talk about the gossip he'd heard about the owner of the chain. "It says in the tabloids that the owner has a lavish estate in every city in Ireland." The man pointed at a candy-blue and yellow motorcycle. "And that's his bodyguard's motorcycle. A real burly fellow, I've heard. And they say the owner's got wealthy women dangling all around him, but he never keeps any one on for long. He gets tired of them fast."

Clara hung back and concealed a yawn behind her hand. Any woman, wealthy or otherwise, who was foolish enough to dangle over a man who was obviously a cold-hearted seducer deserved her deepest sympathy.

As the women neared the entrance, Clara opened her own compact and cast a critical gaze on her reflection. The late-night trauma on the bridge combined with the early-morning tending to Seamus had left shadows beneath her eyes. She adjusted her turquoise headband, securing her hair, dark roots to blonde tips, away from her face, and pinched her cheeks.

"Where does the guitarist live?" Anna transferred her attention from the wooly-haired man to Clara.

"Dublin."

"Does he have a home there?"

Clara bubbled a laugh. "How should I know?"

"You never ask the right questions when you're with men. You could've offered to show him our local pubs while he's here."

"I don't go out much anymore."

"Where's that fun-loving sister I used to know, the woman who fancied a good time? Don't let your ex ruin your future relationships. Remember, he's safely locked behind bars."

4

The tang of fine gourmet coffee permeated every inch of space as the two women stepped through the brick entrance of the coffee shop. Lighting had been softened to a rosy tint, and piped-in Irish folk music, featuring tin whistle and drum, enhanced the welcoming setting.

The Ground Café, crammed with customers, was cleverly named, since the coffee shop was situated on the second floor of an old factory building. The first floor was comfortably furnished with couches, books and magazines, and free Wi-Fi. The women passed reclaimed wooden tables, each featuring a single, fresh pink rose in a glass vase. They rode the escalator, passing large wall murals depicting Ireland's famed castles, craggy coastlines and windswept cliffs.

Anna cocked her head. "Gorgeous, isn't it?"

"I would've liked to see more local artists' paintings featured along these walls," Clara said.

"You always had an eye for decorating." Anna stepped

off the escalator and arrowed straight for the coffee and dessert counter.

A stunning young woman, whose name tag, pinned to her starched cotton blouse, identified her as Kathleen greeted Clara and Anna once they stepped up to the counter. Kathleen's strawberry blonde hair was brushed into a classic top knot, her smoky-black eyes accented by shimmering gold eyeshadow. She wore a pair of black cotton slacks that hugged her rounded hips and long legs.

Behind Kathleen, a long list of beverages, from different-bean coffees, to Americano and cappuccino and lattes, hot or iced, were listed on a cork board. The glass shelves in the display case offered rows of bread and butter puddings and Irish coffee cakes. The cashier at the register poured free samples of the coffee of the day, an Irish latte described as buttery smooth.

"I'd like a tall iced mocha latte and a slice of orange Guinness coffee cake, thanks," Anna said.

Clara scanned the list of teas. "A tall green mint tea, please."

"Hot or iced?" Kathleen asked.

"Iced. And a bowl of fresh fruit."

"You're the thinnest woman in Farthing," Anna teased Clara. "Aren't you ready to relinquish that title and order something fattening like I did?" Anna swept a hand to her hips.

Whereas Anna's midsection remained flat, her hips, to her constant dismay, were full and rounded.

Clara chuckled. "If I ever stopped teaching ballet classes, I'd gain weight as quick as you can say—" She gaped at the tall, attractive man striding directly toward them. "Danny Brady," she finished.

His slightly tanned skin contrasted with his crisp white

shirt and slim-fitting denim jeans. His piercing blue gaze targeted hers.

"Clara Donovan, you're looking brilliant today. If I'd known what time you were coming, I'd have reserved a table for you. Did you wait long?" He grabbed both her hands. His fingers were long, the tips callused.

Her nerves fluttered. Unsettled, she retreated a step. "The queue moved fast."

Slowly, she became aware that customers in the coffee shop were staring, and conversations had been reduced to a whispered hum. Bewildered, she attempted to wrest her hands from his grasp.

He smiled and subtly tightened his hold. "Thank you for accepting my invitation."

That slow and engaging smile. He'd used it the previous evening when he'd mentioned he had a "thing" for Irish damsels in distress.

Anna crossed her arms. "Well, aren't you two the cat's pajamas? Apparently you know each other?"

"Danny is the man on the bridge I was telling you about. He helped me with Seamus."

Clara carefully ignored the gawking, the waitresses who had stopped bussing tables to gape.

"I merely offered my support." His gaze lingered on Clara's face before moving to Anna. "And this lovely woman who looks nothing like you is …?"

"Anna is my older sister who was adopted from Portugal," Clara replied. "Our parents adopted two girls from entirely different countries when Seamus was seven."

"They must've realized that one Seamus was enough for any family." Anna laughed. "He was mad as a ditch even then."

"Mr. Brady." Kathleen focused her beaming smile on him. "Does the counter meet with your approval?"

"Aye, the shop looks grand." Apparently to ensure that Clara's hands were still tucked in his, Danny glanced down.

Somewhere, a spoon clattered to the floor.

In the momentary silence that followed, Kathleen announced that their order was ready. Her eyes narrowed, she bestowed a frosty glance on Clara and then set the beverages, fruit, and coffee cake near the cash register. Danny instructed a waitress to bring their order, along with an assortment of sandwiches and desserts, to the third level.

Clara grinned at him. "I hope you're well-compensated, if you're some sort of manager as well as the guitarist. I've heard the owner of this company is very rich. Tell him to give you a raise."

"I'll pass that along." He seemed impervious to the commotion he was creating. "Let's go to the third floor where it will be quieter."

"We haven't paid," Clara reminded him.

"I'll take care of the bill."

Anna's eyebrows rose. "This boy's a dear. Who said there's no such thing as a free lunch?"

Danny kept hold of Clara's hand as they weaved through the customers. Anna pulled out her cell phone and followed, continually glancing down at her phone.

A woman approached, and Clara immediately recognized her as Maeve Flanagan, the reporter from Farthing Bridge. "Mr. Brady, may I request a few minutes for an interview?"

Another reporter held out a microphone, chiming, "I'm from the *Dublin Times*. Is it true you'll be offering franchises globally?" The woman peered at Clara. "And who is this woman?"

"No comment," he said.

A round of flashes went off, and Danny held up a hand, shielding Clara's face. He peered around. "Where's Ian?" he asked no one in particular.

Clara blinked and yanked her hand from his. "Who's Ian? And what's this all about?"

"Lunch hour." He shepherded Clara and Anna to a private door. "Watch your footing. There's a tangle of wires from the cameramen."

Puzzled by the odd behavior, Danny's and the reporters', Clara asked him what time he was performing that night. "We can return then," she added.

He seemed confused. "I play guitar when the place is ready to close."

But that didn't make sense. She opened her mouth to tell him that if he was any good as a musician, he shouldn't allow himself to be slated to perform at the end of the night. He'd never be discovered if no one ever heard him.

Anna spoke first, though. A slow, incredulous smile had spread across her face as she studied her phone and then gawked at Danny. Her ebony hair swung from side to side as she shook her head and planted a fist on her hip. "The cheek of ya, Mr. Danny Brady. When were you planning to tell my sister that you owned this shop, as well as forty-nine others?"

5

───────

Clara snapped her chin up at Danny. "You lied to me! Do you think—"

"Not here." He shook his head as another round of camera flashes went off. He placed his hand on her elbow as he pushed open the private door, ushered them through, and then latched it behind them. He directed the women down a long corridor until they came to the lift.

Clara jerked free. "I'm going home."

"You and your sister are riding the lift to the third level with me. Get in."

"No!"

Danny exhaled heavily. He'd certainly made a bag of this, totally botching what he'd originally planned. He'd wanted to play guitar and sing for Clara, later in the evening when the coffee shop was quiet.

In contrast to Clara's scowl, Anna beamed good-naturedly. "I'm certain he'll offer a good reason for his deception. Won't you, Mr. Brady?"

"Please call me Danny."

"Won't you, Danny?"

He nodded, then focused on Clara. "I can explain when we get upstairs."

She drew back. "You'll likely spin more lies."

"I haven't lied. Your brother was our concern last night, not me."

"You lied by omission."

The lift door pinged open.

"Come with me." He captured her elbow again and guided her and Anna onto the lift. "We'll talk in my boardroom. I deserve a chance to explain."

Except he didn't know what he'd say.

Earlier, while unloading supplies in the storage room with several of his employees, he'd scanned the security monitors and noticed Clara walking into the coffee shop. Without a word, he'd rushed to the front of the shop to greet her. Aye, this was unlike him because he never acted impetuously. However, he had good reason because the woman was Clara, his captivating non-Irish Irish damsel.

Since his newfound prosperity, he'd learned, much to his dismay, that the prestige that went with dating wealthy men was immensely important to most women.

Not the man. Just the wealth.

Clara hadn't seemed to be one of those women. Consequently, he'd wanted to see her again, hoping the trappings of his success wouldn't color her interest. He'd wanted to tell her who exactly he was when he felt the time was right. And, he'd assumed she'd come by later in the evening, as he'd suggested.

He sighed. So much for that assumption.

Clara stood in the far corner of the lift. When the doors opened, he and Anna stepped out. Clara remained rooted inside.

"The lift doesn't go any higher. Are you waiting for something?" he asked.

She crossed her arms. "I presumed you were a guitar player."

"I am a guitar player. I told you last night how much I love music." He extended his hand, which she refused, although she stepped from the lift.

As the doors closed behind them, Danny's bodyguard, Ian, a brute of a man, barreled down the hallway toward them. His leather jacket was partially zipped, as if he'd been in the process of putting it on. Danny had met Ian in a soup kitchen in Carlow when Ian had been dirty, full of anger, and off the rails. They'd formed a friendship, and Danny had sponsored Ian's six-month stint in a rehab center. As a result, Ian was fiercely loyal, as well as brutally honest.

Danny had hired Ian as his bodyguard when he'd found that one disadvantage of being in the public eye was that customers were contacting him through email and phone, most of the time with complaints. Usually, those complaints were easily pacified, and Danny was always more than generous. He knew the value of one pleased patron was worth hundreds of euros in advertising.

Ian pushed a sturdy hand through his thinning, honey-gold hair. "Boss, you were unloading supplies, then one of the employees said you'd disappeared."

"I didn't have time to let you know that I'd gone to the front of the shop." Noting Ian's inquisitive grin as he glanced at the two women, Danny continued, "I'd like you to meet Clara Donovan and her sister Anna. They live in this charming town of Farthing. Ladies, Ian is my ... bodyguard." He grimaced, knowing another explanation was in order, yet preferring to skip the subject altogether for fear of sounding arrogant.

Clara nodded a greeting, looking thoroughly unimpressed.

"Hi, fella. What's the craic?" Anna cocked her head and laid a hand on Ian's shirtsleeve. "Your boss was looking for you because walking through that crowded coffee shop with all those photo flashes going off was murder."

"I'm here now," Ian said with a laugh. His eyes sparkled, a brilliant hazel, the center a warm, reflective brown.

"And I'm relieved," Anna rejoined, fanning herself. "Clara turned scarlet because everyone stared at us. She loathes that sort of thing after that awful newspaper article written about her."

Danny rubbed his chin. "What newspaper article?"

"Nothing of interest," Clara said, glaring at her sister. Anna didn't seem to notice. Instead, she lingered by the lift and chatted animatedly with Ian.

"They're hitting it off well," Danny said.

Clara fastened the buttons on her coat. "And I'm going home."

"Please stay," Danny said, gesturing down the hall to his boardroom. "I want the privilege of treating you and your sister to lunch."

"The privilege?" Clara came to a standstill. "Don't use my sister as an excuse, you good-for-nothing bowsie."

He lifted a brow. "If I ever grow overconfident, I'll know who to turn to for a set-down. Will you accept dinner as my apology for the deception?"

She tossed her luxuriant hair over her shoulders. "I won't be coming back here."

"I'll deliver it straight to your door because I know where you live." He winked. "In fact, I can walk to your flat from the coffee shop."

She plunked her hands on her lean hips. "Don't threaten me."

"With dinner?" He pressed a forefinger lightly to her lips, silencing her protest. "My offer isn't a threat, it's an olive branch."

Her gaze seemed to warm, although she jerked her head away from his touch. She toyed with the strap of her purse, then resumed her pace, keeping one step ahead of him. "I accept your olive branch. Nevertheless, you're still a bowsie," she called over her shoulder.

He began singing "When Irish Eyes Are Smiling," and she rewarded him with an exasperated head shake. "You're singing so off-key, it sounds like the tune the old cow died of."

"I'm more in tune when I'm strumming my guitar as accompaniment. Or when I play my Celtic harp," he told her.

"Should I be impressed?"

"Absolutely not. I don't play either instrument very well."

She stopped at the closed door, and he took a moment to admire her shapely calves and graceful bearing. Aye, she was appealing, quick to temper, quick to forgive. As he took out his keys, he glanced back to see where Ian and Anna were. Anna had stopped in front of a collection of Waterford crystal vases and was talking about them with Ian.

Danny opened the deadbolt lock on the door, and, with a smile, led Clara into his boardroom. A tall fern stood by the entrance. The room was sparse and masculine, exactly the way he liked his decor, the walls lined in richly carved mahogany. An espresso-colored leather sofa and coffee table were placed beneath a large picture window. The window offered an unobstructed view of the southern bank of the

River Farthing, as well as the entrance to the coffee shop. In the distance, the ruins of an old Norman castle stood atop a steep cliff.

"Very high-end," she said. "And your view is picture-perfect. You might consider rearranging your furniture so that the view is the focal point rather than the sofa."

"Thanks for the excellent decorating tip." He accepted her coat as she slid it off, signaling, he assumed, that she'd be staying for lunch. He hung it on a coat rack by the doorway and then seated her at the boardroom table in the middle of the room. After pouring two glasses of water from the pitcher on the table, he perched carefully on the narrow arm of her chair.

"Would you care for some ice water?" He leaned over to nudge the glass in front of her. Her fragrance reminded him of lemon and wholesomeness, sensual and citrusy.

She tensed, her frown pronounced. "I'll wait for my iced tea and fruit, thanks."

"How is Seamus faring?" Danny asked.

"He suffered dry heaves when he woke. I offered to cook eggs and rashers, but he refused. So I gave him some water and he went back to sleep. His friend Liam came to my flat to spend a few hours. I don't feel comfortable leaving Seamus alone."

"Aye." Danny placed his arm around her chair, earning another piercing frown. "I'll send eggs and rashers along with herbal tea to your flat for them both. I'm well acquainted with hangovers, and Seamus will be hungry once he feels better." He grabbed his cell phone from his shirt pocket and dashed off a quick text to one of his staff, acknowledging with some guilt that he should be available for his employees. Lunch hours were hectic, especially on opening day, and business could suffer from his lack of attention.

"You're experienced with hangovers?" Clara asked. "I'm surprised. You seem so, I don't know, so in control."

"I haven't had a drop in fifteen years, although I still remember the really, really bad headaches the morning after a night of drinking."

And the sadness and anxiety that had followed.

Somehow, at twenty years old, he'd come out of his alcohol-induced haze long enough to realize that alcohol had destroyed those he loved most. His chest still ached at the image of Glenna, his toddler sister, and her cherubic laughing face. He'd nicknamed her his little leprechaun.

The world hadn't stopped spinning when both his parents had committed suicide soon after Glenna's death. The short-term relief they'd sought in alcohol had ultimately killed them.

Danny gripped his glass and sipped his water. As a young lad, he'd trusted his parents to take care of him and his siblings. Instead, they'd scorned him, then abandoned him.

"Thanks for arranging to send lunch to Seamus and his friend," Clara was saying.

Danny set down his water glass and shook his thoughts back to the present.

She was staring at him. "You looked like you were a million miles away."

"I was thinking about the past when I should be enjoying the present and your lovely company," he said.

She continued to study him. Whatever she was searching for, she wouldn't find. He'd learned to keep his expression carefully neutral.

"Seamus and Liam will enjoy the sandwiches," she added.

"No bother. Let me know if I can do anything else." He didn't mention that he could recommend a good rehab for Seamus, and that Seamus's condition cried out for detoxification, which required medical supervision.

Instead, he simply enjoyed the fact that Clara had allowed him to sit so near, even if she was treating his closeness with chilly formality.

Kathleen swung into the boardroom ferrying a tray of chicken salad sandwiches, chocolate orange Guinness coffee cakes, a bowl of fresh fruit, and iced beverages laced with sprigs of fresh mint. She set the tray on the table beside a ceramic vase filled with pink roses, then arranged their place settings with gold-plated utensils, and snowy-white linen napkins.

"The waitresses are all busy downstairs, so I told them I would help. You know I'm here to be sure that everything runs smoothly and that the new employees all know what they're doing," she said.

"Thank you, Kathleen. You're an excellent manager." He indicated she could leave.

She briefly pouted. "Aye, Mr. Brady."

"Kathleen's been working with me since my shop's inception," he explained to Clara.

In fact, Kathleen had insisted on traveling with him from Dublin to open the new Farthing store. She was a dedicated employee, and, in turn, had accompanied him to several company functions. Up until now, he'd enjoyed her lush beauty, as well as her dedication to his business, although today she lacked something. Perhaps it was because her eyes weren't a deep, soft brown and her grin wasn't infectious.

He scanned the beverages on the table. "No coffee?" he wryly asked Clara.

She granted him a mischievous smile. "Coffee's too bitter, remember? My favorite is green mint tea."

"The coffee of the day is mild. And I have it on good authority that every cup of The Ground Café's coffee is brilliant because the owner uses fresh coffee beans and local spring water."

"Yeh, and the Irish latte is buttery smooth, based on the description," Clara said.

"Will you try a cup of my Irish latte? We add non-alcoholic whiskey."

She grinned. "After that fancy description, how can I resist?"

He glanced at Kathleen, who was still standing in the doorway. "Please bring Clara a cup of Irish latte."

"Whatever you say, sir." Kathleen's smile was blatantly sensual. Wheeling on her heels, she sashayed out.

Clara sniffed the flowers on the table. "Roses are my favorite. Why pink and not red? Did you run out of money because red is more expensive?"

He laughed. "All the roses I purchase are the same price. However, a deep pink rose expresses gratitude. Every customer is important, and it's my way of saying thank you."

"I'm impressed by your attention to detail." She retied the belt of her ruffled blouse around her slender waist, and he felt his insides warm. She was so pretty, as pretty as a wild Irish rose. "I'm impressed by your courage, Clara Donovan."

She nodded sagely. "It's not courage. I've simply learned to rely on myself."

"As have I," he said quietly.

At that moment, Ian and Anna entered. Anna shrugged

off her biker jacket and handed it to Ian. He hung it with Clara's on the coat rack near the door.

"There's plenty of room at the table for all of us to enjoy lunch." Danny gestured for the pair to seat themselves around the nine-foot table. He kept his arm securely around Clara's chair.

"Then perhaps you should take your own seat," she said.

He waited several beats. This was his coffee shop, his boardroom, his chair.

She glared at him, the flecks of gold in her brown eyes sparking dangerously.

He complied and stood quickly.

6

———

Danny hadn't intended to break for lunch. He hadn't intended to be sitting in his boardroom when a thousand decisions clamored for his attention. Instead, his mind was filled with Clara, and he couldn't look away from her exquisite profile. What was it about this spirited woman? She'd saved her brother, disregarding the danger to herself. She was proud and brave, yet humble.

He glanced at his cell phone, relieved to see that no employee had texted him. He'd allow himself fifteen minutes before focusing again on his business.

"You're obviously a guy who goes straight after what he wants in life," Anna said. "I admire you." She looked around, indicating a wall mounted security camera. "And you're cautious."

Clara didn't seem to ooze with the same admiration for him.

The food sat uneaten as silence settled over the room. Ian lumbered to the mounted television and grabbed the remote. "Wonder if the football match is being televised?"

Idly, he flipped the channels, groaned at the latest scores, and settled on the local news. He lowered the volume, glanced at his watch, then at Danny. "I'll show Anna your famous painting in the hallway while we're waiting for Clara's latte, boss. Our lunch can wait a few minutes." He glanced meaningfully at Clara's pressed lips.

"Aye, brilliant idea." Danny silently thanked his friend for allowing him more time alone with Clara.

"Do you appreciate fine art?" Danny asked Anna as Ian helped her from her chair.

"Does fine art include graffiti, Danny? If so, I'm interested." She looped her hand around Ian's arm and fairly danced to the door with him. "Lead the way, you fine thing."

After Anna's platform booties had clattered down the hallway alongside Ian's heavy-booted shoes, Danny dragged his chair a hairsbreadth closer to Clara.

She kept her gaze on her glass. "Tell me, do you lie to every woman you bring into your boardroom?"

"Truly, I'm sorry for any deception regarding my identity." He reached for his water and gave his brightest smile. "Aren't you curious about my famous painting?"

"I'm certain your painting cost more than my wages for an entire year."

"You're probably right. And, I admit, one part of me is ashamed. However, the other part is proud that I'm able to afford a widely recognized painting that I consider an investment."

She was silent, nursing her iced tea.

"The painting accompanies me whenever I open a new store."

"So your fancy, expensive painting is an investment?" Her tone held more politeness than interest. "Or is it a good luck charm?"

"Both. This particular painting is one of Francis Bacon's most praiseworthy. His boldness inspired me." Danny caught her inquiring expression. "Bacon's life was as chaotic as mine was."

Her eyes widened. "I assumed you were born into wealth and lived a charmed life."

"Me?" He laughed, the idea so absurd.

She glanced down. "I shouldn't have judged you."

"Is that an apology?"

"I don't manage apologies well."

He accepted her explanation with a brief nod. "My aunt brought me to the Hugh Lane Gallery in Dublin every Saturday afternoon. I should backtrack. After my parents' deaths, my elderly aunt and uncle took me and my two siblings, Erin and Eamon, to live with them. We were chiselers." Clara looked up. Danny avoided her scrutiny, preferring to study the mahogany paneling on the opposite wall.

"I am very sorry." Her gaze strayed to her glass, her voice heavy with sympathy. "Were your parents' deaths unexpected?"

Absently, he plucked a pink rose petal from the vase and rubbed the smoothness between his fingers. "Long story," was all he could manage.

Suicidal depression and alcoholism were signs of a serious mental illness. Nonetheless, his parents' deaths had hit him like an unexpected punch to the stomach. He should've heeded the warning signs after Glenna's death—his parents' withdrawal from family and well-meaning friends, their loss of jobs, their loss of interest.

Danny dropped the petal onto the table and focused on his response. "My younger sister died a few months before my parents."

"Care to talk about it?"

He stared down at his hands and shook his head. He still couldn't say Glenna's name aloud. The weight on his chest and limbs would press too heavily and crush him with guilt. He should've been home the afternoon Glenna died, to attend to her, instead of sneaking off to get drunk with his teenage friends.

"Do Erin and Eamon live near you?" Clara asked.

He noted the softness in her voice. "Both of my siblings live in Dublin." Danny had learned, though, that proximity had nothing to do with how close you lived to one another. Eamon, his brother, was too busy establishing a successful medical practice in Dublin to care about anything or anyone except himself. And Erin, his sister, well, she drifted from one bad relationship to another.

Danny reached for the water pitcher and topped off his glass. "And that's enough questions about my family."

"Indulge me."

He usually resisted answering questions regarding his personal life, but Clara's interest seemed genuine. He held up an index finger and relented. "One more question."

"How was a poor kid like you able to gain entry to fancy art galleries?"

"The galleries were free. My aunt and I had to take a bus to the city centre because we lived too far away to walk."

"I'm not familiar with Dublin. I only visited there once when I was a child."

He inclined his head slightly away from her. "We lived on the north side."

The run-down, seedy section where people living in four-room tenement buildings were buried in dirty grave plots in Glasnevin Cemetery.

Not anymore, he amended. His parents now rested in peace inside an Italian marble tomb, quiet and serene beneath a mature oak tree. And Glenna's little cemetery plot sat beside theirs. He'd added a pot of gold and a rainbow to the top of her headstone.

He leaned closer to Clara. "I'd like to know more about your adoption if you're comfortable talking about it."

She returned her gaze to her iced tea. "There's little to tell. After Seamus was born, my adoptive mother and father said they'd wanted the sound of girls' laughter to brighten their home, so they adopted two girls from abroad. And Anna and I were those two little girls. We provided the laughter my parents sought, and topped it off with female drama." Pensively, Clara swirled the ice in her glass. "In his teens, Seamus was often on a drunken tear. So, my parents got more than they bargained for raising the three of us."

Danny chuckled. "Have you revisited your Italian orphanage?"

"No, and I won't be able to afford the trip anytime soon. I might have an older brother who was also born in Italy. I'll probably never meet him. He's long-lost to me now."

"I'll take you to Italy, luv. The country is magnificent." He stopped himself from saying more, surprised that he'd offered her a trip without thinking it through first.

She was a complete stranger. Nevertheless, he felt like he'd known her a long time. He reminded himself that they'd shared a traumatic experience rescuing her brother, and that people in those types of situations often felt a closeness to one another afterward.

"I'll pay my own way if I ever have the opportunity to go," Clara responded matter-of-factly, as if accepting charity from anyone was unthinkable. "And while a trip to Italy sounds exciting, it's also terrifying."

"Are you afraid of flying?"

"I've only flown once in my life, and I was young when I

traveled from Italy to Ireland. I hardly remember the flight, although we landed in Dublin." She straightened and set her glass down, perfectly aligning it with his.

"Aren't you curious about your Italian roots?"

"Of course. It's the memories ... my poor judgment ..." Tears brightened her eyes and she made no attempt to hide them. "Forgive me. I didn't sleep well and last night's events —" She accepted his offer of a linen napkin and dabbed at her eyes. "Only the present counts, right? That's what everyone says. Keep looking ahead."

"Your past mistakes will haunt you if you don't confront them."

Who was he to give advice? his conscience admonished.

She smiled wryly and placed the napkin on the table. "Have you ever thought about writing your sage words down in a song?"

"I've written several songs. Perhaps you'll inspire me to write another."

"First, a title is essential."

Clara. The title came instantly to his mind. Her name meant bright and clear. A perfect title for a woman who brightened any room.

"Write a song about coffee beans." She offered an audacious grin. "You can begin with 'How warm and robust is the scent of coffee.'"

He laughed. *Forget the coffee. I'd rather sing a song about you.*

She continued to the tune of "Irish Rover," and he hummed along. He knew the melody well.

She exaggerated the high note of the chorus and raised an elegant brow. "No word rhymes with coffee."

"Toffee?"

She took a breath and continued singing.

Her deep set eyes were ringed by thick black lashes and sparkled with amusement. Once, he'd been looking for a woman like her—a woman who was beautiful, kind and brave.

Once. Not anymore. Kyla, his ex-wife, had cured him of pursuing relationships with women. Women were better kept at arm's length. He enjoyed their company, but in the end they'd only betray him, betray his trust. He'd grown immune to their charms.

He rubbed his forehead. He'd tried to make his marriage work. And he'd failed. All his relationships with the people he cared about—his parents, his siblings, even his ex-wife—had proven disastrous.

However, not his business. His businesses flourished and never disappointed him.

So what was it about Clara Donovan that started a thaw in his frozen heart?

He folded his arms and admired her entrancing face as she sang several more bars. "'Convincing me to like Irish lattes is your intent.'" She hesitated and looked at him. "What rhymes with *intent*?"

"Relent. 'If you try my latte, you'll relent.'"

She chuckled. "Or *you'll* lament ... the loss of a sale."

"Money doesn't mean everything to me," he said.

The room grew quiet, the silence interrupted by the murmur of the television.

"I think it means a great deal," she said softly.

His thumbs longed to stroke the blush of enjoyment highlighting her smooth, unblemished features. She was a compelling woman, a surprising treasure he'd never expected to find when he came to the unsophisticated town of Farthing. Firmly, he reminded himself that he'd only be in town a short while; and treasures proved fleeting and were seldom worth the effort because whatever shimmered on the surface was rarely found inside.

"I can't think of any word to rhyme with 'lament,'" she said.

"Neither can I." Perhaps it was because he couldn't tear his gaze away from her moist lips. "Am I forgiven for all my missteps today, luv?"

"Some of them." She smiled, that same vivid smile when he'd teased her about the rain the previous evening.

He relinquished his plan to return to the coffee shop in fifteen minutes.

As if on cue, his cell phone buzzed, intrusive and insistent.

"Are you needed downstairs?" Clara attempted to tuck an errant strand of hair behind her ear, though it wouldn't cooperate.

"In a wee bit." He wanted to spend time with her, not his unrelenting business. "What do you do for a living, Clara Donovan?"

She seemed to make a valiant attempt to keep her features impassive. "I try to keep my brother out of harm's way, which is a full-time job. I also work in a factory, RJ Dougal Restaurant Supplies, plus I teach dance classes at the dance studio in town."

"That's a lot of work for one person."

"I like my factory job, but I adore teaching dance because I love children. You should see how enthusiastic the kids act when they practice their ballet steps, their little faces all puckered with concentration."

Danny noted the gentleness that had crept into her voice when she spoke about children, her cheeks stained with a spark that also lit her eyes.

"So, you're a dancer," he said. "Last night on the bridge, I noticed how graceful you were."

She settled back in her chair and gave a self-deprecating chuckle. "You must've been looking at someone else. I slipped more than once."

He lightly pushed that wayward strand of hair from her face. "And I was there to save you."

"Thank you." Her expression softened.

"No bother." He shifted. Perhaps if she sat on his lap, she could thank him with a kiss.

A clicking and clattering of heels echoed from the corridor.

"Quite an impressive business here, Danny!" Anna announced, strolling into the boardroom with a moon-struck Ian behind her. "And all these pink roses." She nodded to the vase on the table. "Nice touch."

"And I just learned roses are your sister's favorite flower," Danny said.

"Yeh, she's always loved roses," Anna said. "I got restless staring at that one Francis Bacon painting so Ian showed me the kitchen. I didn't realize there was an art to making coffee or that there was so much equipment required—coffee grinders, espresso machines, refrigerators, dishwashers. And you sell your CDs in the lobby."

At Clara's inquiring gaze, Danny explained, "They're mostly instrumental CDs."

"And more money in your pocket," Clara murmured.

He chuckled.

"Your employees are extremely helpful and knowledge-able," Anna continued.

"My staff is very dedicated," Danny said.

Ian's thick blond brows furrowed. "What the boss isn't

telling you is that he works sixty hours a week alongside his employees, and that's why they're so dedicated."

"I'll submit an application to help you out, Danny," Anna dove in. "Both my sister and I need jobs. I've always wanted to try waitressing."

"I could certainly use good waitresses," Danny said. "And I offer complementary food and beverages to all my employees before and after their shifts."

"As you know, I already work two jobs, although thanks for the offer," Clara demurred.

"I don't work any jobs and I love free food." Sitting down, Anna grabbed her chicken salad sandwich, coffee cake, and latte. She peered at Clara over her cup. "Wouldn't it be brilliant to make ends meet for a change? The government doesn't pay me nearly enough money for the pain and suffering caused by my terrible accident."

"That was a year ago, and you've conceded you're much better. And you can't work in the coffee shop until you're off disability allowance," Clara reminded her sister.

"The allowance ends very soon," Anna said.

"Let me know when you're available, Anna," Danny put in. "The offer's open."

"Perhaps you'll consider hiring Seamus instead of me," Clara said to him.

"You should know up front, Danny," Anna said, "before you do a security check, that Seamus spent some time in Farthing prison. It was nothing serious."

Clara glared at Anna. "After Seamus finished secondary school, he enrolled in computer classes online. He's very smart when he applies himself."

Danny hesitated. His business didn't call for office help because he employed professional accountants. And Seamus could cause serious problems if he reported for work drunk. However, if Ian befriended Seamus, then Ian could recommend a good rehab. Knowing her brother was safe and employed would lighten Clara's emotional, as well as financial, load.

Danny extracted a business card from his wallet, dashed off his phone number and handed the card to Clara. "Assuming Seamus can stay on the rails, he's hired once I interview him. I don't require a computer person, but more kitchen help is always appreciated. Here's my cell phone number."

Ian grinned and snatched up his sandwich. "The boss fancies you, miss. He never gives his private number to women. They'd badger him relentlessly."

She leveled a stare at Ian and then Danny. "Please tell your boss that he never need fear badgering from me." She examined Danny's script, then stashed his business card in her purse. "Assuming Seamus is agreeable, I'll send him around tomorrow. I promise I'll keep him straight."

"And I'll want a job as soon as my disability allowance ends," Anna said. "Someday I'll tell you all about my accident and how I wasn't at fault." She lifted a forkful of Guinness cake. "And that the paltry sum the government awarded me wasn't nearly—" She broke off as she ate a bite of cake. "Wow, this cake is deadly. Do you give out your recipes?"

Danny shook his head. "Sorry, my company doesn't share any recipes."

"Top secret?" Anna barked a laugh. "Crack on, because I don't bake."

"My specialty is lemon scones," Clara said, "and I'm not giving away any of my secrets, either."

Danny smiled. "I'm intrigued."

"Nothing else to say," she averred. "That's why they're secrets."

"I'd consider buying your recipe." Very quietly, very slowly, he whispered, "If I'm around you much longer, you'll be privy to all my secrets."

She quickly looked away and toyed with her bowl of fruit.

Between alternating bites of sandwich and cake, Anna pointed to the television screen. "Hey, Danny, you're on TV."

Ian grabbed the remote and turned up the volume.

The television came alive. A familiar face, the reporter from the bridge, came into focus.

"I'm on the scene of a suicide attempt," she said into the microphone. "The incident happened around midnight on Farthing Bridge, and Channel Four News arrived first at the scene. Fortunately, this story has a happy ending, thanks to Mr. Danny Brady, owner of The Ground Café." The camera panned out to the bridge, showing a dejected Seamus and furious Clara, shouting and shaking her hand at the camera.

Clara stared at the television screen, and her face whitened. She shoved back her chair and stood. Danny came to his feet as well, reluctantly watching the TV screen.

"Mr. Brady is considered one of the wealthiest men in Ireland," the reporter was saying. "He's in Farthing to open his fiftieth coffee shop." She extended the microphone to Danny. "Can you tell us what happened on the bridge?"

The camera focused on Danny's face. "I was nearby and immediately phoned the Gardaí."

AND YOU BRAVELY CAME TO a desperate man's rescue," the reporter chimed in.

"I did what I could to help."

The camera swung to the reporter. "Whether he's in the kitchen brewing his famous coffee or saving a despondent man, Danny Brady is Ireland's national hero. This is Maeve Flanagan reporting from Farthing Bridge."

Ian grinned as he strode over to Danny and clapped a hand on his boss's shoulder. "Fair play! That's a load of brilliant publicity. The customers will surely rush the place."

True. Except that Clara's nostrils were flaring and fury blazed from her eyes, which wasn't quite so brilliant.

"You and I know that's not what happened," Danny said to her. "The media sensationalizes everything."

Her hands were braced on the table. Her look was hurt and reproachful. "How dare you use my brother's desperation to promote your wretched coffee chain? Is that the reason why you were so insistent on helping me?"

"Of course not. I'd never circuit a terrible situation into one for my advantage."

Clara threw her purse over her arm and marched to the doorway. "Let's go," she directed Anna.

"I haven't finished my absolutely divine dessert." Anna was attacking her orange Guinness coffee cake like she'd never eaten before. "Besides, Mr. Brady promised us all jobs."

Clara spun. "You'd actually work for this swine?"

Anna put down her fork. "If I hope to attend university, then, yeh, I'd gladly work for him. Ian said Danny pays excellent wages."

"You'd go against your own family?"

"Have you noticed there's no jobs in this town?" Anna's gaze raked furiously over Clara's stung expression. "I don't see any dancing schools beating down your door. Now sit down and wait for your Irish latte."

"I've waited long enough." Clara's gaze fired up as she

whirled on Danny. "You'll lose customers in droves if your barista spends an hour preparing one latte." She grabbed her coat. "Money isn't as important as families sticking together."

"And our family needs to eat," Anna said. "Anyway, how are you getting home? I drove."

"I'll ring a taxi."

"I'll take you home after you've finished your lunch," Danny said, walking over to Clara. "Please don't leave." He placed a hand on her shoulder, assuming she'd shrug it off.

He was right.

"I won't accept charity from a good-for-nothing bowsie." She quit the boardroom, almost knocking over a stone-colored wastebasket set near the tall fern by the doorway.

"Don't go after her," Anna advised as Danny started for the hallway. "Give her time to cool off. You're better off waiting until tomorrow."

Ian sank into his chair and pulled a roll of antacids from his pocket. He popped one into his mouth. "And send a bouquet of roses to Clara's house in the meantime." He clutched a linen napkin and mopped the perspiration settling on his forehead. "I didn't intend to offend her, although it's brilliant you're the town hero, right, boss?"

Danny sighed, crossed his arms, and slumped against the doorway. "Aye, just brilliant."

7

He was riding the city bus, Clara was sure of it. She'd been walking to the dance studio to teach her evening ballet class when she'd spotted him.

Jack Connor's thick features had been pressed against the bus's grubby window. He'd waved, and she'd almost lifted her hand to wave back, a reflexive reaction. Then she'd shivered, drawing her jacket close around her shoulders.

Those cold, leering eyes, that lecherous grin. She'd recognize Jack anywhere. But he was locked away in a prison near Cork, miles from Farthing. Wasn't he?

She rubbed at her eyes. Seamus hadn't slept well the previous night, alternating between shaking uncontrollably and cursing her for being a "rugger bugger" and separating him from his whiskey. Which, in retrospect, meant she hadn't slept well because she'd lectured and cajoled him, insisting he required lots of rest so that he'd be clear-eyed for his interview at The Ground Café.

Yes, she'd relented, because Anna had been right. Their brother needed a job.

Seamus had phoned the coffee shop to schedule an interview, and Clara rang a taxi for him, although her flat was only a short distance from the shop. A threat of rain was in the forecast, and she'd wanted him to look his best. Her car's brakes were still being repaired, and, cell phone in hand, she'd decided to take a chance on the rain and walk. Her quilted jacket sported a hood to keep her dry.

She'd treaded across a handful of puddles left over from a recent rainstorm while her cell phone buzzed three times, the caller ID flashing *Danny Brady*. He wasn't phoning from the coffee shop. He was ringing from his private cell phone number.

When she reached the dance studio, she changed into her leotard and tights and retrieved the three missed calls. Danny's first message sounded professional, confirming that he looked forward to meeting Seamus at the interview.

Expectation and optimism had brightened Seamus's eyes when she'd assured him that he'd probably be hired, and would keep the job as long as he never reported to work ossified, drunk.

The second voice mail from Danny assured her that Seamus had interviewed well and had gotten the job.

"Your brother is very intelligent and witty, exactly like his sisters," Danny said. "I'm starting him off as a dishwasher, though he can easily work his way to a more lucrative position—depending on his interests—whether they be in the office or interacting with customers." Then, in an apparent side note, Danny added, "I trust you enjoyed the dinner I sent last night and didn't throw it out your flat window. I'm hopeful you'll come by the coffee shop after you're finished teaching your ballet class, because I've thought of some new lyrics for our song. I'm tied up with business appointments for a few hours and I'll ring you when I'm finished. Seamus told me about your ballet class, in case you were wondering how I knew. He said you finished around seven o'clock."

She frowned, bristling like an out-of-sorts porcupine. Why was her brother so long-winded and loose-tongued? She valued her privacy, and Danny Brady didn't need to know where she was every minute of the day.

The third message from Danny was brief. "I apologize for the article in the newspaper. There's a photo of us when we walked through the coffee shop, although I had shielded your face. And I've refused to give your name to the reporter who wrote the article."

There was a newspaper article with a picture of her and Danny? Clara groaned aloud.

Assuming Danny wouldn't answer his phone because of his meetings, she punched in his number and left a brief message. "Hi. It's Clara. Pink roses were sitting on my doorstep last night when I returned home. Thank you, they're cheery and ... extravagant, and dinner was lovely. Oh, and I'm certain your song will be the next top hit and receive loads of radio play. Sorry, tonight isn't good for me."

She was meeting her brother outside The Ground Café so they could walk home together. Danny would be preoccupied and never know that she'd come and gone. She'd learned that trick from her orphanage days, slipping in and out of places quickly and unseen.

CLARA WIPED the sweat from her hairline, exhilarated and exhausted from teaching her ballet class. The five-year-old girls in matching pink tights and black leotards, the boys in black leotards and tights, had been squirmier than usual.

She'd abandoned her lesson plan, instead engaging the children in imaginary play and movement games, twirling about with them on the hardwood floor. Afterward, several parents had detained Clara with endless questions regarding the upcoming dance recital. Her phone had buzzed and she hadn't dared answer the call.

Madame Sophie, the director of the dance studio, had stood at the rear of Clara's class and taken copious notes, presumably assessing Clara's teaching. Madame Sophie held absolute control, partly because of her longevity, and partly because her late grandfather had founded the studio three decades earlier.

Once the parents and students had departed, Clara stepped to the side of the ballet barre and retrieved her voice mail message:

"Your class was done at six forty-five. Where are you? You always pick up your phone and it's only a short walk from the town centre to the coffee shop," Seamus said.

I'm leaving now, she texted quickly. That is, as soon as she'd spoken with Madame Sophie. The woman now stood at the far end of the ballet barre, her platinum-white hair pulled into a tight bun, which only emphasized, rather than enhanced, her scowling features. Her top-heavy body was hidden beneath a hip-length tunic. Her long blue-grey jacket and matching pants disguised her stout midriff.

I got the job, Seamus texted back. *The boss is grand.*

Clara choked on her salty retort. Why did everyone raise Danny Brady to such an exalted position? So he'd deigned to step down from his lofty boardroom to offer Seamus a job as a dishwasher. It was insulting, degrading. Nonetheless, it was a stable job in a depressed town offering little employment.

She managed to text back, *Congrats, Seamus!*

As soon as Clara closed her phone, Madame Sophie trooped over. She adjusted her blazing-blue reading glasses while blasting a barrage of complaints, concluding that "Ms. Donovan's" recital choreography wasn't on par with the studio's standards. Another half hour went by, and Clara had rearranged the choreography six times before Miss Sophie finally nodded her approval.

In the employees' locker room afterward, Clara changed into street clothes. She was ready to leave when Colum O'Brien, a fellow dance teacher, entered. Colum had been a principal dancer for the Dublin Ballet. Nearing fifty, he'd returned to Farthing to care for his troubled nephew, a nineteen-year-old boy who'd launched a graphic design business.

Clara could always count on Colum to come to her defense, and oftentimes she believed that he was the only reason she still held her teaching position.

Now he regarded her with his kind, green-eyed gaze. "My dear girl, have you had a rough day? You look as weak as a kitten."

With a sigh, Clara leaned against her locker. "Nothing I do seems to satisfy Madame Sophie."

"She's tough on you because she sees your talent."

"Either that, or she'll only be satisfied when she drives me out for good. I'm certain she'll keep me on probation forever."

"Two years have passed since you were arrested."

"Yeh, and my one night in jail was wretched." Clara rubbed a hand through her hair. She'd been so frightened, her fear of being locked in a small, airless space. "Do you recall when Madame Sophie told me that she kept me employed part-time as a favor, because 'convicts shouldn't be around small children'?"

"Since that incident, you've taught so many dance classes at no charge that I've lost count," Colum said. "You've more than made up for your mistake and I don't believe that Madame Sophie feels that way about you anymore."

"I want the children to embrace dance and movement, to be comfortable in their bodies." Clara scanned her surroundings, taking in the studio she'd come to feel such affection for. The worn pink ballet shoes and cotton balls strewn on the floor, all those years dancing with bloodied toes and aching muscles, because she'd valued the discipline and art of dance.

"You're an excellent teacher who clearly adores children." Colum threaded a hand through his salt and pepper hair, revealing trim, muscled arms, the result of lifting ballerinas in the air for twenty-five years.

She smiled. "How do you always know the right thing to say?"

"Age and experience oftentimes brings a wee bit of knowledge."

"Thanks for being one of the nicest men I've ever met." Clara buttoned her jacket. "I'm meeting my brother at the new coffee shop in town. He got a job."

Colum bent to retrieve a pair of light pink ballet slippers and fiddled with the elastic drawstrings. "I hope he sticks with it."

"He will."

"You're his sister, so you should know him better than most." Colum set the ballet slippers near the changing cubicle and grabbed his camouflage-colored parka. "I'll walk you out and grab a smoke before my next class."

"You realize that a dance teacher who smokes in front of a dancing school sticks out. Kinda like selling candy outside of a health club."

Colum tossed a contrite smile. "I'm quitting next week." He pulled out a pack of cigarettes as they left the locker room. With a quick farewell, Clara headed in the direction of the coffee shop.

Her wristwatch showed seven thirty, and she followed a short cut through one of the alleyways to make up time. The neighborhood was safe, and the Keegan sisters, who were Clara's former school chums, had lived on the street for years. The night sky was somber and overcast, the streets silent. Wild, overgrown brush haphazardly lined the broken sidewalks, a litter of mismatched, cracked cobblestones.

Clara peered at the Keegans' second-story flat windows. All the rooms were dark. She'd heard that their grandmother had been hospitalized recently, and made a mental note to ring them.

That was why, she later rationalized, she hadn't heard heavy footsteps pounding through a puddle she'd just crossed. She'd been pondering Grandmother Keegan's ill health.

"Howya, Clara. Are ya on your way to meet that fancy guy from Dublin?" Behind her, the man's voice rang frighteningly familiar.

Jack Connor.

She felt the gut-wrenching slice of fear, a chunk carved from her belly, before she whirled around.

Too stunned to move, she stared into his pale eyes. The lurid tattoo of a spider seated on a web ran along Jack's neck, a manifestation of the man himself. His hulking body sported a stained leather coat, the collar frayed. She had bought him the coat three years earlier from a thrift shop, that first Christmas when he'd exuded charm and chivalry.

She blinked, shuddered. She'd been a dense fool. She should've realized all that trumpery was for show. But somewhere deep inside, in a place she didn't want to admit, she'd been secretly pleased that a guy had showered her with gifts and undivided attention.

"You're a cute one, ain't ya?" Jack's furry brows knit in a glower, a predictor of the utterly callous fury sure to follow. "Surprised to see me? Or upset that you're on the front page of the newspaper again?"

"I haven't seen the papers." It was a miracle she spoke so calmly when her insides were churning like mad. Surely he could hear her shallow breathing.

He stepped closer, smelling of old sweat and cheap leather. "I'll steal you a paper. Then we'll go for a cold pint and laugh at the want ads, just like old times."

She retreated a step. Her terror came with her.

"I don't drink anymore. I don't steal, either." She attempted to scoff and wheezed instead. And the wheeze, she noted distractedly, sounded far away. "Why are you here?"

He kept his hands beneath his coat. "The weather's nicer in Farthing than in County Cork."

"And what about your prison sentence? You're supposed to be behind bars."

"My brother knows the judge. We appealed, and I was released for good behavior." Jack's menacing sneer sent a string of goose bumps along her arms.

Silently, she chided herself. She hadn't kept track of Jack's prison sentence. Instead, she'd trusted a judge and legal system to keep him locked away.

"The court ordered me to rehab," Jack said.

"Did you go?" she asked.

They were a scant three feet apart. Her gaze flew to the main road, and she counted off the number of seconds it would take to reach the intersection.

"I don't need more rehab and I don't take orders from no judge. You and me, we make our own rules, remember?" Jack's chilling monotone pinned her to the sidewalk. "Now I'm homeless, Clara. You were an orphan and you know what it's like. Will you take me in? I still love ya."

"Leave me alone. Our relationship was over a long time ago."

Why had she once confided to him that she had been a waif, wandering the streets of Italy, then stealing after she was placed in a neglectful orphanage? And why had he conveniently forgotten that she'd subsequently been raised by a loving family?

She lifted her chin. If he saw her fear, he'd use it against her. "You're a grown man, and I haven't been homeless for a long time."

"We're alike, you and me." He slurred each word. "Our past is who we are."

Time stopped. She scanned the overcast sky and gathering clouds. Somewhere in the distance, thunder rumbled. She assessed the alleyway, the clumps of open dirt behind random shrubs. The intersection was closer, a few yards in the opposite direction. She could outrun him.

Before she could take a step, his fingers clamped down roughly on her arm. "You can try, but I'm faster."

She flung off his hand. "Stay away or I'll call the Gardaí.

"I can handle them, as long as your yoke of a brother doesn't come near me. He's touched in the head, you know."

"I'm leaving."

"Without this?" He reached into his coat and brandished her purse. "Didn't even know I'd lifted it, did ya?"

Her purse had been hanging from her shoulder, and she

hadn't even realized he'd taken it. He'd always been able to whittle her down with threats, quick actions she didn't expect, so that she felt like a complete idiot.

Despite her fluttering nerves, she managed to speak dismissingly. "You're a disgrace."

"I've been called worse." There went his high-pitched laugh before he narrowed his glassy stare. "You were good at stealing, remember?"

Remember this. Remember that. She'd pushed it all away to a locked compartment in her mind, and now he was forcing every horrific occurrence to the surface.

She stiffened her spine. No. She'd promised herself that she'd never be controlled by a man again.

"I'm not proud of what I did," she said.

Jack sighed dramatically. "I'm locked away for a couple donkey's years and now you've grown soft. Guess I can't fault ya because you're surrounded by such good friends." He inflated his words by scanning the dark flat windows. "Although the Keegans moved out a while ago, so maybe you need new friends."

Her cell phone rang incessantly from inside her purse.

She stretched out her hand. She was shaking. "Give me my purse."

"Is that your new fella ringing, that Brady millionaire?" Tauntingly, Jack swung her purse in front of her. "He'd better not fancy my fine oul doll or he'll be digging himself an early grave."

"It's Seamus," she said.

And Danny was most likely a billionaire, not a millionaire.

"I saw you on TV," Jack went on as if she hadn't spoken. "They're making that Brady fella out to be a Holy Joe for saving your crazy brother. Seamus was about to jump off that bridge."

"Go back to Cork." This was the brave new Clara, fortified by a strong will, protected by a restraining order. "You'll be thrown in jail if you stay in Farthing."

"I'll be here a while. There're some scores needing settling."

A garda drove past the main roadway and idled at the traffic light.

Jack's eyes widened. He wavered. Clara grabbed her chance and screamed as she dashed for the garda. "Please help! This man is—"

With one vicious jerk, Jack ripped the sleeve of her jacket and hauled her into the bushes.

The traffic light changed, the garda kept going, the distance between them widening.

But there was another car, and she heard the engine before Jack did. A metallic-silver Mercedes sped directly down the alleyway. And the garda had reversed to the other end of the alleyway. Clara and Jack were blocked from both sides.

The Mercedes bulleted in their direction, its headlights blinding them.

"My darling Clara," Jack growled, "you'll be lookin' at heaven's gates for this."

"Stay away from me!" she shouted.

A deluge of rain soaked through her jacket as the skies parted.

Jack raised his fist, and she winced, an old reflexive reaction, preparing for his hard blow. Instead, he shoved her. As she fell to the ground, he threw her purse into the bushes and sprang into the shadows.

8

Danny screeched his Mercedes to a stop. He vaulted from the car, his breath freezing in his chest. In the pouring rain, Clara was lying on the ground face-down.

He knelt beside her. "Clara!" He lifted her, shook her shoulders. "Clara, are you all right?"

She wiped at her face, smearing mud across her temples. "I ... I'm grand."

She didn't look grand. She looked dazed, her complexion ashen.

With an anxiety that made his hands shake, he searched her face for signs of bleeding and ran his hands along her torn jacket sleeve. Big droplets of rain ran down her face, her hair. There were no cuts and no bones seemed broken. He jerked off his wool coat and tucked it around her, wiped the mud from her temples with his shirtsleeve. "Does anything hurt?"

"I ... I don't think so." Sobbing, she mumbled and ferreted through the bushes. "Where's my purse? I can't find my purse."

"I'll get your purse." He retrieved it and guided her to her feet.

"I'm cold," she whispered.

"Aye, it's damp." His legs were unsteady as he brought her to his car. Pure, blind fury had surged through him when he saw the hulking man shove her.

Danny eased her onto the passenger seat and bit back his fury beneath a reassuring smile. He set her purse on the floor mat. "You'll be warmer in a wee bit when you get out of this night air."

She wrapped her arms around herself and rocked. Water dripped from her clothes. "Thank you for—for finding my purse."

He leaned into the car. "It's more important that I found you." He closed the door, catching his breath, gripping the handle until his knuckles whitened.

The garda was walking from his car at the end of the alleyway toward him. "It's necessary that we file a report, sir," he called out.

Disregarding the rain, Danny stalked to him. "This woman was attacked and all you're concerned about is filing a report? Find the man who attacked her!"

"We need names." A thick fringe of bangs hung beneath the garda's peaked hat. He peered at the Mercedes. "I recognize the woman. Clara Donovan, correct?"

"How would you know her?"

"She's been at the prison before."

Most likely Clara had visited her brother when Seamus had been in prison.

"What's your name?" Danny asked.

"Doherty. Jimmy Doherty, sir."

In a sharp, authoritative tone, Danny said, "The only

report you'll be filing is when that man is thrown in prison, Garda Doherty!"

"Aye, sir." The garda got back into his car and gunned down the roadway.

Danny's fury was interrupted by a heavier rain bucketing down as he strode to his car. He pushed his wet hair from his forehead, settled into the driver's seat and set the heat blasting. The windshield fogged, and he switched on the defroster.

He focused on Clara. "Better?"

"A little." She was trembling, shaking her head as if in denial. He wanted to hold her tightly in his arms, although she looked so fragile, he feared she might break if he squeezed too hard.

Instead, he gazed at her wet, tear-stained face and took her hands in his. "We'll sit in my car a while."

"All right." Her soaked hair curled in ringlets around her heart-shaped face. Her dark eyes were overly bright. She licked her lips. "How did you find me?"

"My appointment finished early, and I noticed your brother waiting outside the coffee shop. He kept checking the time and mentioned you were meeting him and that you were late. The weather looked like rain, so I volunteered to pick you up at the studio. One of the instructors, Colum, I believe, was standing outside on the stoop, smoking, and said you'd left. We chatted a bit. He seemed like a nice chap."

"Yeh, I consider him a trusted friend. We've worked together at the dance studio for a while, and he always looks out for me."

"He pointed toward this alleyway," Danny continued.

She leaned against the seat. "And you alerted a garda."

"Aye, a precaution. You didn't answer your phone, and

Seamus and I were concerned." Danny shook his head. That was an understatement. His pulse was still racing.

She stared straight ahead at the windshield wipers swishing away the rain.

Danny took a deep breath. "Clara, who was that man?"

She pulled from his hold and rubbed her hands along her muddy leggings. "Jack Connor, my ex-boyfriend."

Danny nodded slowly. "I assumed so."

"How would you know about Jack?"

"After Seamus finished his interview, we chatted. He told me more about you, including your relationship with Jack."

"My brother has a tongue that would clip a hedge. Sometimes, he never stops talking."

"Fortunately, I'm a good listener." Especially, Danny was coming to realize, if the subject involved Clara.

She chewed her lower lip. "I could've headed Jack off if he hadn't caught me unawares and lifted my purse."

"Aye. You're fearless." Danny offered a supportive smile. "However, for my peace of mind, will you promise to ring me if you see him again? He's a dangerous, unpredictable man. You have my number and can put me on speed dial."

A pair of mutinous eyes stared back at him and she didn't reciprocate his smile.

"Give me your word."

No answer.

"Give me your word," he demanded sharply.

Time ticked in charged silence before she finally swung her gaze to the windshield wipers and muttered, "Yeh."

She was a stubborn, foolish woman if she believed she could outwit a man as ruthless as Jack Connor. From what Seamus had revealed, Jack was prone to fits of unpredictable rage.

Danny stared at Clara's delicate profile, the dogged set of

her chin. She was a spirited, splendid woman who needed him, whether she admitted that fact or not. Despite her rebellious gaze, she was as tense as when she'd raced up the rusty stairs to the top of Farthing Bridge.

She tucked her hands beneath the warmth of his wool coat. "So you offered my brother a job today and then the subject swung around to me."

"Something like that." Danny stroked the damp hair from her forehead. "I'm grateful to Seamus, because I couldn't have helped you if I didn't know about your situation with Jack. Now that I do, I can assure you that you should never be afraid again. I'll protect you."

She waved a dismissive hand, although her soulful brown eyes seemed to seek reassurance. "And how will you manage to protect me?"

His wealth. His resources. He'd garnered respect and influential friends because of his prosperous business. Aye, some enemies in the guise of disgruntled customers too. That was the reason he'd hired Ian.

Danny paused. He could enlist Ian's help to ensure Clara's safety. He hadn't used Ian as a bodyguard for months. Besides, Danny thought, he was a coffee shop owner, not a head of state. He didn't need a bodyguard.

"I'll protect you the way I manage everything in my life," he answered. "Every detail is arranged so that nothing will go wrong."

A fresh stream of tears slid down her cheeks. "Jack will make certain he can't be found, and no one will talk. I know how living in the streets works."

So do I, Danny wanted to say. And people living in the streets answered questions if the right amount of money was offered.

He placed his arm around her and she bent her head to

his chest, soaking his shirt with her sobs. He let her cry, all the while whispering soothing assurances, hugging her closer. When her tears subsided, she wiped at her eyes. "The judge assured me Jack would be locked in prison and never bother me again."

Danny lifted her chin. Solemnly, he said, "I assure you that Jack Connor will be found, then locked away for a very, very long time."

CLARA DREW A LONG, inward sigh. Danny was offering assurances because he felt sorry for her. She'd known well-meaning people when she'd lived in the Italian orphanage. In the end, she'd fended for herself.

No doubt Danny pitied her because she'd cried so hard. Her chin trembled. She was pathetic.

She didn't know what was worse—false assurances or pity. However, Danny's conviction that he'd find Jack Connor and send him back to prison was the only promise she had, and whether it was true or not, she clung to it as a lifeline.

Despite Danny's calm assertions, his expression had changed from frantic worry when he'd first spotted her, to composed decisiveness. Beneath his quiet exterior, she could sense his anger was simmering, albeit carefully restrained.

He adjusted the heater on the dashboard. "Comfortable?"

"Yeh, I'm about dried off."

"Care to tell me exactly what happened tonight?" he asked quietly.

She watched him from beneath her lashes and briefly

nodded when it became apparent he was waiting for a response.

"Did Jack say anything to you?" he pressed.

She waffled, played with the strap of her purse. "What do you mean?"

"Did he threaten you?" Danny grabbed her hands and waited until she met his gaze. "Did he say where he was going, or anything that might assist me and the garda in finding him?"

"I can't recall specific details. It all happened so fast."

Except when Jack had said, *You'll be lookin' at heaven's gates for this.*

She feared Danny's reaction if she told him. He'd most likely find an excuse to drop her off immediately at her flat and then attempt to find Jack himself.

No, she told herself firmly. She had placed Danny in too much danger already. He owned coffee shops for a living. He wasn't a private investigator. He'd grown up in Dublin and visited art museums with his elderly aunt on weekends.

Resolutely, she squared her shoulders.

Danny leveled her with a bold stare. "Should I believe you?"

"Of course," she lied.

"You'd have no reason to protect Jack, would you?"

She bridled. "When we were together, he beat me so often that I lost count and he ruined my life for a long spell. Of course I wouldn't protect him."

But she *did* want to protect Danny.

She tucked her purse neatly on the floor. She should tell Danny everything. She should. She would. Just not tonight. Her emotions were poised to career out of control at the slightest prompting.

"Anything else?" he asked.

"I told you. No." She responded louder than she'd intended, torn between her decision to protect him and the pressing, unexplainable fear that her decision, either way, would result in disaster.

"You're a magnificent, although imprudent woman if you think I believe for one second that you're telling me everything. Don't forget, I'm available anywhere, anytime, whenever you want to talk."

She gazed at his face, so recklessly good-looking, nodded briefly, and resumed her absorption of the rhythmic swishing of the windshield wipers.

With a sigh, Danny pulled his cell phone from his shirt pocket. "Your brother is probably pacing every inch of the coffee shop. He's waiting there in case you arrived there before I found you. Do you want me to call him?"

"Seamus," she groaned. "How could I have forgotten about my dear brother?" Mentally chastising herself, she elected to spend extra time with him over the next few days to make up for her absence.

Danny punched in Seamus's number, waited for the phone to ring through, then spoke quickly. "Aye, lad, Clara's with me and she's safe. Get yourself into the shop, enjoy some dinner, and we'll be there in a wee bit. We'll explain more when we arrive. Aye. Aye." Danny clicked off. "Be prepared to answer a thousand questions. Should we call your sister next?"

Clara hesitated, trying to recall Anna's whereabouts. Her hesitation was punctuated by a wheeze, which Danny politely ignored.

"Anna's visiting a university in Wicklow and she's seeing Ian afterward. I'll phone her tomorrow morning." Clara attempted a half smile. "Thank you for everything, Danny."

"Please, don't thank me. I'm excelling in the course,

Rescuing Lovely Farthing Damsels in Distress 101 ever since I met you. Besides, I had an ulterior motive tonight. We can all dine together at the coffee shop. The owner said it's all right."

His joking did exactly what he'd most likely intended and roused her into a full-fledged smile. "I can't eat. My stomach's in a knot, and the desserts at your shop are too heavy."

His brows rose. "They are?"

"Yeh, beginning with the Guinness coffee cake my sister devoured yesterday."

He chuckled. "Will you join me for a cuppa tea then?" The kindness in his tone, his earnest blue-eyed gaze, made her feel ungrateful and impolite for refusing his dinner offer.

She nodded. "A cuppa tea sounds brilliant." The strain of the evening had brought a catch to her voice. "And despite what happened yesterday in your boardroom, I appreciate all you've done for Seamus."

"It's no bother. And I admire you because you've gone way beyond the definition of a devoted sibling."

"You don't know what Seamus has sacrificed for me."

"Care to elaborate or should I speculate?"

She shifted. "Seamus was devastated after his wife, Fiona, died. And although I knew he was depressed, I didn't offer him any support. Instead, I was self-absorbed with my own problems because of Jack."

"Very understandable," Danny said.

Silence settled. He seemed to be waiting for her to say more.

She continued to stare straight ahead. The wipers were relentless, the Irish rain incessant. "I'd assumed our relationship was over. Then one night, Jack crept through the kitchen window and broke into my flat. I screamed, tried to ring for help ... he grabbed the phone from me."

"Is he the reason your windows are bolted?"

"Yeh." She tightened her hands into small fists. "At the time, I hadn't seen Jack around Farthing for weeks and I'd started to feel safe again. If Seamus hadn't arrived when he did ..." She squeezed her eyes shut to block the memories.

"Go on."

She stole a peek at Danny's concerned expression. "I can't."

Danny laced his long fingers around hers. "I didn't mean to upset you."

She accepted his hold, admiring the quiet authority surrounding him, evident in his deep, calm voice and bold, certain strides. He was a man, a real man, unlike any man she'd ever known.

She didn't continue her Jack story, didn't say that Seamus had rushed her to the hospital because she'd suffered a broken rib and numerous bruises from Jack's beating. Or that Seamus had hunted down Jack once she was settled in the hospital. Her brother had never revealed the details. Jack had simply disappeared from her life and been locked in a Cork prison soon afterward.

And now Jack had returned. It couldn't be possible. Not again, when she'd fought so hard to be rid of him. She shook her head in denial, pulled from Danny's grip, and clenched her clammy palms together.

"Your brother told me the same story," Danny said quietly.

"Then why did you ask me?"

"I'm a good listener," he reminded.

"And Seamus could talk the teeth out of a saw." She closed her eyes to stop her weeping. What had started as a conversation about her ex was quickly becoming a crying free-for-all.

Danny reached across the seat. "I carry paper napkins in the glove compartment, which I reserve for crying women I've rescued," he said with amusement.

She gave a self-conscious laugh. "You've known that many?"

The amusement vanished from his face.

She grimaced. Of course he'd known many women, all of them much prettier and more sophisticated than she.

"Actually, you're the first crying woman I've ever cared about." He feigned levity, although his expression had sobered. The sincerity in his voice, the smiling gentleness that returned to his gaze, chipped a piece of the wall away from her fiercely guarded heart.

He pulled out a paper napkin. Stamped on it were the words "The Ground Café" and the recognizable pot-of-gold logo.

She dabbed at her eyes and grinned, before tucking the napkin in her purse. "Always the businessman, yeh?"

He grinned. "I might meet a potential coffee customer passing through the alleyway."

She managed a trembling smile. "You should warn them about coffee being bitter."

Lightly, he touched her cheek. "Not my coffee." His hand traveled to her nape, a light, soothing caress. She should push his hand away, she told herself. Her breath felt thick and heavy in her throat, and she didn't move.

"Somehow, someway, I'll convince you to love my coffee." His arms shifted protectively around her. "You're an extraordinary woman, Clara."

He bent his head. His lips hovered only inches from hers. He smelled of coffee and cream, the scent reassuring.

A breath away. She saw the banked fire of desire in his gaze, and deep inside her a response rose, a longing for his strength, the safety of his powerful, gentle embrace.

She leaned into him, didn't resist when he kissed her, savoring his hard mouth pressing against hers.

He lifted his lips a fraction. "I will protect you, luv." Affection burned in his eyes, deepening them to a rich indigo, the blue specks reminding her of an ocean, deep with complications.

"I'm glad I came to Farthing," he said. "I wasn't supposed to be here. At the last second, one of my managers called in sick, so I drove from Dublin to oversee the grand opening. If I hadn't, I never would've met you."

His hair gleamed the color of a rich mahogany, damp with rain. He'd pushed a strand off his forehead, which only accentuated his sharp Irish features. His well-built arms swelled beneath the sleeves of his work shirt.

Her heart gave a lurch. He was so handsome, so fearless, and he gazed at her with such affection.

"I'm glad you came too," she said softly.

The rain had softened to a light pattering against the windshield. She snuggled closer to him, her cheek touching his chest, and she accepted his comforting embrace.

Practicality intruded. Danny Brady moved in wealthy circles she could hardly fathom. And she'd pledged to safeguard her heart and never be any man's fool again.

Just for tonight, she'd accept his thoughtfulness, his solid arms keeping her secure. Just for tonight she'd focus on the safety he offered, assuring herself that she'd never be imprudent enough to fall for him. She could never love anyone. She'd thought she loved Jack and he'd left her bruised, vulnerable, and ashamed.

Danny tipped up her chin. "Nor would I have had the

pleasure of saving you and your family at every juncture if I'd stayed in Dublin and lived my quiet, uneventful life."

She smiled slightly. "Somehow, I'm sure that your life is the opposite of uneventful. And I could've handled the dire situations myself."

His eyebrows came together in a mild scowl, and she chided herself. She shouldn't repay his kindness with churlish responses. If Danny hadn't rescued her in the alleyway, she could've ended in the hospital. Or worse.

The image of a hulking Jack, the unnerving spider tattoo on his neck, prompted her to shiver.

Danny brushed a kiss on her temples. "You'll catch a chill if you sit in your damp clothes much longer. Let's get back to the coffee shop." With noticeable reluctance, he dropped his arm. "I wrote new song lyrics. Would you be interested in hearing them?"

"You're trying to take my mind off what happened tonight with a song?"

"Aye."

"Sing away."

A combination of affection and incredulity tapped through her. Something as average as writing a song and wanting her to hear it actually gave joy to a successful man like Danny Brady.

As he merged the car into the traffic on the main street, he sang to the tune of "Irish Rover": "My lovely Irish damsel would rather eat an English toffee, if she drinks my Irish lattes, she will relent."

She laughed out loud. "You changed the words."

"Aye, and the changing of the words was intentional." He clicked his blinker and passed a slow-moving car. "Are you working this weekend?"

Now where had that come from?

"I teach a dance class on Saturday morning. Why?"

"On Sunday I'm headed to my main office in Dublin to update several computer files. My lawyer's been researching the specific laws and regulations regarding international franchising, because each country is different. The paperwork is all signed, but I need to reword a couple paragraphs of the agreement and it shouldn't take long." He began singing again. "So will you accompany me on our first date? I'm hoping you'll *consent*."

"I've never been asked out on a date to the lyrics of a song before."

"Should I switch my Irish charm on high to persuade you?"

He'd done enough of that for one night, she thought, feeling a funny squeeze in her stomach at his inviting smile. His damp work shirt hugged his strapping shoulders, and the spell of his heavy-lidded gaze kept her eyes riveted to his. He seemed to grow handsomer by the hour.

"I'd like to go, although I can't," she said. "Anna is counting on our weekly picture show outing, and I'm treating."

"She can go with Seamus. I'll treat them both, and that way Seamus won't be alone. Any other excuses?"

"Housework?"

"Your flat is immaculate." A roguish gleam came to his eyes, and he sang in his baritone voice. "I've invited her to Dublin and hope she will *consent*." He emphasized the last word with an infuriating grin.

She gave in. "All right, yeh, I'll go with you to Dublin. Teresa's Irish Dancers is a prestigious dance academy in the city centre. Perhaps they're hiring instructors. I've always dreamed of owning my own dancing school and naming the school after myself. Does that sound vain?"

"On the contrary, I'm very impressed. If anyone can succeed, you can."

"Unfortunately, funding is required to set up and design a studio." She sighed. "Followed by advertising costs, insurances, permits, leases. Perhaps once Seamus's gambling debt is repaid, I can apply for start-up financing."

"I can lend you the money."

She shook her head. "Thanks. However, if I ever open my own business, I'll do it on my own." She gazed at him for a moment to make sure he understood, and then glanced at her watch. "Doesn't your gig begin at ten o'clock?"

"There'll be no guitar playing at The Ground Café this evening." He leaned over and brushed a kiss on her hair. "The guitarist had a much more important engagement tonight rescuing a damsel in distress."

Later on at her flat, after Seamus was settled on her couch, Clara went to her bedroom and dressed for bed. She tried to sleep. Instead, she stayed awake for hours listening to the rain drumming against her bedroom window. Despite her best efforts, the frightening image of her ex haunted her. Jack was supposed to be behind bars. He wasn't. And because he wasn't, her life had veered madly off course.

The hours passed and her thoughts swirled. Why was Jack in Farthing?

There're some scores needing settling.

That same gut-wrenching slice of fear she'd felt earlier fairly hissed through the air.

She sat upright and slapped a hand on her forehead. Revenge. Of course. Jack wanted revenge, the man who had once-upon-a-time professed undying love. Now she knew better. He'd been professing a controlling, selfish love. Looking back, she realized that his declarations were an elaborate scheme to exert a tight hold over her.

Clara furiously plumped her pillow before abandoning sleep altogether. This situation with Jack was all her fault. How could she have been so thoroughly blind and gullible when the signs of his brutal and controlling nature were evident early on? She longed to retrogress and give that Clara from two years ago a hard shake. Why hadn't she seen what was so evident to everyone else?

The moon was high overhead when Clara came to an irrevocable decision. She'd created her own twisted, difficult mess, despite her family's warnings, and she'd be the one to rid herself of Jack for good. She'd ask about his whereabouts on the streets until someone led her to him. She knew his old hangouts. She'd start there.

And then, once she found him … then, what?

She took in a long breath, blew it out slowly. And then she'd order him to leave town. Surely he'd listen to reason when she reminded him about the restraining order. Violating that alone could send him back to prison for a long time.

Danny, on the other hand, relied on the Gardaí.

Although she appreciated his offer to help, he lived in a different, high-class Dublin world, far removed from the everyday life of common Irish folk. He didn't understand the cold, calculated life of the streets. And if he'd once been there, he'd banished that existence a long time ago.

She swung her feet to the floor and padded to the window. The rain had stopped. She drew aside her lace curtains and peered at the empty, quiet streets.

Except the streets weren't empty nor quiet because a

hulking man, illuminated by a full moon, stood by the stone wall across from her flat.

Her breath hitched. The space in her bedroom filled her ears with a dull roar.

The figure moved, and she blinked for a second, disbelieving.

She rubbed her eyes and drew the lace curtains together. Her blood thrummed in her ears. She flew to her bedroom door and flung it open, fully intending to shout for Seamus.

His thunderous snores resounded from the living room couch, stopping her short.

She withdrew to her bedroom. Without making a sound, she closed the door. She wouldn't wake him. Her dear brother had endured too many hardships already.

She went to the window and slowly drew back the curtains again, scanning the street for signs of movement. The sidewalk was bathed in the light of a clear moon. There was no man, not even his shadow.

She ran her hands through her hair and shook the tension from her neck. Clearly, she was becoming a raving lunatic. She was supposed to be moving forward in her life.

She sat on the edge of her bed and regarded her pale, thin face in her full-length mirror. Should she ring Danny and let him know?

And let him know what, exactly? That she'd imagined the hulking shadow of a man lurking in the dark streets near the stone wall across from her flat?

Adamantly, she shook her head. No, absolutely not.

You promised, a nagging voice reminded. *Danny was there for you tonight when you needed him.*

I didn't see anyone for certain, she sternly prompted herself. Why get Danny all nettled up for nothing? Her mother had lectured her once on the wisdom of silence, quoting a traditional Irish proverb: Melodious is the closed mouth.

There was no disputing the fact that Danny Brady had extended himself for her and her family. He'd established a flourishing business and managed a stunning number of coffee shops and staff. Nevertheless, without a blink of hesitation, for the past three days, he put her catastrophes above his endless responsibilities.

More important, he was caring. And intelligent. He'd said little about his family, off-handedly mentioning a brother and sister who lived in Dublin, as well as his parents and young sister, unexpectedly deceased. He'd kept his features carefully neutral while he'd spoken of them.

And then there was Danny, the musician. He'd framed clever, funny lyrics to his song, all geared to asking her out on a date to Dublin while diverting her attention from the upsetting events of the evening. Considering his jam-packed schedule, he hardly had enough time to devote to his coffee shops, let alone his music. However, *despite* his busyness, he'd treated her as if she were the most important person in the world.

She climbed into bed, mulled her thoughts around. There was definitely more to the man than she'd realized when she'd first met him at the bottom of Farthing Bridge.

So she'd go with him to Dublin. Someday, she'd look back on her date with one of the most eligible, famous bachelors in all Ireland and shake her head in disbelief. He wouldn't be in Farthing long, so she might as well enjoy his consideration and attention.

She stared stiffly at the ceiling as unexpected tears welled. Why did the thought of him leaving create such an unexpected emptiness in her heart?

She yanked her night shirt to her ankles and brushed

away her tears. She could scarcely understand herself anymore, let alone a successful, fetching Irishman with sharp cheekbones set off by eyes the color of a cloudless spring day.

She reminded herself that he was hardly a saint. He'd begun their relationship by choosing to keep his identity a secret from her. Sure, she'd been furious when the truth had been revealed. However, he was also the same man who made her laugh out loud at his teasing banter. And she hadn't laughed, truly laughed, in a long time. And it felt so good.

Will you accompany me? I'm hoping you'll consent. His eyes had sparked with devilish gleam as he sang that, before lingering on her lips.

There was no use in waffling. He wanted to be with her and, in truth, she enjoyed spending time with him. He'd chosen his life's course as she'd chosen hers. So what if they were different? In the short time she'd known him, she'd come to believe in his honesty and integrity.

I will protect you, luv.

His lips had moved tenderly on hers.

Aye, he desired her, though if the tabloids were accurate, he desired many women. And she'd be the biggest fool this side of Sunday if she believed he cared. She was simply a diversion while he established his thriving coffee business in her economically depressed town. Still, no one could fault his generosity, earnest spirit, or easy smile.

She moved her musings ahead to Sunday. Perhaps he'd end their day together in Dublin with another kiss. Perhaps he'd write a love song for her.

She sank against the pillows and smiled. There was absolutely no substitute for a road trip to Dublin with a heartbreakingly handsome musician.

9

A ll week, artfully-arranged bouquets of light-pink roses had been waiting at the doorstep of Clara's flat when she came home from work. One dozen roses. Every evening. She'd asked Danny why he'd chosen the lighter shade, and he'd responded that a light pink rose meant admiration.

"Do you like them?" he'd asked.

"I love them. The fragrance is exquisite." She didn't want to hurt his feelings, nor sound unappreciative by adding that one bouquet of a dozen roses would have been more than enough. Seven dozen was a bit extreme.

Her flat was beginning to smell like a florist shop, until Anna volunteered to help Clara disperse the flowers to a hospital in town.

The cards attached to the bouquets were always written in Danny's confident scroll:

"So glad I'm in Farthing, luv," one had read. "Ring me as soon as you read this so I know you've arrived home safely from work. Your favorite barista, DB."

Their week together had been delightful, save for one

ongoing disagreement. Danny had mentioned, much too casually at dinner that first evening, after he'd rescued her from Jack, that Ian would be escorting her to and from work each day. Ian was pleasant and loyal, Danny said, an asset to Danny's company, but he needed more to do and—

She'd checked Danny's suggestion in midsentence and flatly refused his offer. She could handle her affairs perfectly fine by herself, and, she'd added in a blandly polite tone, "A bodyguard isn't necessary for a small-town woman like me. Thanks, anyway."

After several heated disputes, Danny had reluctantly agreed.

Since Danny's shop had opened, her shifts at work had doubled. The factory supplied local restaurants, and The Ground Café was placing large orders. She had gladly accepted the overtime hours, hoping to use the money to help pay off Seamus's gambling debt. Anna had volunteered to stay with Seamus when he wasn't working so he wouldn't be alone.

Adding to her hectic week, Clara had filed another restraining order against Jack, although he'd disappeared. She'd checked some of his old hangouts and no one had seen him. She held on to the guarded hope that perhaps he'd forgotten about her and taken himself back to Cork.

At the end of the workweek, Clara was walking the two short blocks from her flat to the coffee shop. The air was unseasonably warm, the rain a light misty sheet. Her car's brakes still weren't fixed, and the mechanic had explained it was a bigger job than he'd first estimated. Her car would be in the shop at least another week.

She pulled the hood of her quickly mended quilted jacket over her head and checked her wristwatch. Nearly eight o'clock. Seamus would be finished with his shift.

Tonight, Danny had invited them to stay on at the coffee shop, enjoying dinner and desserts, while he sang Clara the song he'd recently composed.

"I'd appreciate honest opinions," he had joked, adding, "Keep in mind that musicians are fragile, so don't say anything too honest unless it's complimentary."

Five minutes later, she'd arrived at the shop. As always, the exterior was well-lit, the pot of gold mounted on Kelly-green signage and illuminated by a strong spotlight.

Seamus stood smoking near the entryway. He adjusted a brimmed plaid tweed hat to sit lower on his forehead.

"Nice hat," she acknowledged.

"Thanks. It's from Donegal."

How and when had Seamus been able to travel to Donegal? she wondered. The town was several hours north of Farthing.

"What's the craic?" She pecked a kiss on his cheek, surprised when he recoiled.

"No craic or fun to be had working in a hot kitchen all day." He threw the cigarette down and ground the butt into the grass.

She gestured to the cigarette. "Your boss won't approve. Danny enforces a strict no smoking policy in his coffee shops."

"We're outside," Seamus said. "The nicotine calms my nerves after being around those chirpy employees all day." He fidgeted with the buttons of his jacket. He'd seemed edgy the past few days.

"The employees are cheerful because they're working for a good, fair boss."

"Mr. Brady has favorite employees and I'm not one of them. He works me too hard."

She arched a brow. "I'll tell him to ease off. He knows what you've been through."

"Won't do any good." Seamus lit another cigarette, hoisted his pants over too-skinny hips and tightened the worn belt around his waist. He'd lost weight. She'd encouraged him to eat more, although from what Danny had mentioned, Seamus enjoyed two good meals at the coffee shop every day that he worked.

"Ian is probably Danny's favorite employee. I know they're good friends," she told him.

"I haven't seen much of Ian. However, Kathleen, the gorgeous barista, is never far from Mr. Brady's elbow. Is she his personal assistant?"

Clara struggled to keep a bland expression in place. "I don't know. I only met her once."

Dazzling, sultry Kathleen and her devastatingly handsome employer. Kathleen knew everything about his business. She had started with him on the ground floor when he'd begun establishing his coffee empire. They shared a past, a history together.

Feeling an unexpected jolt of jealousy, Clara dragged her gaze from her brother's smug smile.

"Sometimes," Seamus went on, "Mr. Brady and Kathleen disappear for hours and go upstairs."

"Danny's boardroom, offices, and computer are all on the third floor."

"He keeps a small flat on the third floor. I thought you ought to know, sis, before you became too involved with him. I don't want to see you made a laughingstock again, like when Jack was seeing other women while he was controlling you like a marionette."

"Danny Brady and I are just friends. He can do whatever he pleases."

"He certainly has the money for it." Seamus flicked the cigarette ashes on the ground. "Any word on Jack Connor?"

"Nothing." She rubbed her arms to stave off the sudden chill in the air. "Danny nearly ran Jack over with his Mercedes the other night. Jack may have been scared off."

Seamus's fists tightened. "The Donovan family doesn't need no fancy Mercedes to scare off Jack Connor."

"Please, Seamus. Control your temper or you'll make a complete mess of a good thing. Your life is finally changing for the better." She peered at her brother's rough face, the dark circles under his eyes, the tufts of burnt-orange hair poking from his chin. "Are you sleeping okay?"

He rubbed his neck. "Why?"

"The last few nights I heard you pacing the living room. And I thought the front door opened and closed around two in the morning."

His brows pulled together. He drew a last drag, threw his cigarette on the grass and grabbed a fresh one. "You're mistaken, sis. I always—"

"I assumed you'd gone outside for a smoke," she interrupted.

Like Danny, she enforced a strict no-smoking policy in her flat, and Seamus had agreed to smoke outdoors. However, that was the only request Seamus respected. She usually came home after work to a pile of dirty pots and pans in the sink, as well as his soiled wash strewn in the bathroom.

It was okay, she reminded herself. Small stuff. Everyone went through hard times. Seamus required all his strength to recover from his sadness over Fiona's death, plus recover from his addictions.

He dragged more nicotine in his lungs. "I sleep like a newborn babe at your place."

"You'll always have a home with me, because we're family."

Despite his punched-tight body language, a smile lit the creases on his freckled face. "You're a fine, pretty thing, you know?"

"You're mistaking me for Anna." She linked her fingers together and regarded her navy-blue jacket and khaki slacks. Her plain wardrobe lacked color and style, and she couldn't recall the last time she'd purchased anything new for herself. Perhaps, using some of her overtime money, she'd purchase a fashionable outfit for her upcoming date to Dublin. Something light and bright. The weather forecast for the weekend called for sunshine.

Regretfully, she shook her head. Perhaps in Danny's world a woman could shop on a whim, but certainly not in hers. She couldn't afford a new outfit of any sorts. Seamus still owed the bookies over five hundred euros, a near fortune on their combined salaries.

He had become unnaturally quiet and covered a yawn. "Mind if I head to your flat? The boss spent the last half hour looking out the shop window waiting for ya, and he saw enough of me for one day."

She hesitated. "We agreed someone will stay with you at all times."

Seamus shifted from one leg to the other. "Aww, Clara, trust your big brother. What will I be tempted by? One of your lemon scones? There's no liquor in your flat."

Several customers exited the coffee shop talking and laughing, but then sneaking uneasy glances at Clara and Seamus. Danny followed the last customer through the entry, and stood on the threshold to his shop, his arms crossed.

He regarded Seamus and Clara before he spoke. "Am I interrupting something?"

"My younger sister is being overprotective, telling a grown man he can't be left alone for a couple hours. I can't talk to her without getting lock-hard, unsolicited advice. She's making me feel like a child." Seamus threw his cigarette on the grass. "That's not the way to help a man, is it? She's stealing away my self-confidence."

Danny frowned at the smoldering cigarette. "Did you tell your sister you received your first paycheck today, Seamus?"

"I was just getting around to that." Seamus did a change about. "Sis, I made—"

"Congratulations, Seamus! Your first paycheck in over a year," Clara broke in.

Despite his unmistakably unwelcome body language, she hugged him.

Seamus stood stiffly and stuffed his hands into his jacket pockets. "I figured on walking to the city centre and buying you a gift with some of the money I earned. You've ruined my birthday surprise for ya by all your harping."

She dropped her hands. "Seamus, I'm sorry."

Danny looked at Clara. "You're celebrating a birthday?"

"Not for a while. My adoptive parents decided to celebrate my birthday on Saint Joseph's Day, which is two days after Saint Patrick's Day. The Italian orphanage didn't have a record of my actual birth date. My parents wanted to honor my Italian heritage in an Irish country so they chose Saint Joseph, the Italian saint. Too much information, right?"

"So your birthday is March nineteenth," Danny summarized.

"Yeh."

"Welcome to the thirties. I'm thirty-five."

"How did you know I was going to be thirty?"

"Your brother told me."

"Of course." She laughed and shook her head. Sometimes she believed the only reason Danny had hired Seamus was to glean information about her. Which was ridiculous, of course, because her ordinary life wasn't of interest to a billionaire. And any dirt on her had been spread across the front page of a two-year-old newspaper. She was old Farthing news.

She suppressed the inclination to pick up Seamus's discarded cigarette and throw it in the garbage. Instead, she stared into Danny's laser-beamed gaze. He was so fine-looking, his strong build reminding her more of a leading man in a Hollywood picture than a coffee shop entrepreneur. His gaze was thoughtful, his full mouth turned up into a grin.

Mesmerized, she felt a piece of her heart melt. Perhaps he was more interested in her than she realized.

She released a ragged sigh. Umm, no. Everyone knew that rich people weren't the least bit interested in poor people. Still, the thought that he might be a wee bit taken with her made her pulse unexpectedly quicken.

Seamus widened his stance and focused on Danny. "Clara and I enjoyed a lovely chat last night over a pot of tea. Whenever I'm thinking of going astray, she sets me straight."

"I'm very proud of you, Seamus," Clara said. "Please, go ahead and—" She stopped in midsentence. "Are you going to my flat first, or the city centre?"

Seamus pulled at the collar of his ill-fitting cargo jacket. "I'll walk to the city centre first and browse the shops before they close. I might meet Liam."

Danny's expression became watchful. "Seamus, you're welcome to spend the evening with us and visit the shops in the morning. Ian and Anna are stopping by, and I can drive you and Clara home later."

Seamus threw Danny a look of mock disgust. "Don't take offense, boss. I've been running the dishwasher ten hours today in your hot, steaming kitchen and I'm knackered. Besides, you two couples will want to spend time together without a big brother in the way." He pivoted back to Clara. "So, I'll meet you at your flat later."

There was no mistaking the urgency in Seamus's voice. He was curt, defensive. Had he always acted like that? No, not always. The shift had been gradual.

"I thought you were walking to the city centre," she said.

"Clara, you're always analyzing every word I say. I meant *after* I shop for your gift."

Danny stepped forward. His gaze was sharp, carving a warning. "Don't talk to your sister in that derogatory tone."

Clara started at the bite of anger emanating from Danny's six-foot frame.

"My brother is only teasing," she said, attempting to diffuse the situation. "He often speaks to me that way."

Seamus seemed to shrink a hair. "Only joking, boss. I'm just a big brother winding my baby sister up. If you had a baby sister, you'd understand."

Danny hesitated. He stiffened. "I did," he said after a long pause. "She's dead."

Clara flinched. "Danny, Seamus didn't know about your sister's death."

She was making excuses, she realized. She was always making excuses for her brother.

As if reading her mind, Danny ran a hand through his hair, then pulled a business card from his wallet and gave it to Seamus. "Ring my office any time."

"Yeh, thanks." Seamus lit another cigarette, swung around, and strode briskly in the direction of the town centre.

Later, when Clara reflected on their conversation, she wondered why Seamus had rushed past her like a man who'd been given a reprieve from the guillotine. And why she hadn't realized that all the shops in town closed at six o'clock.

10

The atmosphere in the after-hours coffee shop was so different from during the day, Clara mused. Quiet and calm, the customers gone, only a few employees organizing the shelves and polishing display cases. An Irish ballad about a fair maiden who'd lost her true love in Galway played softly in the background.

The scent of chocolate and butter cream, and, yes, the aroma of rich coffee beans caused Clara to halt in the middle of the lobby and sniff approvingly. Sea salt caramel candies were set in covered glass jars behind the counter. The sleek coffee shop boasted large, comfortable couches, Wi-Fi, computers set at various tables, and muted television sets. Half of the lobby was shelved with current books and magazines.

Danny stood at the cash register ringing receipts while she wandered to a display of CDs. She scanned the titles, noting his name on several covers. She picked one featuring an Irish fiddle and bagpipe and skimmed the list of songs.

"Who's Glenna?" she asked.

Danny glanced up, his hand hovering above the cash register pad. "Why?"

"Because the name of this instrumental piece is 'Ode to Glenna.' Was she a former girlfriend?"

"My ex-wife's name was Kyla," was all he offered. When Clara raised her brows, he finished, "My marriage was disastrous and short-lived. Unfortunately, we couldn't come to terms on our initial agreement, which resulted in a heavily publicized and ugly divorce."

So he'd been married. And Glenna was someone else.

"Can I take the CD home? I enjoy traditional Irish music, and I'll pay you, of course."

"Didn't I tell you that everything in my shop is free for you?" he said with a teasing smile.

She grinned. "No, but thanks. Are you singing on the CD?"

"Just one selection."

"I look forward to listening." She perused the song list until Anna rapped loudly on the front glass plate window.

"Anybody home?" Anna shouted above the Galway ballad.

Danny strode to the door and unlocked it. Ian stood at the entry beside Anna, fumbling with a set of keys. Both Anna and Ian removed their motorcycle helmets as rain pelleted the windows.

"I couldn't find the keyring to the shop and upstairs office, boss." Ian hurried Anna inside. "Do you have an extra set for the boardroom?"

"I should." Danny shook his head as he walked back to the cash register. "Last month you couldn't find your motorcycle in the shopper's mart parking lot. Took you an hour to find it parked at the end of the plaza. You're becoming more and more forgetful."

"Now I park my motorcycle near the entrance, and haven't lost it since."

"How can you lose a motorcycle?" Anna reached around the counter for a caramel candy and chewed appreciatively. "A keyring maybe, but a candy-blue and canary-yellow motorcycle with shiny metal fenders?"

"Lots of people are absent-minded," Danny said. He looked at Ian. "Perhaps you're working too hard."

Anna stopped chewing. "Then this is the perfect occasion to offer him a holiday, somewhere sunshiny and warm with his girlfriend. I've always wanted to revisit Portugal, my birthplace. I may have birth siblings there."

All gazes turned to Anna. "Thanks for the broad hint. Glad you joined us," Danny said.

"A free meal, coffee, and dessert at the newest hot spot in town? Who could resist? This entire plaza was a kip, a dump, and your transformation is amazing." Anna smiled broadly. "Be warned that you've taken on an expensive venture offering free food to our family. We love to eat."

Clara grinned. "Don't tell him that. He'll worry we'll cut into his profit margin."

"Enjoying time with you and your family is my pleasure." Danny closed the cash register and placed the receipts in a drawer. "That's why I'm working. To keep you all well-fed, employed, and happy." He strode back to Clara and whispered, "And to keep you safe and protected."

Before she could take a breath and remind him that she didn't need protecting, Anna laughed and said, "We're singing with joy ever since you came to town, Danny."

"Don't tell him that, either." Clara rolled her eyes. "He's likely to burst into song at the slightest provocation."

"You have one of the boss's CDs, Clara?" Ian eyeballed the CD she held in her hand.

"Yeh. He's feeling generous and said I could take it home. No charge."

"Did he tell you that all the proceeds from the sales of his CDs are donated to a children's charity in Dublin?"

"No, he didn't." Hurt and annoyed that Danny hadn't mentioned anything about the proceeds going to charity, Clara tucked the CD in her purse and glared at him.

"I'm sorry, Clara." Danny complemented his apology with an easy smile. "Am I forgiven?"

Ian shot Clara a look of wounded dignity on Danny's behalf. "You'll soon learn, Miss Clara, that the boss says little about his good deeds. Nevertheless, he's known throughout the world for his philanthropy."

The absurdity of Clara's annoyance prompted her to shake her head. She shouldn't be infuriated at Danny because he was generous and didn't flaunt his good deeds.

"You're forgiven," she hastened to assure him.

Still smiling, Danny poured two steaming cups of herbal tea from a dispenser behind the counter, secured the lids, and handed one to Clara. "Even *I* think it's too late for coffee."

"Tea is brilliant, thanks."

He took her hand and led her to the door marked *private*, calling to Ian and Anna that he was writing a song he wanted Clara to hear. "Help yourselves to whatever, sandwiches, desserts, beverages, in the kitchen, and we'll join you later."

"Just in case your song takes longer to sing than you anticipated," Anna said with a knowing grin, "are there any slices of your divine Guinness cake left in the kitchen?"

"Aye. And tomorrow there will be an even better offering." Danny exchanged a glance with Clara. "Will you share your prized lemon scone recipe?"

"Do I get a commission?"

"How does a flat fee of ten thousand euros sound?"

"Twenty thousand is fairer," she quipped.

"Agreed." Setting his tea down on the counter, he grabbed a pad and handed her his gold pen. "Can you write the recipe down for me?"

"Sure. It's easy and I have it memorized." She set her tea beside his and jotted the ingredients and recipe on the pad. "Tell your bakers to knead the dough first," she instructed as she handed the sheet to him. "And drizzle the glaze on the scones when they come out of the oven and are still warm."

He examined the paper and placed it in his pocket. "Thank you." His gaze dipped to her mouth before he led her through the private door. The reward for her recipe was a caress of his strong fingers against her nape and an unexpected, passionate kiss that took her breath away.

DANNY CLUNG to the feeling of Clara's lips pressed against his as they rode the lift. He'd watched the conflicting reactions flicker across her beautiful face. She'd been obviously surprised by his kiss, feigning indifference at first. He'd deepened the kiss and, with a sigh, she'd wrapped her hands around his neck and kissed him. When the lift doors opened and the kiss came to an end, he drew a shaky breath. Slowly, his hand roved up her back.

"Fast lift," he remarked.

Less than a minute later, they stood facing the door to his boardroom. He rattled the locked door handle and released it.

"Where is that keyring?" he muttered to himself. He

glared at the door with one hand on his hip. "All the files are on my computer, including the song I was writing for you."

"How're you going to get in the boardroom?" Clara asked.

"How do you think?" He handed her his cup and lifted the decorative doormat in front of the door.

"My boots aren't muddy, are they?" She raised one foot and then the other, checking the bottom of her boots.

He held up a keyring that had been under the mat and smiled. He inserted a gold key into the lock, swung open the door, and gestured for her to enter as he flicked on the lights.

"A billionaire hides a spare keyring to his boardroom under the doormat?" she asked.

"Soon-to-be billionaire," he corrected with a grin. "Although I plan to become a billionaire once my franchises go global."

"Why go global when you're so successful right here in Ireland?"

"Because I'm a driven man and never satisfied." He grabbed his cup of tea from her. "I can enter new overseas markets, gain additional customers, and double the coffee shop's net worth. Someday I'll tell you more, if you're interested."

"I'm interested." She quirked a delicate eyebrow and said wryly, "No one can fault your ambition, Danny." Her statement was followed by a prominent wheeze.

He shoved the keyring into his pocket and smoothed his fingers over her shoulders. "How are you feeling?"

"Couldn't be better."

"Aye, so it seems."

There could be a remedy to soothe her breathing, although she would probably resist his suggestion that he help her pursue that. Nevertheless, he would try. "My doctors in Dublin are excellent. Would you like me to make an appointment with one of them?" He kept his tone light as they walked into the boardroom, their feet sinking into the thick wool carpeting.

She studied the carpet before meeting his stare. Her huge, dark eyes showed exhaustion. "Absolutely not. My cough will subside now that spring is approaching and the weather will be getting warmer."

Her airy response despite her obvious fatigue was so typical that Danny almost acted unconcerned. "And then autumn will arrive again. And then what?"

She rubbed a brow as if to ward off the question and didn't respond.

He set both cups atop ceramic coasters on the coffee table, pushed a pile of magazines aside and gestured to the espresso-colored leather sofa. "Please sit and rest a bit."

She collapsed against the sofa and sighed. "The money part of the overtime is grand, while all those hours lifting heavy boxes is difficult. Between taking care of Seamus and juggling my jobs, I haven't slept much."

He sat beside her, wanting to take her into his arms. She shouldn't work so hard, struggle as much as she did. A woman like Clara deserved to be sheltered and pampered, spoiled with extravagant gifts and a magnificent home.

"Shouldn't you check your computer files?" she asked.

He opened her tea and handed the cup to her. "The files can wait."

She took a sip. Several beats passed.

"What are you thinking?" he asked, deciding to engage in pleasant conversation to divert her from her tiredness.

"I'm thinking about how much my family's life has changed this past week."

"Hopefully for the better?"

She set her cup precisely in the middle of the coaster and fixed her gaze out the picture window. The view captured nighttime in the little town of Farthing, all smudged by a misty rain. The Farthing streetlights gleamed, creating a shadow play on her smooth cheeks.

"You've offered endless kindnesses—the flowers, meals, employment ..."

He moved closer and draped his arm around her. "And you can repay me by accepting my protection. Please consider my offer to enlist Ian as your bodyguard until Jack Connor is safely behind bars."

She shot him a frown. "Did anyone ever tell you that persistence isn't always a good quality?"

"It's one of the best qualities for running a successful business."

"However, I'm not a business, I'm a person."

Danny had the uncomfortable feeling he'd somehow managed to say the wrong thing, despite the fact that most everyone knew that successful businesses and persistence went hand in hand. Successful personal relationships, on the other hand, required caring and ... affection.

He stood and cleared his throat. "I won't be long checking my files."

She plucked an issue of *Entrepreneur* magazine off the stack and began leafing through it. "I assure you I can amuse myself."

He took a seat at his computer and scanned the files, relieved to find the coffee shop's invoices, balance sheets, spreadsheets, and banking information hadn't been tampered with. For some unsettling reason, he'd feared someone had hacked into his files, most likely because of the unnerving mystery of the missing keyring. Satisfied, he shut down his computer and settled onto the leather sofa beside her.

She didn't glance up, apparently deeply engrossed in *Entrepreneur*.

Briefly, he closed his eyes, counting how many days remained before he was scheduled to depart for London. His lovely companion didn't seem remotely interested that he was sitting so close. He propped one foot on the opposite knee and regarded her. As always when she was near, he could think of little else. Her beauty distracted him.

He shook his head. He didn't have room in his life for distractions. He needed to concentrate on one goal, offering franchises worldwide to secure his wealth. Then he would find the peace that he'd been searching for, insulated from the poverty and insecurity he'd known.

He watched Clara in the silence. Soon, he'd be required elsewhere, although he refused to dwell on that thought, the absolute finality of his departure. After spending the week with her, he didn't want to leave her picturesque town, her quirky family. Dining with her every evening, laughing together as they walked the rainy streets, writing lyrics to a song ... These simple activities had caused him to stop and reflect on everything that had been missing in his life. Snippets of the ordinary. He'd forgotten they existed, and the joy those moments brought to his hectic, demanding world.

In the reasonably short amount of time since he'd become successful, he'd known plenty of attractive, ambitious women who had eagerly accepted any invitations he'd casually extended. Yet Clara was hesitant to spend one day in Dublin with him until he'd convinced her with a song. She wasn't a woman who'd wanted to date him for his money or fame. If anything, Clara was furious when she'd learned who he really was.

The object of his thoughts studied the open magazine in her hands and murmured, "Did you know that one of the characteristics for a successful entrepreneur is to be passionate about your work?"

"Aye. And you have a passion for teaching dance," he pointed out.

She straightened. "Once Seamus is better, I'm applying for city funding to open my own dance studio. I want to teach underprivileged preschoolers. These children have nowhere to go after school except an empty house with a disinterested sitter."

He considered her remark. "Sounds good." He emphasized the good, in case she didn't believe how much he believed in her. And he did. He couldn't recall the last time anyone's face had lit up like Clara's when she'd described teaching the young boys and girls.

"My options are limited because Miss Sophie, the director, won't allow me to teach any more classes."

"Why not?"

With a small, grim smile, Clara said, "I was in trouble a while back and she won't let me forget it."

Danny caught Clara's chin and pressed her to look at him. "What kind of trouble?"

"Browse an old copy of the Farthing newspaper." Her expression turned guarded, and she didn't meet his gaze. "Just remember there's more to the story than what's printed on the page."

He waited for her to explain further. Instead, she turned back to her reading.

He picked up his tea, now lukewarm, and gazed out the window. The sleepy Farthing streets radiated in four different directions off Main Street, the backbone of a town with ten thousand people. The six pubs were undoubtedly open and ready for business. Farthing was so different from the bustling city of Dublin, which boasted an international airport, world-famous statues and landmarks, and restaurants too numerous to list.

Once, as a child, he'd loved Dublin. Now that he was an adult, the city brought regrets and remorse, tied to a sadness that wouldn't leave his gut despite the three-story mansion he'd built. His home was ridiculously large. Located in the coastal area, its view of the sea was jaw dropping. He rarely visited the place.

His gaze traveled to Clara, and he studied the fine contours of her features, her natural, flawless complexion devoid of makeup. If he'd met her sooner in his life, would she have been able to teach him tolerance for his parents' shortcomings, the tolerance she'd exhibited so freely and patiently with Seamus? Could Clara have given him a purpose grander than procuring wealth, the pursuit that shaped his entire adult life? Could she have reignited his joy so that he felt free to compose and sing whenever he wished? In the throes of building his business, he'd regrettably put his music aside.

Danny took a deep breath and slowly let the air out of his lungs. Someday, after his international franchises were secured, he'd return to his music making. At present, though, wealth brought well-being and self-respect. He'd met hunger firsthand and preferred luxury.

Despite his ambitions, he didn't know how to quell the "what if" questions racing through his mind. His gaze perused Clara's lovely figure, the silky hair gliding across her shoulders. And her soft lips, the pouty, full outline that encouraged his kisses.

He shifted. "Whenever you're done reading that riveting article, we can chat."

Clara set the magazine on the coffee table. "What do you want to talk about?"

"Tell me about yourself."

"Haven't you learned enough about me through my chatterbox brother?"

Danny sipped his tea. "When it comes to you, my curiosity is insatiable."

She changed positions on the sofa to face him, pulling her knees to her chest. A mischievous grin played on her features. "Well, for one thing, I could've broken into the boardroom for you."

He stopped in midswallow. "What did you say?"

"The deadbolt lock. I know how to break in most anywhere. I learned to pick a lock when I shoplifted in Italy." She wiggled her fingers. "It's easy. You take a credit card, slide it into where the barrel connects with the doorjamb, wiggle the door handle a wee bit, and—"

He gaped, setting his tea on the table before he dropped it. "You stole?"

"Mainly food for me and the other kids in the orphanage, sometimes warm clothes for the toddlers."

"You stole?" Danny repeated again in sheer disbelief. She was certainly a woman full of discrepancies—unafraid, impulsive ... enchanting ... and full of surprises.

"If I hadn't, some of the littler ones in the orphanage wouldn't have survived the winter. They most likely would have died from starvation."

"How old were you when you were adopted?" He touched his throat, somewhat surprised that he hadn't been rendered speechless by her admission.

"Almost six. The older boys and I snuck out of the orphanage a lot. We learned how to dodge the security cameras in the posh shops."

"Risky business for a five year old, wouldn't you say?"

She straightened. Her defensiveness filled the air. Remorse came with it. "The orphanage didn't feed us nearly enough. I had no choice."

Danny shook his head. He visualized Clara, the protector, spine erect, brown eyes flashing, ready to take on the world for her suicidal brother at the top of a precariously high bridge. And Clara, the thin, five-year-old street urchin, sporting short wispy bangs and a helmet of shaggy hair, ready to take on the rough Italian streets so that she could steal food for the orphanage children.

Her devotion to the people she loved was incredible. He watched her stunning smile and felt a bump in his pulse. She must've been born with that smile on her alluring lips.

And then he felt it again. Another bump, followed by a curious, urgent tug on his heart.

"The older boys taught me lots of criminal tricks," she went on. "Just think of the notorious career I could've had if my parents hadn't adopted me."

Danny's shout of laughter ricocheted off the walls. He drew her near and buried his face in her luxuriously lemony-fragrant hair. "No one except me could have come to Farthing on a business trip and met Italy's greatest crook. Do I dare ask if you were ever caught?"

"Only once, when the matron in charge of the orphanage found out." Clara's demeanor changed. She clutched her arms to her stomach, her expression revealing surprising vulnerability. With a sigh, she rested her head against his shoulder.

"What happened?" he asked softly.

She chewed her bottom lip. "The matron locked me in a closet. It was so cold in there, so dark, like the walls were closing in on me. The matron said she wanted to teach me a lesson."

"Did you learn any lessons?" Danny tempered his voice. Inwardly, he envisioned wrapping his hands around that particular matron's neck and squeezing tightly.

"I learned not to get caught."

Danny smiled. It was just like Clara to grow weary of an establishment that didn't care properly for its own and take matters into her own hands.

"You're certain that stealing was the best solution?"

She looked up at him with a wounded expression. "If I didn't steal, I would've been forced to beg."

"And you're too proud to beg?"

"I felt embarrassed sitting on a corner, rattling a tin cup and asking for handouts. I relied on myself."

He settled an arm around her. "You're not desperate anymore. You're a determined, sometimes stubborn woman who insists on assuming every burden by herself. However, if you are ever in a pinch, you have me."

"I've learned to be independent because I've been let down before. I can assure you that it will never happen again."

"I'll never let you down, luv." His profession came clear and simple. He stared into the depths of her determined, chocolate-brown eyes. She was fascinating and ingenious and resilient. And more of the pieces of how she had been formed were coming together. "Sometimes I wish you were weaker so that I could be stronger for you."

She squared her shoulders and seemed to push out her words. "You don't want my problems added to your all-too-full plate. You'll be leaving soon."

"Not yet."

"Soon enough." He felt her withdrawing, despite the fact

that she hadn't moved. "So now that I've told you about my life, can you tell me more about yours?"

"Perhaps."

He knew that if they spent more time together, ultimately he'd tell her all of it—his parents' suicides, his young sister's death, his strained relationship with his siblings. And the guilt. Always the guilt. Although he didn't know why he felt compelled to share his story with her. He'd never told anyone about his past, not even his ex-wife. Only his siblings knew, and they never spoke of it because too many other sentiments from the past would roll to the surface. They'd decided years ago to bury the past alongside the gravestones in Glasnevin Cemetery.

Perhaps he'd tell Clara because she'd already inspired him much more than she'd realized—by her wry humor, her fortitude, her willingness to carry other people's problems without harboring a shred of resentment.

He tightened his arm around her, tilted her chin, bent his head.

Her eyes twinkled up at him. "You really want to kiss me after my confession?"

"Did you ever botch a job?"

"The older boys in the orphanage said I was so good I could've stolen the sugar out of their punch."

His lips were a breath from hers. "I'm delighted to know a first-class thief in case I'm desperate for coffee beans and my finances run low."

"I'm a reformed crook. I may have lost my touch."

"If I were a betting man, I'd wager some skills are never truly lost." He buried her laughing lips against his, pleased that she'd yielded so sweetly.

An hour later, they'd finished their tea, accompanied by increasingly light banter. As they were leaving the boardroom, Clara glanced at her phone. "Seamus texted me. He went to visit Anna and should return to my flat shortly."

The hour was late, the streets murky, when Danny drove Clara to her flat.

"I could've walked home," she protested for the second time.

He'd insisted. He certainly wouldn't allow her to walk home alone in the dark.

He went around his car to open the door for her. "And deprive me of an excuse to escort you to your door and kiss you good night?"

They stood on her front steps, and as she looked into his eyes, he felt his chest grow tight. The lyrics from "Oh Danny Boy" flooded his mind, the song they'd sung together in her flat only a few short days ago. So much had happened since then. He tried to push away the thought that he'd be leaving Farthing soon. He would be forced to travel the world in order to promote his international franchises. He had no other choice, his climb to success outweighing all other options.

Oh Danny Boy.

Were the pipes truly calling him?

He pulled in a shaky breath.

Droplets of rain began to fall, mingling with the fog.

From under the awning over the front entrance, they took in the quaint stone buildings on her cobblestoned street and the craggy hills in the distance. She ran a hand through her damp hair.

"What do you love most about Farthing?" she asked.

He smiled. "The wet weather?"

"It's a fine night for young ducks."

He framed her face in his hands. "What I love most about Farthing ... is you."

Her gaze darkened with an affection she didn't attempt to hide. He touched her lips in a soft, warm kiss.

And in the space of a heartbeat, he knew that leaving Farthing was going to be far more difficult than he'd imagined, more difficult than his decision to quit school, or his decision to leave the safe confines of his aunt's home to start his own business.

He buried his face in Clara's hair and closed his eyes.

Her fingers spread across his jaw, urging him to look at her. "When are you leaving?"

She'd read his mind, their thoughts in unity.

"I'll be required to attend business meetings in London by the middle of next week."

"I wish you could've stayed longer. I wish ..." Her voice sounded broken, a shattered whisper.

He touched her lips with his fingers, quieting her. "Don't. Don't make it more difficult than it already is."

She actually flinched from his firm tone.

"Your business is more important. I know that, I just thought ..." She looked away and raised her chin. "No worries. I won't mention your departure again."

Clara and Danny climbed the hallway stairs and stepped into her empty flat. Clara's gaze darted around the living room. "It's so quiet without Seamus here. I'd expected him to have arrived by now."

"Why did he visit Anna at this hour?"

Clara glanced at her watch. "Why not? He's a grown man. He told me to give him more space and I agreed. I can't be hovering over him every second."

"Do you want me to stay until he returns?"

Her fingers waved an airy dismissal. "I'll be fine."

"Then thank you for a delightful evening." Danny kissed her one more time, another excuse to hold her. "And I promise I won't share a word of your secret with anyone."

She cocked her head. "What secret?" she asked with sham innocence while smiling like an angel.

He grinned all the way to his car. Out of the corner of his eye, he detected a man's silhouette. Danny waited, peering into the darkness. Seeing nothing, he reached for his car keys, but then decided to retrace his steps. The foggy night brought a disorienting inky somberness to the streets. Hadn't there been a streetlight lit on the corner the last time he'd visited her? If so, the light had gone out, leaving only a slant of moonlight sifting through the clouds.

Danny pulled out his cell phone and switched on the flashlight app, searching for footprints near the stone wall. A pickup truck's headlights switched on and unexpectedly swerved, blinding him. He shielded his eyes. The truck rammed into his parked Mercedes, leaving the front fender scratched and damaged.

"Hey! What the—" Immediately spoiling for a knock-down fight, Danny was already pulling off his coat and rolling up his sleeves as he rushed toward the truck.

It quickly sped past. "You're an eejit, a bloody eejit!" the driver yelled. The man in the passenger seat wore a brimmed hat drawn low over his forehead. He sank down in the seat and quickly averted his face.

Danny shook his head in mock disgust at himself and returned to his car. He should've reacted quicker, raced faster. He'd fought his way through the Dublin streets when he'd lived with his aunt and uncle, and was considered a pro when it came to a good, solid fistfight. He hadn't tolerated his family being called drunken meads, not by the rough, secondary-school lads, not by anyone.

He thrust aside the memories.

The rain had stopped. The air felt heavy, the sky was tar-black. He shivered, kneading the tight muscles in his shoulders. He'd been working too hard, while preoccupied by a stunning Italian Irishwoman. He pulled on his coat and checked the damage to his car. Scratches and minor dents, he determined. He'd take the car to the garage when he returned to Dublin.

As he turned the car's ignition switch, he decided he

would employ Ian to keep an eye on Clara whenever she commuted to and from work. And he wouldn't tell her.

He didn't want to keep his decision from her, didn't want to unduly frighten her. However, he had no choice, and her protests be damned. Jack Connor was, in Clara's own words, dangerous and unpredictable, and Danny refused to leave her vulnerable and unprotected. This latest incident could've been a coincidence. The men in the truck were plastered, very drunk, out for a good time. They seemed to be of university age.

No. He corrected. They were older. One of the men's hair was platinum blond, probably why he had first assumed the men were younger.

Danny returned to the coffee shop and rode the lift to his small flat. He stopped in midstep before he started down the hall.

He'd never sung his new song for Clara. He'd forgotten. His thoughts had been diverted by something much deeper than his beloved music. And he recognized that his carefully controlled emotions were slowly becoming unhinged by an angelic smile and a reformed thieving orphan.

12

Sunday morning had sped by. After Clara had attended church services, Danny's Town Car had arrived at exactly ten o'clock. The chauffeur, wearing a coolly crisp uniform, had opened the back door of the sedan, and she'd bade him a cheery good morning. With a broad smile and a good day, the chauffeur had driven her the short blocks to The Ground Café.

Two jazz clubs at the end of the renovated plaza displayed "Coming Soon" signs, and an ice cream shop announced an early May opening. Danny had single-handedly breathed new growth into a tired town and rundown square.

He stood outside his shop waiting for her. His navy wool pants appeared expertly tailored, contrasting with a cadet-blue button-down shirt that outlined his muscular build. A long camel-colored coat was slung over one arm; he held a leather briefcase in the other hand.

"How are ya?" Danny nodded to the chauffeur.

Ducking into the seat beside her, Danny deposited his coat and briefcase near him. Then he greeted Clara with a broad smile and light kiss, his gaze drifting over her admiringly.

"You are gorgeous." He nuzzled her neck. "I love when you wear your hair away from your face. Your eyes remind me of a dark, rich espresso."

"My eyes remind you of coffee?"

"I love coffee."

The unflinching approval in his tone did amazing things to her pulse. She felt her cheeks heat as he helped her off with her jacket and placed it beside him.

She'd shopped at the thrift store in town, thrilled to snag a new, fitted multi-colored paisley top that she wore over a bright-red tank. Charcoal-grey cotton slacks completed her outfit. She'd secured her hair from her face in a thick, wavy ponytail.

The heady effect of their anticipated afternoon in Dublin combined with Danny's male nearness, the tangy scent of his cologne, prompted her to say, "You're gorgeous, too."

A wide grin lit his face, lending him an endearingly youthful appearance. She couldn't help but smile at his response.

Clara leaned her head against the luxurious headrest. Seamus and Anna were seeing an afternoon matinee, and Ian was stopping by Anna's flat afterward. For the first time in a long while, she'd be able to enjoy a worry-free afternoon. As her entire body lightened, her eyes drifted shut.

When she opened her eyes, afternoon sunlight filtered through the windows of the sedan and trees went by in a blur. A Celtic harp solo strummed delicately on the CD player. She blinked and took a second to consider where she was. Danny's arm was firmly around her. She sighed with contentment, settled deeper into the sedan's comfortable leather seats and snuggled nearer his warm, strong body.

His fingers brushed her cheek. "Clara, we're nearing Dublin. Time to wake up, luv."

She offered a weak grin. "I slept the entire trip?"

"All two hours of it." His chuckle was muffled against her hair. "You fell asleep so quickly, I didn't want to wake you. This week has been exhausting for you." He pulled his arm from around her and sighed. "I have some work I should review."

In the serene haze that comes after sleeping so soundly, she studied him while he leafed through a stack of documents he'd extracted from his briefcase. His spiky dark lashes offset the brilliant crystal-blue of his eyes. His face was all strong angles and chiseled features.

His entire demeanor changed as he reviewed his paperwork. Even his voice, when he said he had some work to review, had taken on a more professional tone. No longer was he the relaxed guitar player who'd sung "Oh Danny Boy" in her Farthing flat. He'd transformed into a man firmly in control, his mouth set, his posture strong. His straight coppery-brown brows drew together as he shuffled papers scribbled with numbers. He caught her staring at him and offered a rueful grin.

She let down the window and the wind whipped her hair, the air smelling of mustard-yellow blossoms and freshness. She breathed in and slowly exhaled.

"You haven't coughed," Danny noted.

"The brilliant weather and bit of sun eases my symptoms."

"Perhaps you should move somewhere exotic and sunny?"

She shook her head. "I love Ireland and would never leave."

As they entered the city, she saw sprouts of glade-green grass lining the cobblestone sidewalks, and people walked at a brisk pace, smiling and talking to one another. Dogs barked eagerly, running after rubber balls and wagging their tails with excitement. Everyone was having a love affair with the vibrant spring day. Clara lifted her face to the sun shimmering through mere wisps of clouds, brilliant streams of light. Dublin was exactly as she'd envisioned, vibrant and energetic.

Near the city centre, they drove past the famous Molly Malone statue on the corner of Grafton and Suffolk Streets.

"Tart with a cart," Danny provided with a laugh.

"Please don't start singing 'Cockles and Mussels,'" Clara warned.

Too late. He'd already begun. Clara couldn't resist joining in.

She admired Trinity College, and even the ashen-grey smoke from dilapidated smokestacks that dappled the sky. Pearls of sunlight sparkled on the River Liffey, and silently, Clara thanked Danny for the opportunity to see Dublin.

As they neared Pearse Street, Danny knocked on the window partition between the front and backseats, and instructed the chauffeur to park in a side parking lot.

"This is my flagship store." Danny pointed to a brick cornerstone building. "All my stores are set up with the offices located on the third floor."

"And a flat for you?"

"Aye." He clicked off the harpist. "Oftentimes, I work late. Otherwise, I drive to my house in Howth."

"You own a home in Howth? I've heard lots of famous people live there, including my favorite Top 40 Irish singer."

Danny placed his paperwork in his briefcase and snapped it shut. "I haven't met my neighbors. I'm so busy traveling, I don't get home often."

As the chauffeur pulled into the parking lot, Clara gaped. The large stone building extended across an entire street corner. Burgundy-striped canvas awnings ran the entire length. An outdoor seating area featured moss-green wrought iron tables and chairs. Vintage-style lightbulbs were strung in private alcoves, and outdoor heaters stood waiting to be used.

Danny assisted her on with her coat, then captured her hand as they exited the sedan and walked to the main entrance. Barring a lone security guard stationed in the lobby who respectfully stood and touched the brim of his cap as they passed, the building was empty. Danny explained that his shops were closed on Sundays in order to give his employees the day off. The scents of strong coffee and sugary caramel lingered in the lobby's air.

"Any decorating suggestions?" Danny asked. "Since this was my first store, it probably requires updating to your trained eye."

"I'm hardly trained, though I love decorating." She crossed to the far end of the lobby and looked around. "I'd strive for a cozy, contemporary feel. Concrete floors are trendy, and salvaged-wood walls would add contrast. Mix the old with the new. Antique velvet furniture could create more inviting seating areas."

"Can I hire you as my interior designer?"

She waited for him to walk over and touched his sleeve. "At present, two jobs are all I can handle. You don't get my life."

"I get more of it than you think, and the offer is open if you ever change your mind."

They spent the next hour touring the coffee shop while he explained that dozens of fresh pink roses, one for each table, would be delivered on Monday morning.

"I sincerely appreciate all my customers." He inspected a row of enormous glass jars filled with chocolate-covered coffee beans that stood behind the counter, ensuring that they hadn't been placed in direct sunlight.

She lifted the lid of one of the jars, filling her nostrils with the rich, tangy aroma, then popped a chocolate-covered coffee bean in her mouth. The taste was surprisingly sweet and bitter, and she enjoyed the different, creamy flavors mixed together. Perhaps, she thought, she might grow to like the taste of coffee after all.

Her fingers stole into the jar for another coffee bean, and she savored the intense bitterness on her tongue. "If you remodel, place the pink roses in galvanized buckets on each table."

"Aye. Good idea." He seemed to want her to keep talking about her ideas, so she did.

As he showed her the enormous kitchen stacked with commercial coffee grinders, flavored syrups, condiments, and numerous coffee supplies, she could hear the pride swell in his voice. He selected two Irish ham and cheese sandwiches topped with Dijon mustard from the cooler as well as bottles of water, and grinned at her approval.

As they rode the lift to the third floor, she asked him what the benefits of international franchising were.

"Do you want the short or long description?"

"Short."

"Typically, it involves a franchisor, in this case, me, granting an individual or company, the franchisee, the right to run their business using my business model, identified by my trademark. 'The Ground Café' will be used for logos, and our coffees and recipes will be provided. In return, I'll receive an initial upfront fee."

"And my lemon scone recipe?"

"I'll feature the scones daily."

"Have we negotiated what I'll receive in return?"

His chuckle was impenitent. "Aye. My undying devotion and lots of euros."

She fell in with his teasing mood. "Is that all?"

"We can negotiate the details in my office." His eyes gleamed with a sensuality that made her catch her breath.

His hand firmly on her elbow, he piloted her from the lift when they reached the third floor. She paused at a bold-stroked painting. "Francis Bacon hangs here too?"

"Aye. Besides greatly admiring his work, I'm also known for quoting his sayings."

"Should I ask?"

"Francis Bacon said, 'It is impossible to love and be wise.'"

She absorbed the saying delivered in Danny's husky voice, and navigated through her emotions by trying to ignore the heat radiating through her body. "You're a shameless flirt and a true blue dub, Danny Brady."

"I'll take that as a compliment." He led her to a large mahogany-paneled office and hung their coats by the door. At one side of the office sat a trio of potted philodendrons next to an enormous bay window. The window offered an unobstructed view of the city of Dublin. A Tuscan-bronze wastebasket sat neatly in the corner. An acoustic guitar stood on a stand nearby.

"Do you play guitar often?" As she asked, she realized she'd never heard him play.

His face fell a fraction. "Not as often as I'd like."

He gestured to a grey settee flanked by two cobalt-blue pillows. "Will this area be comfortable while I work?"

She scanned the magazines fanned out on the end table alongside the settee. "Is there a copy of *Entrepreneur* in the pile?"

"*Business Weekly.*"

"It'll do nicely." She sank against the pillows.

He pressed a kiss on her cheek, and set the sandwiches and water on the table. Then he straightened, strode to a large desk, and switched on a computer.

"One of my tech geniuses is developing a software program to connect all my coffee shops to one program, allowing me instant access to financial information wherever I travel." Danny typed in a password and waited. His brows knit into a frown when the computer wouldn't fire up.

An article in *Business Weekly* entitled "How to Start a Small Business with Little Capital" had caught her attention. When she finished reading the article, she glanced at Danny. He was still hunched over his computer and frowning.

"Hopefully, no computer problems?" she asked.

"I've been intending to change my password. Should've done it to begin with instead of spending so much effort trying to figure out what happened." He anchored his attention on her, grinned, then went back to his computer. With a chuckle, he typed in five letters followed by numbers and special characters, swiveled to meet her gaze, and winked.

"Problem solved?"

"Aye, with a brilliant new password." He propped back in his chair with his hands behind his head as his computer files opened.

She didn't hazard a guess. There was no need to. She'd noted the purposeful gleam in his eyes. Somewhere in that jumble of numbers and characters, he'd typed her name as part of his computer password.

Clara.

Now he'd think about her countless times a day, whenever he opened his computer files. She smiled, the smile of a woman who felt truly cared for. Although he was leaving Farthing soon, she was important to him.

She gazed out the window, over asphalt and metal rooftops, and sighed heavily. The thought of never seeing him again sent a quiet sadness through her. They wouldn't be discussing his departure; he'd made that point clear.

She punched up the cobalt pillows and curled up on the settee. He was bent over his computer, his brows furrowed as he concentrated on a screen teeming with numbers.

The afternoon sunlight flooded through the window, highlighting his hair's deep cinnamon tones. He'd rolled up his shirt sleeves. Crisp, reddish-brown hair glanced through the open collar of his shirt. Besides being devastatingly masculine, Danny Brady epitomized every inch of the wealthy Irish entrepreneur. He'd succeeded because of his drive, persistence, and aptitude for business.

She could easily fall under his persuasive spell, the glamor and enchantment of the rich and famous, although she would never allow that scenario to occur.

He swiveled his chair and slanted her a smile. "We'll eat our sandwiches in a wee bit, all right?"

"Yeh, no hurry." She pulled her phone from her purse and texted Seamus. *What's the craic?*

Home from the picture show, he texted back. *Ian's here at Anna's flat. R U in Dublin?*

Yeh.

Busy with the boss?

We're sitting in his office. Danny wasn't able to log into his computer so he changed his password. Now he's working on franchise agreements.

There was no response from Seamus for a full minute. *How do you know he changed his password?*

The way he looked at me.

Hope he's hiring more dishwashers, though he hates to part with his money.

Danny's an absolute gent. You said he was grand.

What time R U headed back to Farthing? Seamus texted.

A few hours. Stay with Anna and Ian until I return.

I'm a grown man and can take care of myself. See U later.

About to text Seamus a rejoinder, Clara saw Danny was studying her. His hands were folded at his waist, his manner relaxed.

She placed her phone in her purse. "How's business?"

He logged off. "Brilliant and, thankfully, done." Seating himself beside her, he unwrapped their sandwiches. "I'm sorry we didn't have time for a proper meal today."

She heard the sincere regret in his tone and nodded.

"My business is pressing because of these international franchises and my imminent travel schedule. America will open vast and unlimited opportunities, and I'm a wee bit nervous. Can I admit that?"

"Of course," she said. A man like him was actually nervous. She couldn't help but smile.

"There's a new restaurant in Dublin," he continued, "the Ballyburren Smokehouse, set in a traditional thatched roof cottage. And you wanted to visit Teresa's Irish Dancers, the dance academy. I checked and they're not open on Sunday. Next time for both dinner and the dance academy, all right?"

Clara concentrated on her sandwich, knowing there wouldn't be a next time. Danny was simply making small talk to avoid an issue that neither of them wanted to broach. Soon, he'd be miles away, and he'd offered no promises of continuing their relationship. Their worlds were too far apart.

She swallowed. No matter. She'd visit the dance academy and the Ballyburren restaurant on her own.

"I'd invited my sister, Erin, to my office today because I wanted you to meet her," Danny was saying between sandwich bites. "She's the proud mother of Michael, my six-year-old nephew. However, my sister's out of town because she's visiting her latest boyfriend."

Clara detected a note of sarcasm. "You don't approve?"

Danny swigged some water, polished off his sandwich, and shoved the wrapper aside. "Erin can date whomever she chooses as long as her boyfriend takes care of her and her son properly."

"And does he?"

"I wouldn't know. She's never allowed me to meet him. She said I'm too judgmental."

"I'm certain Erin is a grown woman who can make her own decisions. I can't imagine your sister's life requires your help."

"*You* are trying to run your brother's life."

His remark made her cringe.

She arranged the *Business Weekly* magazine, fanlike, on top of the others. "That's different. Seamus needs me in order to get better."

"Or maybe you want to *think* he needs you. Maybe he needs more than you can offer."

She pushed to her feet. "He's an alcoholic who's vowed to stay away from the drink because of the long cozy chats I've had with him."

"He's suicidal."

She rubbed a hand over her face, as if she could scrub away Seamus's troubles. "He's suicidal because he drinks. If we solve that, then all Seamus's other problems will go away."

"Until he realizes that he actually has a problem and he sincerely wants to fix it, he won't relinquish the drink no matter how many 'cozy chats' you have."

"Thanks for your unasked-for opinion." She picked up the discarded sandwich wrappers and tossed them into the wastebasket.

"Do you always organize and clean when you're uneasy?"

She saw the quiet tenderness in his gaze and regretted her outburst. He was well-meaning, truly interested and trying to help. Danny had given Seamus a job, hadn't he?

Clara softened her tone. "I don't like to see anything messy. Blame it on my orphanage days when everything was chaotic in my life—meals, bedtime, caretakers. In spite of that, the woman who ran the orphanage screamed for order. So I was pulled in opposite directions at a very young age."

Danny's dark brows rose. "Consequently, you like to control your surroundings and don't appreciate any inter-ference?"

"Yeh. So occasionally when I'm upset, I tend to straighten things. It gives me something to do." She looked down at her hands. "Once, when Jack left me home alone in our flat all day, I felt so isolated. He'd forbidden me from seeing or talking to my family or friends. So I alphabetized all the spices in the spice rack. It didn't take long. We only had salt and pepper."

"Do I upset you because I want to protect you?" Danny asked quietly, ignoring her attempt at humor.

Her vision blurred. This strapping, powerful man had a

way of tapping into her emotions when she least expected. And nothing broke down her guard as effortlessly as kindness.

She braced herself for another of his sympathetic remarks.

A few seconds passed. When one didn't seem to be forthcoming, she offered, "Yeh, my spine goes up because I can take care of myself. I was duped once before into believing I should depend on someone. I wasn't strong enough. This time, however ..." She balled a discarded napkin she'd overlooked and threw it into the wastebasket.

Danny came to his feet. "Don't ever do that."

"What?"

"Compare me to your ex."

"I didn't. I wouldn't." She met his steel-blue gaze. "I just meant—"

"That guy almost broke you. If you want to insult me, you're at the top of your game."

She heard the Dublin in Danny's voice—that hard, previous life he kept firmly under wraps. Attempting to avoid a heated conversation, she started for the door. "Let's ride the lift down to the kitchen. I noticed a couple slices of Guinness cake in the cooler."

He rubbed a hand across his temples. "Forgive me, Clara, if I sounded harsh. This Jack Connor thing has me so frustrated and worried for you."

"No bother."

"You've become very important to me."

She took a half-step back. No, forward. "I'm still hungry. Are you ... hungry?"

His voice deepened. "Only for dessert."

Off-balance, she contemplated how best to resist him. He'd mentioned his flat on the third floor. Did he expect her to sleep with him in exchange for a trip to Dublin and a ham sandwich?

She gave herself a firm mental shake. If he assumed she'd be another one of his conquests, a brief fling after their briefer time together, he'd be sadly mistaken. He'd offered no commitment, only the assurance that he'd be leaving.

She tossed him a guarded look.

"Do you know how beautiful you are, luv? Clara, you are so damn beautiful."

His gaze caressed her with gentleness.

That was good, right? No demands. Although she'd learned from her ex that gentle words were a façade to reeling a woman in. And gentleness didn't last. Gentleness made a woman weak and pliable and trusting.

She wrenched her gaze from his and studied the philodendrons.

"Did you hear me, Clara?"

His voice warned that he would persist until he'd gotten an answer. She turned her head slightly and watched him. Danny's molten gaze offered another layer far more dangerous than gentleness. Desire simmered in his eyes, deepening them to a dark, rich blue with flecks of navy.

She grabbed her water bottle from the table and finished it off.

She couldn't afford to be hurt again, to rely on someone other than herself. Soon, when Danny was gone, she'd be left alone, the dreaded constant in her existence. And she'd manage, just like always.

Which was better—gentleness or desire? Neither. Both. The question with no answer lodged in her throat.

She stifled an urge to find a dust cloth and begin dusting the room.

Instead, she went over to the window and watched the lively atmosphere of the rooftop pubs, the patrons soaking up the sun. She heard Danny, his stride sure and steady as he came behind her.

"I can take away those bad memories," he said. "The ones that are frightening you." Lightly, he rubbed his hand against her cheek. "If you'll let me ..."

Her mouth went dry. She could resist him. A nonchalant comment swirled in her brain, the word *no* on her tongue, a knee-jerk reaction, protection for her heart.

She pasted on an expression devoid of emotion and swung around to face him.

13

———

Danny stared into Clara's fathomless eyes. The way she was looking at him filled him with the agonizing longing to hold her tight and never let go. Grimly, he reminded himself that Jack had hurt her deeply and her earlier life had been ridden with hardships.

"No one can make me forget the awfulness of the orphanage," she said. "We were hungry and cold and always dirty. The caretakers tried, although there were too many of us and too few of them. Remembering those times ... It makes me so sad."

He suppressed a shudder at the deprivation she must have suffered. No one had held her. No one had loved her. Everyone needed love and acceptance, especially when they were children, especially when they were adults.

"Can you teach me how to break into a place?" He attempted to disrupt her solemn remembrances with levity. "There's a competitor's coffee shop down the street I've intended to visit. Unfortunately, they're closed on Sunday."

She rewarded his levity with a small smile. "I've never broken into a coffee shop."

His mouth quirked. "A new career path for you, perhaps?"

"That particular career path was a small part of my long-ago past."

She shook her hair with an impatient shake, and he longed to loosen her waves from their loose ponytail and run his hands through them. Did she have to be so perfectly shaped, so slim and willowy, her mouth so curved and inviting? He stroked his hands over her shoulders. Her fitted paisley blouse made her look small, fragile, defenseless.

"Someday," he promised, "you will own your own dancing school."

"It'll take me a year to dig out from Seamus's debt and then there'll probably be other bills I didn't anticipate. Maybe I'm a fool for suppressing horrific experiences, but if I dwell on them ... I should look to the future, yeh?"

He felt himself becoming lost in her glorious eyes, the dark recesses pulling him in. Lightly, his thumbs stroked her cheekbones. "You're smart and you've accomplished so much since you left Italy."

She rolled her cheek against his palm. "And yet, somehow, Jack has reappeared in my life. Once, I was dependent on him to fill a void. Not anymore." She seemed to dwell on the thought, seemed to search for the right words. "Now it's up to me to make him go away—not you, nor Ian, nor Seamus. Nor a justice system that can't be counted on."

Her response brought a deluge of his own remembrances—his uninterested parents and Glenna, his beloved spit of a sister. Was he, in his effort to move forward and succeed, putting off dealing with his heartache from long ago, just like Clara? Would the past forever be nipping at his heels? No matter what he'd accomplished, he'd always label himself a poor chiseler, a child born to suicidal parents, a weak sibling who hadn't saved his younger sister. No amount of wealth would ever change that.

He bent his head and lightly rubbed his lips over Clara's.

She kept her hands at her sides.

Rather than intensifying his efforts, he reasoned that it was necessary to meet her where she was in her life. Her feelings were raw and vulnerable.

The older boys in the orphanage said I was so good, I could've stolen the sugar out of their punch.

She'd joked to hide her mortification for stealing. She was too proud to beg, aye, and too stubborn to accept the fact that Seamus's recovery required more than her love and support.

Danny slid his arms around her, relishing her nearness, the scent of freshly squeezed lemons on a warm spring's eve.

"Have I told you how much I admire your thievery skills?" he murmured with a laugh.

"Unfortunately, being a thief isn't a talent I can list on a resume. However, *your* achievements are amazing."

The sincere compliment and admiration in her gaze was his undoing. "Thank you. I'm truly happy when I'm with you."

She smiled.

His heart exploded. Their growing relationship was brilliant, delicate. Delightful.

He touched his lips to hers again. He felt her resist, her indecision, knew the exact second when she yielded. His heart raced madly when she allowed him to lock his statement with a scintillating kiss. Blood pounded in his ears as he savored the sweetness of her mouth. For a fleeting second, he considered taking her to his flat, just down the hallway. In his reckless past, he hadn't been one to let an opportunity slide by.

He lifted his head and she took a guarded retreat. "Danny, I won't sleep with you."

He rested his chin on her hair until his breathing slowed. "I know, luv."

And he wouldn't ask, because he respected her too much.

Because Clara meant more to him than an insignificant tryst. And if he was honest with himself, he'd admit that as sure as the hills of Ireland were a lush, emerald green, he was falling in love with her.

AN HOUR LATER, Clara and Danny headed to his Town Car. The chauffeur opened the door, and Clara and Danny slid into the backseat.

The sedan merged onto the highway. An early evening sun shone through the windows and cast a golden glow on Clara's features. With his legs stretched out, Danny wrapped an arm around her. She'd pulled out her ponytail, and her tumbling waves fell past her shoulders. Leisurely, he ran his fingers through her glossy hair.

As the sedan took the Dublin airport exit, traffic picked up, then it calmed again when they passed the National Botanic Gardens.

"Are we headed to Farthing?" Clara asked. "Seamus is waiting."

"Your brother will survive brilliantly without you." Danny fiddled with the CD player, deciding on silence. "I've instructed the chauffeur to stop at Glasnevin Cemetery since I haven't visited in several months. My parents are buried there, along with ..." He paused, staring out the window at a curving brook running alongside the roadway.

"Along with?" Clara tipped her head to one side.

"Along with my young sister," he continued softly. "Her name is Glenna."

Clara's eyes widened. "Glenna is your sister?"

"Aye. Didn't I mention her to you?"

"Not by name." Clara gazed past him. "I assumed Glenna was one of your past wives."

"I've only been married once, to Kyla." He thought about glossing over the details before forging ahead with the truth. "I was young and married her for the wrong reasons. Her wealthy family invested a large sum of money in my fledgling coffee company, assuming they'd reap a huge profit. They did. And I repaid her parents the money they loaned me. Soon afterward, Kyla and I divorced."

"What happened?"

He tapped his foot to a silent beat. "We were never suited. I tried to make the marriage work, but in the end, I was the one who filed for divorce. Kyla was furious. Nevertheless, she was well-compensated. She called me a money-monger and informed every tabloid who'd listen to her that I'd used her family's wealth for my business venture, then cast her aside. I didn't refute her claims." He shrugged. "A month later, I discovered that she'd stolen a great deal of money from my business. I confronted her and she said I owed her the money because I'd been such a disinterested husband throughout our marriage."

"Although I don't condone Kyla for what she did, she must have loved you and was probably hurt when you filed for divorce."

He answered with a derisive snort. "She didn't love me. She loved my money."

They soon reached Glasnevin in the northern section of Dublin, and the car chauffeured quickly past the trademark high walls and round watchtowers of Glasnevin Cemetery.

Danny directed Clara's gaze to the watchtowers. "Those were erected to scare away the body snatchers in the eighteenth century."

She shivered. "Body snatchers?"

"Aye. Body snatchers stole corpses for money, usually selling the bodies to medical schools."

They passed simple stone gravestones covered in a jumble of ivy, and elaborate gravestones topped by Celtic crosses. On the street near his parents' marble tomb and Glenna's grave, Danny asked the chauffeur to park the car.

Clara leaned on the door, her gaze on the rows and rows of headstones. "Glasnevin Cemetery is massive."

"One and a half million people are buried here." Danny stepped from the sedan and strode around to open her door. He took her hand, and they walked slowly on the path leading to the tomb and Glenna's grave.

Danny breathed in the cool, damp breeze and eyed the clovers dancing along the path. As he'd directed, shrubs and evergreens, offset by red begonias and silvery dusty miller, had been carefully tended at both Glenna's grave and his parents' tombstone. A field of violet and sugary-pink wildflowers bloomed nearby, the uncommonly warm winter beckoning the flowers open. So much promise blooming so close to so much sadness.

Paying no heed to the damp grass, he knelt by Glenna's grave, keeping his focus on the granite headstone. Clara knelt beside him and bent her head. When they were finished praying at Glenna's gravesite, then his parents' tomb, he brushed the grass clinging to Clara's pants as they stood.

"We'll be going back to Farthing with green knees," she

said. "Though kneeling to pay our respects is more important than any grass stains."

"Infinitely more," was all he could manage. Tears he'd bottled swam precariously close to the surface.

"You live in Dublin. Why haven't you visited the gravesites more often?" she asked.

He took a deep breath. His chest ached. "Busy with work," he murmured. In truth, he'd found one excuse after another for not visiting, when the reality was he couldn't manage the grief.

A cold sadness clogged the late afternoon air. The space where they stood was fragrant with the scent of pine needles. Nearby, a liver-colored tree sparrow perched on the branch of an elm tree, greeting them with a nasally *chu-wit*.

"Glenna's gravestone is strong and erect, just like she must have been. So beautiful."

"Sorry. What did you say?" He looked at Clara. He'd gotten caught up in staring at the intricately carved Celtic cross topping Glenna's polished headstone.

"The gravestone is beautiful." Clara pointed to the brilliant rainbow etched on one side of the somber stone, the pot of gold and flaming-orange-bearded leprechaun on the other.

Danny focused blindly ahead, concentrating on the scarlet sunset tucking itself behind rolling hills. In the pressing weight of the bleak graveyard, he could almost feel Glenna's childlike presence.

"I used to call Glenna my little leprechaun. She was so mischievous and innocent."

A poignant memory rose unbidden.

"Leprechauns are real, Danny," Glenna said, crossing her thin, freckled arms. "And I'm gonna catch one and he'll lead me to a pot of gold so we won't be poor anymore.'

Danny tousled her flaming-red hair. "Aye. Well, if I find that wee man smokin' a pipe, I'll take off his buckled shoes and carry him to you myself."

And Glenna had giggled with delight.

For one heart-stopping beat, Danny thought he could hear her trusting voice calling out to him.

She had enjoyed every moment of life with the pure unworldliness of a child. If she were alive, she would've been in the middle of the wildflower field performing cartwheels and chasing butterflies, rather than gazing somberly at a frost-grey headstone.

"How did she die?" Clara asked gently.

He looked off toward the watchtowers. Dusk was creeping in, the cemetery becoming deserted, the other mourners returning to their cars. Soon it would be pitch-dark. The chauffeur got out of the sedan and motioned Danny with a slight wave. Danny nodded, delaying, the memories nudging him.

He shifted. "Glenna was always searching for a pot of gold. Sometimes we'd spend hours in the hedgerows adjoining our land, playing, making up games. She loved cow parsley. We used the stalks as pea-shooters while we chewed on the leaves."

Clara nodded, her expression encouraging him to continue.

"And then one afternoon in late September, Glenna was poisoned by the leaves of a hemlock bush she'd apparently found growing at the edge of our yard. I found her lying on the cold grass, limp, unresponsive. Did you know that cow parsley and hemlock look very similar?"

"No, I didn't." Clara hesitated. "Was she alone in the yard?"

"Aye. And if you're thinking she was too young to be out

wandering alone you'd be right. My parents had been inside our house, passed out drunk on the couch. The judge ruled Glenna's death an accidental poisoning."

A kind understatement. Glenna's death was partly the result of his alcoholic parents' inadequate supervision and neglect, and partly because he hadn't been with Glenna when she had needed him most.

He kept his tone carefully controlled. "My little sister never lived long enough to find her pot of gold. I blame my parents. I blame myself."

He glanced around. Had he said the words aloud? Judging by Clara's expression, her fingers that had somehow become laced tightly with his, he assumed he had.

All his life he'd tried to save what inevitably couldn't be saved. He'd talked, he'd argued, he'd shed tears. Despite his best efforts, he couldn't seem to control other people's actions.

"Absolutely not your fault," Clara said adamantly. "You were a kid too. You were probably at school right then."

"I'd skipped school that day. I'd decided to get drunk with my friends. If I had come directly home, Glenna might still be alive." He pushed a hand through his hair, attempting to push away the inevitable self-disgust swelling like poison in his veins. "At the burial, I begged my parents to add a pot of gold to Glenna's headstone. They refused. They were hardhearted bastards. I told them that it was their fault Glenna had died—they were neglectful drunks. They shouted that I should slither back to the streets where I belonged, because I was the drunk who would never make anything of himself. My brother Eamon was the smart one."

She shook her head. "You shouldn't speak ill of the dead. They were probably lashing out at you to cover their own grief."

He pulled his hand from hers. "You don't understand. It was their fault, and they wouldn't accept the blame."

She stiffened at the dangerous edge in his tone, but then sympathy and support flooded her beautiful eyes. "You're not justifying their negligence. You are strong and brave. Forgive so that your own healing can begin."

"I can't be disloyal to Glenna and forget what happened."

"You're not forgetting." She lifted her gaze to his. "You're finding your own happiness. Otherwise, these resentments will gnaw at you and you'll never be at peace."

He ran his fingers across the stony Celtic cross, the faded etching of Glenna's name, the absolute finality of her death. Bottled rage at his parent's neglect simmered beneath his own fury at himself. He didn't want to deal with it. The subject was too painful. Work was the answer, the only alternative, immersing himself so that he could prove his worth.

A heaviness settled in his heart.

Prove his worth to whom? His book-smart brother, who had been their parents' favorite child? His dead parents?

And for what?

So that he could boast that he was the richest man in Ireland, thereby showing his dead parents that he hadn't been a failure? That Eamon wasn't the only one who could be successful?

"The pot of gold on The Ground Café's logo is your tribute to Glenna," Clara said softly. "Soon, that logo will be seen throughout the world."

"Wealth buys many things, fixes many things," he murmured.

"But not this."

He drew in a breath. Waited. "Not this."

Glenna's last day of her life was seared in his brain. He'd begged her to hold on, squeezed her fragile, cold hand tightly in his.

"Don't you dare leave me alone with Ma and Da, Glenna. They don't care about us. We only have each other," he'd pleaded. "Don't leave me."

It was too difficult, all those terrible recollections emerging. He knuckled away a tear, attempted to find some sense in the tragedy that shouldn't have happened.

The wind picked up, more frigid than slight, rustling the leaves on the thin and spindly tree branches.

Clara gave his fingers a gentle squeeze. "You were a devoted brother and Glenna's death wasn't your fault. You were only a teenager and despite what you believe, your parents must've been devastated. Losing a child so young … I can't imagine."

He wanted to accept her grasp, her reassurance. "If my parents were devastated, I never saw a shred of remorse. If anything, they drank even more those months following her death. I damn well tried to stop them from drinking and I damn well failed. I thought I could fix them. I couldn't. They both committed suicide a few months later. They needed more help than I could give them."

She seemed to absorb every word, every sadness, into her own heart. "So then you went to live with your aunt and uncle and finished secondary school."

"I never finished. I left the schooling to my brilliant older brother. Eamon's an esteemed physician in Dublin now, very up-and-coming in the medical field."

"Experience is more important than any schooling." She stepped in front of him and offered a quivering smile. "Danny Brady, I believe you've achieved great things and the best is yet to come, although I'm still waiting for your apology."

Momentarily speechless, his lips parted with no sound. "For what?"

"For talking so unnecessarily harsh to me a few moments ago, in that imperious tone of yours. And here I was nice enough to accompany you to Dublin and missing the Sunday matinee picture show."

Taken aback, he brushed his knuckles against her cheek. "Will you still let me buy your recipe?"

"My price keeps increasing for every second that you don't apologize."

"You said that you don't like to apologize."

"This is about your apology, not mine."

"You drive a hard bargain."

She was the only woman he'd ever met who could take him from sorrow to laughter to passion in under one minute. "And I sincerely apologize for my earlier rudeness."

As they walked to the sedan, Clara gripped his hand firmly. In times past, he'd wanted to be alone in his grief. Today he was grateful for her presence.

He glided his thumb against her fingers. "I've never asked anyone to accompany me to Glasnevin before."

"Thank you for sharing your past with me." And before they slid into the sedan, she gave him a kiss.

Clara, his enchanting Clara, brought balance to his unsteady, demanding world.

The chauffeur pulled the sedan into traffic. Clouds were gathering in the twilight sky, promising rain as the Dublin streetlights stretched farther away. Clara rested her head against his shoulder, and he stroked her hair.

She'd listened to his tale about his parents and young sister without judgment, urging him to forgive. In the end, it wasn't Clara's reassuring words that had moved him. It was the respect shining from her chestnut-brown eyes, her unabashed belief in him, her ability to see only the good. Her affirmations meant more than all of his extravagant estates and luxury cars combined.

He pressed her nearer. "May I take you out to dinner tomorrow evening? I've heard there's a posh restaurant in the next town over from Farthing, The Duckling and the Quail. Do you fancy duckling?"

She shook her head. "Never had it."

"Mouthwatering quail?"

Another head shake. "We're of the fish and chips mentality."

"Me too." He laughed and pressed a kiss on her cheek. "Surely there'll be some type of normal food on the menu we can eat. I'll make reservations and ring Ian and Anna to stay with Seamus."

After a lengthy, relaxed silence, Clara remarked, "You've managed to find the most expensive restaurant within thirty miles of Farthing. My dance class finishes at seven. I'll need to go home to shower and change first."

"I'll come by your flat at eight."

He held her tightly, wanting to escape the tragedy of his past in her goodness. And he wanted to make their last few days together as unforgettable for her as they would be for him.

14

———

The following morning, Clara lingered in bed later than she'd planned. Seamus had kept her awake the night before, complaining that both Ian and Anna had lectured him about "staying on the rails ... or else."

"Or else what?" Clara had inquired while she'd started the wash and tidied the kitchen. She was too tired for this conversation, she thought. She stayed, although she would have preferred to go to her room and think about her day with Danny and what she had learned about him.

"Or else they'd force me into a treatment center," Seamus had replied.

At midnight, Clara had finally pleaded exhaustion while making assenting noises in Seamus's direction before bidding him good night.

Just now, she'd been relieved when the door to her flat had opened and closed at seven, the exact time Seamus departed for his shift at the coffee shop.

She smiled. Despite his ranting the previous evening, Seamus had proven himself a responsible worker, reinforcing her belief that nothing was more important to his recovery than his family's love and encouragement.

She sank deeper under the covers and listened to the soothing sound of rhythmic rain against her bedroom window. Stretching, she sighed contentedly and closed her eyes.

She and Danny were getting on brilliantly. Although they'd known each other for only a short while, they'd formed a strong connection, a bond she couldn't deny.

And tonight she'd be seeing him again.

Mentally, she went through her closet, deciding what to wear to the posh restaurant. Months earlier, she'd purchased a ruby-red silk cocktail dress at the local thrift shop. The dress was stunning and sophisticated, its sheath design clinging subtly to her slim curves.

She'd called Anna the previous evening and asked to borrow her beaded faux-crystal headband. Danny had said he'd liked Clara's hair best when she pulled it back to show off her dark eyes.

And dinner with him at such an exclusive place. Why, hadn't the prime minister himself dined at The Duckling and the Quail?

The meal would be superb, coupled with Danny's easy laughter and impeccable manners. At the end of the evening, she envisioned him wrapping her in his arms and kissing her in that sensually confident way of his. Just thinking about his kisses heated her entire body.

On her nightstand, her cell phone chimed and her eyes fluttered open. Noting Danny's caller ID, she picked up on the first ring.

"Good morning, Clara. It's your favorite barista."

She grinned into the phone, basking in the warmth of his deep voice. "Good morning."

"You still in bed?" His tone took a husky turn.

She sat up and propped the pillows behind her. "How did you know?"

"Your brother reported for work at the coffee shop and he's a virtual chatterbox, remember?" Danny's soft laugh sounded tired. "Sorry to ring on such short notice. Unfortunately, I need to cancel our dinner tonight. My lawyers are convening in Dublin this afternoon, and I was just informed that I must be present. More papers require my signature and I need to go over some eleventh-hour details regarding my trip."

The laughter, she noted, was gone from his voice.

"When are you leaving?"

"Shortly."

She slumped against the pillows. "Is your chauffeur driving you?"

"No. My car needs some repair work done. I'll drive it to Dublin myself." Danny seemed to falter for a second. "Ian may come with me. He has ... a project in Dublin to attend to."

"That's a fret. We were in Dublin yesterday."

His weary sigh was followed by a pause. "Aye."

She accepted his response. He sounded as frustrated as she felt. Noting the clock, she pushed to her feet. Cradling the phone against her shoulder, she pulled on her robe and padded to the kitchen. "How long will you be gone?"

"I'll fly directly to London from Dublin because there's no sense delaying these meetings. I promise I'll make it up to you when I return to Farthing in a couple of weeks."

"No worries." Deflated, she lowered herself onto the kitchen stool.

Two weeks without him.

She stood and started the kettle to boil. "Will you ring me?"

Immediately she regretted her question, hated the underlying neediness. Her wounded self-respect prompted her to add, "Of course I'll want to know you've landed safely."

"I'll ring you tonight when I arrive in London." He punctuated the silence by clearing his throat. "I'm going to head on then."

A woman was talking to him in the background. Clara sensed he was rushed.

She squeezed the phone. "Safe travels, Danny."

"I'll miss you." He waited for a beat. "Will you miss me?"

She brought the phone close to her ear. Perhaps he wasn't handling his unanticipated departure as dismissively as she'd thought.

"I'll miss you a great deal," she replied honestly.

"Imagine my arms around you while I'm gone, ensuring that you are safe." He lowered his voice. "Keep your thoughts on last evening, when we were in the backseat of the sedan. Remember that."

They'd kissed as if they were a couple of love-struck teenagers.

Briefly, she closed her eyes. "I will."

"I'll return as soon as I can, luv." He hung up with a quick click.

She stared at the phone. Should she be a little hurt that he hadn't offered more than a quick farewell? For a man who'd seemed so concerned about her welfare, he was leaving on extremely short notice with only the promise of a memory.

Frustrated, she showered quickly, got dressed, and ran a hairbrush through her damp hair. As she sat finishing her morning tea and lemon scone, a pounding on her entry door brought her quickly to her feet.

"Anybody home?" Anna waltzed into the kitchen with her purse slung haphazardly over her arm.

Clara put a hand to her heart. "I nearly had 40,000 canaries. You scared me half to death."

"Only me." Anna screwed up her face and shook the wetness from her hair. "It's raining stair rods out there." She bent and smiled at her reflection in the stainless-steel toaster on the counter, then fluffed candy-blue hair strands to frame her face. "How do you like my new hair color?"

Clara chose her words carefully. "It suits you better than royal purple."

"I chose this color to match Ian's motorcycle."

"A perfect match."

"He's a cupcake. Tonight, we're riding his motorcycle to a pub the next town over. I'm wearing a candy-blue sweater too."

"Even better." Clara muffled a smile, then frowned, considering. "Ian's staying in Farthing this evening?"

"Yeh, where else?"

Clara sank onto the kitchen stool, pushed her teacup aside and started to ask about Ian. Hadn't Danny said that Ian would be driving to Dublin with him?

"You should lock your flat door, by the way," Anna interrupted before Clara could speak. "Your useless toe rag of an ex is roaming somewhere around Farthing and you don't want him barging into your flat unannounced."

"Jack Connor would never be awake before noon. Besides, Seamus asked on the streets, and word is that Jack returned to Cork and is living with his brother."

"He's not back in prison then?"

"Nope."

Anna shook her head. "Sometimes I still can't believe that you were once arrested and put in prison because you stole from our friends. The Murphys, of all people. They'd owned their furniture store for years."

"Jack was so controlling. I did whatever he said to do. I was in a fog."

"Seamus and I tried to tell you that he was manipulative. You wouldn't listen."

"I wasn't myself. I was with Jack every second. He was all I heard, all I saw ..." Clara wiped at her eyes. Her cheeks felt hot. Shaking away her thoughts, she glanced at the clock and stood. "I'd wet some tea for you, except I'm already late for the bus."

Anna set her biker jacket and pink suede purse on an empty stool, plunked herself down, and forked the last bite of Clara's scone. "I'll drive you to work. You'll be soaked before you reach the bus stop."

"Thanks. I don't know when or if my car's brakes will ever be fixed. Now the mechanic's saying the cost to repair the brakes will be more than the car's worth. His advice is to give up the car. I don't really need one, anyway." Clara went to the stove and threw two teabags into the teapot. She poured Anna a cup and brought a sugar bowl and two more scones to the table.

"True." Anna added several heaping teaspoons of sugar to her tea before biting into another scone. "So, on a much more fascinating topic, I assume you had a whale of a time yesterday in Dublin with Danny? Happy out?"

Clara sat opposite Anna. "Dublin was grand."

"There are definite advantages in dating a billionaire. By the way, the reason I burst in this morning was to bring you my headband." Anna reached into her purse and brandished the sparkly headband, waving it gaily in Clara's direction. "Tonight you're actually dining at The Duckling and the Quail!"

"Not anymore." Clara attempted a swallow of tea. The warm liquid stayed trapped in her throat as a nagging realization struck her. Danny Brady would always choose his business above his personal relationships. And that realization brought a clearer insight into his priorities.

He had to have known how unpinned she would feel, how much she'd been looking forward to their evening together. Sure, she'd had plans canceled on her before. And she'd carried on, just like she would this time.

She swallowed the tea, set down her cup, and pushed it aside. She'd never mention her disappointment to him. Her pride was too fragile. Besides, she'd vowed she'd never allow a man to make her feel vulnerable again. "Danny's leaving for Dublin today because of some unexpected meetings. Then he's off to London for a couple of weeks."

Anna pushed the sparkly headband back into her purse. "You sound disappointed."

"A little." Clara went to the sink and rinsed a clean cloth, then returned to the table and wiped bits of crumbs onto her plate.

Anna finished off her scone and licked her fingers. "He'll be back."

Clara feigned absorption in the crumb-wiping. "If he returns, it's because he'll want to ensure that his fiftieth coffee shop in Ireland is a huge success before he enters the international franchise market."

"He employs at least one hundred other employees who could oversee his coffee shop in our little town," Anna said with insolent amusement. "He'll return to Farthing for one reason. You."

Clara stopped in mid-swipe. "What do you mean?"

Anna appraised a third scone before biting into it. Chewing, she dabbed at her lips. "He talks about you all the time. Ian told me, so the info is straight from the horse's mouth. And anyone can see Danny has a glad eye for you. He's in love with you."

Clara went to the stove to freshen her tea while Anna's remarks swirled through her mind. The persistent drumming of raindrops against the window had stopped. A thin ray of sunlight wafted its way through the window and into a corner of the kitchen.

Shaking her head to emphasize her point, Clara turned to face her sister. "Danny and I have become good friends because he's seen me through a couple trying ordeals."

The truth was, they'd become more than good friends. The heat in his kisses, the kindness in his smile, the tenderness in his gaze, were all evidence that he cared. If they kept seeing each other, their relationship might develop into something more, something deeper. Something lasting.

She curved back to the sink and switched on the faucet, washing imaginary bits of food down the drain.

Will you miss me too? The caring in his voice, like a honeyed caress, had effortlessly brought down her defenses.

"So you're just good friends?" Anna asked.

Clara slanted a glance at her smugly beaming sister.

Anna washed down the scone with her tea in a poor attempt to hide her glee. "I've seen the secret smiles you two share."

Clara shut off the faucet. "Get outta that garden before your imagination wanders too far," she warned with a half smile. "Will you promise that you won't talk of my relationship with Danny Brady again?"

"Yeh, I will promise," Anna said, and both women burst into laughter. In Ireland, many times "Yeh, I will" actually meant "No, I won't." And in that instance, Clara knew Anna would never change. Anna loved romance and happy endings and good craic. Besides, they shared a sisterly bond.

The women were still chuckling as they left the flat. Clara locked the door, and the women walked arm-in-arm to Anna's parked car.

A blink later and unbeknownst to the women, Seamus and Liam entered Clara's flat through the same door.

CLARA HAD DECIDED that a fortnight without seeing Danny was long enough. She'd missed him more with each passing day.

Every evening, he'd rung from London. Besides entertaining her with hilarious accounts of pompous lawyers conducting their endless business meetings, he'd encouraged Clara to recount details of her childhood. She'd told him about her brief time in the orphanage in Italy and her happier upbringing in Ireland. The wonderful life she'd enjoyed with her loving, adoptive Irish parents had dimmed her memories of her desolate orphanage days.

He'd listened intently, interjecting affirmations, urging her to talk for hours. During their lengthy conversations, he'd listened as though she were the most important person in the world. On several occasions, she'd attempted to shorten their nightly talks, reminding herself that he was a billionaire businessman with a thousand other concerns vying for his attention. Still, his interest in her seemed insatiable and the affection she felt for him had only deepened.

Now she counted the hours until his return.

During Danny's two weeks away from Farthing, she'd thought she'd seen Ian several times as she'd walked to and from the city centre. After all, the burly guy was hard to miss. She'd asked Danny once about Ian's whereabouts. He'd denied that Ian was in Farthing, vaguely remarking that Ian was working on some project in Dublin before changing the subject.

Even stranger, Anna had also denied that Ian was in Farthing, offering an ambiguous excuse that Ian was needed in Dublin for some project. Anna had kept herself scarce, explaining that she was applying to several universities and working on applications.

Despite all that denying, Seamus, on the other hand, had never seemed happier.

On March 17, Saint Patrick's Day, Clara returned home immediately after work. The night hummed with festivity, and as she'd walked from the bus, her nostrils had been overwhelmed by the smells of pub food and thick, dark beer.

She met Seamus outside the street door to her building. He was dressed in a new pair of denims, an indigo-colored hoodie, and his brimmed tweed hat.

They faced each other with only a patch of moonbeam lighting the sidewalk between them. The streetlight had been broken weeks before and had never been fixed.

Clara fished in her pocket for her keys. "Where are you going?"

He lit a cigarette, the flare of the match showing every unshaven stub on his square chin. "I'm workin' on a deal to buy a new car. You've said that your car isn't worth fixin'."

"It isn't. However, the car dealers are all closed at this hour."

"This here's a private negotiation, Clara," Seamus drawled in an icy tone.

"We don't need a car. We can walk most places and I ride

the bus to work. If you've saved any extra money, use it to pay your gambling debt."

"It's paid."

"How?"

"I'm savvy with my money, Clara, and I worked out a deal with the bookies." He smoked silently for a beat. "And now I want a car. Furthermore, I won't allow my little sister to catch a bus to work anymore."

"You don't earn enough money to afford a car." Nasty little tendrils of suspicion began to take root in her mind. Was he gambling again? Was that how he'd gotten so much money in so little time?

"The car is an old banger, but it runs." Seamus frowned at her censorious tone. "Don't fret. I'm takin' on extra hours at the coffee shop and your man has actually given me a raise."

"He's not my man."

"Yeh, right." Seamus flicked the ashes of his cigarette in quick, juddering movements. "Besides, my friend's letting me buy the car on credit."

"Who is this mysterious friend?"

Seamus expelled an enormous ring of blue hazy smoke and squinted at Clara in the patch of moonbeam. "She's a fine, large doorfull of a woman. I'll let you meet her soon."

Clara smiled, trying to think positively. A good, sturdy woman would bring joy to Seamus's life. A good woman was exactly the person he needed.

She drew back to admire him. Her strong-willed brother, so brawny, so dapper in his new clothes and tweed hat.

"I'll be home for the evening," she said, "and Danny's ringing me at nine. You'll not be out late? Saint Patrick's Day is always mad here, and there'll be trouble brewing." She extended her arms for a hug. He narrowed his eyes and tapped his foot, visibly fidgeting.

She dropped her arms. "Good luck with your car deal."

Seamus threw the still-smoldering cigarette on the ground and crushed it with the heel of his shiny black boots. "I'm always in the field when luck is on the road. This time, however, my luck is changing. I guarantee it, Clara." His eyes darkened to slits of charcoal. His expression gave away nothing.

He spun decisively in the direction of the city centre. He had a little too much swagger in his walk, she decided later on. And his eyes had been too bloodshot.

Luck. Gambling. She wanted to call out a warning for him to be careful, although her mouth went dry. For a second time, she worried that he might be wagering on the horses. However, after all their long cozy chats and his sincere reassurances, that troublesome thought was simply unthinkable.

15

———

Two days after Saint Patrick's Day, Danny returned to Farthing.

Without fanfare, he knocked on the door to Clara's flat at six o'clock on a rainy March evening.

She opened the downstairs door and her mouth flew open. She'd resigned herself to spending her birthday by herself, half deciding to tackle the thankless job of cleaning her refrigerator and oven.

"You're looking brilliant, luv." He favored her with a look of unabashed approval.

He needed a shave, and the rain had given his hair a copper sheen. One of the buttons of his linen sport jacket had been buttoned in the wrong hole, as if he'd been in a hurry. He looked incredibly tall, devastatingly handsome, and completely desirable.

She blinked back tears of delight at the invitation in his compelling blue eyes. Without words, he was telling her how much he'd missed her.

"Danny, you're ... not in London?"

In a laughter-tinged voice, he said, "I don't think so." He

smiled, that primal, intimate grin that ignited her insides. His feet were braced apart, a bouquet of a dozen red roses clutched in his hand. "Happy Birthday."

She shoved a hand through her hair. "I expected to spend the night alone. Seamus hasn't been around much lately and Anna said she was busy studying for some university entrance exams. I even offered to assist Colum with a very active preschool class at the dance studio because he says he can't control that age group. However, he said the attendance was small and he could handle the children by himself."

She knew she was babbling and immediately quieted.

Danny smiled. "Is that all?"

"Thank you." With a prim nod, she accepted the roses from Danny's outstretched hand and inhaled the delicate aroma.

The rain finally registered, and she pulled him into the foyer.

Caught between delight and confusion, she added, "This morning when you rang, you said your meetings in London ran longer than you'd anticipated. I didn't expect to see you until tomorrow."

He grinned. "I'd planned to charter a private plane to Dublin if I missed the flight from London. And that's what I did."

"You didn't tell me *that* part."

"I wanted to see you. Judging by your smile, you wanted to see me too."

"How many hours have you been traveling?"

"I was up before dawn. Seeing you was more important than a few hours of sleep."

She bit back a teary chuckle, fearful to show too much emotion, powerless to stop the joyful sniffles because she'd missed him. He'd effectively dissolved the pity party she'd decided to have for herself because no one had wished her a happy birthday.

Danny tenderly wiped the corners of her eyes. "I thought we'd enjoy your birthday celebration in my flat at the coffee shop, nice and quiet, just the two of us. We'll have dinner there."

"I should change first." She gestured to her worn denim jeans and ripped grey sweatshirt. "And I'll place your beautiful flowers in a vase with water."

He glanced at his watch. "Will fifteen minutes allow you enough time to get ready?"

"Are you in a rush?"

He averted his gaze, looked at his watch again. "I'm only in a hurry to be with you." He added a swift, nipping kiss on her lips that made her smile. "I'll wait here in the foyer."

She whirled toward the stairs and called over her shoulder, "Give me ten minutes." She'd change into the ruby-red silk cocktail dress that she'd contemplated wearing to The Duckling and the Quail. And she'd twist her hair into a quick French braid, using her faux-pearl clips to hold it. Silver hoop earrings would complete her outfit. It was her birthday, after all, or at least the day her adoptive parents had designated to celebrate her birthday. And it was Saint Joseph's Day, a traditional day to wear red.

She didn't know the date of her actual birthday, a quiet voice in her mind prompted, because she'd come to Ireland as an unruly, untidy, and uncombed shoplifter from a dirt-poor orphanage.

She chased away her negative thoughts. The drop-dead handsome man who'd appeared at her door had remembered her birthday. He'd grinned at her, all male charisma, and her heart had taken a solid bump. She had so much to be thankful for.

She met Danny in the downstairs foyer in ten minutes flat. He was standing exactly where she'd left him and was texting someone. He glanced up, quickly snapped his phone shut, and held out his hand.

"You look exquisite, Clara." He flashed a gleaming white smile so appealing, her knees felt watery. He reached into the inside pocket of his sport jacket and pulled out a box wrapped in luxurious gold foil.

"Happy Birthday."

"You already brought me flowers and—"

"And you would deny me the pleasure of buying you two gifts for your birthday?"

She hesitated.

"Open it," he prodded. "I hope you like it."

In her shabby foyer, Clara unwrapped the most beautiful diamond necklace she'd ever seen. Eye-catching and brilliant, several heart-shaped diamonds in an exquisite white-gold setting. She fingered the stones. "Surely these can't be real diamonds."

He seemed taken aback. "Of course they are. Eighteen carat. I insist that my girl have only the best."

My girl. Her heart squeezed.

She leaned nearer him. "I could never wear a piece of jewelry this extravagant. Suppose I lost the necklace? Suppose—"

"Suppose I put the necklace on you? It would please me greatly if you'd wear it tonight." He fastened the necklace around her throat. She glanced at her reflection in the entry-door window and smiled shyly at herself.

His mouth captured hers in a breathless kiss. When the

kiss ended, she stayed in his arms. Her hands stroked the beginning of a beard on his chin.

"Do you like the necklace?" he murmured against her lips.

Her eyes welled with tears of joyfulness. "I love diamonds. They're beautiful, although I've never owned any."

"Be prepared," he teased. "This is only the beginning of what I plan to give to you."

When they reached The Ground Café, Danny helped her out of his Mercedes. Because of the rain, she'd donned a khaki raincoat to protect her silk dress. Fortunately, the earlier rain shower had settled to a light drizzle.

"The parking lot is empty," she said. "Where are all the customers?"

"I closed the coffee shop at six because of your birthday."

She lifted her brows. "You? Giving up business and losing money?"

He accepted her barb with a glint of amusement, which seemed to lighten his eyes to a cornflower blue. "Only for you, luv."

As they entered the empty shop, Danny flipped on the lights and gestured to the tea dispensers behind the counter. "Would you fancy a cup of green mint tea?"

"You remembered my favorite tea."

"I remember everything about you." He poured the tea. Then he tidied a bagged coffee display and refilled a bin of sugar. Another thirty seconds, and she imagined him grabbing a broom and sweeping the floor.

He seemed as jumpy as a schoolboy, humming the tune to "Oh Danny Boy" as they made their way through the empty shop to the lift.

She grinned over her tea and drew in the nutty, toasty aroma combined with strong, refreshing mint. This exquisite-tasting tea was one of the many reasons why his businesses had flourished; because of his attention to excellence, cleanliness, and detail. His standards were high, reflected in his first-rate products. Customers had shown their appreciation by patronizing his coffee shops in droves.

When they reached the third floor, they passed his boardroom, and Danny waved to a young guy with sparse carrot-red hair and thick glasses hunkered over a laptop. He nodded in return.

"Aiden is my top accountant," Danny explained. "I depend on him because he never gets rattled. He's also honest to a fault. He came in tonight to begin working on our yearly audit, and he's checking the numbers for the Farthing store to ensure that the spreadsheets balance out. It's imperative that I demonstrate to my potential franchisees that I run a sound business."

"So, is your business venture in my modest town successful?"

"I haven't checked the numbers in a few days, though the shop has shown a bigger profit than expected." His gaze shot to hers. "You've never seen the inside of my flat."

She didn't reply as a previous conversation with Seamus sprang to mind.

"Sometimes Mr. Brady and Kathleen disappear for hours and go upstairs."

Could the gorgeous Kathleen have shared hours with Danny in his private flat? How many nights had they spent together? Could that striking woman with the strawberry-blonde hair have experienced his sensual kisses, the delightful pleasure of his hard body pressed close to hers?

She was utterly devoted to him and had been with him since, literally, the ground floor of his coffee shop endeavor.

Despite the warmth of the tea steaming from her cup, Clara's fingers felt chilled. She tried to reassure herself that Danny had chartered a private flight to see her, not Kathleen.

"I've arranged for a dinner to be sent up at nine o'clock," Danny was saying. "Nice and quiet, just the two of us."

Clara shot him a look of annoyance. Why did he keep repeating himself?

They reached a closed door. "I'll hold your tea," he said, gesturing to the door handle. "The flat's unlocked, although I know that breaking into a place is one of your—"

"I can certainly hold a cup of tea and open a door at the same time," she snapped, his drollness irritating her. Not to mention his ear-to-ear grin.

She clicked the handle and stepped inside. The room was dark and silent, except for a muffled giggle somewhere in the room.

"What's going on?" she asked.

The lights came on and a crowd shouted, "Surprise!"

16

"Happy thirtieth birthday!"

A cacophony of tin whistles and shakers greeted Clara. She yelped and jumped back. All around the room were people wearing iridescent-green party hats, laughing and playing a variety of musical instruments—tin whistles and hand drums and tambourines. Colum grinned and waved, along with Ian and several of Clara's friends. Anna stood next to Ian in the middle of the room. Besides holding a party-blower, Anna threw Kelly-green confetti into the air and waved a pastel-green balloon emblazoned with the number 30.

Clara blew out a suspended breath. Wasn't Anna supposed to be home studying? And Colum should've been teaching his preschool dance class. And wasn't Ian working on a project in Dublin?

Anna snaked her way to Clara and bussed a kiss. "Wow! That shocked look on your face was priceless." She blew into her party-blower, then inspected Clara's necklace. "Umm, are those real diamonds?"

Clara fingered the heart-shaped stones and nodded.

"The necklace is a birthday gift from Danny. Isn't it gorgeous?"

Anna gave a triumphant giggle. "I told you there were advantages to dating a billionaire."

Clara smothered a laugh. "He really is so good to me."

"And because of him, I've avoided you like the plague this past fortnight. I was so nervous that I might spill your surprise birthday after he rang me to work out the details."

Clara grabbed her sister's arm. "Details? Who? What? How?"

"Ask him." Anna's accusation came out in a rush as she pointed to Danny. "He arranged everything. Do you know you're called the surprisee?" Anna whirled, all animation, her pale-pink floral dress swaying, her leopard stilettos accenting her shapely legs. "He instructed me to decorate his living room in green because he said green's your favorite color. Isn't his place posh? I love the sleek, modern fireplace. Imagine what you could do with a place like this with your decorating ideas."

Clara surveyed the large living room, the bright-green streamers wound around every lampshade, the table towering with platters of sandwiches, coffee, and fruit punch. On a side table, an etched silver tray held sliced red apples and fresh strawberries.

Clara caught Danny's guilty, albeit pleased, expression. Laughingly, he shrugged and held up her green mint tea. She hadn't realized he'd taken the cup out of her hands.

"You planned all this?"

"I'm the culprit." He set the tea on a cherry-wood credenza and came to stand beside her. He helped her off with her raincoat, slung his arm around her, and kissed her. "Happy birthday, beautiful," he whispered. "I'm sorry that I haven't finished writing my song for you. I really wanted to sing it to you tonight."

She heard the suppressed excitement in his voice and smiled. No wonder he'd been so jittery. He'd acted like a fresh-faced lad, bursting with his secret surprise ever since he'd knocked on her door.

"Will you have your song finished by tomorrow night?" she teased.

He hung her raincoat and his jacket by the door before returning to her side. "No. Unfortunately, I've been too tied up with meetings."

Clara recognized two of Danny's employees from the coffee shop. They were dressed like waiters and traveled through the crowd offering appetizers to the guests— smoked salmon in new potatoes and cucumber-ham rollups, as well as nonalcoholic emerald-colored cocktails and chocolate mint shakes in glittering crystal glasses.

Danny plucked two cocktails from a tray as one of the waiters passed them and handed one to Clara, then he asked everyone in the room to take a glass for a toast.

A burst of pride surged through her as Danny stood alongside her. Tall and elegant, he projected an impressive, take-charge appearance, an aura of capable command that was an integral part of his character.

He centered his gaze on her. His eyes sparkled, a beam of forget me not blue, mesmerizing and oh so attractive. Raising his glass, he said, "Several weeks ago, I came to Farthing to open a coffee shop. Clara and I hadn't known each other twenty-four hours before this charming, gorgeous woman accused me of being a bowsie, a good-for-nothing male. I'd told her that I was a musician and loved music. She advised me to stick with making coffee because I sang so off-key that I sounded like the tune the old cow died of."

The group laughed.

With a smile and shake of his head, Danny continued, "Many of you know that one of my life-long aspirations was to open a chain of successful coffee shops. This aspiration was far easier to accomplish than my second—to live up to the example this fearless woman has shown me." He lifted his glass higher. "Sometimes I don't understand her ability to forgive so freely, but to quote our great Irish poet and novelist, Oscar Wilde, 'Women are made to be loved, not understood.' Slainte!"

Clara flushed as she met Danny's tender gaze. When the surge of toasts ended, she nodded at Seamus. He'd stood in a far corner of the room, and when she caught his glance, he tipped a glass in her direction. "Happy birthday," he mouthed. Then he turned to Ian, and the two men started talking.

What was Seamus drinking? Water? The liquid in his glass looked clear. The question nagged, even though Danny was leading her to the CD player and asking if his music selection was to her liking. Seamus was soon forgotten.

The hours went by in a fairy-tale haze. Clara noted that Danny spent a good deal of time speaking with Colum. She smiled, listening to the two men before she continued mingling with the other guests.

As the evening progressed, Danny's employees lit a fire in the grate and set apple-green tea lights and votive candles on the credenza. The candles added a soft shimmer to the room and a scent of spring to the air. The overhead light was lowered to a mellow afterglow, and on the CD player, The

Dubliners, a popular Irish folk band, sang a ballad about how lonely life was around Athenry fields.

Danny took Clara's second emerald cocktail out of her hand and set the glass down. "One last dance?"

"Of course." She smiled. "I am having a brilliant time tonight. Everything was planned perfectly."

He led her to the middle of the living room. As he took her in his arms, his gaze kindled with the promise of tantalizing kisses. She felt her own response, yearning for his body to stay pressed to hers, the softness of his caress. As they slow-danced, she listened to the heartbreaking lyrics of "The Fields of Athenry," which told the tale of a man sentenced to forsake Ireland because he'd stolen food for his starving family.

When the poignant ballad came to an end, Danny gathered her nearer and placed his chin on her upswept hair. "Thank you."

She toyed with the reddish hair at the nape of his neck. "For what? I should be thanking you."

He tipped up her chin and held her gaze. "For your smile, your love of life, your appreciation. For being you—breathtaking, valiant and incredibly dazzling in that red dress. And for making my time in Farthing so memorable."

She touched her fingers to his cheek. "It sounds like you're ... you're leaving?"

"Armed with my franchise agreements and a half-dozen lawyers, my franchise expansion begins in Europe."

She had difficulty swallowing the ache in her throat. "When?"

His arms tightened around her. Briefly, he closed his eyes. "Tomorrow I leave for London. And then ..." He gestured wordlessly, indicating more places and miles than he could name.

There it was. The irrevocability in his tone, the finality of their relationship. It was useless to reply with any note of longing in her voice. A while ago, he'd let her know in no uncertain terms that his departure was not open for discussion.

She lowered her head and studied his broad chest, his forest-green cashmere sweater reminding her of a woodland filled with lonely pines. "How long will you be traveling?"

He shifted. "A few months, which may be extended, depending on any unforeseen red tape along the way. It'll definitely be a long while."

She avoided his probing gaze. Her heart beat sluggish.

She should be happy for him, she told herself, because the business venture he'd worked on for so many years was coming to fruition. Victory was well within his grasp. And she should tell him how happy she was—except that a sharp sadness threatened to carve a hole in her lungs every time she took a breath.

Somehow, she managed a weak smile that she was certain didn't reach her eyes. In an effort to dispel the melancholy mood settling over them, she changed the subject. "Thanks for giving Seamus extra hours at work this week. And his substantial raise has been brilliant. He bought a new car, because it was going to cost too much money for my car to be fixed. Seamus is putting his hard-earned money to good use."

Danny cocked an eyebrow. "I haven't given him a raise, Clara. And your brother called in sick the past seven days, although he reported for work today."

"You must be mistaken." She scanned the near-empty room, realizing that Seamus must have slid out of the party without a word. She considered the time, just before eleven o'clock, then zeroed in on her sister. Anna and Ian were sharing bites of salmon hors d'oeuvres while Ian dangled Anna's leopard stilettos from his beefy fingers.

Clara pulled out of Danny's arms and headed toward her sister.

"Hi Clara! Great party—which is why we're still here." Anna laughed. "You know me, the type of person who comes for the wedding and stays for the christening, just like the old Irish saying. Of course, we were also waiting for the rain to stop because getting soaked while riding a motorcycle is no fun."

Grinning, Clara hugged her sister. "You and Danny managed to pull off a wonderful shocker birthday celebration that I'll reminisce about for the rest of my life."

Anna's own smile was just as wide. "And I got a job at his coffee shop. I start tomorrow."

"Congratulations."

"Yeh, it'll be grand. Now that my disability insurance had ended, I realized it was time to get a real job with a great boss." Still grinning, Anna's honey-colored eyes met Ian's hazel gaze. "We danced every fast dance and my feet are never going to forgive me. Tonight, I'll be riding on your motorcycle barefoot, cupcake."

A moonstruck-looking Ian gawped at Anna. "I love your feet."

"And I love yours." Anna and Ian glued their lips together, the irresistibly offbeat couple clearly in love.

Clara folded her hands together and waited. When their kiss ended, she said, "I was so preoccupied with all the guests, I didn't realize Seamus had snuck out early. He wasn't with a woman, was he? He said he'd met someone."

Anna shook her head. "He hasn't been with any woman since Fiona."

"And he looked half-cut again after drinking all that vodka tonight," Ian put in.

"Seamus doesn't drink vodka. He used to drink whiskey, but not anymore." Clara touched her neck and asked haltingly, "Again? You've seen him out drinking?"

Ian kept his arm firmly around Anna. "Aye. We talked on several occasions at the local pubs this week and got along well."

"Seamus has an addictive personality, especially when he drinks and gambles, and one drink can easily lead to more." Clara chewed her bottom lip. "You must be mistaken about the vodka."

"Vodka is the drink of choice for an alcoholic because it's clear and can go undetected."

"Where would Seamus get the vodka? Did Danny—"

"The boss instructed no alcohol at your party," Ian said. "Your brother must've walked in with his own drink."

"Wait." Clara paused, letting the conversation lag as she rewound Ian's earlier remark. "How could you have seen Seamus in the local pubs? You were in Dublin this past fortnight." She narrowed her eyes. "Weren't you?"

Ian pulled at the collar of his beat-up leather jacket and shot Anna a helpless glance. "I have a terrible memory," he began. Ian yanked a roll of antacids from his pocket and dashed one in his mouth as Clara saw Danny approaching in groundbreaking strides. "Sometimes I lose my motorcycle and ..."

A knot was forming in Clara's stomach. "Surely you'd remember where you were all week." She whirled on Danny, feeling a swell of genuine wrath. "Your bodyguard's been following me, hasn't he?"

"Aye."

"Aye? Aye? You've all lied to me!" She whirled to her

sister, but Danny stopped her with his hands on her forearms.

"I couldn't leave you alone in Farthing without my protection, Clara." He held her firmly. "Not until Jack Connor ..." His voice trailed off.

"I told you I could take care of the Jack Connor problem by myself."

Danny quirked a brow. "You haven't done a very good job. However—"

She flung off his hands and cut him off with an abrupt shake of her head. "Neither have you."

"I couldn't bear the thought of you possibly getting hurt. Do you truly believe that I deserve your animosity for wanting to protect you?"

Slightly mollified, she replied, "I can take care of myself."

"Let's talk this out alone, all right? There's something I need to tell you." He looked around the room. Except for the four of them, the only people left were the waiters. He gave Ian and Anna a meaningful look, dismissed the waiters, and then gathered some empty plates and headed for the kitchen.

"We were about to leave, anyway," Anna said, grabbing her stilettos from Ian. As he went to retrieve her leather biker jacket and their motorcycle helmets, she spoke to Clara in a low voice.

"Don't be angry at Danny. He's an honorable man. And he loves you, and he declared it to all your guests tonight when he gave his toast."

"He quoted Oscar Wilde, whom he admires as much as Francis Bacon," Clara refuted. "I've been Danny's diversion while he's spent his working hours in Farthing opening another profitable business."

Anna scoffed. She took Clara's cold hands in her warm ones and nodded toward the kitchen. "You're wrong. Go to him."

Clara yanked her hands from Anna's grip. "Don't pass that yoke to me. I have little enough self-respect to salvage after what Jack Connor did to me. And I won't sacrifice any progress I've made these past two years to appease a billionaire businessman just because he's given me a surprise party."

Ian reappeared, assisted Anna with her jacket, and handed her a motorcycle helmet. "The rain has let up. We should head off."

Clara turned away from them, intending to tear down all the decorations and straighten Danny's flat. Then she'd extinguish the votive candles and fold the linens into a neat pile. And then she would walk home.

Anna's stern tone checked her in midstep. "You know that progress you refuse to sacrifice? That's what Danny admires most about you—your indomitable spirit. Go into the kitchen, apologize for your uncalled outburst, and thank him for arranging such a lovely party." With that, Anna tucked her hand into the crook of Ian's elbow and exited Danny's flat.

CLARA WALKED over to the cherry-wood credenza, piled high with an assortment of birthday gifts. So considerate of all the guests, she thought, examining each brightly colored tag. Every person had brought something, except for Seamus. Odd, considering their conversation in front of the coffee shop a few weeks prior.

I'd figured on walking to the city centre and buy you a gift with some of the money I earned. You've ruined my birthday surprise for ya by all your harping.

She fingered the exquisite diamond necklace around her neck.

For you, luv, Danny had said eagerly, a tender, expectant gleam in his eyes when she'd unwrapped his gift. *I hope you like it.*

With her sister's advice overriding her excuses, Clara silently counted to sixty. Tackling difficult discussions and admitting she was wrong didn't mean she'd lost control, she told herself.

She took a deep breath and joined Danny in his small, efficient kitchen. She noted his stiff back as he dried forks and spoons on a dishtowel.

Obviously aware of her presence, he turned and said, "Tea?"

Despite his rigid stance, his voice was gentle. He looked tired, a weariness softening his handsome features. He'd been awake since dawn.

"Thanks." She smoothed her dress. "Look ... When I—I realized that Ian had been following me and everyone had been lying, I overreacted. Jack lied many times and I always felt so hurt and defenseless when I found out the truth." She shook her head. "I was so gullible."

Danny's hand tightened on the dishtowel. "You're doing it again, daring to compare me to that monster."

"I'm not. Let me finish explaining."

"Your brother told me that your ex would beat you when he was drunk." Danny dropped the dishtowel on the counter. "Do I seem that type of man to you? Someone who would drink, and beat you, and manipulate you?"

"Of course not." She dug her nails into her palms and let

a slow breath in and out of her lungs. "The reason you asked Ian to stay in Farthing was for my benefit."

Danny swerved to the sink and filled the electric kettle with water. When he curved back around to face her, his jaw was still tense. "I knew you were against the idea. However, your safety was more important to me."

She twisted her hands together. Her voice cracked. "Then afterward, Jack would apologize over and over until I'd relent and forgive him."

His cell phone in his pants pocket buzzed several times. He scowled.

She shifted. "Shouldn't you answer? The call might be important."

He slipped the phone from his pocket and glanced at it. "It's Aiden. He's busy doing whatever accountants do best. He can wait." Danny sent a quick text and shoved the phone back in his pocket. He gazed at her for a long while and his features softened. "My apologies for the interruption, Clara. Please continue."

She swallowed. Tears burned her throat. He always placed her needs above his own.

"I'm not used to a man being so kind to me and sometimes I don't know how to respond. I ..." Her voice cracked again.

It was the closest justification she could offer. Danny would understand. He knew how difficult it was for her to apologize after dealing with Jack. She'd been so confused. After a while, she hadn't known what was wrong, what was right.

Danny didn't respond. Perhaps he wanted more. More of an apology, more awkward reasons that might only justify his anger. Or perhaps this entire argument gave him the opportunity to sever a break—from her, from her family, from Farthing.

He leaned against the kitchen counter and closed his eyes.

She waited, watching him, remembering his generosity, his thoughtfulness, and her defenses crumbled. Sadness and despair welled at the realization that he was leaving in a few hours and, if she didn't right her wrong, she might never see him again.

"I apologize," she said. "My reaction to your protection was unwarranted."

She lowered her guard because she trusted him and wanted to be close to him, leaving no emotional barriers between them. And if apologizing to a considerate and kind-hearted man made her vulnerable, so be it, because it was time to break loose from the damaging, traumatic chains that Jack had shackled around her.

Danny opened his eyes. Understanding, affection, and unmistakable desire smoldered in his gaze. "I accept your apology. And I was wrong, too, for being dishonest. I should've risked your anger and told you that Ian would be staying in Farthing to ensure your safety."

She smiled at him. "So you're afraid of my anger?"

"You put the heart crossway in me, especially when your eyes shoot daggers." With a chuckle, he brought her into his arms. His mouth came down ravenously on hers. She parted her lips to receive him and looped her arms around his neck, forming her body to his, softening against his solid form. When the kiss ended, he kept his arms around her.

Clara didn't move, protected in his embrace, feeling safe and secure and cherished.

He pressed his lips to her hair. "Your apology means so much to me."

She brushed a single tear from the corner of her eye. "I was afraid I'd open an emotional floodgate that I'd be powerless to stop, that I'd feel defenseless and out of control."

He cradled her in his arms. "And now?"

"I was wrong about that too."

And with that admission, she felt empowered, not defenseless.

He rested his cheek against her head and sighed. "It's late, and I should start preparing for my departure tomorrow morning. However, I'd like to continue our relationship long-distance." He lifted her chin and stared at her. "I hope you feel the same way."

She nodded.

"While I'll be traveling a great deal, I should have reasonable Internet connection, and we can talk by phone every evening. You know I'm a planner."

"I know."

"Are you willing?" he asked quietly.

Her throat clogged. She couldn't find her voice.

He cupped her chin. His blue eyes gleamed with purpose. "Long-distance relationships require a great deal of commitment. Network connections are spotty, plus I'll be circumnavigating language barriers, time changes and jet lag. If your schedule allows, perhaps you can meet me on occasion? I'll arrange and schedule your flights." He brushed his lips across hers. "I'll miss you too much if I don't see you every day."

Through happiness and unabashed tears, she managed, "I can't fly to a different country every day. However, I will try to see you as often as I can."

"What more can a man ask for?" Slowly, he bent his

head, his mouth lingering over hers. Their breaths merged. His kiss was longer, primal, claiming her.

When he lifted his head, he said with a grin, "One of my international franchisees is in Rome. You can join me there and show me all the shops you pilfered. That is, *if* they're still in business." He waited for a beat, the teasing grin gone. "I also want to see your orphanage. Do you remember the town you were in?"

She shook her head. "My Irish mom said the town was close to the Egadi Islands. She may have mentioned Palermo. That town may be miles away from your coffee shop."

"No matter. We can fly there or take a train. I'll investigate. Also, we can research your long-lost Italian brother's whereabouts."

"I remember his name was Luciano." She ran her hand along the sleeves of Danny's sweater. "I don't know if my orphanage is there anymore, or if my adoption records are available."

"We'll find them. In addition, the weather will be warmer in Italy, which will help your breathing."

"Yeh." Because in that moment, she knew. She needed to be with him.

"That's it? You're agreeable?"

"I don't strike you as the agreeable type?"

He laughed and kissed her. "Good. Everything's settled." He drew out a copy of his itinerary from a kitchen drawer. "Take this so that you can keep track of me. And I assume you'll be in Farthing, waiting for my return. The key word is that you'll be waiting for me." Although his tone was light, the heat from his smile warmed her blood.

Briefly, she closed her eyes, then smiled at him and nodded.

His cell phone buzzed, persistent, and Danny uttered a quiet Irish curse. His laughter had faded. "My business leaves me no peace," he muttered.

"Your business is a large part of your life."

"Too large a part, I'm beginning to realize."

An insistent knocking at the door drew a more colorful oath from him.

She pulled out of his arms and tucked his itinerary in her handbag. "Go. I'll follow. It must be important."

Danny stalked to the door and threw it open.

A disheveled Aiden raked a hand through a knot of his carrot-red hair. "I'm sorry to bother you, Mr. Brady."

"Perhaps I wasn't clear enough." Danny placed his hands on his hips. "I texted that I wasn't to be interrupted."

"My apologies, sir. Could you step into your boardroom? Your computer files—there's an alarming discrepancy. The numbers don't add up—at least not accurately." Aiden, the bespectacled guy who was never rattled, was wiping his hands against the thighs of his pants as he spoke.

Standing behind Danny, Clara clasped her fingers and glanced outside as an explosion of hard rain hit the glass.

"Can't this wait?" Danny was asking Aiden.

"I was vetting all the payments, and one particular invoice did not go through the proper procedure," Aiden said.

"What's the name of the company?"

"RC Dougal Restaurant Supplies."

Danny scrubbed a hand over his face and hesitated. She caught the hesitation before he said, "That's the name of the factory Clara works for."

Aiden shook his head. "The factory in town is RJ Dougal Restaurant Supplies."

"I don't understand," Clara murmured, willing her heart to stop racing.

"I suspect that your Farthing business account has been compromised, sir," Aiden continued, "I've summoned the Gardaí because this incident has all the makings of a cybercrime."

17

———

Aiden and Danny hastened to the boardroom with Clara at their heels. Danny quickly took a seat at the computer desk while Clara and Aiden stood behind him.

"There, sir." Aiden leaned over Danny and pointed to the computer screen. "An invoice for the café in the amount of fifty thousand euros was submitted by RC Dougal Restaurant Supplies, and our accounting program paid it."

"Normal," Danny said.

"However, this payment did not go through the proper procedure. The banking information for this supposed company is not valid because the company doesn't exist."

Danny's fingers tightened around the computer mouse.

"At first, I assumed the money transfer was normal—"

Danny lifted his brows. "Transfer? To where?"

"Most likely to an existing hijacked account. All of this was done outside of normal banking hours. My assumption is so that it would go undetected. Did anyone else have access to your boardroom?" Aiden asked.

Danny frowned. "No. This room is always locked with a deadbolt."

"I checked the lock. It doesn't appear to have been broken." Aiden enunciated each word grimly. "What about your computer files, sir? Who has security access and pass-word information?"

"No one except you and me." Danny clicked to another screen and said absently, "This Internet connection seems slow."

"Aye." Aiden's eyes narrowed through his thick glasses. "If someone took control of your computer from a remote location, both computers are connected. However, slipping in and out of the boardroom would have been easier *if* the hacker knew your account password. Then it's simply a matter of logging onto your computer and doing whatever you want. Like uploading a phony invoice from a flash drive and telling the accounting program to pay it."

"Who could have done this?" Danny tapped his fingers on his desk and glanced briefly in Clara's direction. "I changed my password a few weeks ago."

She stiffened. Her mind raced with possibilities. Had she mentioned to anyone that she suspected Danny had used her name in his new password? Anna? Seamus? Colum? Even so, he'd used a combination of characters for his password.

Still, was this entire incident somehow her fault?

She braced her hands on Danny's chair for support. Her knees had started quaking.

"An employee, perhaps, who's down on their luck?" Aiden was asking.

"I trust my employees with my life." Danny leaned back in his chair. "Ian, Kathleen, and several others have been with me since I started my first coffee shop. I only hired one new employee, a dishwasher, within the past couple of weeks." Danny lifted his gaze to Clara. Under his breath, he asked, "Any thoughts on this matter?"

"Thoughts?" she echoed, surprised that she'd managed to keep her tone composed and reasonable. Very softly, very carefully, she asked. "Perhaps your computer has a virus?"

"A computer virus can't lift fifty thousand euros from a business account," Aiden said sharply.

Of course, she realized that. And through her mounting apprehension came one adamant denial: Seamus, Danny's notable and newest hire, couldn't possibly be at fault, no matter if all the evidence in the world pointed to him.

Her dear brother had lost his beloved wife, and then had turned to alcohol and gambling for consolation. That was understandable. Everyone made missteps and needed a second chance. With the help of his loving family, he was slowly piecing his life together. Hadn't he seemed more upbeat lately? The job at the coffee shop had given him self-respect, as she had hoped. Besides, if Seamus was hiding any illicit, secretive activities, she would know. He lived with her, and, for the most part, she knew his whereabouts. Furthermore, her brother was a chatterbox who couldn't keep anything to himself. A cybercrime took advanced, careful expertise.

Through the boardroom's window, flashing red lights from the street below brought her rioting thoughts under control.

Danny, Clara, and Aiden leaned forward and peered out. Under a sky filled with angry, ragged clouds, two Gardaí stepped from a patrol car. One of the men looked retirement age; the other was stout with a fringe of brown bangs. They both wore peaked hats and formal uniforms and swung their nightsticks in unison. Opening identical black umbrellas to protect themselves from the heavy rain, they marched briskly up the steps to the coffee shop. Clara's heart beat more slowly with each of their quick strides.

CLARA CHECKED HER WATCH, noting that it was well past midnight. A long, excruciating hour had passed. She stood to the side as the stout garda--his name was Jimmy Doherty--squinted at Danny's computer screen, while the older garda went over a report with Aiden. This was Danny's world, where staggering sums of money were invested.

Garda Doherty leaned forward to get a closer look at the security camera's video feed. "Nothing is showing on the DVR for the night of March eighteenth. The adapter, cable, and power port seem to be working."

"Then how could there be no feed?" Aiden asked.

"It may have been cut off." Doherty unbuttoned the top silver button of his black jacket. "Did the coffee shop experience a power outage?"

"Not that I was made aware of," Danny answered.

Clara glanced at him. He stood to the right of his computer desk, his features drawn. His replies had been thorough and composed as he'd answered unending questions. All the while, he'd seemed to be moodily contemplating the situation and never met her gaze. Exhaustion, she'd decided. He'd been awake for almost twenty-four hours and had to catch an early plane to London.

"It doesn't look as if anyone broke into the boardroom," Aiden commented.

The older garda returned to the door and inspected the lock. "The doorframe hasn't been forced in and the deadbolt doesn't show indications of being visibly tampered. We'll send a locksmith out tomorrow to be certain. Might've been a professional break-in. These types of thieves are savvy and don't usually leave a trace. The chief constable will want to have a look too."

"An extra set of keys to the boardroom went missing recently and haven't been found." Danny rubbed a hand through his hair. "Regardless, someone hacked into my computer files. And my email. And my online identities."

"Happens all the time, sir. We'll report it as a cyber-crime," Doherty replied.

Clara concentrated on his shiny black boots, the silver buttons of his somber uniform that seemed ready to burst around his thick waistline, his fringe of thick brown bangs.

A recollection flickered. Wasn't he the garda who had arrested her the night she and Jack had attempted to steal money from Clara's friends, the Murphys?

She shuddered. Garda Doherty had hauled her to the dank, cramped cell and locked her in. The peeling blood-red paint and sharp walls had reminded her of the suffocating closet she'd been locked in all those years ago at the orphanage.

She fingered the cold stones of the diamond necklace around her neck. "Computer hacking is a crime?" she asked.

"Aye, and punishable with a fine and imprisonment from one to twenty years." He tipped his head. With a dawning look of recollection, he asked, "You're Clara Donovan?"

She chewed her bottom lip and nodded.

"It seems as if I've seen a lot of *you* these past couple of years." He spoke loudly, bluntly emphasizing the word *you*. He caught the older garda's gaze, who lifted his brows in amused derision.

Danny turned a questioning look on Doherty. "Where? When her brother was in prison?"

"Ask her. The Murphys are such nice people."

With a curt nod to the men, Danny drew Clara into the hallway and closed the door behind them. "Am I missing something?"

"Is this an interrogation?"

"It's simply a question demanding an answer. Who are the Murphys?"

She paused. His abrupt demand fired her indignation. "I told you to check the past copies of the Farthing newspaper."

"I obviously haven't had time to be going through old newspapers."

She threw him a scathing look to match her tone. "Why not? Because you've wasted so much time in Farthing around me and my family? Sorry that we've become such a burden to an important man like you." She whirled, intending to walk away.

He grabbed her by the forearm and angled her to face him. "Clara, what did the garda mean?"

She thrust her hands against his chest, forcing a space between them. "He was in the patrol car the night Jack Connor shoved me."

"Jack did more than shove you, so don't cover up for him."

"I'm not. I—"

"And that incident didn't happen two years ago." Danny released her forearm so suddenly that she reeled. "So tell me what everyone seems to know except me."

She took a deep, pained breath and closed her eyes, torn between indecision and decisiveness. *Help me to be forthright,* she prayed, before realizing that the person she was praying to was Danny. He was compassionate, and kindhearted, and possessed an integrity and empathy rarely found in a person. He of all people would understand.

She could lean on him, be honest with him, trust him, because ...

Dear saints in heaven. Because she loved him.

She could scarcely move because of the realization. Her heart filled to bursting. Had her deep feelings been there all the while, tamped down by her shame, her denials, her struggle to be totally self-sufficient?

She'd told herself that she and Danny had grown close because of the traumatic events they'd shared. Yes, they'd become good friends. She cared a great deal about him.

She fought the impulse to grab his hand and declare her love.

She didn't. Instead, she fastened her gaze on his face, taking reassurance from his calm expression.

Cautiously, she began answering his question. "A couple years ago, I stole money from my friends, the Murphys. They own a furniture store in town. Jack had convinced me that we needed the money for the rent and that we would repay them." She swallowed, the memories pressing so close that her ribs felt squeezed together. "I was so nervous that I stumbled out of the store while the burglar alarm was going off. I lost one of my shoes and dropped my purse when I started running. And what I did was so very, very wrong." She trembled. The sound of Jack's drunken, high-pitched laugh still sounded in her ears.

Danny's blue eyes were inscrutable. "You knew it was wrong and you still went along with Jack's scheme? The Murphys were your friends."

She flinched at the sting in his tone. "Before the robbery, Jack had assured me that the Murphys were rich and would never miss the money. He said they'd never suspect me because I was 'their charming and honest friend.'" She squeezed her eyes shut, humiliated and furious at herself. And the shame, always the shame.

Why had she believed Jack? She'd been in a daze when she'd been with him, constantly responding to his demands as he manipulated and altered her beliefs. As a result, she'd lost sight of her own values. And, in ironic hindsight, he hadn't cared about the rent. He'd wanted the money for his drink and drugs.

The older garda opened the boardroom door. "Do you want to press charges if we pick up any suspects, sir?"

"Absolutely," Danny said. "Whoever did this will pay for their crime."

"Can you both step into the room in case we have any further questions?"

Danny nodded. His expression had changed from alarm, to anger, to carefully neutral. And he hadn't commented on her admission.

As the men formed a conclave in the boardroom, Clara pressed a hand to her forehead. Fifty thousand euros was an astronomical sum. No one in Farthing would ever be able to reimburse that amount of money.

In a swish of ruby-red silk, she sank onto the espresso-colored leather couch. She eyed the doorway, noting that Danny's fern needed watering. Plus, the magazines on the coffee table were in disarray. She'd neatly sort the pile and then water the fern. Surely, there was a sink and watering can somewhere.

However, her nerves were playing havoc. Deciding that she couldn't sort, or water, she laced her shaking fingers on her lap. Listening to the men's muted voices, she closed her eyes.

When she heard Danny say thank you to the Gardaí and *slán* to Aiden, she opened her eyes. He came to the sofa and took a seat beside her.

"How are you faring?" he asked. "You must be exhausted."

"Not as exhausted as you, I'm sure. What time do you leave in the morning?"

"Seven." He pulled his phone from his pocket and texted someone. "I'll sleep on the plane."

"Don't you need to go to Dublin first?"

"Aye." He snapped his phone shut and slipped it into his pocket. "Ian will drive me. He just left your sister's flat and is on his way here. He'll take you home. He can use my car."

"You're ... you're not taking me home?"

"I have a lot to wrap up before I leave. Aiden is contacting a few of my accounting and computer employees. They'll be changing and safeguarding all my computer accounts after this hacking."

She tried to swallow and had difficulty. "That's understandable, considering you'll be gone for several months."

He hadn't smiled, hadn't wrapped an arm around her, hadn't so much as met her gaze. His manner was coolly polite, as if he was speaking to an acquaintance, someone he had little interest in conversing with.

His gaze shifted to his watch, and he rose. Without a word, he walked over to the picture window. Despite the hour and steady downpour, the town was aglow with corner streetlamps and bustling pubs, typical for a Saturday night in Ireland.

With his back to her, he stared out at the rain for a long while. He was so still, she wondered for a moment if he were breathing.

His cashmere sweater fit his broad form splendidly. He

was athletic, commanding. He was a man who would always succeed, able to carry any burden weighing down on his strong shoulders.

Although the boardroom was warm and brightly lit, an unsettling chill settled over the room. With a determined lift of her chin, she decided to venture into the deafening silence. They only had a few minutes before Ian arrived.

"Are you angry at me for some reason?" Despite her resolve, she heard the tremor in her voice.

He swung around. Anguish and hopefulness, two contradictory emotions, flickered across his face. He rubbed the back of his neck. "Should I be angry? Angry at you?"

"No, unless you've suddenly grown an aversion to celebrations and sur-surprise birthday parties." She hadn't meant to stammer. And she'd spoken louder than she'd intended.

He didn't seem to notice. Instead, he expelled a long sigh. His sharp gaze seemed to pierce through her, and she directed her own gaze at the rain spitting against the window. She kept her head high, her chin determinedly set. And she waited, although she wasn't sure what she was waiting for.

"Clara, where was your brother last evening?"

She heard her own sharp intake of breath. Danny's voice was so implacably calm.

Very deliberately, she shook the wrinkles from her silk dress and stood. "You know where he was. He spent the day working in your hot kitchen and attended my surprise party."

"I meant last evening. March eighteenth."

"I don't know. I'm trying not to nag Seamus about his whereabouts because he gets furious when I do."

Frantically, she sifted through her memory. Seamus had

gone out to settle a car deal on March 17, St. Patrick's Day. And tonight, March 19, was accounted for. Her mind was in turmoil as she tried to recollect the day in between. Hadn't Seamus said that he was working on March 18?

A vision of her brother from two years ago, strong-willed and protective, a sprinkle of reddish-brown bristles along his chin, flashed in her memory. He'd safeguarded her from Jack Connor so bravely.

And then another image from a few weeks past. Seamus, his mouth twisted in hopeless despair, that heart-wrenching night atop Farthing Bridge when he'd contemplated suicide.

"It's better if I end my life. I'm on me tod, I'm all alone," Seamus had sobbed.

"You mentioned that Seamus was buying a car," Danny was saying. "Where did he get the money?"

"He said it was a private deal. Why? There's no crime in a man buying an old banger of a car to get around. It's further proof that he's exchanging his bad choices for good ones."

She could see the conflict in the set of Danny's jaw as he stepped forward, his tall form seeming to loom over her. Automatically, she stepped back before changing her mind and standing her ground.

He put one hand on her arm. "I don't believe that Seamus pulled off a cybercrime from a remote computer location. He must have either stolen the key to the deadbolt from Ian when the keys went missing, or broken into the boardroom. Somehow, he managed to avoid the security camera."

"How dare you accuse my brother!" Angrily, she shrugged off Danny's hand. "Seamus would never do such a terrible thing and steal money right out from under you. You're his employer and his new job is the main reason he's finally beginning to respect himself. You saw him tonight at my party. Did he look like a criminal to you?"

"Did you talk with him?"

"No. Although I wanted to, I never had the chance."

"Because he was probably avoiding you. He was buzzed on vodka most of the night."

She didn't speak as a glacial blast of silence encased them.

"Unfortunately," Danny finally said quietly, "I may be forced to press charges against Seamus, now that Aiden and the Gardaí are privy to so much information."

White static went through her brain, a forewarning of impending disaster. She knew that he might suspect Seamus, and had half expected his questions. However, she hadn't expected his unsympathetic confrontation and accusation, and a fierce wave of protectiveness for her brother rose in her.

In quiet defiance, she repeated, "My brother is not a thief."

Danny looked away, seeming to mentally review the evidence. "Perhaps he's been gambling again. Perhaps he was desperate."

She bristled. "He has no reason to be desperate. He lives with me and we share the cost of his food and I charge no rent. Plus, one of the reasons he's buying a car is so that I won't have to use public transportation to travel to and from work anymore. Please." She reached out and touched Danny's sleeve. "Seamus is kind and considerate and generous. We all go through hard times and he's made a remarkable recovery. He's vowed that he isn't gambling anymore. And, emotionally, he wouldn't be able to survive being hauled into a garda station for questioning."

"And I have a cyber nightmare ahead of me. The need

for all these fixes will impede the smooth flow of my businesses as the computer system is being changed and upgraded. Not to mention the money taken—"

"It's all about the money for you. Not about people, nor their lives, nor their hardships. And—"

He interrupted with an ironic laugh. "Despite what you may think, I don't care about the money."

She almost lost her determination to continue. However, Danny had shown her that persistence paid off, and *that* realization gave her resolve.

"You care about being a winner." She stiffened her stance, meeting his cool gaze with as much confidence as she could muster. "You're so driven. And for what? Coffee? Can't you be satisfied with all that you've already accomplished? You *are* successful. You don't need any more money or international franchises to prove that."

In the glare of the overhead florescent lights, she saw the fury, then sadness, emanating from him. They were standing so close, within arm's reach, yet so far away. She dropped her hand.

"You don't understand," he said softly.

"Help me to understand."

A heavy-booted stride had them glancing toward the hallway. Ian had undoubtedly arrived.

Clara started for the door. "I'll get my things from your flat."

"I told Ian to retrieve your gifts and personal belongings and pack everything into my car."

She pressed back the tears threatening to flood her eyes. "You're quite efficient," she managed to say. "Of course, you're an entrepreneur, and all your jobs and appointments must be completed on schedule."

He jerked, then said curtly, "Aye, they must."

She swiped a tear that had managed to trickle down her cheek. Surely, he would take her in his arms and reassure her that this was all a grave misunderstanding.

At first he didn't move. He folded his arms, seemed to think better of it, and stepped forward. Lightly, he placed both hands on her shoulders. Any hint of the sparkling, teasing gaze she'd come to treasure had long disappeared from his eyes.

"Clara."

She stared up at him, at the persistent pulse drumming at his temple. Hesitantly, she laid a hand against his cheek. "Please, don't do this to Seamus, to us." She felt more tears, made no attempt to wipe them. "Please. I love—"

He shook his head, effectively stopping her from continuing.

"I must ask you one more question," he said. "This is difficult for me. Please understand that I have no choice." He blew out a ragged breath. He couldn't quite meet her gaze. "Clara, where were you the evening of March eighteenth?"

18

She visibly whitened as his words registered. And Danny knew, having asked the question he didn't want to ask, shouldn't have asked, that she'd never forgive him.

He wasn't prepared, however, for the sharp crack of her hand against his jaw.

"You think it was me? You think I was the one who hacked into your computer and stole your precious money?" She reared back and hurled a curse at him. "How dare you? You are nothing but a wastrel, a no-good bowsie who only thinks about himself!"

She lifted her arm, ready to strike him again.

He grabbed her hand. "Of course I don't think it was you. I think it was your conniving brother who coerced you into committing this crime."

"Did I waltz past your fancy security surveillance camera, your always devoted barista, Kathleen, plus shut the power to your entire shop so that I could steal fifty thousand euros?"

He shrugged with an indifference he didn't feel. "If anyone could pull off a crime like that, you could."

Her eyes widened in confusion. "Because I stole from some shops when I was five years old?"

"You're conveniently forgetting your crime from a couple of years ago."

Her lips parted and she blinked rapidly. "My crime? My *crime,* like I'm some sort of hardened criminal? I never ended up stealing any money from the Murphys, and I served my night in jail." She visibly shuddered and rubbed her hands up and down her arms as if to warm herself. "My crime was splashed on the front page of the Farthing newspaper and I felt such shame afterward. Wasn't that punishment enough for my foolish mistake? Or would you prefer that I serve my sentence for a lifetime?"

"Of course not." He released his grip on her wrist. His gaze raked her features, searching for guilt. He saw only her anguished expression and her trembling chin; heard her soft sobs. And in that instant, he knew that no matter how much misguided devotion she felt for her brother, she would never have taken part in Seamus's misdeeds.

Danny swallowed the unaccustomed tightness in his throat. "I'm sorry, luv."

She was sobbing harder now.

"I'm ... I'm sorry. I—I didn't mean to sound so harsh. It's late." His excuses were hollow, because there were no excuses.

He watched her exquisite features crumple, and his heart seemed to crumple too. Her shiny hair had fallen from its upsweep, tumbling in waves around her face.

She twisted from him, her shoulders shaking. She was crying, and she didn't want him to see. She was so proud, had fought so hard to break free from her shameful past.

And he was driving her away, just as he'd driven away everyone he had ever loved with his harsh judgments.

Instinctively, he placed a hand on her shoulder. "Luv, please don't cry. I never meant to hurt you. I'm not thinking straight. I'll make it up to you. I'll buy you—"

"Don't touch me." She shrugged him off. "Don't ever touch me again. Don't ever come near me or my family. We don't need you, your posh gifts ..." She whirled, unfastened the diamond necklace around her throat and threw it on his computer desk as if the stones were filthy.

He ached to take her in his arms and absorb the hurt he had caused with his terrible charge. He wanted to thread his fingers through her hair, kiss her nape, inhale the fresh, lemony scent of her. "Please, keep it. I picked it out in London especially for you. It's my birthday gift."

She tightened her fists at her sides. "I don't want anything from you." Her voice was fainter, her tone broken.

"Seamus coerced you," he said quietly, trying to talk reasonably. "He's obviously off the rails."

"No. He lives with me, we have long chats." She drew in a shaky breath. "He wouldn't need fifty thousand euros."

"Gambling debts add up quickly, and unscrupulous men may have pushed Seamus to the brink of desperation. And, if you'd be honest with yourself concerning your brother for longer than ten seconds, you'd realize that Seamus has had a lot of extra time and money unaccounted for."

"People fall ... people fail ... Everyone deserves a second chance. He's doing well, has a job ..."

"Your brother has perfected the art of persuading you to feel sorry for him. It's time he stood on his own two feet without you making excuses for him every inch of the way."

She cut him off. "He said he was working and saving his money. He said—"

"And I'm his employer, and I can say for certain that he's hardly put in one full day of work since he was hired."

"Seamus leaves my flat at the same time every day."

"And where he goes is anyone's guess. My guess is liquor and gambling." With a heavy sigh, Danny looked up at the ceiling. "Clara, please. At least, entertain the thought that Seamus may have committed this crime."

She shook her head. "No."

A click of boots in the hallway was followed by a knock on the door.

Ian entered the boardroom quietly. Working an antacid around in his mouth, he kept his gaze on Danny while handing Clara her raincoat. "I'm warming the car, boss, and ready to return Clara to her flat."

"Not yet, Ian." Clara lifted her hand and turned to Danny. "You've forgotten about Jack. It could easily have been him. He's stolen plenty of times. He gambles. He drinks."

She waited until Danny met her gaze. Everything grew quiet.

Danny drew in a heavy breath and released it before he spoke. "Clara, that's what I've wanted to tell you all evening and I haven't had the chance. Since the Gardaí haven't been any help, I hired a private detective to follow Jack Connor. He was picked up a few days ago near Dublin."

Her hands went to her face. "What was Jack doing in Dublin?"

"Apparently, he was trying to get to me," Danny said, half to himself. "Aiden said the money lifted from my Farthing account occurred on March eighteenth and Jack wasn't anywhere near Farthing. He's been locked in county Dublin prison the past three days for violating parole."

DANNY STOOD by the window in his flat. He'd abandoned the task of sorting files, leaving the computer fixes to his experts. For him, the burden was emotional. He felt violated. Someone had accessed his online information, which he considered private.

Silently, he replayed his last scenes with Clara before he finally shut down his computer. She'd hardly bidden him a civil good-bye, even when he'd assured her that he wouldn't press charges against her brother, although he would be forced to dismiss Seamus from the dishwasher job. He'd also offer Seamus a month-long compensation in wages.

She'd said nothing in return, silently assessing him and then requesting that he never contact her again. He'd insisted she take the diamond necklace because it was a gift, and she'd reluctantly placed the necklace in the pocket of her raincoat. Then he'd watched her walk away. Her spine had been straight, her chin held high.

Her unconquerable spirit had been ever-present, even when he'd charged her with theft. He kept envisioning her in that silky dress, its deep red color enhancing the creamy olive tones of her flawless skin, her silver earrings glinting in the overhead lights. She'd been enraged, her face heated, her hand raised, ready to strike him a second time. She'd resembled a stormy, outraged goddess.

And she'd never looked so irresistibly gorgeous.

He walked down the hall to his flat and fixed a cup of tea. Clara's lemon scone recipe, written in her scholarly scroll, sat on the kitchen counter. He'd shared the recipe with his bakers and kept her hand-written recipe for himself.

He stared at it and sighed. He wasn't certain what made

him more furious—his infatuation with her, or his inability to concentrate whenever she was near. He was in his thirties, considered one of the most successful businessmen in all Ireland, and she'd trimmed him down to staring at a lemon scone recipe.

Somewhere along the path of his disillusioned, cynical life, Clara Donovan had taken the eye out of his head. He'd been smitten with her, a part-time dance teacher who lived in a small town that he hadn't even known existed. Despite the turbulence surrounding their relationship, he had enjoyed every minute of their time together. He'd started to dream that their moments together could last forever.

He wet his tea and added a great deal of cream to cool it. He sipped. Still too damn hot. He shook his head.

He'd seen what he'd wanted to see—a life with his precious Clara. He loved her desperately. And now, somehow, he needed to come to grips with the fact that her engaging smile, her eternal optimism, was gone from his life.

He carried his steaming tea to the living room and stood at the window, looking down at the street. Rain bore down endlessly, beating against the cobblestone sidewalks. The roads were rapidly becoming infinite lakes of grey, mud-spattered water.

He took a dull swallow of tea, quelling the urge to ring Clara, closing his eyes to memorize every detail of her exquisite features—as well as her wit and her jaunty smile. For he knew, he'd never see her again.

With a rough sigh, he shoved away from the window and set his cup on the cherry credenza. He'd instructed Ian to return before dawn so that they would reach Dublin by early morn.

He should be packing, Danny's practical side insisted.

Six months of travel was a long time. Instead, his gaze canvassed the remnants from Clara's birthday party. The green balloons were sinking. The slices of apples had browned, and the strawberries smelled unpleasantly pungent. Kelly-green confetti littered every inch of the cream carpeting.

If she'd seen it, Clara would have begun straightening the mess immediately. Except that Clara wouldn't ever know, because she wasn't standing beside him.

With a vicious jerk, Danny tore the festive streamers from the lampshades and threw them on the floor. This was all her brother's fault. He'd been a dark cloud, hovering above every moment of Danny's relationship with Clara. He was the painful trigger, and Danny resented Seamus more and more. Seamus's drinking and gambling, his resultant lies, had set off this devastating chain of events.

Why did people—his parents, Seamus—act the way they did and not overcome their addictions? He didn't know. He just knew that Clara was still crying when she left.

On his way to his bedroom to begin packing, Danny picked up several discarded napkins. *The Ground Café* was proudly stamped on each, along with the recognizable pot of gold logo.

"Always the businessman, yeh?" Clara had said, grinning while she'd sat in his car and dabbed at her eyes, the night Jack Connor shoved her.

Or when she'd sat pertly, engrossed in *Entrepreneur* magazine, a frown of concentration on her beautiful face. She'd mentioned her hope to someday open a dance studio in town, and that she required money for expenses.

Danny crushed the napkins in his hands. His mouth twisted. Perhaps Seamus had convinced her that they would split the fifty thousand euros so that she could open her own business. After all, Jack had convinced her to steal from the friends.

Danny threw the crushed napkins in the wastebasket.

No.

His exquisite Clara would never have stolen from him, certainly not for her own gain. Moreover, he'd offered the money outright to open her business. She'd looked him straight in the eye and refused his offer.

Women couldn't be trusted, a small voice argued in his sleep-deprived brain. Hadn't his ex-wife, Kyla, proven that? Women wanted him for his wealth, the prestige of dating an up-and-coming billionaire. No woman wanted him for himself.

Except for his Clara. She'd been furious at his deception when she'd found out his real identity that first day at the coffee shop. The bittersweet memory made his heart skip a beat. He'd vowed that he wouldn't fall in love, because love had no place in his demanding, stressful life.

But he had. He'd fallen in love with a magnificent, tenacious woman who saw the good in everyone. Once, he'd dreamed about marriage to a woman like her, settling down in a small town, having children.

Restlessly, he paced the soundless room which no longer radiated with her disarming humor and jaunty animation. Hours earlier, she'd chatted and laughed, her splendid silk dress rustling gracefully as she'd engaged with her guests. Now she'd walked out of his life.

And with her departure, he felt empty.

Perhaps the mellowing effect of the rain against the window was why he'd slumped on the couch and eventually closed his eyes. He awoke to the harsh sound of Ian knocking on his flat door. He opened his eyes with a start and gazed out the window. Dawn was streaking across the early morning sky.

"Ready, boss?" Ian stepped in and peered at Danny. "I'll drive. You look terrible."

"Thanks," Danny said wryly. As quickly as he could, he packed his bags and briefcase, and then went to the kitchen and grabbed Clara's hand-written recipe, putting it in the inside pocket of his sport jacket. He'd have just enough time to shower in Dublin before boarding the plane for London.

"Remove the Francis Bacon painting and deliver it to my home in Howth," he instructed Ian as they passed the watercolor in the hallway. "And instruct Kathleen to return to my Dublin shop by the end of the week, then meet me in Italy. She wants to work there a few months and brush up on her Italian, because she met some Italian guy online. I assume you'll be in Farthing a while longer to look after the coffee shop?"

"Aye. Anna lives here." Ian bent a thoughtful eye toward Danny. "Does that mean you won't be returning to Farthing, boss?"

"Never again will I set foot in Farthing."

The men rode the lift to the main floor of the coffee shop in silence.

He wouldn't look back, Danny told himself. He wouldn't look back.

Mist swirled around him as he stepped outside. He slid into the passenger seat of his silver Mercedes and Ian took the wheel. As the car glided through rain-slicked streets, Danny snapped open his briefcase and leafed through a stack of documents, looking for the paperwork he'd need in London. Only once did he peer out the window to admire the early sun rising against a crimson sky. The way the sun filtered through tawny clouds signaled an end to the rain, at least for a day or so. Clara wouldn't need to worry about a downpour when she walked to the bus stop.

The quaint town of Farthing was Clara's town. It had never been his town, just as she had never been his damsel in distress, because she hadn't been the one in distress. In the end, he'd needed her more than she'd needed him.

Muttering an Irish curse, Danny extracted his gold pen and a pad of white paper featuring The Ground Café logo from his briefcase. He ignored Ian's brutal set-down that he get some sleep before he collapsed from exhaustion.

"I am so exasperated," he said, shaking his head. "So frustrated with Seamus. Doesn't Clara see he's the problem? He's impossible. He's an addict. Why doesn't he change his behavior?"

"Perhaps you can't change him," Ian said softly. "Perhaps you can only change yourself."

"What's that supposed to mean?"

Ian's sigh was polite. He added a small shrug.

With unswerving determination, Danny wrote up a formal deed, including instructions to draft a check to Clara Donovan in the amount of thirty thousand euros. On a separate sheet, he added a note: "Per our agreement, this check is for your lemon scone recipe, and to assist Seamus in repaying his gambling debts. It is my hope that you enjoyed our time together as much as I did."

He hesitated. She would probably be furious when she received the check. However, the thought of her struggling each day to make ends meet was intolerable. If, by God's good grace, her brother actually stayed on the rails, then Clara wouldn't need to keep bailing him out of debt, and she could use the funds to make her life more comfortable. She deserved this check, and so much more.

He folded the papers, instructing Ian to get them to his

solicitor in Dublin and tell him to draft the check to Clara immediately.

"The funds may take a wee bit longer to clear because of the cybercrime and resultant investigation," Ian reminded him.

With a clipped acknowledgement, Danny shoved the deed and note in an envelope, sealed it, and placed the envelope on the dashboard. Leaning his head against the leather seat of his Mercedes, he resisted the impulse to rip the envelope open and write the words to Clara that were in his heart:

"Please, luv, can we start again? I'm sorry for my hurtful accusation. It was so wrong. This wasn't the way I wanted your birthday celebration to end. If I can take you in my arms once more, I promise I'll brighten every hour of your life with love and laughter. I'll make it up to you. We can visit Italy together, the Egadi Islands, and you can show me ..."

No.

Danny discovered that he could swear fluently in Gaelic. Disregarding Ian's scowl, he reached for the documents in his briefcase that he'd neglected. He'd plunge himself into the minutest of details involving each franchise in Europe and America, thereby occupying every second of his waking hours with one mission in mind.

Forgetting Clara.

19

As the following week went by, Clara found that she could sometimes go an hour or two without thinking about Danny. Anna knew better than to mention him, or her new waitressing job at the coffee shop, or Ian, for that matter, although Clara knew that Ian was still in Farthing.

Gradually, Clara was finding a quiet stability in her routine, although her eyes were continuously red from crying and her heart was broken. Danny had called every day, his caller ID flashing across the screen of her cell phone. She'd refused to pick up the phone. She'd told him not to contact her, but he made his own rules. Besides, she didn't want to risk speaking with him, fearing that she'd burst into tears before she was able to utter a word.

In her flat one damp, grey evening, she lit a fire in the hearth. On impulse, because she missed hearing Danny's voice, she played his CD, the one he'd given her from the coffee shop.

His soft Irish ballad brought her to her knees, and she wept so hard that she feared she might never stop. When there were no more sobs left inside her, she stared at the cheery fire in the hearth and forced herself to stand. Her throat ached as she vowed she would never cry for him again. She was self-reliant, dependent solely on herself. Stiffly, she placed the CD in its case and tucked it in the bottom of her bedroom bureau.

To make matters worse, Seamus had grown more difficult. Since losing his job at the coffee shop, his temperament had been surprisingly mellow. That is, until he erupted in anger and aggression because of something she'd unintentionally said. He'd blame her, and she'd apologize. Somehow, his mood changes were always her fault.

He slept in most mornings, often waking famished, and constantly sipped from a coffee thermos. Despite his overeating, he seemed to be rapidly losing weight and spent a great deal of time in the bathroom.

Her workweek ended with the same routine she'd established before she'd met Danny: walking to her preschool dance class. The days were getting longer, and for a change, the twilight sky was devoid of clouds. The warmer weather had soothed her cough, and her disposition lifted with each step. Teaching dance gave her such delight and took her mind from her melancholy. If only she could do it full-time. She so enjoyed her young students' energy and imagination, their bright-eyed sparkles of giggle.

When she arrived at the dance studio, Colum O'Brien stood in the middle of the rehearsal room amidst seven active preschoolers.

"Who can jump on one foot all the way to the barre?" he was asking.

A freckle-faced little boy hop-scotched to the ballet mirror and made a funny face, while another ran in rapid circles around Colum.

Giving Clara a wave, Colum wiped his sweaty brow and declared, "I am so relieved you are here, Miss Donovan. Things were getting a wee bit chaotic."

"My pleasure, Mr. O'Brien," she returned with a laugh. "Children, let's join hands and sing our good-bye song. Show me how *slowly* you can move."

When the parents entered several minutes later, Clara hugged each departing child. Afterward, Colum perched his slim hip on the reception desk and silently applauded. "One would think that a grown man with over twenty years of professional dance training and experience could handle a group of four-year-olds," he said.

Clara grinned. "The key is structure. Children like routine, including a clear beginning, middle and end."

"I prefer teaching adults. At least they listen to my instructions." Colum grabbed his parka. "After that energetic class, I need a smoke."

"I thought you were quitting?"

"Next week." He dug around in his pocket and drew out a cigarette and lighter. "Can we chat?"

"Sure. My class doesn't begin for another hour."

They made their way to the front stoop.

While cars whizzed by, Colum assessed her with an astute, green-eyed gaze. "So, I enjoyed your birthday party," he said, a bit too pacifyingly.

The slight wind burned her puffy eyes and sent the hood of her jacket fluttering behind her. She jammed her hands in her pockets. "Thanks. Everyone seemed to have a good time."

"Your Brady fellow worked hard to pull off the surprise. He wanted each detail to be perfect and rang nearly everyone himself, making them promise to keep your party a secret."

She stared fixedly at a rut in the road and pinched her lips together.

Colum paused, seeming at a loss for words, and blew a ring of smoke in the air. "I caught one of his interviews on television the other night. He was leaving London and flying to ..."

"Spain," she provided. She'd memorized Danny's itinerary. "And before you ask, he won't be returning to Farthing."

"So I've heard." Colum scowled, then patted her shoulder. "If you ever want to talk about what happened, I'll be happy to listen. I like Danny Brady. He's a good chap."

She bent her head, attempting to dull the longing she felt whenever she heard Danny's name.

Colum was so understanding. Their friendship made her want to babble, to tell him that her heart had been shattered, but the words lodged in her throat.

"Danny's doing what he does best," she replied tonelessly. "He's making a fortune and—"

Colum checked her words. "He rang me this week. He wants to talk to you. He said he's called you numerous times and you haven't picked up."

"He never left a message."

"A hollow excuse and you know it." Colum waved one hand in the air. "You can't resolve a disagreement by not speaking to one another. Mr. Brady and I enjoyed a lengthy chat the night of your party, and he couldn't take his eyes off you the whole while. It was obvious that he's in love with you. In my opinion, his love is so strong that even *he* doesn't recognize it." Bleakly, Colum smiled. "Judging by the shuttered look in your eyes every time his name is mentioned, you feel the same way about him."

"He's undoubtedly regretting the day he ever met me."

Ruefully, Clara dragged her thoughts away from her first meeting with Danny at the bottom of Farthing Bridge. "He came to our town for one reason, the successful opening of his fiftieth coffee shop."

Colum's forehead knit into a frown. "Don't fault him for his ambition. Recently, I read a magazine article featuring an account of his early years and his very difficult upbringing. He's accomplished everything on his own."

She rolled her eyes. She wasn't in the mood to extoll Danny's virtues. "As a result, his priorities are expensive homes and cars and his precious money. Not people. Not—"

Before she could finish, a yellow taxi pulled to the curb. Madame Sophie stepped out, scowled at the cigarette dangling from Colum's fingers, and marched to the stoop. Neatly installing her matronly form between Clara and Colum, Madame Sophie adjusted her hip-length kimono wrap and greeted them.

"Good. I need to speak with both of you." She peered over yellow reading glasses at Clara. "Ms. Donovan, your teaching this year has been—"

"I'll pack my things," Clara broke in, blindly grabbing Colum's arm for support. Her feelings were raw, and two letdowns within a few days would undo her. Wildly, she rehearsed how she was going to accept the fact that Madame Sophie was firing her in front of Colum without running down the street like a blubbering fool.

"Ms. Donovan, your teaching this year has been exemplary," Madame Sophie finished. "So, I loathe being the person to break bad news on such short notice. However, I'm closing the dance studio at the end of March. We can't afford to make ends meet and I'm retiring gracefully."

"Which means that both Clara and I will be losing our jobs in less than a week." Colum's ruddy complexion turned so ashen, Clara feared he might get sick. Already, he was reaching for another cigarette.

Madame Sophie's index finger pointed reprovingly to a rundown building across the street, another building with its paint peeling, the potholes in the street. "This little town doesn't have the resources to support the arts."

Tears brimmed in Clara's eyes. "What about our end-of-the year dance recitals? The students will be so disappointed. They've been practicing all year long."

Madame Sophie cast the dance building a swift, fault-finding perusal. "I've exhausted all our resources—fundraising, begging for corporate donations, raising our tuition. Maintenance costs are rising. The studio requires a major updating."

Colum leveled Madame Sophie a furious gaze. "I've taught dance my entire life, plus, my nephew relies on me. His graphic design business is in the beginning stages. If you had shared the studio's dire financial problems, I would have been looking for another job."

He inhaled a final puff and threw his cigarette to the ground. Head down, his shadow lengthened as he stalked away.

THERE WERE two reasons why Clara scrubbed her flat the following day.

The first was because she was upset about the dance studio closing, and her restless fingers needed something to do.

The second was because the diamond necklace that Danny had gifted her the night of her birthday party had gone missing. Panicking, she'd retraced her steps and scoured every inch of her bedroom. After she'd returned to her flat the night of her argument with Danny, she'd been certain that she'd placed the necklace in her jewelry box.

She took a few deep breaths, trying to focus and keep her mind clear. She'd chased away Seamus's clutter and checked under every piece of furniture.

Perhaps Seamus had seen the necklace. She made a mental note to ask him when he slipped in for the evening. *If* he slipped in for the evening. Offhandedly, he had mentioned that he and Liam had gambled all week because Seamus was on a winning streak. He'd assured that the pastime took away his thoughts of suicide and depression, and that gambling was harmless. After all, he wasn't bringing illegal drugs into her flat.

Clara had lectured him about the dangers of addiction before he'd stormed out and slammed the door behind him.

She'd brushed off his terseness. He was still having a hard time coping with Fiona's death. Plus, he was under stress because he'd lost his dishwasher job and was having difficulty finding employment.

In the meantime, he'd purchased an orange sports car to "cheer him up," and had parked the car ostentatiously outside her flat. And the car wasn't an old banger, as he'd initially claimed. When she'd questioned the expense—a new convertible, no less, in a country that experienced rain over two hundred days a year—he'd snapped that he'd received a generous compensation from Mr. Brady and needed transportation because he was looking for a job.

All of her cleaning hadn't turned up the necklace, so she went to the kitchen to bake. She started to dice lemons for a batch of scones, and then switched on the television in the living room. The low hum was company in her quiet, lonely kitchen while she measured flour, baking powder, and sugar for the dough. She set the dough to settle and reached beneath her kitchen cupboard for cleanser to scour the sink, surprised to find a half-empty bottle of clear liquid that she hadn't noticed before.

Detergent? She opened the bottle and sniffed.

No. She wrinkled her brow. Her stomach clenched. Vodka.

A deep, familiar Irish brogue coming from the television brought her into the living room with the half-empty bottle of vodka in her hand. Danny Brady appeared on the screen. Sounding like a Dubliner, he spoke at length into a microphone, explaining— to a well-known, gorgeous female newscaster—his newest coffee franchise in the south of Spain.

Her gaze riveted to the television, Clara assured herself that she wouldn't be affected by watching him, and that she'd view the interview only for a second and then return to the kitchen to finish the scones.

The harsh studio lights brought out the reddish tinge in Danny's brown hair. He was so handsome, looking into the camera with his china-blue eyes, suited in a navy sport coat and white button-down shirt. The newscaster gushed throughout the interview, and Clara didn't miss how she lightly touched Danny's sleeve. When the interview ended, Clara felt her insides die a little beneath an anguished pang of jealousy. Her hands were cold, her legs were trembling.

Women had always made themselves readily available to him.

Fifteen minutes later, with tears streaming down her cheeks, Clara clicked off the television and crossed to her bedroom. She placed the bottle on her bureau and cried out her sorrow in her pillow—for the half-empty bottle of vodka, for the dance studio's closing, for her lonesome life without Danny.

An hour later, she was still huddled in a cocoon on her bed when an insistent rap on her flat's door forced her to answer. The postman stood at the entry and handed her a thickly padded sealed envelope. She brought the envelope into the kitchen, unsealed it and pulled out official-looking papers. A check for thirty thousand euros was clipped to the top of the documents.

Thirty thousand euros.

Clara dropped the check on the table. She'd never seen such a large sum. Her hands shook as she read the documents, punctuated by legal terms she scarcely understood. "In consideration of the Buyer," and "Bill of Sale," and "The Seller." At first, she assumed the packet pertained to Seamus's sports car and that she'd mistakenly opened a post intended for him.

And then she realized that the check was signed by Danny Brady.

Her fingers shook as she spread out the neatly folded note, stamped at the top with The Ground Café's logo. In Danny's bold scroll, he'd written: "Per our agreement, this check is for your lemon scone recipe, and to assist Seamus in repaying his gambling debts. It is my hope that you enjoyed our time together as much as I did."

She squeezed her eyes closed.

"I'd consider buying your recipe. How does a flat fee of ten thousand euros sound?" Danny had asked.

"Twenty thousand is fairer."

Her eyes snapped open.

Her pride insisted that she tear up his check and toss it into the fireplace to burn. He had shattered her to the core, taken away her self-esteem and proven that he didn't trust her.

Her heart, however, whispered otherwise.

An image of Danny's tormented face when he'd apologized for his accusation rushed into her thoughts: *Luv, please don't cry. I never meant to hurt you. I'm not thinking straight. I'll make it up to you.*

He was good-hearted, so generous to her and her family. And Colum said Danny loved her, and that nothing could be resolved if she and Danny never spoke.

Colum was right. She'd never been so unhappy. She was living in a suspended state, flanked by memories of her joyous past days with Danny and a desolate future without him.

Anxious and indecisive, she rubbed her neck, took a deep breath and slowly exhaled. Perhaps they could begin where they'd left off, before the terrible accusations and bitter argument.

She envisioned Danny's face, and a deep longing swelled in her heart. He was so splendid, and she missed him so much. Perhaps she should call him, thank him for his generosity. She'd begin by telling she forgave him. Everyone made mistakes and he had apologized.

She reached for her cell phone. Smiling, she envisioned the broad grin spreading across his face when he answered and heard her voice.

But what would she say?

She took a quick breath, a fluttery feeling in her stomach. She stared at the phone, her mind groping frantically for reasons why she shouldn't call him. He would be busy, he wouldn't have time to listen to her. He probably was angry because she hadn't picked up his calls. Or worse, he'd act cool and indifferent. Furthermore, there was a time difference and it was an hour later in Spain. He might have retired early for the night.

She set the phone down.

The next time he rang her, she would answer his call, thank him, and thus, salvage her self-esteem.

She stared at the check. With these funds, she could keep the studio open. And she would be able to do what she loved best—teach dance, while creating a lively and diverse cultural centre in Farthing. She could connect with other arts groups and civic leaders, as well as philanthropists like Danny. Together, they could entice families to stay in her hometown rather than relocate to bigger cities.

She could advertise, design a fresh, new look for the studio. To help prevent injuries, she'd install a floating floor for the dancers. She'd paint the studio walls in gentle, inspiring hues—light beige, muted blues and gold. The lobby could incorporate fun, bright colors—teals and shocking pinks. Most important, Colum could continue to teach dance. He wouldn't need to scramble for another job.

She flew to the sink, filled a kettle with water for tea and set it on the stove to boil. Her mind busied with plans because there was so much to tell Danny. And he could offer insight regarding Seamus's behavior. Her pride might suffer considering her refusals of his advice, yet she wanted to discuss the matter with him.

Her spirits lifted. She could lean on Danny's broad shoulders. After all, relationships were a give and take partnership.

She beamed, picturing their joyful reunion. In person, she would finally tell him what was in her heart. Her handsome, bold, sophisticated man.

Her Danny Boy.

20

———

Danny attempted to tune out the talkative businessman sitting next to him in first class by staring down at the international permits on his lap, all the while pondering why he hadn't chartered a private plane. They were headed for Rome, Italy, although the plane had been delayed several hours in the Spanish airport. Consequently, he was several hours behind schedule.

In three days, he'd be in America. His coffee franchises were scheduled to open on the east coast in New York City, Atlanta, Miami, Charlotte, and Boston.

He scrubbed a hand over his face. The Spanish coffee shop, located near Malaga in southern Spain, had experienced unexpected complications. Furthermore, although his expert staff had reinstated his computer accounts, the continual phone calls and meetings had been a cyber nightmare.

He tipped his head against the seat and tried to rest. He couldn't seem to keep his mind on his work. Every time he closed his eyes, the image of Clara's stricken face when he'd accused her of stealing tore at him. When would he be able to arrange his thoughts back into a semblance of working order?

When she finally decided to answer her damn phone, that's when. He needed to talk to her.

"Beautiful scenery."

Danny opened his eyes.

The businessman's gaze was roving appreciatively over Kathleen's voluptuous curves. She sat across the aisle, attractively dressed in a clingy jersey knit top and short skirt. She met the man's gaze with a teasing grin before crossing her legs and returning to the magazine on her lap.

With a lingering, leering chuckle, the businessman looked back to the window. "We're flying over the three Egadi Islands."

"Aye, I've heard of them," Danny said.

Do you remember the name of the town?

No, although my Irish Mom said the town was close to the Egadi Islands.

He stared out the window, watching the loops of clouds swirling in the sky, evolving from white to grey. He yearned to have the swirls block out the ever-present sting of memories and resultant pain in his gut.

To distract himself he turned to chat with Kathleen, asking if she'd heard anything recently from her Italian boyfriend.

She shook her heard. "Not since yesterday. I hope his villa is actually as nice as the internet photos he texted."

She'd flown from Dublin to Spain to meet with him to help with the opening of the Spanish coffee shop. She'd help with the launch of the Rome coffee shop as well, and then stay to oversee it after Danny departed. The Italian coffee market was highly competitive, and Kathleen was ever competent in dealing with distributors. Besides, her new Italian boyfriend lived there. Or at least, she assumed he did.

"Hopefully, you're not in for a surprise—with either the boyfriend or his villa," Danny said. "Internet relationships can be tricky, and people are sometimes not who they portray themselves to be through texts and photos."

"How close is your hotel to the coffee shop, just in case?" Her low laugh had a slight catch.

She was too accessible, Danny thought, too willing to please men—any man. And her eyes weren't a deep, warm brown.

He glanced at his watch. The plane was scheduled to land in forty-five minutes. As soon as he reached his hotel, he'd ring Clara. If she didn't answer, he'd leave a message this time, then continue ringing until she picked up. Persistence. It had worked well in business, it would work well with—

He didn't complete the thought.

Hoping it would soothe him during his whirlwind journey, he'd brought his acoustic guitar with him. So far, he hadn't had the opportunity to strum a note, neither in France nor Spain. Perhaps in Italy, on a warm, balmy night, he'd sit on his hotel balcony and finish his song for Clara.

"I'm American," the businessman said. "And I own a home in Italy and speak fluent Italian."

Danny nodded absently. "Bravo."

"You?"

"Irish. I own a home in Ireland and speak fluent English and a wee bit of Gaelic."

"Gaelic is a difficult language."

"Aye."

The businessman pressed closer to the window. "Looks like a storm brewing."

Danny resumed his appraisal of the permits.

A bump. An unexpected jostle. No warning.

The businessman lifted the plane's shade higher. "Turbulence from the winds," he observed knowingly. "I'm a seasoned world traveler."

"Good to know," Danny replied, thinking he would have been better off saying nothing, because the businessman would probably start talking again.

The plane shuddered and dropped altitude. The pilot came on the loudspeaker and advised passengers to fasten their seat belts because they were making an unexpected, forced landing at a small airfield near Cosenza, Italy.

"Not an emergency." The flight attendants reassured passengers, scurrying down the aisle as the plane continued to dip. "Only a precaution. Brace, brace, brace."

Danny felt woozy, his brain drifting.

The plane tilted and oxygen masks were deployed.

The last thing he remembered was smelling smoke, followed by a loud bang.

21

———

Clara stood on the stoop of the dance studio with Colum. The two of them had just spent the day painting the interior of the studio.

She pulled in a deep breath and pointed to her new sign, large pink letters against a white backdrop. "Hang the sign a little more to the left," she instructed Colum's nephew.

"Miss Clara's School of Dance." Colum gazed at the sign and smiled broadly. "Congratulations. You've saved the arts in our little town. Not to mention my job."

"And my thanks to your nephew for designing the sign so quickly. He's very artistic. We should consider offering art classes in the future." She couldn't help an entrepreneurial smile. "Remember, this is all because of a lemon scone recipe."

"A fair exchange. I'm sure Mr. Brady was delighted when you told him about your business venture."

Clara shoved her hands into the pockets of her new, caramel-colored jacket and released a ragged sigh. "I haven't heard from him since his check arrived. Maybe he sent me the money to assuage his guilt for his accusations. Now his conscience is clear because he's paid for his recipe and is well rid of me."

"I like him," Colum replied, giving her a hard, quick embrace. "However, I like you more. And I don't like the idea that he's hurting you, whether intentional or not."

As she brushed away a tear, her cell phone buzzed. She'd become an expert in the art of weeping, she thought sheepishly. Ever hopeful, she glanced at the caller ID before answering the call. She sighed again and then said, "Hi, Anna."

"Don't sound so thrilled to hear from me."

"Sorry. I'm at the dance studio with Colum."

"You've been very mysterious the past few days."

"I'm working on a surprise." Clara glanced at the sign. "You'll see it tomorrow."

"I have a surprise too. Can you stop by the coffee shop? I'm finishing my shift and I want to show off ... the baked goods display. Your lemon scones are selling well."

The thought of entering the coffee shop, especially since her last encounter with Danny, caused Clara to falter. "I've seen my lemon scones before and they're not a surprise," she evaded.

"This is important to me."

Apparently eavesdropping, Colum mouthed, "Go ahead. We're done here."

"I'll head over now, Anna." Clara nodded and bid Colum a silent farewell. With her cell phone pressed firmly to her ear, she headed toward the coffee shop.

"The lobby is near empty." Anna continued their conversation while Clara walked. "Ian is in Dublin and Kathleen flew to Italy."

"Kathleen flew to Italy?" Clara parroted. She stopped, swaying in place as the realization hit her. Danny was in

Italy with Kathleen, which was why he no longer bothered to ring. He'd lost interest, pure and simple.

She shook her head. She should've called him but she'd gotten cold feet. And she'd wanted to salvage her wounded pride, plus give them both a cooling-off period before they spoke. In the meantime, he'd moved on, resuming his affair with the sultry and dazzling Kathleen.

Clara frowned at the wetness burning the back of her eyes. Now she knew exactly what being in Danny's arms meant—and Kathleen might be enjoying his breathtaking kisses and warm, teasing smile.

Her shoulders shook with soundless sobs as Anna clicked off.

The coffee shop hadn't changed, Clara mused, when she pushed open the door ten minutes later. The aroma of dark, rich coffee beans surrounded her. An Irish fiddle and harmonica were the featured instruments on the Irish music piped in the background.

She rode the escalator to the second floor and spotted Anna behind the display counter. As usual, Anna oozed attractiveness. Her name was pinned to her starched white blouse, the dazzling white in sharp contrast to her tanned skin. Her black slacks hugged her appealing curves.

"What's the craic?" Anna asked.

Clara gave a noncommittal shrug. "I don't have much of a life at the moment."

Anna's response was a half smile. "You look wrecked, as if you haven't slept."

"I've had a difficult week."

Anna added a look of frustrated annoyance. "You're not answering Danny's calls."

Clara didn't respond. Anna had obviously been talking

with Ian. Or Colum. It seemed like the entire town knew about the argument.

"The coffee of the day is hazelnut. Wanna try some?" Anna busied herself behind the counter.

"Coffee's too bitter. I'll have a glass of mint green tea."

"Our hazelnut coffee is sweet. We add cinnamon and a touch of sugar."

Clara shoved her hair off her forehead. "No, thanks. I'd like iced tea."

Anna poured the tea and set the cup on the display case between them. She huffed an overstated sigh. "You're so bullheaded, you know that? Once you get something in your mind, you don't listen to reason."

Clara grabbed the cup, squeezing it with a death grip. "I'm unreasonable because I don't drink coffee?"

"You're just … unreasonable."

"In case you're confused, Danny was the person with the unreasonable accusations," Clara reminded with a broken laugh.

"Then you're merely bullheaded. You've been seeing a man who owns a chain of coffee shops and you refuse to try his coffee."

"Don't patronize me."

Anna grinned. "You realize that we're quarreling about coffee?"

"Coffee, tea. All roads seem to lead to Danny Brady." Clara attempted to keep the sadness from her voice. "I wish …" That torrent of tears threatened to emerge.

When she couldn't continue, Anna softly said, "I invited you here to see your lemon scones. Aren't they brilliantly displayed?" Anna's fingers, their nails sporting a deep purple polish, fluttered in the air around the display case. A shining diamond ring glittered on the fourth finger of her left hand.

Clara grabbed Anna's hand. "You're engaged?"

Anna hooted elatedly. "Ian taped my engagement ring inside my motorcycle helmet. I went to put it on last night and nearly had a cow when I saw the ring. Then he got down on one knee and proposed, right in the middle of a rainy street. My fiancé is a romantic."

"So you accepted his marriage proposal?"

"Of course! He's a romantic cupcake." She sighed. "Today he had to drive to Dublin for business but he should be back later this evening. I haven't seen him all day and I miss him."

Clara's lips trembled with elation for her sister while she blinked back hopeless tears for herself. "Have you told Seamus about your engagement?" she asked.

"I haven't seen much of Seamus these days."

"Neither have I." Clara chewed her bottom lip, undecided if she should tell Anna about the half-empty bottle of vodka she'd found, and that the diamond necklace had gone missing.

Anna's cell phone buzzed. She fumbled in her pocket for it and read the text. "Ian can't remember where he left the keys to his flat, and he wants me to check in the boardroom," she reported, and then tsked. "Danny will personally wring Ian's neck if Ian lost another set of keys. Come upstairs and help me look for them."

Clara lowered her eyes. "I'll wait in the lobby."

Anna's exasperated frown swung in Clara's direction. "I was in the boardroom earlier because I brought Aiden a cup of tea while he labored over the coffee shop's yearly audits. I left it unlocked, so you won't be blamed for breaking in. No worries."

Anna's bluntness jerked Clara out of her tortured reverie. "No, I'll—"

Too late. Anna was already pushing her in the direction of the door marked Private, then onto the lift to the third floor.

"Francis Bacon is gone," Clara noted as they crossed the hallway.

"Ian returned the painting to Danny's home in Howth," Anna explained as the women stepped into the boardroom. She tossed her hands to her hips. "Now where could my forgetful cupcake have misplaced the keys to his flat?"

While Anna went through computer desk drawers, Clara examined the drooping fern by the doorway. She knelt and began pulling dried leaves off the bottom stem. Out of the corner of her eye she spotted a familiar looking men's cap, half hidden and wedged between the fern and doorway. Doing a double take, she slowly and deliberately fingered the stiff brim and plaid tweed. Then she gasped.

Anna hurried over. "Nice cap." Her statement held a question.

Clara moved back slightly, staring at the cap as if it were about to begin speaking. "This cap belongs to Seamus. He bought it in Donegal."

And when had she last seen Seamus wearing the cap? Surely it must've been before her birthday.

Anna lifted her eyebrows and grabbed the cap from Clara. "What's it doing here? He worked in the kitchen."

Absently, Clara rubbed her forearms. All the pieces of Seamus's never-ending mysteries registered in mere seconds. His excuses, his denials, slipping in and out of her flat at all hours. The missing diamond necklace. The half-empty vodka bottle.

Her mouth opened, closed. Her chest tingled. "Seamus

was in the boardroom on March eighteenth." She tried to rein in her disbelief, heard her voice choke up. "I can't believe this. Seamus lied to me. He's lied all these months."

Anna's face had gone pale. She openly gaped. "Seamus stole the fifty thousand euros?"

Clara's thoughts scrambled. No, it couldn't be true. No one could spend that amount of money, although Danny had said that gambling debts added up quickly.

Feeling lightheaded, she rushed to the leather sofa and sank into the cushions.

Anna followed.

"This explains ..." Clara covered her face with her hands. "This explains Seamus's new sports car ... and all the other unanswered questions that have baffled me." Repeatedly, she shook her head. "I chose to ignore what I didn't want to see."

Dear saints in heaven. Seamus, her dear brother, was an addict. A gambler, an alcoholic and a liar. And his suicide attempt had been a cry for help.

She dropped her hands. Her job title as loving sister hadn't been sufficient. She hadn't helped him. She'd only enabled him.

Anna was gaping at her. "Now what?"

Clara leapt from the couch, grabbed her sister's hand and dashed for the door. "Now we can only hope it's not too late."

22

———

"**B**oss, where have you been?"

Danny leaned forward in the ripped bus seat, straining to hear Ian's voice crackling through his cell phone's static interference. He rubbed his bleary eyes. He'd had little sleep, and weariness had taken a firm hold in his veins.

The small airport where the plane had landed three days earlier had boasted no showers, rigid benches that ensured impossible sleeping, and a near-empty vending machine selling stale candy and bottled water. The bus was the opposite of luxury, smelling of chewed tobacco and diluted diesel. With any luck it wouldn't break down, Danny thought, although the brakes squeaked at every twisted turn in the road.

"I've been holed up at an Italian airfield in a remote town with no cell phone connection," he explained.

"I thought you and Kathleen were flying directly to Rome."

"We hit a bad storm as we approached Italy. One of the plane engines stalled and we had to make an emergency landing. They found significant damage to one of the blades. No worries," Danny hastened to assure Ian. "Our pilot was very competent and got us safely on the ground. I was able to shower at a youth hostel in Cosenza this morning. However, I've lost three days of valuable time, plus have been virtually unplugged from the rest of the world."

He'd found a quiet seat in the rear of the bus, setting his briefcase and carry-on luggage beside him to dissuade anyone from joining him. Intent on working the entire six-hour bus ride, he'd extracted the Spanish permits from his briefcase. Sleep would have to wait.

The talkative businessman and Kathleen had ... well, never stopped talking since they'd landed at the small airfield. Danny flashed a look at them a few seats ahead of him and grinned slightly. Heads together, they sat deeply engrossed in conversation. Again.

"I'm in Farthing," Ian was saying through the static. "Anna and I are engaged."

Squelching his unexplainable annoyance at that announcement, Danny asked a bit too abruptly, "Should I be surprised?"

"Not at all. You are aware of how close Anna and I had gotten."

He seemed to be waiting for a reply.

Danny tried not to sound irritated. He tapped his gold pen on his knee. "Ian, I am genuinely happy for you both. However, to ring me with this news when I have so many important matters facing me seems—"

"Have you ... spoken to Clara?"

"Not since the night of our argument." Danny softened his curt tone. "I've tried, although she hasn't responded."

"She's staging an intervention for Seamus."

Danny sat straighter. "What? When?"

"Seven o'clock this evening. I'll be there with Anna and Colum. We're meeting at the dance studio in Farthing." Ian hesitated. "You should be there too, boss."

Slowly, Danny set down the permits and pen on the empty seat beside him and stared out the graffiti-stained window. He shifted in his seat, and one shoe seemed stuck to the floor. He lifted his foot. A thick wad of bubblegum was stuck to the sole of his shoe. He picked at the gum with his fingernail. It had to be at least ten years old. "I'm in Italy, remember? Once I arrive in Rome, I'll only have three hours to open my new franchise."

An uncomfortably long silence ensued.

"You should be in Farthing," Ian said again.

Danny's jaw tightened. "I leave for America in the morning."

"We all have a copy of your itinerary, boss."

Was there really a note of sarcasm in Ian's voice, or was it the terrible static on the line?

"So then you know what you're asking is physically impossible. My franchise agreements are all legally signed and sealed, and my biggest profits await across the pond."

"She found Seamus's tweed cap in your boardroom."

Danny was silent as he envisioned Clara's pain at that discovery.

"You charged Seamus with stealing, and you were right," Ian continued.

Of course he was right. Seamus needed professional help. Clara had attempted to solve Seamus's problems, deflecting his troubles by taking on his burdens.

Danny forced a laugh. "I saw through Seamus's lies all along. If she'd only listened instead of—"

More static.

"What's that, boss? I can hardly hear you."

"I said that she should have listened to me."

The phone went silent. Ian hadn't hung up, had he?

He resisted the urge to fling it out the bus's grimy window.

He shook his head, steepled his hands. He should be feeling satisfaction.

Instead, he felt shallow.

Why?

Seamus was the reason he and Clara were separated, and, if Danny was honest, he resented Seamus. Although resentment didn't feel very good.

Didn't matter. How could he let Seamus off the hook after the havoc he had caused? Danny could never forgive him. Just as he couldn't forgive his parents. They'd caused Glenna's untimely death. How could he ever forget their mistakes?

He reached for his permits, intending to drown himself in his work.

A picture came to mind, frozen in his memory.

Clara, at Glasnevin cemetery: *You're not forgetting. You're finding your own happiness. Otherwise, these resentments will gnaw at you and you'll never be at peace.*

This anger. These resentments. He blew out an exhausted sigh and set the permits aside. He had to let it all go.

He didn't understand people's mistakes. And he didn't need to understand. Or judge. He couldn't change Seamus nor his parents. He *could* change his reactions. Perhaps he'd been angry at them because of his own addictions and inability to forgive himself.

He drew in a long breath. Seamus had held Clara as an emotional hostage, manipulating her so that she felt guilty whenever she confronted him. However, enabling Seamus had come from a good place in her heart, and she'd freely forgiven him for his mistakes. Sure, she'd been sidetracked and in denial. But she was also the closest Danny had ever come to meeting an angel.

His sweet, non-Irish damsel.

She had tried to tell him that she loved him and what had he done? He'd held up his hand to interrupt her. All he'd offered in return was his distrust and crippling accusations.

And still she'd rallied, dauntless and spirited.

He grinned. She could be a real spitfire.

He placed the pen and permits in his briefcase and retrieved her lemon scone recipe from his jacket pocket. Aye, he'd carried it with him, Clara's recipe written in her scholarly hand.

He ran his thumb along the recipe and pressed it to his lips. He detected a subtle fragrance of lemon, cheerful and uplifting. Clara's fragrance.

His heart thumped in slow, aching beats.

He missed her desperately. He missed their connection. They'd been separated far too long.

23

———

Clara pushed open the doors of the dance studio with her spine straight and her shoulders set. Today was the day.

She had told Seamus to come by after her class ended at seven o'clock. She hadn't told him why, giving only a brief excuse about seeing her new studio.

Two days earlier, she had contacted the Flyaway Treatment Center to stage his intervention. She had presented the center with a large donation, thanks to Danny's generous check. Bryan, the interventionist, had arranged everything, beginning with choosing Ian to act as the point of contact. The plan was for Ian to meet Seamus at Clara's flat, then the two men would ride Ian's motorcycle to the dance studio.

Liam hadn't been informed, as Clara had feared he might sabotage the intervention. And, she suspected that Liam was also involved in the cybercrime. Perhaps he had guided Seamus on the phone through the entire process when Seamus had been in the boardroom.

She took a calming breath, arranged bottles of water on a round table, and glanced at her watch. Time ticked slowly, although only a few minutes remained until the men were scheduled to arrive.

For the umpteenth time, she straightened the five chairs she'd set in a circle. One for herself, Ian, Anna, Seamus, and Bryan, who would orchestrate the intervention. Colum would wait outside the building, standing by to lend moral support. These were the team members. Together, they'd rehearsed a consistent message and well-thought-out plan. They'd gathered their information and shared it with one another. The entire picture of Seamus's destructive behaviors was now clearly mapped out. Besides his gambling and alcohol addiction, he'd been stealing. The diamond necklace and hacking into Danny's accounting system still hadn't given him enough funds. He'd obviously risked his money gambling beyond his ability to pay, because Seamus owed a large amount of money to numerous bookies reaching as far as Donegal.

The previous day, the team members had staged a rehearsal, deciding who should speak and in what order, and the general thrust of what each person would say. It had been a long and intense training session. There would be no room for indecisiveness once the intervention began.

An addiction specialist had counseled the team, and Clara had gained a better understanding of Seamus's compulsive actions. His suicide attempts had been an effort to alert those around him that something was seriously wrong. He was obviously depressed. Despite the negative consequences, he had been struggling to find an escape from his grief and hopelessness after Fiona's death. He'd denied and hid and refused to acknowledge that he had a problem.

Clara had arranged for Seamus to travel directly to the treatment center following the intervention. His admission was set, his suitcase packed. A specialist stood ready to escort Seamus quickly out of the studio through a side door.

Bryan drew Clara and Anna aside. "No half measures. No caving in," he reminded the women. "Your brother has fallen off his tightrope for the last time. He's holding on by the proverbial thread. Don't waste this opportunity, and keep in mind that it's not your job to help him back up. I'll guide you through the confrontations."

Clara nodded. She wanted her brother to be able to walk with his feet firmly planted on the ground. This intervention was his opportunity.

The outer door slammed. All heads jerked up.

"Here they come." Anna gestured to the lobby and grabbed a bottle of water. "Remember, I'll go first."

Clara glanced at the note to Seamus that she had drafted, and then nodded to Bryan that she was ready.

Seamus and Ian walked in, their shoes echoing on the new floating dance floor.

"What's the craic?" Seamus's bewildered gaze shot around the studio.

Clara wiped her sweaty palms on her slacks, pushed her hair from her forehead, and rose swiftly to her feet. She looked at Seamus. Her gaze never flinched.

DANNY TOLD himself that if the Gardaí wanted to stop him for speeding, first they'd have to catch him. He pressed his foot on the Mercedes's gas pedal, grateful for the long stretch of open road. He was not grateful, however, for the rain that had decided to beat against his windshield, nearly blinding him as he took the last curve into Farthing too fast.

He found a spot a half block away from the dance studio, and parked behind a familiar candy-blue and yellow motorcycle. The rain had stopped as quickly as it had started.

Ireland. Who said it always rained?

He checked his watch. Seven thirty. He was late for the intervention, although considering he'd flown from Italy to Dublin, then raced to a Dublin florist shop to pick up two dozen red roses, he'd completed the journey quickly. The one-hour time difference between Italy and Ireland had worked in his favor.

He observed an unfamiliar sign hanging above the entrance as he approached.

Miss Clara's School of Dance.

He grinned, mesmerized for a moment.

Colum O'Brien, wearing a camouflage-colored parka, was perched on the stoop. He held a cigarette in his hand and seemed to be having a love/hate relationship with it.

Danny nodded a greeting. "How are ya?"

"Grand."

"Is Clara inside?" He attempted to step past Colum, who was doing a brilliant job of blocking the doorway.

"Of course she's here. She owns it." Colum eyed Danny with a suspicious frown and then glanced at the roses. "And where has the likes of you been lately?"

"Traveling."

Danny was preoccupied in trying to find the best way around Colum without shoving the man out of the way.

Colum scraped back his thick salt and pepper hair. "Now you're in a hurry? After breaking her heart?"

Silence for a beat.

"Let me pass." Hadn't he said that once already?

Colum rose, staying right in front of Danny. "You left her in Farthing to deal with Seamus, to pick up the pieces of her life after your accusations. I hope she tells you how much she's accomplished since you decided to disappear."

Danny glanced at the sign, then meaningfully toward the door. "That answer is perfectly obvious."

"You'd better be planning to make it up to her."

Danny had immediately liked Colum when he first met him. And, although it was absurd, he was coming to like Colum even more. The man was proving to be Clara's devoted friend, a man of honor who expected the same integrity from those around him.

"That's why I'm here," Danny replied evenly. "I'm going to try very, very hard, as soon as you let me in."

Colum's expression softened. With a sigh, he threw his half-smoked cigarette to the ground. "It'll take more than roses."

"I can't change what I've done, but I can learn from her how it's supposed to be done. I'll do whatever's necessary. I love her."

"I know." Colum appeared to smile, although he crossed his arms. "Sorry. I still can't let you inside. There's an intervention going on, and only family is allowed."

"Ian's back there. He's not family."

"Ian and Anna are engaged. He's considered family."

"Clara and I are engaged too."

Or at least they would be, if he ever was able to actually talk with her.

Colum's eyebrows flew up. "You and Clara are engaged? Since when?"

Danny paused. "We'll be engaged in less than two hours."

The last of the hostility in Colum's face faded. Mischief flickered in his green eyes.

"I'll hold onto your flowers and walk you inside. You may need a friend with the crowd you're about to face."

24

The entire intervention had taken less than thirty minutes.

"Thank you for all you've done for me. I love you." Clara fiercely hugged her dear brother before he turned and started for the door.

The love and support from his sisters, and the fear of looming consequences, had prompted Seamus to go willingly to the Flyaway Treatment Center. Bryan had told Clara that quick action was necessary, before Seamus's defense mechanisms and excuses kicked in. The window of opportunity was a small one.

Seamus had been quiet and reflective when the intervention was over. He'd seemed to appreciate the objective competence of the specialists, and had paid especially close attention to Ian.

"I will be there, every step of the way," Ian had assured Seamus. "I'm a recovering addict too, you know."

As Seamus left with the two professionals and Ian, Clara lifted a prayer of thanks. The first step to Seamus's recovery had begun. And it had all happened in thirty minutes.

Anna gulped her water and sank into a chair. Her hands trembled. "You know what it's like to have the wind knocked out of your lungs? That's how I'm feeling—physically and mentally exhausted."

Clara drew a deep breath and nodded. She felt the same —emotionally drained.

"I'm meeting Ian outside as soon as Seamus is safely on his way. Wanna join us?"

Anna's tone was genuine and imploring.

Clara shook her head. "You need time alone with your new fiancé. You don't want a sister tagging along. I'll head back to my flat." Her cold, empty flat. "Besides, Colum and I need to straighten the studio before we leave."

"You can always change your mind. I told Ian that this intervention either called for a swear word or food."

"And you picked?"

"Food. Join us if you want." Anna stood and finger-combed her canary-yellow hair strands into place. "What do you think of my new hair color?"

"Still matches Ian's motorcycle."

"Ian likes it. He's thinking of dying his hair to match mine."

"Now there's a visual."

Laughing, Anna slung her purse over her shoulder. Then she paused, studying her sister's face. "Have you heard from him?"

Anna didn't need to say Danny's name. Clara knew who she meant.

"He hasn't made the slightest effort." Somehow, she kept her voice from breaking. She looked away for a moment and focused on the ballet mirror. "And it doesn't matter anymore."

She knew that she wasn't fooling Anna for a second.

Tears sprang into Anna's amber eyes. "You managed a wonderful intervention, Clara. You did the best thing for Seamus."

"Thanks. It was a concerted effort. We're a great team."

"Ring me if you change your mind and would like to join us." After a nod of assent from Clara, Anna headed for the lobby.

Clara turned to face the mirror again, allowing her relief at the successful intervention to flow through her. She still held the note she'd read to Seamus, and she looked down at it, reading the last line aloud. "So you see, Seamus, the Flyaway Treatment Center is your best option."

She looked up to see a tall, handsome man with reddish brown hair and china-blue eyes step into the room.

Their gazes met.

"Missus, are you trained for this?" he asked.

25

————

anny kept walking toward her and without hesitation took Clara in his arms.

Desperately, she tried to understand what was happening. Danny was here. He was here. This good-looking, grave man who was staring down into her eyes.

Slowly, tears slid down her cheeks. She stood motionless, unable to move, scarcely breathing.

He hadn't uttered another word.

"Danny," she whispered. "How? When?"

His strong arms held her closer, as if he could absorb the sadness he had caused her.

"If you ever think again of not answering the phone when I ring, I'll put you on redial and never give you a moment's peace."

She tipped her head back and saw the anguish on his face, raw and exposed.

"And if I answer on the first ring?"

Tenderly, he kissed her cheeks, her temple, her hair. "Then I'll finally be able to talk to you."

She reached her arms around his broad shoulders. "And what will you say?"

"I only know a few words." He framed her face, brushed his lips against her temple. "Clara Donovan, I'm sorry. And I love you so very, very much."

His mouth captured hers. She kissed him back with an eager desperation equaling his. When the kiss ended, she stayed in his arms. Her fingers stroked the silky hair at his nape.

"I can't believe you're actually here, in Farthing. This past week, everything's felt so—"

"Desolate? Empty?" She loved his persuasive baritone voice, the voice that had haunted her dreams.

"Lonely." Her voice broke. "Danny Brady, I've missed you more than you will ever know."

His response was his lips parting hers.

CLARA LOOKED SO beautiful and Danny concentrated on memorizing each detail of her exquisite face and perfect figure. For several minutes, he hadn't been aware that anyone else was in the dance studio. That is, until he heard two people clearing their throats.

"You're kidding," he said, glancing over his shoulder to a beaming Ian and Anna.

"What's the craic?" Anna's face was wreathed in mischievous laughter.

"How long have you two been standing there?"

"Only a minute," Ian replied. "I didn't know anyone could travel that many miles so quickly."

"Now you know."

"Glad you could make it, boss. Are you flying to America in the morning?"

Danny shook his head and held Clara tighter. "Kathleen is handling the American franchises."

"I thought she was staying in Italy with a new guy she met on the Internet."

"That guy turned out to be a thirteen-year-old kid playing a hoax. However, she met a hotshot American businessman on the plane, so they'll fly to Boston together. And there are competent employees to handle the Rome coffee shop." Danny kissed Clara's shiny hair. "I need to spend my time on more important things."

"Well, I'm glad you two are all settled, because I'm starved." In the true nature of a matchmaker whose mind turned to food once the match was settled, Anna added, "Danny, Ian and I are headed to your shop for free Guinness cake. Then we're taking a week's vacation because Seamus's intervention wore us out."

Ian sheepishly looked at Danny. "Hope you'll agree, boss. Anna wants to visit Portugal."

"My birth country," Anna declared. "I can hardly remember any details from when I was a child and I want to visit with my favorite cupcake." She blew a kiss in Ian's direction although he was only standing a foot away from her.

"Perfectly fine. Enjoy your time off," Danny said.

"There goes a week's profit," Clara murmured.

Danny laughed and shrugged. "We'll walk out with you and Ian, Anna."

Clara perused the chairs, the empty water bottles. "Not yet. I need to clean—"

Danny shook his head and firmly took hold of her hand. "Tomorrow."

Colum sat on the stoop as the foursome stepped outside. He held two dozen roses. "Forgetting something?" he asked Danny.

"A wee bit wilted," Danny apologized as he handed the roses to Clara.

"They're beautiful. They just need a little water. Thank you."

They all wished Colum a good evening and started to leave. Colum called after them, "Congratulations on your engagement."

Anna glanced back. "You already congratulated me and my cupcake."

Colum shook his head. "Not you. Clara and Danny."

Clara stopped in midstep. She turned to Danny. "We're engaged?"

"Aye," Danny said. "I wanted Colum to be the first to know."

The rain had started as Anna and Ian hopped on his motorcycle. "Does it ever stop raining in this country?" she asked him.

"How would I know? I'm only in my thirties." Ian laughed at his own joke.

With a grin and a farewell, Clara slipped into Danny's silver Mercedes.

He turned on the engine and let it idle. Then he reached for her and held her in his arms for a long while. "For our honeymoon we'll travel to Italy," he said. "I've seen the Egadi Islands, from the air, at least. They look beautiful. Then after our honeymoon, we'll find your orphanage. If it's still there, I'll set up a fund for the children. And together, we will confront your bad memories."

"Always the planner. Don't forget my brother, Luciano."

"Aye."

"Where are we going?" she asked.

"Your flat."

She stared up at him. "Can I tell you something?"

He nodded.

"I'm sorry that I didn't listen to you about Seamus."

"The main thing is that Seamus is going to get the treatment he needs." Danny pulled her closer. "You'll see, he'll be better soon."

"And I'm sorry about the diamond necklace. During the intervention, Seamus confessed that he stole the necklace you gave me, but Ian and I will check the pawn shops and try to find it."

"No worries. You're more important than a thousand diamonds." He gazed into her glorious eyes. His precious Clara.

She snuggled nearer and he kissed her tenderly.

When the kiss ended, she asked, "Now can I ask you a question?"

"Always."

"Why did you return to Farthing?"

He grinned. "I like your smile. I like your lemon scones. And I love you."

He waited a beat for her reply. When one wasn't forthcoming, he continued, "And I want to sing the last two lines of my favorite song to you. I hope you will finish it for me."

"Is it the song you've been working on?"

He shook his head. "It's better than anything I ever attempted to write. May I?"

Tears welled in her eyes. She nodded.

To the tune of "Oh Danny Boy," he sang, "'Oh Clara Donovan, if you'll not fail to say you love me—'"

Clara's smile was radiant as she finished the chorus:

"'Oh Danny Brady, Oh Danny Brady, I love you so.'"

THE END

A NOTE FROM JOSIE

Dear Friend,

Thank you for reading *Oh Danny Boy*. I hope you enjoyed my sweet romance. I have had the opportunity to visit Ireland many times and wanted to capture the essence of one of my favorite countries in the world.

If you loved this uplifting romance as much as I loved writing it, please help other people find *Oh Danny Boy* by posting your review.

Oh Danny Boy is available in ebook, paperback, Large Print paperback, Hardcover, and audiobook.

I'd love to meet you in person someday, but in the meantime, all I can offer is a sincere and grateful thank you. Without your support, my books would not be possible.

As I write my next sweet or inspirational romance, remember this: Have you ever tried something you were afraid to try because it mattered so much to you? I did, when I started writing. Take the chance, and just do something you love.

My Spotify Playlist for Oh Danny Boy is here.

With sincere appreciation,
Josie Riviera

IRISH SCONE RECIPE

Enjoy this Irish Scones recipe, brought to you by a granny in County Derry, Ireland.

Irish Scones:

    2 cups flour

    1/2 tsp. salt

    1/4-1/2 stick margarine

    2 tsp. baking powder

    4 oz. buttermilk

    Set oven to 450F. Grease cooking tray and sift dry ingredients. Cut and rub in margarine.

    Mix quickly and lightly to a soft dough.

    Turn onto a floured table and knead.

Roll and cut out small scones.

Brush with egg or milk.

Bake 10-15 minutes in preheated oven.

I have converted grams and milliliters and rounded off. Hopefully errors have not occurred! I also learned that sweet milk is buttermilk, and cooking butter is margarine.

ACKNOWLEDGMENTS

An appreciative thank you to my patient husband, Dave, and our three wonderful children.

ABOUT THE AUTHOR

Josie Riviera is a *USA TODAY* bestselling author of contemporary, inspirational, and historical sweet romances that read like Hallmark movies. She lives in the Charlotte, NC, area with her wonderfully supportive husband. They share their home with an adorable shih tzu, who constantly needs grooming, and live in an old house forever needing renovations.

To receive my Newsletter and your free sweet romance novella ebook as a thank you gift, sign up <u>HERE.</u>

Become a member of my Read and Review VIP Facebook group for exclusive giveaways and ARCs.

josieriviera.com/
josieriviera@aol.com

ALSO BY JOSIE RIVIERA

Seeking Patience

Seeking Catherine (always Free!)

Seeking Fortune

Seeking Charity

Seeking Rachel

The Seeking Series

Oh Danny Boy

I Love You More

A Snowy White Christmas

A Portuguese Christmas

Holiday Hearts Book Bundle Volume One

Holiday Hearts Book Bundle Volume Two

Holiday Hearts Book Bundle Volume Three

Holiday Hearts Book Bundle Volume Four

Candleglow and Mistletoe

Maeve (Perfect Match)

A Love Song To Cherish

A Christmas To Cherish

A Valentine To Cherish

A Christmas Puppy To Cherish

A Homecoming To Cherish

A Summer To Cherish

Romance Stories To Cherish

Romance Stories To Cherish Volume Two

Cherished Hearts Six Book Volume

Aloha To Love

Sweet Peppermint Kisses

Valentine Hearts Boxed Set

1-800-CUPID

1-800-CHRISTMAS

1-800-IRELAND

1-800-SUMMER

1-800-NEW YEAR

The 1-800-Series Sweet Contemporary Romance Bundle

Irish Hearts Sweet Romance Bundle

Holly's Gift

A Chocolate-Box Christmas

A Chocolate-Box New Years

A Chocolate-Box Valentine

A Chocolate-Box Summer Breeze

A Chocolate-Box Christmas Wish

A Chocolate-Box Irish Wedding

Chocolate-Box Hearts

Chocolate-Box Hearts Volume Two

Chocolate-Box Double Hearts

Recipes From The Heart

Leading Hearts

New Year Hearts

SENIOR HEARTS

Summer Hearts

Christmas in the Air (1-800-Book)

A Very Christian Christmas

Most books are available in ebook, audiobook, paperback, Large Print paperback and Hardcover.

Many are FREE on Kindle Unlimited!

Perfect Match
Maeve
USA Today Bestselling Author
JOSIE RIVIERA

Maeve

by

Josie Riviera

Cover by Raine English
Elusive Dreams Designs
http://www.ElusiveDreamsDesigns.com

INTRODUCTION

You're cordially invited to spend an all-expenses-paid week-long trip to the island of your choice, courtesy of Perfect Match Online Dating and Travel Agency.

This is Maeve's story...

Maeve Doherty needed a hard-earned break from Ireland's rainy weather, as well as from caring for her younger brother. When the offer from Perfect Match to enjoy a week on an island of her choice arrived, she hesitated. But not for long.

She'd always wanted to visit Corsica. Besides, who passed up free?

All right, so she'd spend the week with a match. On her dating profile, she'd added that she was a workaholic. Hopefully, so was he.

Edward Newell had one thing on his mind when he reached Corsica, and it didn't involve meeting a perfect match. Dating? Love? Romance? Not for him.

He was determined to find the picture-perfect location for his thriving hotel chain.

When unexpected attraction burns for the beautiful Maeve, and business conflicts with pleasure, what could possibly go wrong?

PROLOGUE

Maeve's Perfect Match Dating Profile ...
Miss Irish Independence, Age 26

"When he takes me in his arms, he speaks to me softly, I see the world through rose-colored glasses."—Edith Piaf, French singer, songwriter, and film actress.

I live for a hot cuppa tea and will share it with you.

I'm a good listener. But make no mistake, I follow my own dreams, not yours.

Love comes in many forms, and I believe in a commitment to one person.

Be warned ... I'm a workaholic.

1

"It'll do you good to get away from Ireland. We've had a rainy summer."

"Rainy summer?" Maeve Doherty grinned at her best friend, Colleen O'Keefe, who was busily swiping Maeve's phone. "When can you recall a non-wet summer in Ireland?"

"A year ago. It was on a Thursday."

Maeve laughed out loud. As always, her flaming-haired friend's sunny disposition lifted her spirits.

Colleen chuckled in return. Her tailored canary-yellow pantsuit, with matching pumps, fit her full-figured body impeccably. Maeve glanced at her own worn linen skirt and smoothed her wrinkled polyester blouse. When had she last taken time for herself? She'd forgotten, it had been so long ago, with all the worry and sleepless nights.

Colleen plunked into an oversized chair in the lobby of the building that housed the Merrimac Company. The women were purchasing agents for a small Irish hotel chain. Their duties included placing orders for everything from hotel furniture to cleaning supplies, and comparing various prices and the quality of the merchandise.

Colleen pointed with one of her French manicured fingernails at Maeve's phone screen. "If I'm reading this email correctly, you've been offered a free week at the paradise island of your choice, compliments of the Perfect Match dating agency."

Maeve pulled up a chair across from her friend. "Aye."

Keeping her fingertip on the blinking cursor, Colleen paused. "You plan to accept, don't you?"

"Whatever the catch is, it's not worth a week anywhere on the globe."

"This offer is from Amy Yates, your friend from America, and her husband, Dawson. And it's a personalized invitation." Colleen scanned Maeve's phone screen. "A free vacation, a romantic getaway, a chance—"

Maeve held up a hand. "Aye."

"So it's legit," Colleen declared gaily. "I remember you said they owned the agency."

"Aye."

"Which island are you choosing?"

"I'm not choosing any island because I'm not going."

"How about Corsica, France?" Colleen obviously pretended she hadn't heard Maeve. "You've always wanted to learn French. And isn't there a famous museum there you've always wanted to visit?"

"Maison Bonaparte, the ancestral home of the Bonaparte family." Maeve nodded. "The museum is located in Ajaccio, Corsica."

"Then go."

"Yes, someday, on my own, using my own money—not obligated to a matchmaking agency."

Colleen pushed her glasses up her nose and peered at

the phone. "All expenses are paid and the terms and conditions are clearly spelled out. All you have to do is agree to spend the week with your match or risk being charged for the vacation."

Maeve lifted a skeptical eyebrow. "That's all?"

"It's a massive marketing campaign to introduce their new business," Colleen reminded her. "You're helping them as much as they're helping you."

"I love history, but I'm not that desperate to see Napoléon Bonaparte's death mask. I'd prefer spending a cozy week in my flat reading a pile of European history books." Maeve tapped her fingers together and drew in a breath. "Figure in a hot cuppa Irish tea and lemon scones from The Ground Café and I'll be merry as a leprechaun."

"You're emotionally spent," her friend said quietly. "And you gave Amy Yates permission to plug your name into the Perfect Match database."

Maeve turned a despairing look on Colleen. "Aye, in a flash of desperation when I feared any opportunity for love was passing me by. I'm over that."

Was she?

Once she'd recovered from the sadness and shock of learning her twenty-year-old brother Owen had been diagnosed with cancer, she'd settled into the daily task of tending to him when he opted to move in with her rather than live with their mother. She'd given up every pastime she enjoyed to care for him, including auditioning for minor acting roles, something she loved.

Now that Owen's radiation treatments were over and his caregiving routine had become stable, perhaps she could ease up a bit, take a breather. Perhaps ...

"Maeve?" Colleen prodded. "Owen is in remission and he can go live with your mother for a week. She's able-bodied and can tend to him. You're only twenty-six. Live your life."

"Most days my mother isn't capable of washing a dish, let alone attending to a sick adult. She had a hard-enough time being a parent when Owen was well."

"Your mother lands in the middle of drama because of the type of men she sees, and her ongoing dilemmas can't always be your problem." Colleen leaned back in her chair. Her normally keen bright-blue gaze softened. "Enough about your mother. What's the craic with you? Are you sleeping okay?"

Maeve shrugged. "I'm always tired, although everyone is exhausted nowadays because of our hectic lifestyles."

"Grab this chance. Go. Believe me, if it weren't for my boyfriend, Colin, I'd take your place."

Colleen and Colin had an on-again, off-again relationship that had lasted for over a year. Currently, it was on again.

A reassuring grin crossed Colleen's freckled face. "Along with Owen's healthcare providers, your mother will mind him brilliantly. I want to see an optimistic smile on your face again. I'm sure you'll have a lorry-load of stories to share when you get back."

Maeve shook her head. "Because of all the days I missed when Owen became ill, I'm on the verge of losing my job. I certainly can't afford to take off any more time. Besides, his medical bills are mounting, and our private insurance only covers part of them."

"You're physically and mentally exhausted. *Your* health is important too. You need the time away to maintain your sense of balance."

"Aye, perhaps," Maeve admitted. Her brother's cancer journey had been a lengthy road crowded with difficult decisions and the challenges of radiation treatment.

"The Merrimac Company wants to branch out of Ireland and explore resort areas for other hotels. Pitch the idea to our manager. Tell Mrs. McShea it's a working holiday. Just think you'll get paid for sitting on a beach in a bikini."

"I don't swim, and I've never worn a bikini."

"Live a wee bit, Maeve. Spend your days lying in a lounge chair and looking out at the Mediterranean. You once told me there are over two hundred beaches in Corsica. Imagine the sun, the surf—"

"Colleen—"

"The sand." Colleen laughed. "It's a win-win. Besides, who can pass up the chance to meet Mr. Right?"

"I'm too busy to fritter away my valuable time on a man. And there's no such man as Mr. Right, at least not for me."

"How do you know? Make the time."

"Suppose he's not interesting?"

"Suppose he is?"

"What about Crinkles?"

"Your dog is accustomed to your ma's flat." Colleen tapped the phone screen again. "Amy says her agency's matchmaking algorithms are the best and they're launching this campaign to prove it."

"And if you keep scrolling, you'll see they want people who've been unlucky in love."

Like her.

Maeve studied Merrimac's lobby—a gleaming brown floor, mahogany table, anything but her friend's sympathetic stare. She'd spilled out more than she'd intended.

A year ago while visiting a cousin in America, she'd met Amy while shopping in an exclusive boutique, not realizing at first that she was chatting with the owner of the boutique.

They'd become instant friends, and they shared coffee and heartfelt conversation after the store closed. That evening, Maeve had poured out her sadness to her new-found confidante.

Finbar, Maeve's boyfriend of two years, had broken up with her—not even in person—but through a dismissive text.

"No more," she'd declared to Amy. "Men and their hollow promises are not to be believed."

Wasn't Maeve's father, who'd left her mother without an explanation, further proof of her statement? He'd said he'd return. He never had.

"Maeve? Maeve?" Colleen yanked Maeve from her upsetting remembrances. "I'm partial to the final line of your dating profile." She read aloud: "'Love comes in many forms, and I believe in a commitment to one person.' Colleen looked up at Maeve. "Aww, that's very sweet. You expressed yourself perfectly."

Heat rose in Maeve's face. "I'm starry-eyed and foolish for writing something so reckless. No one stays with one person forever."

"Some do. Some people have a love that lasts. Where are those rose-colored glasses you used to wear?"

"I've put them away and become realistic."

"Dust them off. What if Mr. Right is waiting for you in Corsica?"

"He won't be, although just to be sure ..." Maeve grabbed her phone from Colleen and included another line at the bottom of her dating profile.

Be warned ... I'm a workaholic.

Colleen squinted at the screen. "Being a workaholic is supposed to deter him?"

"I'll plead nine-to-five obligations."

Plus, any other excuses necessary to safeguard her heart.

"So, it's settled." Colleen flashed a quick smile. "You'll accept Amy's offer and choose Corsica."

"Aye." Maeve feigned enthusiasm, then blew out a breath.

She'd go, she'd rest, she'd work. But she wouldn't risk falling in love.

Once was enough. Besides, if there was a perfect match for her on God's emerald-green planet, she'd have found him by now in Ireland.

"That's grand," Colleen said. "Finally, you're doing something for yourself." With a flourish, Colleen stood and walked over to Maeve, throwing her arms around her. "Get ready, my dear friend, for an amazing adventure!"

2

———

Edward Newell arrived in Corsica aboard his family's private jet. He'd initially flown from London to Nice, where he'd spent the night so he could check on a family-owned resort property. From there, he'd flown on to Corsica, an easy forty-five-minute trip.

The Perfect Match agency had offered to arrange his travel; he'd declined.

Bidding the limo driver, a thank you and farewell, he strode into the marbled lobby of La Bonaparte Resort, pausing to admire wall hangings that depicted Corsica's famed cliffs and its nature reserves. He passed a scattering of loud tourists and headed toward the reception desk.

In a reasonably short while he was greeted by a skinny, clean-shaven man. His tawny-colored hair was raised and swept to the side, giving him a James Dean appearance.

"*Bonjour, monsieur.* My name is Pierre Martin, and I'm the head concierge. Please allow me to welcome you this Sunday afternoon to our resort." Pierre extended his hand for a shake, then produced a flute of champagne and a cool lavender-scented washcloth.

"Good afternoon." Edward accepted the washcloth and refused the champagne. He drank on rare celebratory occasions, and this wasn't one of them.

"Your name, monsieur?"

"Edward Newell."

Cheerful and energetic, Pierre clicked on his computer while briefing Edward on the hotel's amenities and Wi-Fi. "Ah, you're staying for *une semaine, oui*?"

"One week. That's the plan."

"We hope you enjoy your stay with us." Pierre boasted a reedy French accent and a broad grin. "If you need anything, please don't hesitate to call on my services."

"A glass of iced tea sounds good."

"I'll send it straight to your suite, along with today's newspaper."

"No paper. I can catch up on the news tomorrow."

"Excellent." Pierre typed into his computer and then reached behind the desk. "May I also present your Perfect Match?" He kept his face bland although Edward detected a slight raising of Pierre's carefully tended eyebrows.

"*Merci*." Edward placed the washcloth on the counter, stuffed the sealed envelope into the inner pocket of his tweed suit jacket, then pulled out his wallet. "Here's a little something—"

"*Non*, monsieur, I don't accept tips. Always my pleasure." He glanced at Edward's woven leather bag and matching briefcase. "Do you need assistance with your luggage?"

A bellhop appeared before Pierre finished his question.

"No, I can manage," Edward said.

"But of course. The young lady ... your match ... hasn't arrived yet. Her flight from Dublin was delayed."

Dublin. The woman hailed from Ireland? Probably pale-

skinned and frail. She'd be sun-burned within fifteen minutes in this blasting heat.

Edward gazed out the floor-to-ceiling windows that stretched across the far end of the hotel. Picture-worthy, the three-tiered infinity pool appeared to collide with the turquoise waters of the Mediterranean.

"I'll alert you when the lady arrives," Pierre was saying. "I'm sure you're anxious to meet her. Mr. and Mrs. Yates arranged a dinner date for you and your match this evening."

"Who are the Yateses?"

"The owners of Perfect Match, monsieur."

"Right." Edward dismissed this fact with an absent wave of his hand. How could he forget? Perhaps he needed this getaway more than he'd figured. As vice president of his father's luxury hotel chain, he was responsible for steering the family fortune in the resort industry's fast-moving climate. If only he had twenty-five hours in a day instead of twenty-four.

He checked his cellphone. He was expecting an important business call from his sister Karen—who was in charge of operations—regarding another acquisition. Briefly, he frowned, noting she hadn't rung yet. She'd probably gotten caught up in her investigation. Her current husband's illicit liaisons, although elusive, had been a source of upset for her and the entire family and she was attempting to find enough proof to end the marriage.

With a sigh, he stepped back and took in the ornateness of the lobby. A trickling fountain, showy-blue sofas and scores of dense-green houseplants created a restful ambiance. He particularly liked the touch of tropical fish swimming in the two-story aquarium. Perhaps his next resort property could feature ...

No, no, no. He needed to think of something other than business. He needed to allow himself time to unwind.

Pierre spoke to him, drawing his attention from the hypnotic aquarium. "May I also mention les Calanche Cliffs are nearby, monsieur? They are world renowned." Pierre displayed a mouthful of white teeth, smiling as if he were imparting the most exciting announcement of his career. He'd obviously been well-schooled in the art of hotel service.

"Very good." Absently, Edward checked his cell phone again.

"And dinner will be served at eight o'clock on our terrace overlooking the sea."

"Then I'll meet this Perfect Match woman at dinner. No need to alert me of her arrival ahead of time."

Pierre raised an eyebrow in seeming approval. "We'll keep the special unveiling of your match a surprise then, oui?"

Edward inclined his head but couldn't help his grimace. "By all means."

He didn't like surprises. This one couldn't be helped.

Pierre tended to folding the washcloth on the counter, politely ignoring Edward's lack of enthusiasm. "Will that be all, monsieur?"

Edward hung back. He'd acted curt to the friendly concierge. To make amends he offered, "Those cliffs you mentioned ..."

Pierre brightened. "Les Calanche Cliffs."

"Are they conducive for hiking?"

"Oui. Miles and miles of trails. The entire island features numerous activities, both tamed and untamed."

"Excellent." Edward grabbed his luggage. "I'm an outdoorsman."

Pierre handed him two keys. "One is for the pool and gym space," he explained. "The other is for your suite, number 201A. Take the elevator or staircase on your left."

Edward turned away. "*Merci,* Pierre. Cheers."

"May you find your true love in our one-of-a-kind paradise," Pierre called after him, loud enough for the entire lobby to overhear.

Edward swiveled. At his raised eyebrows, Pierre explained, "Mr. Yates's words, monsieur, not mine."

With a succinct nod, Edward turned away again, but then he lingered, his gaze fixed on a pair of cardinal tetras swimming in the aquarium. A host of other tropical fish in neon colors, silvers and stripes, swam alongside.

An all-expense-paid holiday in stunning Corsica wasn't the reason he was here, and he was tempted to tell Pierre that. Nor was it to find the woman of his dreams, as if such a woman existed.

He pursed his lips together and blew out a long breath.

To his knowledge, his two younger adult brothers had never experienced love, that warm, tingly sensation that prompted besotted men to write poems and become blind to common sense. And his sister was certainly nowhere near genuine love in her married life. Only their parents seemed to have found it, their time-tested marriage having lasted thirty years.

Briefly, he considered strangling his friend Bentley for setting him up for this promotion. Bentley was in the hotel business also, although lately Edward had heard that Bentley's business had dipped, largely due to being nudged out by competitors' renovated hotels and absentee ownership. The fact was, Bentley was never around. He preferred partying and spending any profits.

At any rate, this Perfect Match prank was characteristic

of Bentley, always out for a laugh at someone else's expense. But what had started as a practical joke had quickly ballooned into two demands from Edward's entrepreneurial father when he'd gotten wind of the news.

Demand one: Edward was to stake out Corsica for any available property to build another family-owned resort, preferably on a beach. Demand two: Edward was advised to seriously consider making Davinia DeVito, an Italian clothing-line heiress he'd been dating, his wife.

"Settle down, get married. A man needs stability in his life," his father had fussed. "Marriage is what your late mother wanted for you, not you off philandering with every attractive woman in England."

He wasn't philandering, he'd wanted to tell his father. He was simply enjoying his twenties, and now his thirties.

Despite the lush surroundings of La Bonaparte Resort and its breathtaking view of Bonifacio, the old town in the distance, reservations about agreeing to this Perfect Match escapade were growing more well-founded by the minute. And any hopes that this pint-sized island was undiscovered had been dashed by the heavy traffic and congestion he'd experienced on his ride from the airport.

Glancing back at the reservation desk, Edward noted Pierre still observed him, albeit discreetly. A well-trained concierge who could double as a mind reader was an asset to any hotel, but they were sometimes a little too ... curious. With a final nod in Pierre's direction, Edward climbed the stairs, found his suite, and swung open the heavy door.

Outstanding. Posh and proper, decorated in creams and golds and navy blues, with gleaming natural light streaming through the windows. The suite boasted a living room, efficiency kitchen, large bedroom, and a bath with a raised marbled tub. Bottles of chilled mineral water and vases of orange lilies enhanced the sense of privilege.

He loosened his silk tie and set his luggage and briefcase near the cream-colored couch, decorated with throw pillows in rich tapestry.

A crystal bowl piled high with ripe peaches sat artfully on the coffee table alongside a glass of iced tea, sliced lemons and cubes of sugar. Somehow, an invisible employee had reached Edward's room before he'd finished climbing the stairs.

He drained the tea, snagged a peach and unlocked the French doors leading to a railed balcony that held a wrought iron table and chairs. In the center of the table sat a terra-cotta vase brimming with tiny purple blooms.

He slid the vase aside, relaxed on a checkered pillowed chair and took a bite of the peach. The flowers' fragrances and the salty sea scented the air, the peach was tangy and flavorful, and for the first time in months his muscles untightened.

He shrugged off his suit jacket, draped it on the other chair, and closed his eyes. After a quick shower, he'd take an invigorating swim.

And then he'd meet his Perfect Match ...

Right, a bit of a damp squib.

He swallowed and shook his head. Anyone who knew him would vouch that he wasn't husband material. And after dessert this evening, he'd present his side of the equation to the Perfect Match lady, before she pegged him out as the passport to remedy her no-doubt desperate marital status.

All the same, he grabbed the Perfect Match envelope from his jacket pocket and unsealed it.

The opening information stated he and the woman were

meeting at eight for dinner. He already knew that thanks to the ever-efficient Pierre.

He unfolded the second sheet and read her profile:

MISS IRISH INDEPENDENCE, *Age 26*

"WHEN HE TAKES *me in his arms, He speaks to me softly, I see the world through rose-colored glasses."—Edith Piaf, French singer, songwriter, and film actress.*

I LIVE *for a hot cuppa tea and will share it with you.*

I'm a good listener. But make no mistake, I follow my own dreams, not yours.

Love comes in many forms, and I believe in a commitment to one person.

BE WARNED *... I'm a workaholic.*

SO SHE WAS INDEED IRISH, and a feisty independent woman. He chuckled. And a type-A personality from the sounds of it. Just like him.

He turned over her photo and his breath caught.

This was her? This woman was Maeve?

Right ... well ...

Her dark eyes held an impish twinkle. Her chestnut-brown hair was pulled away from her face, enhancing high cheekbones and full pink lips. She was stunning, and he hadn't expected that.

He placed her photo on the table, gazing at her for a long while. Then he reread her profile. *I live for a hot cuppa tea and will share it with you. I'm a good listener.*

Perhaps this Perfect Match setup wasn't such a bad idea.

Maybe she loved the outdoors, as he did. Maybe they'd swim every evening after work, climb the cliffs, dine on exotic Corsican cuisine.

There was no obligation to see her again after the week was over, and enjoying life had always been his motto. In fact, he'd written it on his dating profile.

Emboldened by those thoughts, he grabbed his suit jacket and headed inside his suite to take a shower. He might be a workaholic, but he was still a man.

And besides, they both liked tea.

3

———

Maeve's anticipated five-hour plane trip from Dublin to Corsica had taken ten. After being delayed by inclement weather, the flight was unnervingly bumpy, and she'd lifted a grateful prayer when they landed in Corsica.

She rang her mother, relieved to hear that her brother, Owen, had received encouraging news at his doctor's appointment that morning. The more time that passed, the lower the risk of recurrence. And Owen had been cancer free for over six months.

Feeling that, at least for the moment, that all was well in the world, she stepped from the black limousine that had picked her up from the airport to bring her to the small town in Porto where La Bonaparte Resort was located. The surrounding picturesque region was cited as one of the top ten places to visit in Europe. As she stepped onto the cobblestone street, she lifted her face to the balmy breeze. A bellhop loaded her bags onto a luggage cart, and she followed him up the stone steps of the hotel. Three stories high, the hotel's exterior boasted a rustic wooden pattern. Like something out of this world, she reflected, with the backdrop of the fiery-red Mediterranean sun setting behind the hotel and les Calanche Cliffs spiraling upward in the distance.

She'd assumed the weather might be blindingly hot on the island, but the climate was decidedly comfortable. She was looking forward to a refreshing shower and an opportunity to change into clean, unwrinkled clothes. Her traveling outfit, a linen navy skirt, white cotton blouse and sensible leather flats, had looked polished and put together when she'd left her flat. Not so much now. Ruefully, she evened out her skirt to look presentable, then started to the check-in desk.

Awe at the lobby's elegance slowed her pace, and she fingered the straps of the monogrammed jute tote she carried.

Was it too late to reconsider this trip?

Most definitely, she decided with a sigh. Even a one night-stay in a boutique hotel boasting Michelin status would cost a fortune in Euros to repay.

She caught a glimpse of a well-heeled tourist shouldering a designer purse. Clearly, a working-class woman like herself didn't belong here, she thought. She pretended to look around, intent on studying the marbled floor for several beats rather than meet the other woman's gaze.

Why, oh, why had she let Colleen talk her into this trip? Her chest tightened just thinking about the week ahead.

While Maeve waited in a short line to check in, the family ahead of her argued among themselves before stomping away from the reception desk, and swearing in Italian.

"Good evening, mademoiselle. You must be Maeve Doherty, oui?" Behind the oak desk, an impeccably-suited, tawny-haired man with a disarming smile welcomed her. He introduced himself as Pierre Martin, the head concierge, and didn't seem at all flustered by the group before her.

"I am Maeve. Aye."

"We've been expecting you. Welcome to our island of paradise."

"We?"

"The entire hotel staff and Perfect Match. And, of course, your date for the week. I've met him and can assure you he's a delightful fellow."

Delightful fellow.

She refrained from gaping at the view of the infinity pool through the resort's expansive rear windows and tried to return Pierre's grin. "That's grand."

She had no photo of her match, no dating profile, her mind feverishly reminded her. What if Amy and Dawson Yates and their Perfect Match specialists had made a mistake, and she and this "delightful fellow" didn't share any mutual interests? She imagined elaborate computers and complicated algorithms searching for ... for what? Computers couldn't be trusted on matters of the heart.

But this wasn't a matter of the heart. This was a working holiday.

"You are *tres belle, mademoiselle,*" Pierre said, "and indeed more beautiful than the profile picture Mrs. Yates sent. I'm certain your match will be very pleased." He struck his fingers to his lips with a whoosh, simulating a kiss. "In the meantime, your suite is on the second floor, room 201B, and Nigel will assist you." He nodded to the bellhop leaning against the luggage cart, then handed her an envelope.

"Voila! Your Perfect Match, Miss Doherty. And you'll meet him at eight o'clock for dinner on the terrace."

Voila?

"Thank you," she said. As Pierre went on to describe the highlights of the resort, including the gift shop and a coffee bar, the outdoor pool and a five-star restaurant, she inspected the envelope. Everything vital to accomplish her stay, all the information about her match, was enclosed. This was her week to enjoy herself ... to ease toward relaxation with a man she'd never met.

A few hours spent with him? Aye.

A week?

What would they possibly have in common?

On a half laugh, she debated tearing open the envelope and reading his profile aloud, but didn't want to appear too anxious. Still, her hand shook as she stowed the envelope into her red tote.

Breathe, she chided herself. She'd agreed to the offer and to be spotlighted in promotional publications. She'd redeemed her coupon. She'd signed in good faith, and an Irishwoman stood by her word.

"Pierre, are there any more towels?" a deep male voice called from behind her.

Maeve pivoted and almost collided with a dripping wet man striding to the reception counter. He wore little more than a very tight, very revealing spandex bathing suit. Barefoot, he'd tossed a towel over his shoulders. Water puddled at his feet.

"Monsieur Newell." Pierre's eyes widened. The implacable concierge dashed from behind his desk and pitched himself in front of Maeve. "Your match has arrived."

"The Irish woman?" Mr. Newell strode closer. His sea-green eyes held a gleam; his coal-black hair was wet and slicked back. He was decidedly taller than Maeve's five feet status, and she guessed he was over six feet.

"This isn't the eighteen hundreds, Pierre," Mr. Newell said. "I'm allowed to see my match before our official meeting. I'm sure Mr. and Mrs. ..." He paused.

"Yates, monsieur."

"Right. I'm sure Mr. and Mrs. Yates won't object. Besides, whoever you're hiding isn't my bride. I can take a peek."

"You can take more than a peek, Mr. Newell." Maeve shoved the rigid Pierre aside and held out her hand. "I'm Maeve Doherty."

He seemed stunned for a moment, then delighted, then quickly concealed all reactions. "Very pleased to meet you, Maeve. I'm Edward Newell." He lifted her hand and kissed it. His hand was wet. Drops of water clung to her palm.

He in his wet spandex suit, she in her wrinkled travel clothes, they stood in the marbled lobby of one of the most expensive resorts in the world and warily assessed each other.

At least, Maeve was wary.

She took a quick breath and an even quicker look at Edward. He appeared relaxed, despite his clothes, or lack of clothes. Look up, she scolded herself. Fix your gaze on his face, although her gaze insisted on gravitating downward to his broad, bare chest.

"Hello, Edward." She congratulated herself on being able to speak.

"Now that we've gotten that out of the way," he said. "I recognized you from your photo, although you're much more beautiful in person." His devastating smile held her spellbound. She peered at their hands. They were still connected.

Edward Newell. The name sounded so posh.

His eyes mesmerized her, and she felt a pulse of pure attraction. He could have passed for a swimsuit model. She inhaled a whiff of fresh air and chlorine and affluence. He definitely smelled like a man who enjoyed the good things in life. And if that wasn't enough, she had to concede he was exceedingly handsome.

She could hear Colleen whispering in her ear. *"What if Mr. Right is waiting for you in Corsica?"*

Determined to brazen out their first meet, she turned to the two men beside them. Pierre's features were well-composed, his gaze was riveted on a point somewhere above her head. The bellhop Nigel stood suspended in midstep, holding onto the luggage cart, apprehension furrowing his brow. Baggage temporarily forgotten, he kept his gaze on the same spot as Pierre.

Evidently impervious to the goings-on around him, Edward kept hold of her hand and used his other one to drape his beach towel more securely around his shoulders. Fit and tanned, his physique was lean and well-toned. Well, except for those shoulders capping off a slim waist. Surely, he must bench-press every day.

"I'm afraid I'm at a disadvantage, Mr. Newell," Maeve said. "I've just arrived and haven't viewed your profile yet."

"There's not much to view, although what I wrote was honest." He studied her with candid interest, still holding onto her hand.

She scraped back her hair with her free hand. Before she'd left Dublin, she'd curled it. Now it hung in loose waves above her shoulders, and she was sure it looked tangled and unmanageable. Why hadn't she taken a second to pull a brush through it? She'd been so anxious to ring her mother and brother, she hadn't focused on anything else.

Aware Edward still scrutinized her, she scrambled for

something to say. "I like an honest man," was the best she could come up with.

His lips quirked in a half smile. "And I like an honest woman." Lazily, his gaze dipped, perusing her from the tips of her sensible flats to the top of her hair.

To her chagrin, she felt her cheeks heat.

"So you're from Ireland?"

She lifted her chin. "Aye."

Something flickered in his gaze, and his smile persisted. "You have a lovely Irish brogue, Maeve."

"Thank you." He was a charmer, that was certain. He'd probably dated hundreds of women and planned to cast her onto his list of conquests.

She scanned the lobby. The air hung suspended, and several moneyed tourists openly stared. She imagined Dawson and his crew lurking behind a potted fern and snapping photos of her and Edward.

"I'm from England," Edward continued, "so we don't live far from each other."

"A ninety-minute ferry ride from Dublin across the Irish Sea." She shook her head ruefully. "Of course, you must factor in the additional four-hour train ride from Holyhead in Wales to London."

"Have you ever visited London?"

"Never, although I've known friends who travel to London for soccer matches and concerts."

Edward grinned, his white teeth flashed. "You'll need to update your travel itinerary, Maeve. See the world, live a little."

"Beginning with Corsica, aye?" She drew her hand from his and shot a glance at Pierre. He adjusted his patterned bow tie and patted the yellow square peeking from his breast pocket. "Dinner will be served at eight o'clock this evening."

"We know," Edward and Maeve said at the same time. They shared a chuckle.

"Thank you, Pierre. I'll be there," Maeve agreed.

"Most assuredly, so will I." Very quietly, Edward added, "I'm looking forward to getting to know you better, Maeve."

4

———

Maeve had followed the bellhop to her second-floor suite.

Although she did not expect that she and Edward would be sharing a room, any hopes that his suite was in another building were quickly dashed. In the Yateses' expectation of a match, they'd booked Maeve and Edward into adjoining rooms separated only by an arched door.

Maeve quickly solved the problem by noisily bolting the door, knowing Edward—who'd followed her and Nigel up the stairs—could hear her key turn in the lock.

What would she say when she called Colleen that night, as she'd promised to do, and Colleen asked what kind of a man Edward Newell was.

"He's fine-looking, I'll give him that," Maeve would answer. "And successful, by the way he carries himself. We met unexpectedly in the lobby. He wore a spandex bathing suit that left little to the imagination and ..."

No, that wouldn't do. Colleen would ask one hundred questions and she'd never allow Maeve to get a good night's rest.

Maeve spent the next few hours unpacking, showering, resting, and finally dressing for dinner.

At seven forty-five, she stared back at herself in the room's full-length mirror. She'd decided to wear her favorite dress, a tie-dyed tank jersey that skimmed her slender figure to mid-calf, accenting her left leg with a side slit.

With a last swipe of rose lip gloss, she slipped on her ankle-strap sandals, grabbed her leopard pouch and walked down the one flight curving staircase. As expected, Pierre was behind his desk, his head bent over a computer.

Briefly, Maeve wondered if he ever slept.

"Miss Doherty." Pierre looked up and immediately became cheerful. "May I show you the terrace? We reserved your table overlooking the harbor and Mr. Newell is waiting for you there."

Here goes, she thought, taking in a deep breath. She'd worked herself into a knot of expectation for what the first dinner might bring with the attractive man she could only envision in a skimpy swimsuit.

Before she'd even unpacked, she had read his dating profile. Actually, she'd read it so much she had it memorized.

OUTDOORGUY, *Age 30*

"*NEVER, NEVER, NEVER GIVE UP.*" *–Winston Churchill*

I'M a guy who spends his time outdoors whenever he can get away from work.

It's not often. You see, I'm married ... to my job.

When I do go outside, my dog and I ride my motorcycle as far away from civilization as possible and pitch a tent.

My motto? Enjoy life whenever you can. Every day is a gift.

IN HIS PROFILE PHOTO, he'd obviously just finished playing a pickup football game with friends, judging by the short-sleeved jersey clinging to his muscular shoulders and the beads of sweat on his forehead. A couple of teammates in the background wore wide grins, and they all held up pints of lager. She noticed he didn't.

When Pierre showed her to the terrace, Edward, who had had his cellphone clapped to his ear, immediately disconnected and came to his feet. "Good evening Maeve. You look lovely."

That devastating smile again.

She felt the heat rise to cover her face. "Thank you."

He looked quite fine himself in his elegantly tailored pinstripe suit. His white starched shirt contrasted sharply with his tanned, wind-burned cheeks. His black hair had dried naturally and curled at his nape. Obviously, no fancy hair care products for him.

Pierre bid them a delightful evening as their waiter bore down on them. With a slight bow, he introduced himself as Achille and drew a chair out for her. He had a groomed white mustache and a genial smile.

She paused, taking in the expanse of sea and sky, an occasional whip of a tenacious breeze, the fragrant night air. Realizing Edward and Achille remained standing, waiting for her to sit, she settled into the chair.

Edward sat with his back to the harbor, perhaps out of

consideration for her to appreciate the view, perhaps because Achille had directed him to sit there. Regardless, the sight from the wraparound terrace offered fine dining at its best. The Mediterranean night glistened under a bevy of silver stars, and fishing boats swayed side by side amidst million-dollar yachts, gentle waves lapping at the hulls. An occasional seabird swooped, feeding on the Mediterranean's surface.

Achille returned bearing a silver serving tray with a bottle of Champagne in an iced bucket and two fluted glasses. "Because this is your first date, the Yateses insisted you indulge in our finest French Champagne."

Achille set the glasses and equipment on an auxiliary table, drew the cork with a distinctive pop, and carried bottle and glasses to their table.

"Water for me, thanks," Edward said when the waiter began pouring.

"Very good, sir. And you, mademoiselle?"

"I'd love a glass."

The bubbly Champagne flowed, and Achille waited for her to taste.

She took a sip, and nodded her approval. As Achille marched back to the kitchen, taking Edward's unused glass, she asked, "You don't drink?"

"Not in eleven years." He shrugged. "I take that back. I imbibed at my parents' twenty-fifth wedding anniversary."

"Congratulations on the longevity of their marriage!"

"They were married thirty years." He paused, and his voice was quiet when he spoke again. "My mother passed away a year later. She's been gone five years now."

Maeve hesitated, trying unsuccessfully to think of something to say, and decided to stick with what was in her heart. "I'm sorry. I'm sure you miss her terribly."

"I do. Thanks." He gave her a thoughtful look. "My siblings and I are all still devastated. She was a courageous woman who fought bravely."

"How did she die?"

"From cancer."

"My sincere condolences." Maeve's thoughts scrambled and with effort she gathered them together. She couldn't face where the discussion might lead—to her brother, his cancer—so she modified the subject. "Otherwise, you don't drink, Edward?"

"Rare occasions."

Achille came back to the table with their menus and recited the catches of the day. "Of the choices, I recommend our Corsican fish. It is prepared unassumingly with olive oil and wrapped in foil. *C'est délicieux!*"

On that recommendation, Maeve ordered the Corsican fish, as well as sautéed potatoes and fresh asparagus. Edward asked for the same.

When the waiter disappeared into the kitchen, Edward lifted his water glass. "I believe a toast is in order. Cheers to us!"

"Aye." With their glasses upraised, they clinked.

She rarely drank, but because she was in a country she'd always fantasized about visiting, because a most attractive man sat across from her, because she needed courage to converse with him intelligently, she told herself it was okay.

"I can't believe I'm here," she declared.

"Neither can I."

She grinned. "It's because of my best friend—"

"It's because of my university friend—" They shared a laugh and clinked glasses again "To friends."

He set down his glass. "So this Perfect Match week wasn't something you agreed to voluntarily?"

"To be honest, no." Somehow, she wanted to tell him more. Perhaps about her brother's illness, her mother's never-ending drama.

No, that wouldn't do. She hardly knew him.

Instead, she drained her glass and clarified, "I'm a friend of Amy Yates."

"Who is she again?"

"Amy and her husband Dawson own the dating agency."

"Right."

"How about you? Why are you here?"

"Hmm?"

He was staring at her so intently she didn't know whether to avoid his gaze or stare back at him. She opted for gazing at the boats in the harbor. "You mentioned your friend," she reminded Edward as Achille appeared to refill her champagne glass.

"Oh, right." There was a long silence before Edward continued. "My friend Bentley decided to play a practical joke and signed me up for this, somewhat of an escapade. When he learned about the joke, my father thought it was an excellent idea. He'd just as soon marry me off to the prettiest woman with two—"

Maeve drew back in her chair and raised her glass to her lips. "Two ...?"

"Legs. Two legs." If Edward was trying to look sheepish, the attempt was marred by his boyish grin.

When the meal arrived, she bowed her head and whispered a prayer. Edward didn't participate, although he did bow his head.

More than an hour later, after a lengthy dinner and nonstop conversation, Achille served *fiadone*, a light cheesecake, for dessert. She managed a bite before pushing it to the side. "One word for this cheesecake is a sinful marvel."

"That's two words. Three words if you count the *a*."

"Aye." She laughed. "I wish I could finish it. It's delicious."

"Do you mind, then?" He waited for her assent before scooping the cheesecake onto his plate.

As he ate, she gazed at the spectacular scene behind him, particularly the way the lights from the town glistened on the harbor's glass-like surface. In her mind's eye, she visualized the panorama at daybreak, sunshine dappling across the boathouses, iron benches set alongside wooden paths leading to the sea, violets and orchids blanketing the flower beds.

The little she'd eaten of dinner had been superb—hot crusty rolls, wafer-thin fish, creamy potatoes, and steaming asparagus sprinkled with parmesan cheese, salt and pepper —all served on porcelain dinnerware, cobalt blue and white, edged in gilded scrollwork. The hectic day of travel, the weather fluctuations from Ireland's dampness to this tropical warmth, so utterly different from her rainy climate, had set her stomach aflutter. Wistfully, she eyed the champagne. She didn't want to waste an entire expensive bottle by drinking only two glasses.

Attributing the delicious warmth flooding her veins to a marvelous evening, she debated indulging in more champagne. However, when Achilles started to refill her glass, she checked him at only a half. Over the rim, she observed Edward. All evening, he'd entertained her with fascinating facts about London's off-the-beaten-path book shops and historical sites. Always soft-spoken, he seemed genuinely interested in the latest Irish scuttle-butt she'd shared, leaning closer, encouraging her to continue whenever there was a lull in their conversa-tion. He exhibited the kind of natural polish she'd observed in the well-heeled clients that frequented Merrimac.

No doubt the other women on the terrace coveted Edward as their date, she thought, for she'd caught more than a few appreciative glances sent his way. Amazingly, this sophisticated and urbane man was with her.

She smiled. He caught her gaze and held it.

And there it was, that tug of attraction.

How? They'd only just met.

As she mulled this over, Edward slanted her a long look. "Quite a day?"

"Aye." She held a hand to her mouth, stifling an unexpected yawn.

"Tired?"

"A little."

"I noticed you didn't eat much, luv." Pointedly, his gaze fell to her empty glass. If he assumed she was feeling a wee bit drunk, he was right.

"I'll make up for my lack of appetite tomorrow," she said. "I love to eat decidedly more than I love to cook."

"I didn't read that bit of information on your profile."

"There's a lot about me you don't know, Edward." She was feeling particularly cheery and unconcerned that she was having trouble focusing. "Do you cook?"

"I prefer takeout, and if I'm forced to host a dinner party, I ring a caterer. I look at the menu online, pick appetizers, a main course, and a dessert, pay the bill, and then I'm done. It doesn't mean I'm lazy," he continued. "It just means I'm inadequate."

She grinned. "I can't imagine you being inadequate in anything."

"There's a lot about me you don't know," he said, parroting her earlier phrase. He pushed back his chair and buttoned his suitcoat. "If you're ready to leave, I'll walk you to your room." He winked. "It's not out of my way."

She laughed again. "Aren't we waiting for someone from the Perfect Match staff to explain what's in store for us this week?"

"Are we?"

"Didn't you read the paperwork?"

He gave a rueful smile. "Clearly not everything."

As if on cue, a pert young woman walked over to their table and introduced herself as Carissa Swanson. She looked to be in her thirties, with a stream of blonde hair. She was a member of the Perfect Match staff. She invited them to sit somewhere else on the terrace that was away from the dining tables.

"I will leave the champagne, mademoiselle?" Achille asked Maeve as he and a busboy discreetly removed plates and silverware. He nodded to Carissa.

"Not a drop more tonight, Achille. Thank you." She placed a hand over the ounce left in her glass, then traced a finger along the cork in the basket. "A cup of hot tea with a spot of sugar sounds good, though."

"Very good, mademoiselle."

Carissa encouraged Edward and Maeve to relax in a cushioned loveseat adjacent to her and urged them to sit close.

She began with a brief description of Perfect Match and the algorithms the company had developed for pairing couples. "We are certain," she went on, "that we've set you two up correctly. For example, you're both workaholics, have never been married, and you both own a dog. Of course, there's more to it than that." She smiled. "But we'll let you two find out those things."

She directed her gaze toward Maeve. "Tomorrow

morning at nine o'clock, we'd appreciate footage of you two exploring the island together."

There went her work intentions, Maeve thought. Or maybe she could surreptitiously take notes and photographs of the places they visited to submit to Merrimac Company as potential locations for a new hotel.

"When the sun sets tomorrow night," Carissa continued, "you can frolic in the sea for a swim."

"Frolic?" Edward lifted a dark eyebrow.

"Mr. Yates's word, sir."

"Sorry, but I don't swim." Maeve moved her tea aside. "I don't think I packed a bathing suit ..."

Edward's grin was positively roguish. "If you didn't, there's a natural bay on the west coast where you can swim without wearing any—"

"I'll buy a swimsuit in the gift shop," she interrupted.

"One piece or two?"

"I'm not certain until I see a style I want to wear."

"I'm partial to string bikinis on women."

Torn between humor and shock, she jibed, "I definitely will *not* keep that in mind."

She blushed easily, an embarrassing giveaway of her emotions, and she felt a tint of heat on her face. With a half giggle, she gaily considered her newest predicament— which swimsuit to purchase. If only life in Ireland could be so uncomplicated.

Carissa left a short while afterward, and Edward and Maeve sat in silence while fragments of conversation from the other diners went on around them. Content with the world, Maeve sighed happily and burrowed deeper into the loveseat.

"I didn't know you like dogs," Edward said. Somehow,

his arm had ended up around her shoulders as he grinned down at her.

"Doesn't everyone?"

"No. Some people like cats." He brushed a light kiss on her forehead, sending a disturbed flurry of excitement to her pulse. "What's your dog's name?"

"Crinkles. She's a miniature pug."

"A regular-sized pug is small enough to fit in a suitcase. How much does Crinkles weigh?"

"Less than four and a half kilos. Around ten pounds."

"What can a dog that size do besides yap?"

"She's a lapdog. When I get home from work, I'll settle in a comfortable chair by the fireplace with a book in my hand and the drumming of rain on the roof. She cuddles next to me or sits at my feet."

"Do you enjoy reading?"

"Aye."

"Any favorite books? No doubt romance novels, right?"

She hesitated, went for a sip of tea. "My main interest is history, which is the reason why I wanted to come to Corsica."

His smile widened. "Any particular era?"

"The French Revolution, and particularly Napoléon Bonaparte. I admire him as a military commander who led several successful campaigns. Because he was born in Corsica, there's a museum here."

"Remind me to never quarrel with you, if you've read up on Napoléon Bonaparte."

"No worries. I'm very peaceful and will do anything to avoid a conflict." She helped herself to another spoonful of sugar and stirred her tea. "What about your dog? Is she as cute as mine?"

"He, and I'm sure he wouldn't appreciate being pegged as *cute*. He's a black lab and weighs thirty-six kilos." He grinned. "So, eight of your Crinkles. He's a proper dog who rides my motorcycle with me. Plus, we go camping together."

"What's his name?"

"Harley."

"Aye, thus the motorcycle reference in your profile." Maeve nodded and reached for a last sip of tea. Briefly, she savored the lukewarm brew and closed her eyes.

Edward sat so near, the tang of his aftershave scented the brisk evening air. The night was superb, the meal exquisite, and she felt her cares being lifted from her shoulders.

She was so content, she didn't know how much time passed before Edward stood and offered his hand, waiting for her to accept. She couldn't say no, and didn't. As they crossed the lobby, the ever-present Pierre peered up from his computer. "I trust you two had an enchanted evening?" he inquired.

"If you're partial to beautiful Irish women, then mission accomplished." Edward high-signed a salute. "I'd say it was quite marvelous, in fact."

"And you, mademoiselle?"

"Aye. Thank you. Tell Amy and Dawson it was perfect." *More than perfect.*

Hundreds of white votive candles set in glass jars tied with gold ribbons were set on tables throughout the lobby, shooting shadows of light along the marbled floor. The effect was storybook-like, and very, very romantic.

She and Edward climbed the wide, sweeping staircase to the second floor, stopping in front of her door. She leaned against the wall with its patterned wallpaper, her head whirling, and tried closing her eyes. The sensation that she was spinning made her instantly open them again.

She fixated on the soft glowing sconces on the opposite wall and the painting of Corsican orchids. "I never realized I liked champagne so much," she murmured.

He chuckled. "I'll ask your opinion tomorrow morning at nine."

She turned abruptly to bid him good night, overestimated the distance and smacked into his chest. Immediately, his arms encircled her, and he balanced her unsteady footing.

Afterward, when Maeve reviewed what happened next, she upbraided herself for the way she reacted. Rather than staying where she stood with his arms around her, she should have drawn away.

His green-eyed gaze glided to her mouth and his head lowered. As his mouth met hers, his hands skimmed over her hips, drawing her to his muscular build.

She shouldn't have, but her fragile hold on what she should and shouldn't do slipped away while his lips moved boldly over hers. As if it were the most natural thing in the world, she wound her arms around his shoulders and kissed him back.

Dazedly, when she eventually pulled away, it struck her that he'd already released her.

Several seconds passed.

Drawing an unsteady breath, she squinted at him through a haze, distinctly seeing several Edwards standing beneath the portrait of orchids.

More beats.

Finally realizing he was waiting for something, she lifted her eyebrows and said in an overconfident voice, "Do you think I'm going to invite you to my room? Are you hoping that's what happens next?"

"On the contrary, there's an important bit of information about me I wanted to tell you."

"What?"

Please, she thought, *don't let him be married.*

He took a step back and shoved his hands in his pockets. "I don't know how to start, so I'll just say it. Maeve, you're a charming woman."

"Thank you. And you're quite charming yourself."

He nodded but avoided her gaze. "And because of our earlier talk about honesty, I intend to be upfront with you starting now."

She felt herself go still. "Aye?"

Gently, he grasped her forearms. "This week is a bit of a lark for me. As I started to tell you at dinner, my friend Bentley put me up to this and my father seconded the idea. These next few days are a working vacation for me, nothing more. I'm sure you understand, as you're also a workaholic. And for the record, I'm not the marrying type."

Coolly, ungraciously, she shook off his hold. "And you think I am?"

"Look, no matter what happens, we both walk away at the end of the week. No strings, no promises. Agreed?"

"I'm not desperate for love, Edward."

"Good. I don't want you to get hurt."

"By you?" She heard her laugh. It had a cutting edge.

"By any man."

"So this is all a joke, right? This match, this island, me …"

His eyes flashed. "I wouldn't call it that."

Then what would you call it?

She didn't ask the question out loud as tears of exhaustion and embarrassment sprang to her eyes. The indulgent amusement of the evening had vanished.

He was silent for a moment before he continued. "All I'm saying is we shouldn't spoil a pleasant week with talk of perfect matches or love."

Every muscle in her body quivered. "The last thing I want is a relationship with a man, particularly one who puts his dog at risk."

"What's that supposed to mean?"

She looked away. Heat flushed through her body, which she recognized as mortification for being so impetuous around him. Still, there was no retreating, so she grasped at a flimsy excuse. "I've never seen a dog ride a motorcycle before. What kind of an irresponsible dog owner are you?"

"What? Harley wears goggles and a helmet and rides in a motorcycle carrier, and I'm a most responsible dog owner. Happy now?"

"Nothing you described sounds safe or responsible."

"Take care of your own affairs, Maeve." Edward's gaze narrowed. "Concentrate on what I just said. No strings. Are we in agreement?"

"I haven't the slightest interest in the likes of you."

"That's fine," he said. "But I'm not a betting man, so it's best to clear things up from the starting gate. From what I've gathered, you wouldn't be able to repay such an expensive trip. So let's agree to put on an act for the cameras."

"Actually, I'm a particularly proficient actress."

He shuffled back a step. "Really?"

"Really." She swept out an arm to make her point and knocked the orchid painting to the carpeted floor.

She scrambled to retrieve it, but Edward was faster,

hanging the painting back on the wall before she had a chance to sputter another rejoinder.

"Good, it's settled then." He unlocked the door for her and ushered her into her suite. "We'll work together, play together and make this week a resounding success for all of us."

5

———————

The rap on the door of her suite at precisely nine o'clock in the morning told Maeve it must be Edward. Had she read in his profile that he was punctual, or had she imagined it? He certainly seemed the type ... with his classy ways and ever-pleasant composure.

She'd been frayed the preceding evening and hadn't rung Colleen, although she'd sent a quick text with Edward's name, so at least Colleen had something to go on.

Disheartened by his "honesty," she had tossed in her luxurious king-sized bed and ended up staring at the rotating fan on the high ceiling.

When next she awoke, she saw from her window a golden August moon lighting the sky. She curled onto her side seeking the peacefulness of slumber, but it eluded her. She attributed her restlessness to her pounding headache, which she'd blamed on her champagne overindulgence.

Although she knew it was more.

Edward had informed her in no uncertain terms that he wasn't interested in a romantic relationship.

Which was terrific, because she wasn't interested in one, either.

Although wasn't he the same man who'd seemed mesmerized with her throughout dinner and had kissed her in the hallway outside her suite? She'd seen the desire in his smoky, dark-green gaze. Surely she hadn't imagined it.

Her cheeks burned at how quickly she'd slipped into his arms and returned his kiss. She'd made a brainless fool of herself. And, she vowed, it wouldn't happen again.

She awoke for good at first light, watching the sky transform from blush to peach to vivid orange. She read the book she'd started on the plane, and at half past seven she texted her mother to check on Owen. She had waited because of the one-hour time difference between Ireland and Corsica.

Reassured her brother was doing well, she showered in the spacious Italian-marble shower, and then dressed for the day. She'd pinned her hair in a casual bun, but the sleepless night had left telltale shadows beneath her eyes. However, her jean shorts and a neon-pink tank top made her look fun and young and fit for island exploration.

Again, a knock sounded.

"I'm coming," she called out. She squared her shoulders and dismissed the ruffling in her stomach.

"Corsica discovery, day one," Edward joked as she opened the door. He'd been texting someone. Rapidly, he finished, then stowed the phone into his shorts pocket.

"Sorry. Never-ending business. You know the drill."

No, she didn't. She worked a nine-to-five job at an hourly rate, and wasn't in any position of authority.

He looked exceptionally handsome. He was the sort of man who looked good whether he was dressed for business or leisure. He always looked spot-on. Today, he wore green cargo shorts, a worn navy T-shirt, and black leather mesh shoes. His arms were bare, and a thought zipped through her mind. She wished he hadn't worn a shirt, so she could see his muscled chest.

No, no, no, don't go there. She blamed her speculation on her headache, although despite his dampening comments at the end of the night, his magnetism drew her. She stared at him. Just stared. How could a man be that good-looking?

He strode inside. With a concerned glance at her, he asked how she was feeling.

"Awful." She expelled a shaky sigh. "Most of the night my stomach churned the same as when I arrived, although yesterday I blamed the churning on flight delays and turbulence." She shrugged. "You must have had the same bad weather in London. Did it delay your flight?"

"I flew in from the Continent. I had business to attend to in Nice."

"There's a direct flight from Nice to Corsica?"

"There might be." He shrugged, shifted. "My family owns a private jet."

My family owns a private jet. She massaged her temples and tried to assimilate the information.

"Do you still like champagne?" he asked with a hint of a grin.

"Not nearly as much." She glanced toward the dazzling sunlight filtering through the French doors that led to her balcony and flinched. "My head resembles a soft-boiled egg."

His lips twitched. "I've read it's because of the sulfites in champagne that lots of people have similar reactions, so drink plenty of water today."

She indicated the water bottle she'd placed by her tote bag and attempted a wan smile. "What are sulfites, by the way?"

"No idea." He made a valiant attempt to keep his features straight. "Did you eat any breakfast this morning?"

"Aye, a slice of toast and a bowl of dry cereal."

"Good. I'll order a sports drink for you in the lobby too." He pulled out his phone and quickly texted, she assumed, Pierre.

"Are you an expert on hangovers?" she asked.

"Unfortunately, I am," he said. "Now, ready for a morning of exploration?" He gestured to a daypack thrown over his shoulders.

"Aye." She was wearing sturdy slip-on sneakers and in her jute bag she carried sunscreen, a scarf, and her cellphone for pictures and note taking. She was prepared.

"I went for a run on the beach when I got up and passed Pierre in the lobby before I hit the steam room," Edward said. "As you can guess, he knows our agenda, and it includes les Calanche Cliffs and lunch. Carissa will meet us downstairs." He stared at Maeve's exposed legs, lingering for longer than necessary. "If you stumble and skin your knees, you'll be laid up for the week."

"We're *seeing* the cliffs, not *climbing* the cliffs."

"Right." He took her hands in his. "Did I already tell you that you look lovely today? Despite your fondness for bubbly beverages, you've recovered admirably this morning."

"Thank you. I ... no one told me our sightseeing included cliffs and I'm not changing my outfit."

His fingers tightened around hers, his gaze becoming positively seductive. If he tried to kiss her like he did last evening, she'd—

"No doubt," he said, "you didn't thumb through the promotional material, because if you did, you'd have seen our itinerary this morning, which was all about the cliffs," he was saying.

He included a wink that prompted her to laugh. He wasn't going to kiss her, so she needn't fret about how she'd react. She broke from his grip and placed the water bottle in her tote bag. "For the record, I prefer trolling museums. The more ancient the artifacts, the better."

"Ah yes, the Bonaparte museum. So you've mentioned." He rolled his eyes. "Napoléon Bonaparte is on tap for Friday. The Perfect Match specialists planned our activities around the weather report. Friday it's supposed to rain and the museum is our indoor activity."

When they reached the lobby, they were accosted by a bubbly Carissa wearing khaki shorts and a long-sleeved striped shirt.

The ever-present Pierre, although assisting a stout woman obsessed with the breakfast menu, uttered a cheerful "Bonjour" and handed Edward a sports drink "for the mademoiselle."

"We'll take a footpath to the cliffs," Carissa said as she led the way. "The camera crew will meet us there. They'll get shots of you two sitting on the red cliff rocks, cavorting in the sand ..."

"Cavorting?" Edward held up a hand. "Don't tell me ..."

Carissa nodded. "Dawson's word."

As they trudged the footpath beside roadside vineyards, Carissa spoke nonstop. "After the photo shoot, the waitstaff will provide a picnic lunch for you. Then you're free to spend the afternoon doing whatever you'd like."

A nap, Maeve supposed, but then she remembered she was supposed to be working.

Frothy sea water rolled over the cool, firm sand, and the sea was so blue it was a contest to distinguish where water ended and sky began. Oftentimes both Maeve and Edward paused to take photos with their cellphones, and then Maeve would rapidly type in notes. A spray of salt water often surprised them when a wave crashed close to shore. Boats with billowing white sails navigated the slicing waves in the distant harbor, and the morning sun looked as if it were dusting tiny diamonds across the water.

True to Carissa's word, the camera crew, consisting of a woman and two men, were waiting at the bottom of les Calanche Cliffs when they arrived. Cameras were set up, as well as tripods, light stands and reflectors. A cameraman propped a shade umbrella on a ridge of rocks to protect Maeve's pale complexion from the sun, adding a blanket for her to sit on between takes.

Carissa had even brought along a bouquet of native orange lilies for Maeve to hold while Edward kissed her for a pose.

"Look romantic and affectionate," Carissa directed. "Now can I get a cuddle for another shot? We'll preserve these memories and inspire other couples."

When Carissa announced a wrap at noon, she handed Maeve and Edward clean beach towels. "We're finished for today. You two are so good-looking and natural together. It's as if you've known each other for years and are head-over-heels in love. The chemistry ..."

Edward gave Maeve a pat on the shoulder. "That's because Maeve is a professional actress."

"Don't believe a word he says," Maeve ribbed. "He even fakes his British accent."

"And here I was trying to hide my Englishness this whole time." He nudged her elbow. "Well done on discovering my secret!"

After they'd used a nearby restroom, the camera crew and Carissa packed their gear and headed back to the resort.

Four waiters from the hotel delivered a picnic lunch in a wicker hamper. They also set up rainbow-painted canvas chairs, a portable table and a beach umbrella. Efficiently, they served roasted turkey sandwiches on soft pretzel buns, a selection of brie and gouda cheeses, and sliced tomatoes and olives. Dessert included ripe blackberries and squares of dark chocolate. Both Edward and Maeve declined the recommended wine pairings, compliments of Achille, and opted instead for iced tea, bottled water and Maeve's sports drink.

When the last of the luncheon staff departed, Maeve stared at the rising granite rock formations behind them, looking like a pair of gnarled fingers pierced the sky. "My head is still pounding," she told Edward, "so I'm heading back to the resort to work."

"How? It's a long walk back."

"I'll hail a taxi if I get tired. You?"

He scanned the cliff. "I'd like to see where this path leads."

"Don't you need to work too?"

"Yes, but a hike beckons."

She shaded her eyes and peered up. "It's a steep climb."

"But I bet the coastal views are stunning from the top."

"And I'm positive the drop is terrifying if you look straight down." She snatched her tote bag and pivoted toward the footpath. "Happy climbing."

"Maeve? 'The mountains are calling and I must go.'"

She turned. "You couldn't have made that up. Who are you quoting?"

"John Muir. He was from the UK."

"You didn't use his quote on your dating profile."

"I didn't remember it until now." He gestured to a modest sign on the ground. "This path is for beginners and is an easy thirty-minute hike. Don't you want to explore a famous Corsican rock formation with me?"

"Edward, do I look like a person who hikes? The food and shade helped my headache, but I'm bordering on only 50 percent brilliant at best. Besides, you said yourself I'm not dressed for hiking." She turned toward the footpath, again, then turned back to him.

"You're not up for the challenge?" he goaded. "You, a sturdy Irishwoman?"

She wasn't feeling exceptionally sturdy, but she took the bait, especially when he mentioned the lava rocks were two hundred and fifty million years old, and she being a history buff and all ....

He'd neglected to mention that although there were no words to describe the stunning natural landscape when they reached the top, the hike would leave her breathless. The trail led sharply through the woods. Loose stones were everywhere, and she lost her footing several times on the dangerous, heart-stopping corners.

He frequently steadied her, much as he had the night before, with one arm around her shoulders. Many times she questioned aloud why she'd agreed to go with him; and he smiled, calm and patient, and offered to carry her tote bag. When she told him he didn't need to hover beside her every minute, he went ahead, although he glanced behind often. Moreover, he took numerous breaks, pausing to snap photos of the scenery until she caught up.

An hour later, she wiped her perspiring face and pushed strands of hair from her forehead, as most of her hairpins had fallen to the ground.

So much for a casual bun. So much for a thirty-minute hike.

He yanked a thin jacket from his day bag and laid it down for them to sit on. They rested on a notched rock with a marvelous view of the entire Calanche area. The lights and shadows of the cliffs, the colors, fluctuated with the angle of the sun, and the rough and wild coastline spread far and unknown beneath them. Maeve admired the panorama as the howl of the ocean whistled between the rocks and a light mist of brine settled on her cheeks.

"Corsica is magnificent, isn't it?" she mused.

"Extraordinary." He gestured at the wind-eroded rocks. "How does it feel to be a mountaineer?"

"Exhilarating and exhausting. You were right though. The view is worth it."

He drew two bottles of water from his bag and offered her one.

"What do you do for a living?" he asked when she'd taken a swig of water and rested against the rocks.

From the tangled underbrush, she plucked a fistful of rosemary and sniffed the mint-like aroma. "I work for a hotel firm, the Merrimac Company. I'm one of the purchasing agents."

"What are you in charge of buying?"

"Mostly seating and lighting. I compare prices and quality. We're small, and I pride myself on contracting the lowest bids for everything I order."

"A good purchasing agent can make or break the profits of a hotel."

"I'd like to work up to a position in management. Merrimac is based in Ireland. Have you heard of it?"

He drained his water bottle and jammed it into his bag.

"England and Ireland are separated by a brief ferry ride, if you recall," he teased.

"If it's pouring rain, then the trip wouldn't be quite as brief, I suppose." She chuckled and took another sip of water. "What about you? What do you do for a living?"

"I own a hotel resort firm, Penelope and Edward International. Or rather, my father owns the company and I'm vice president."

She touched a hand to her chest and silenced her gasp.

Penelope and Edward International? The single most distinguished hotel conglomerate in the world, boasting resorts in America, Europe and Asia.

She gazed at a rock formation resembling a staircase so she wouldn't gaze in shock at him. "You actually own Penelope and Edward?"

"My family does, although I'm at the helm now, being the oldest son. Old-fashioned values and all that. My father is impatient to retire."

At her quizzical look he went on. "Penelope was my mother's name. She and my father established their first resort hotel thirty years ago. They learned a lot, struggled a lot and invested judiciously. My father's name is Edward."

"And you're Edward the second?"

That explained it, she thought. *His refinement, his utterly sophisticated manner, his private jet.*

He chuckled. "You make me sound like royalty which I can confirm I'm not."

"So you're not Lord Edward, and I can most assuredly verify I'm not Lady Maeve."

Where was this leading? she wondered, setting her water bottle down. He *owned* one of the most luxurious hotel resort chains in the world. She *worked* at a hotel as an employee in the marketing department. Big difference.

Breaking the silence, he pointed outward toward an inlet. "I'll explore that area tomorrow, along with the lengthy stretch of beach. Penelope and Edward is weighing options for another resort, which is why this is a working holiday for me."

"Coincidentally, my company is seeking a place to expand as well. They prefer a site that has an existing property, thus *my* working holiday."

Before she could react, he brought her hands to his lips and kissed her palms. "Maybe the Perfect Match specialists knew what they were doing after all. We have so much in common."

The light from the afternoon sun enhanced the laugh lines around his sensual mouth, and she was powerless to tear her gaze away from his persuasive green eyes. A gust kicked up, blowing her remaining hairpins onto the rocks and tossing her shoulder-length hair in all directions. Distractedly, she pulled her hands from his grip and reached for the crinkly scarf she'd packed inside her tote bag. She twisted the scarf's edges, folded it around her hair, and double knotted it.

"Wouldn't you agree, Maeve? We get along so well." He checked her busy hands. "We're never at a lack for words. Perhaps we are made for each other."

"You're joking, right? Not for one minute are we alike. First, you're ignoring the fact I'm far from wealthy by your lofty standards, and second—"

"We're both here, aren't we?" His voice was quiet, seductive.

"Aye, for a week. You're either very fluthered or—"

"I don't drink, remember?"

She primly folded her hands on her lap. "I forgot you're a holy joe."

"I'm sensible."

"After your elegant speech last night," she said, "we both know this conversation isn't a good idea. Next time I'll throw more than a wall hanging at you if you try to kiss me."

"And here I assumed you were trying to elbow that painting off the wall just to test Newton's theory of gravity."

Slowly, he drew her to him.

She started to pull back, but his arms tightened around her. At the initial contact of his lips on hers, she froze. He continued, biding his time, his fingers caressing her cheeks, smoothing and shaping, his mouth bold yet tender.

"Edward, I won't be able to forgive you this time," she murmured against his lips.

"I'll take my chances," he whispered.

The taste of his mouth on hers, the hard, male strength of his body, brought a humming to her veins. She tried to keep her hands in her lap, but they slid around his neck of their own accord. The more boundless the kiss, the more yielding she became.

When the kiss ended, she rested her face against his chest. Disoriented, she struggled to analyze her emotions. Although angry at him, she was angrier at herself. She'd vowed she wouldn't become another of his conquests, a woman he had fun with for a week and then discarded. Nonetheless, his charm disarmed her at every corner.

On a sultry August day in Corsica, even the breeze was hot; and the sharp taste of the salty ocean air, even as high up as they were, reminded her of the waves pounding below them.

"Are you ready to leave?" he asked.

After that kiss? She glanced at him, but he'd set his features on neutral. Oh, if only her emotions weren't such an open book.

"We'll go down the same path, as we're familiar with the terrain," he continued, peering at his expensive watch, the dial illuminated. "It's three in the afternoon, and we'll pace ourselves since the grade is so steep. I have responsibilities to attend to before dinner, but I've got five hours to get everything accomplished."

"I have work too, remember?"

"As I pointed out, we're both workaholics." With that, he grabbed her water bottle, tightened the cap and added it to his day bag. He offered his hand and brought her to her feet, then tied his jacket around his waist. "Another reason we should head down is because ..."

"Dinner is at eight," they said together, and laughed.

A low-hanging mist hampered their progress down the cliff. They stopped often, and had to use their hands to keep from sliding downhill.

"Look ahead, stay centered," Edward instructed. "Take small steps. We're nearing the bottom."

"It's steep and slippery in this one patch." She went to grab a slender tree branch and lost her balance. The scenery tilted and blurred. Her muscles knotted.

She was falling and there was no way to stop it.

She screamed, groping blindly. Stone scraped her bare arms and legs. Soon she'd be plunging through empty air.

"Maeve!"

Scrambling for something to hold onto, she caught sight of Edward, his face ashen as he tore downhill and caught her. With her in his arms, he lost his footing, and they landed together on the uneven ground.

They both saw it. The odd twist of his ankle as he rolled to the side.

Immediately, he stood up and limped two steps.

He looked pale. She righted herself and gripped his hand. His pulse was unsteady.

"I think I sprained it." His gaze flitted from his ankle to the path. "I don't think I can walk."

"I'll go for someone. There must be a physician on this island."

He swayed as she steered him to a sheer vertical rock wall. He leaned into her, so much so that she was barely able to support his solid body. Inch by inch she assisted him as he braced a hand behind himself and sat. An oath escaped him.

"I'll ring for help." She snatched her cellphone from her tote bag and punched in the resort's phone number.

Oh no. No service in this remote area.

How was she going to assist a man twice her size down a cliff when he'd twisted his ankle?

She flopped down beside him and ran a shaking hand through her hair.

"Maeve, are you all right?" He gritted his teeth as he leaned forward and brushed her knee where blood streamed from a gash.

"Me? Aye, of course. I'm a sturdy Irishwoman, remember? You're the worry." She pulled the scarf off her hair and patted her knee with it. Then she removed the shoe and sock off Edward's injured foot, untied his jacket from his waist and used it to wrap his ankle. "Just rest for now," she said calmly, much more calmly than she felt. "There are plenty of hours before dark."

She set his day bag on the ground. His ankle was swollen and obviously tender to the touch judging by the way he tightened his fingers around his bag and avoided her gaze.

Carefully, she settled his foot onto her lap. He winced.

"I'll head to the restroom area below," she said. "It's not far. There should be cellphone service there and I'll ring for help."

He grimaced and sat stiffly against the rock. "You're a good caregiver, Maeve."

"Aye, it's what I do best." She considered his handsome face. This close, she could see the flecks of gold in his green eyes, his long, soft lashes. "Does your ankle hurt much?"

"Yes." He managed a smile. "If I were a drinking man, I'd go for a glass of last night's champagne about now."

"Believe me." She gave a doleful laugh and carefully elevated his foot on his day bag. "You'd be sorry tomorrow."

"Maeve." He grasped her fingers as she stood. "Can I admit I don't want you to leave me?"

She saw the effort it took for him to ask the question, his steely self-control exposed.

"You can admit whatever you'd like." She pressed her hand against his cheek, an act of comfort. "I won't be gone long, I promise."

And with that guarantee, she began her descent.

6

———

Maeve was more than an exceptional caregiver, Edward decided the following morning as he finished a business negotiation with his sister. She was an angel.

After she'd gotten him settled against the rock wall, she'd hurried down the cliff and then came back within a few minutes. Winded, she'd apparently run the entire course. She had been able to use her cellphone at the base and had called Pierre, who had immediately contacted the nearest hospital.

Thirty minutes later, medical aid arrived. By stretcher, the medics carried Edward to the main road where an ambulance idled, waiting to transport him to an accident and emergency center.

Maeve remained with him in the rear of the ambulance, lightly stroking his hair, telling him everything would be all right in a voice clogged with tears, which betrayed her assurances. She'd been more worried about him than he was, unable to hide the concern in her eyes, and his heart had filled with appreciation.

When they'd reached the center, Dr. Dubois, a portly man in his fifties, had assessed Edward's range of foot motion. After X-rays and because Edward was able to walk without any aids, the doctor had determined no bones were broken.

"I recommend crutches, and I won't need to see you again unless your ankle isn't healing properly." Dr. Dubois's gaze shot to Maeve. "In the interim, your lovely nurse will help you get around."

"Oui, she's a tremendous support," Edward agreed.

With that pronouncement, every person in the examining room turned to look at Maeve.

She'd laughed a denial, then angled her head to the side to avert their stares. A flattering pink bloomed on her cheeks, resembling an early-summer rose, utterly charming against her creamy skin.

Through his discomfort, her blush had coaxed a grin from him.

Now it was a day later, and nearly noon.

Edward settled into the cushioned chair on his suite's balcony. Despite his original doubts about this trip, the days were passing surprisingly fast.

Maeve stood in his efficiency kitchen, cobbling together a sandwich for his lunch—thinly sliced turkey, cheddar cheese, mustard and a side of crisps. Although the resort had offered to cater their meal, she'd instead insisted the staff provide ingredients so she could prepare the sandwiches herself.

She pleated white linen napkins, then creased the napkins into a three-way pocket and slipped the utensils inside.

"Did you hear what I said, Edward?" she called.

"Hmm?" He'd been staring at her. She looked so

provocative in cut-off jean shorts, bare feet and one of his worn chambray shirts, which she'd tucked into her shorts. She'd spilled orange juice on her blouse when preparing him breakfast, and although she'd unlocked the adjoining door to her suite, she hadn't returned to change after he'd offered one of his shirts.

She tilted her head to look at him. "I said, do you want a cup of coffee with your sandwich?"

"I drank my quota for the day, thanks." Along with eating enough tangy grapefruit that morning to cure the most jaundiced sailor while Maeve had itemized the benefits of vitamin C.

At first, the pain in his ankle had dominated Edward's attention. Now the pain rested quietly in the background, thanks to compression dressing, ibuprofen and Maeve's tender care.

After carefully showering, he'd thrown on a pair of fleece shorts and a Snoopy T-shirt. Now he sighed and stretched, comfortable and content.

"Don't forget," Maeve said, "that the doctor advised the twenty/twenty rule. Ice on your ankle for twenty minutes, then twenty minutes off. We don't want you to get frostbite."

"Oui, mademoiselle," he teased.

"I've always wanted to learn how to speak French." Finished with plating his sandwich and a salad for herself, she poured a glass of cold tea for him and mineral water for herself.

"Because my hotels are international," he said, "I'm fluent in the French language. I can teach you if you're interested."

She smiled over her shoulder at him and set the food and drinks on a tray. "I'd like that."

The way her dark eyes shone a deep, sincere brown, the

way she carried herself—proud and graceful—sparked something inside him. He didn't know what to call it, couldn't give it a name, this strange feeling in his gut each time he looked at her.

Walk off at the end of the week, he reminded himself. *No emotional hassles were the best approach to relationships with women.*

It had suited him well in the past. The women he dated knew the score. No tension, no promise of commitment, only a brief physical connection.

Yet with Maeve, already their relationship spun with warm-heartedness and a joggle of attraction he couldn't deny. He recalled the way her face had lit up when she'd described her dog, her Irish flat, her love of history. He liked a woman with a craving for life. Dating a woman like Maeve, he'd never be bored.

When a knock sounded on the door, Edward called for the person to come in. A ramrod-straight Pierre stood in the doorway. When he spotted Edward sitting on the balcony, his foot elevated, his pained expression affirmed that Edward's ankle sprain had somehow been his fault. "Mr. Newell, I am so sorry about your accident," he apologized for what had to be the six thousandth time. "I telephoned Mr. and Mrs. Yates and they are very concerned."

With a brief nod at Pierre, Edward puffed out a breath, wracking his brain for a way to get rid of the man.

"Must be a busy day for you, Pierre," he said. "I overheard a huge number of people from a cruise ship are checking in around noon."

The concierge gawked at his watch, and his eyes widened. "Oui, monsieur. I almost forgot."

"Well then, au revoir." Edward glanced at Maeve and winked. "That means goodbye in French."

She smirked. "Merci."

Pierre's gaze swung to her. "A staff member will check on Monsieur Newell later. May I remind you both that dinner is at eight o'clock, and Achille is serving roasted boar and zucchini beignets. Does that suit, mademoiselle?"

"We're brilliant here, Pierre," she said. "And I'm sure dinner tonight on the terrace will be magnificent." Maeve continued to slice up strawberries and blackberries, combining scoops of them into a crystal bowl. "Everything is lovely, really. You should go."

A frown creasing his normally good-natured expression, Pierre demonstrated a perfect bow and quit the room.

Maeve carried the luncheon tray onto the balcony. She nodded at his cellphone, which had been attached to his ear for nearly three straight hours. "Edward, I think you should slow down your activities this afternoon."

"You mean I overdid it with my walk from the couch to out here this morning?"

"You should have used your crutches." She set the tray on the wrought iron table. "Crutches aren't doing you any good propped against the couch."

"I don't need them."

"Because you leaned on me whenever you got up and moved anywhere." With that laughing reminder, she went into his suite for a bucket of ice and a thin towel. Reappearing, she enfolded the ice in the towel, then gently wrapped the towel around his elevated ankle.

"The swelling is better," she said. "You're a good and proper patient and do what you're told."

"And you're the first person who's ever claimed that about me, at least the *do what you're told* part."

Her smile dazzled him, and he could think of nothing he would rather do than kiss the mischievousness from her face. Instead, he ran his finger around the rim of his iced tea glass. "Thanks to you I'm feeling better."

"Thanks to Dr. Dubois." She settled onto the chair across from him and peered at the killer-view vista of sea and sky and cliffs.

Edward's gaze shifted to her. "I realize employment calls, and yet you're devoting every spare minute to me. Thank you."

"You're very welcome." She withdrew her fork from the folded napkin, set her napkin on her lap, and said a prayer. Then she poked at the lettuce on her plate. "You have work too."

"Which I attended to this morning and I'm taking the rest of the day off. But you have a boss to answer to."

"Right. Because you're the vice-president and I'm a mere worker bee."

True, he thought, understanding what else she didn't say. The enormous wealth gap between them that she had pointed out the day before. She was dressed in the most casual of clothes, and she'd secured her dark hair with an elastic band in a spur-of-the-moment bun at the top of her head. She certainly didn't have the means to purchase expensive clothes or jewelry like Davinia, the raven-haired heiress he'd been dating on and off for a couple years, yet no one looked as radiantly striking as Maeve, his compassionate caregiver with the gentle mannerisms and dainty, endearing profile.

He took a bite of his sandwich, briefly closed his eyes and sighed. "This is delicious."

"Thanks, I'm an expert at sandwich preparation because I've made hundreds in my lifetime."

He laughed. "Sandwiches for yourself?"

"Aye, and my brother Owen. He's twenty, in case you're interested."

"I'm interested in anything that has to do with you. Is he attending university?"

"He was, but he dropped out. He needs a lot of care."

Edward caught the word *care*. Instantly attentive, he sat straighter. "Why? Is he ill?"

Her earlier smile faded. "He has cancer. Thankfully, he's in remission."

Memories rushed to the fore of his mother's battle with cancer. It had been a life changer as his family adjusted to the new situation, the daily activities, the skilled medical team eventually brought into his parents' home. Even his stalwart father had, at times, been just as anxious and felt just as helpless as his sons.

"I'm sorry." Edward stayed silent for a moment. "I know firsthand how scared you and your mother must be."

"Aye." Maeve laid down her fork. Sadness lived on the edges of her nod. "When you spoke of your mother's passing the other evening at dinner, I considered telling you, but didn't want to burden you with my troubles. Part of my hesitation was selfishness, I suppose, for speaking of Owen's illness makes me sad."

He pondered this before treating himself to another bite of sandwich. "And your mother? How is she handling your brother's illness?"

"My mother ... Well, she has many interests besides Owen, especially since my father walked out on us a few years ago."

Setting his sandwich down, Edward scooped up a handful of crisps. "Somehow I sense you're the strong one in the family."

She waved a dismissive hand. "Truly, you're giving me

credit I don't deserve. Anyone would do the same and take care of the ones they love." She stabbed more lettuce with her fork. "I spoke with my mother last night, as a matter of fact, and she mentioned things are brilliant. You see, Owen moved in with her while I took this holiday. She's enjoying his company so much she suggested he live with her permanently until he lands a job and secures his own flat. It'll be good for them both to grow closer." She sighed. "Still, I'll miss not seeing him on my couch every evening."

Typical Maeve, Edward thought. Concerned about everyone except herself, wearing her sentiments on her sleeve, forever fair and honest. Deep in his chest, a heartrending affection blossomed, a protectiveness to keep her safe from sadness and hardships, and the emotions both bewildered and disquieted him. He chewed a crisp, swallowed, then picked up his iced tea and drank half the glass.

For the first time, he considered that he wouldn't be seeing Maeve again after this week. How could he return to London in a few days with only the remembrance of her lilting laugh, her pleasant ways, her kind compassion? With the afternoon sun illuminating her face, she looked so delicate, so gorgeous, she seemed almost ethereal.

As he set his iced tea glass down, she gave him a curious look. "You said the other night that you don't drink."

"Not a drop."

"May I ask why?" She waited. The silence between them interrupted solely by the sound of splashing waves below them.

He sat back in his chair. "When I attended university, one of my classmates was seriously injured in a car accident. He'd been drinking heavily. We all had been. He should never have gotten behind the wheel. Then, in a blink"—Edward snapped his fingers—"his car ran off the highway.

Now he's paralyzed from the waist down. Fortunately, no one else was hurt."

"Oh my." She held a hand to her heart. "I'll say a prayer for him."

Edward pushed out a sigh. "I make it a point to visit him whenever I can, as he lives near London." He disposed of the towel, now dripping wet from melted ice, that she'd wrapped around his ankle. He stretched out his long legs and glanced at her. She was frowning. "The twenty/twenty rule," he reminded her. "It has to be twenty minutes from now."

"So," he went on, steering the conversation in a different direction to lighten the somber moods of cancer and drunken car accidents, "who's watching Crinkles this week?"

"My mother. And your motorcycle-riding dog?"

"One of my brothers, Justin, keeps him, and you'll be relieved to know Justin doesn't ride a motorcycle." He leaned across the table and tipped up her chin. "So no worries."

Their gazes locked. He kept his hand on her chin.

Her dark eyes flashed. "Edward, remember my warning."

"What warning?"

"You know perfectly well."

He did, but he wouldn't be admitting it.

"Let's talk about your siblings." She shoved up the sleeves of his shirt and sat back. "What are their ages?"

"Twenty-eight, twenty-six, and twenty-four. And you know my age from my profile."

"Aye. You recently turned thirty. And their names?"

"Bryan, Justin and Karen. Bryan's twenty-six and Karen is twenty-four. She's very hands-on and business oriented, and helps me quite a bit with the company, but she's also unhappily married. Justin is in the middle. He was married for five years and is recovering from a bitter divorce that almost destroyed him. I learned something from Karen and Justin."

"Let me guess. You vowed never to marry."

"Guys like me are better off single. My parents worked nonstop to develop our business and I intend to continue the expansion. I'm married to my work."

"As well you should be, with all you own." She set her napkin on the table and glanced at her watch. "Well, it's more than time for me to leave. Thanks for a brilliant lunch."

"You've barely eaten."

"I've consumed more these past couple days than I normally eat in a month. For now, I should head back to my suite and input a couple hours' worth of reports before dinner. I can't afford to lose my job. Owen's medical bills are staggering. He has insurance, though it's not enough. Fortunately, I was able to assure my manager, Mrs. McShea, that I'd be effective this week. So far, I haven't managed to get an ounce of work done and don't even know if my computer works."

Right away, Edward felt remorseful. He was keeping her from her job and monopolizing her. His injury didn't require her to wait on him because the efficient hotel personnel were more than delighted to accommodate his requests. He simply wanted her to stay because he liked being around her.

She came to her feet and began stacking plates. "What about your work? After all those phone calls this morning, I'm thinking you've probably got paperwork to catch up on."

What work? What paperwork?

He stared out at the ocean, the sheer vastness that stretched to the horizon, the waves taking their cue from a sea breeze. What was truly important? Work? Family? Marriage and children as his father claimed?

He'd made a fortune following his father's lead, inputting his own grit and perseverance, along with solid investments. What did he have to show for it? Well, he'd purchased a palatial estate in Surrey in a million-dollar suburb outside London. The six-bedroom home was perched on the banks of a river and surrounded by acres of green space. He rattled around in the hollow house and seldom entertained. He was too busy working.

A golf course was nearby, but he'd never golfed in his life. He preferred a more energetic sport like soccer. To him, golf was a mental game and not physical enough.

In truth, he was too busy ... working.

Seconds ticked by. He noted Maeve watching him.

"My job is challenging," he finally said.

Her eyes widened in mock surprise. "Really?" She broke into a smile. "How do you manage such a huge conglomerate of resort hotels?"

"We employ an exceptional staff. Several smaller chains fall under the Penelope and Edward International umbrella as well, so not every hotel is a large resort. In addition, more than half are franchised."

His cell phone buzzed with a text message. He glanced at it and smiled. "Tomorrow we're going deep sea fishing."

She lifted a delicate eyebrow. "Are we now, knowing I can't swim?"

He grinned. "Our itinerary—"

"What about the Bonaparte Museum, the only tourist site on *my* wish list and the main reason I wanted to come to Corsica?"

He put on an expression of horror. "A *museum*? And here I thought you came here for me."

"If you recall, I didn't even know who you were."

Employing his most charming grin, he said, "Bonaparte Museum is on our schedule for Friday when it rains, remember? On Thursday, I'm interested in exploring the stretch of beach I pointed out to you. Are you okay with that? I'm sure Pierre can provide transportation."

"Aye. Although I'm warning you, I'll be sending a report to my boss too, especially if there's an existing hotel on site." She put on a haughty expression. "And I'll be getting the most excellent prices on the lighting and seating because I drive a hard bargain."

He nodded in acknowledgment of her superiority. "Which companies do you acquire from?"

"Mostly J and J Hospitality."

"An excellent supplier."

She laughed. "So, on Thursday we may be at war over a stretch of beach.

"I'll never be at war with you, Maeve," he said in a tone that brooked no argument. "And if I ever am, with your knowledge of battle history, you'd win."

"Your resources are stronger than mine. Wealth, power—"

"That means little when it comes to you." He hobbled to his feet, grabbed the plates from her hands and set them on the table. "Stay a while longer." He sat down again. "It's quiet and private here."

"Being alone with you isn't necessarily a good thing for me."

"Why not?" He captured her wrists. When she didn't pull away, he drew her down on his lap. Her scent was floral with a hint of citrus, adrift on the warm summer breeze.

"All this is make-believe, Edward, not real life. You and I both know where it ends."

For a long while, he stared at her. "I'm sorry you feel that way. These past few days have been some of the most enjoyable of my life. And I think you're the prettiest, most captivating woman I've ever met."

Silently, she scanned every inch of his face. "You must say that to every female."

"No, just one Irish lady who has me wanting to spend every minute with her." He traced his fingers along her high cheekbones. "When I'm with you, I forget about conglomerates and franchises and high-pressure meetings. You have a sense of serenity about you, Maeve."

She looked down, rerolling one of the sleeves of his chambray shirt. "And now, after all this flattery, you're waiting for an excuse to kiss me, I suppose."

"I don't need an excuse." He gathered her closer. "Although truer words have never been spoken."

Her gaze lifted to his, silently enticing.

It was all the encouragement he needed.

His mouth slanted over hers as he kissed her greedily. She circled her arms around his neck and kissed him back. For an eternity, their lips merged as she molded herself to him. Strands of hair fell from her loose bun, and the fine dark strands brushed against his cheek.

He deepened the kiss, cradling her face, whispering how exquisitely she fit into his arms. When his lips left hers, she drew a ragged breath and snuggled against him.

They stayed that way for an endless moment, and when she began to stir, he tightened his arms around her. "Wait another moment, luv."

The thought that they could stay like this forever, in this halcyon place, her body fitted so perfectly to his, filled him with a joyful spirit, one so happy, he hardly recognized himself.

Somewhere close by, a turtle dove cooed on a bough.

He looked out again at the ocean and the sandy shore, the smudges of royal-blue sky on the horizon. He imagined the waves tumbling over seashells and snatching them back into the ocean.

"Edward."

Her voice drew his gaze back to her. She was looking up at him, desire smoldering in her brown eyes.

"Yes?"

"I should leave. I have my job."

"If you insist on staring up at me with that expression ..." His lips strayed to hers. "I guarantee you won't be getting a morsel of work done today."

She twisted from his arms and leapt to her feet. "Shall we put more ice on your ankle?"

With that, she boosted him to the living room couch. While he dried his foot with a spare towel, she made another ice compress and then wrapped it around his ankle. He dragged a sock over it to hold it in place.

With no more warning than a knock on the door and a "Anybody home?" Carissa pranced into Edward's suite holding the hallway orchid portrait. "This fell off the wall. I'll let Pierre know." She gestured to the cameraman who'd stepped in behind her. "I'm hoping for a brief shot of you two today since we missed last evening's photo shoot on the beach."

"Carissa, I'm a fright." Maeve ran her fingers through her hair, dislodging the elastic that held it in its untidy bun. "Tell Mr. and Mrs. Yates to wait until tomorrow for better promotional material."

Fright was not the word Edward would use to describe Maeve. Her silky waves of hair teased her shoulders. Her lips, he noted, were the color of an enticing plum wine, and she looked like a woman who had just been thoroughly kissed.

"Nonsense, Maeve," Carissa said, "you're always gorgeous. Just stand together near the couch. And Edward —" Carissa clucked at his jersey shorts, then brushed crumbs from the neckline of his T-shirt. "You'll have to do. Sorry about your ankle calamity, by the way."

"I'm recovering nicely." He grinned as Maeve helped him stand.

Carissa regarded them intently, then frowned. With practiced actions, she snagged the orange lilies from the crystal vase set on the coffee table. "Maeve, hold these, and Edward, brace yourself on your crutches or you'll knock Maeve over."

Carissa stepped back, reassessed, still frowned. "Let's prop the orchid painting on the shelf behind you for color interest."

The cameraman shot multiple images until Carissa, apparently satisfied, pivoted on her ruby-red pumps, and headed for the door. "Tomorrow is deep-sea fishing," she reminded them. "And tonight, dinner is at ..."

"Eight o'clock," they all chimed.

Still chuckling as the door closed behind Carissa and the cameraman, Edward turned to Maeve. Her cheeks were flushed with high color, her laughter filling the air with goodness and pure joy. More and more, everything about the tempo of their days together—the sun-drenched island, his attraction to her, spending every waking minute with such an incredible woman—felt absolutely and utterly spot-on.

7

———

Sporting a wide-brimmed straw hat, Maeve took one last glimpse at her reflection before answering Edward's nine o'clock morning rap on her suite's door.

The night before, dinner had been expertly prepared, and she'd eaten her way through the entire meal, having discovered a love for zucchini beignets and all things French.

It seemed half the island of Corsica had dined on the terrace along with them, and Edward had reminded her that a cruise ship carrying hundreds of passengers had arrived that day. And, he'd recapped as he'd stabbed a slice of wild boar, La Bonaparte Resort was a three star Michelin resort —the highest rating—and dining there was a "must stop" in all the guidebooks when visiting Corsica.

She'd rung her mother after breakfast and been reassured her brother was fine, and then Maeve finally called Colleen. As expected, Colleen peppered their conversation with complaints about Ireland's nonstop rain, and then had demanded every detail concerning Edward and his ankle

sprain, which Maeve had texted her about. Maeve acknowledged she was enjoying an altogether marvelous week and
hadn't logged onto her computer once. Therefore, she
hadn't produced a smidgen of work.

How could she when thoughts of romance and happiness consumed her?

Dare she dream?

Love consumed her.

"How's Edward?" Colleen asked, obviously settling in for
an interrogation. "Tell me everything."

"Well, he's drop-dead handsome and kind and charming
…"

"When you sent your text with his name the other day, I
did some probing on the internet. Are you aware he's a
billionaire and one of the wealthiest men in the world? And
he's a member of the three-comma club."

"What's that?'

"Do the math. It's his yearly income, whereas ours has
no comma." Colleen chortled. "His family owns Penelope
and Edward International. You know, that hotel chain
manages over one thousand resorts and rents two hundred
thousand rooms a year."

"He certainly doesn't flaunt his wealth. He's funny and
down-to-earth and smart. And we always eat together for
dinner. In fact, yesterday we had lunch in his suite."

"Go on."

"Even though I'm seeing him often, we never run out of
things to talk about." Maeve rubbed a hand across her
temple. "Colleen, it's beautiful here, and he's so attentive
and—"

"You sound like you're already half in love with him."

"I'm simply a princess in a fairy-tale. He's my prince, and
relies on me to get around."

Truth nudged. She knew he was using his ankle as an excuse to be near her, but she certainly didn't mind.

"You're a caregiver, Maeve, but Edward isn't your brother. He's a rich playboy, if the reports in the tabloids are true. Sorry to burst your bubble, princess, but I don't want you to get hurt again. Remember your last boyfriend?"

"It's different this time. Edward's a good man and the complete opposite of Finbar."

"And you're a good woman. Enjoy yourself while you're there, just keep a clear head."

"I will." With a nod into the phone, Maeve clicked off.

She'd slept deeply and easily the night before, burrowing into the decadently thick covers and dreaming of a tall handsome man with hair the color of ebony and eyes as green as shamrocks. She wanted to deny the magnetism, like a bolt fastening her to him, as if they'd always been together. As if … She sighed.

Still, she couldn't ignore Colleen's warning. Hinging any hopes of a future with Edward, of love and commitment, well, the mere personification of the idea was meant to cause her heartache and pain. The outcome was as plain as a dark, drizzly Irish winter.

She opened her door and Edward walked gingerly into her suite. He wasn't using his crutches, again, and was careful not to put his full weight on his hurt ankle. He wished her good morning in French and then peered at her. "Anything the matter?"

"No, of course not." She swallowed hard against the lump in her throat.

Who were dreams for, she asked herself, all those fabulous Cinderella stories? The young and the foolish. Certainly not for her. Love happened to other people.

"Good," he said. "You're a treat to look at, as pretty as a gourmet candy."

"A compliment, aye?"

"Absolutely."

"I bring out the kid in you?"

"And the adult." He drew her into his arms, cuddling her for a long kiss. "Ready for Corsica Adventure Day Three?"

When she stepped back from his embrace, he scanned her tasseled swimsuit coverup, which featured a glimpse of her bare shoulders. "I'm glad you were able to pick up something pretty at the gift shop."

"I ducked into the gift shop after dinner last night, before the shop closed."

He quirked a dark eyebrow. "Is your swimsuit one piece or two?"

"You're really asking me that question?" She jabbed a playful fist at his forearm. "I'll surprise you."

"Excellent. I have a surprise for you tonight too."

"What is it?"

He grinned. "If I tell you, it would spoil the surprise."

He wore washed-out board trunks, and she was grateful he hadn't worn his tiny spandex swimsuit, for she wouldn't have known where else to look but at his perfectly-toned abs.

Mirrored aviator sunglasses were hooked onto the front of his Linus and Lucy T-shirt.

"Evidently you're partial to the Peanuts comic strip?" she noted.

"I read the daily comics, even now when they're in reruns. Since you're such a history buff, you'll be interested in this. Did you know Peanuts ran from the year 1950 to 2000, and it's been suggested it's the longest running story ever told?"

"Very interesting." She peered down at his ankle. On his feet he wore a pair of slide sandals stamped with a designer logo. "Umm, where are your crutches?"

"Don't need them, as long as I have someone to lean on."

"How's your ankle?"

"Better. Dr. Dubois said everyone heals differently. I'm apparently a fast healer."

She sighed. "And men always hear what they want and dismiss the rest. If you recall, Dr. Dubois also said you could easily injure your ankle again, so to be careful."

She slid into thong sandals and dropped heart-shaped sunglasses into her jute bag. Colleen had gifted Maeve the sunglasses with gold and pink lenses, a fun reminder of rose-colored glasses.

"They suit your outlook on life, Maeve," her friend had said.

As they walked into the lobby arm in arm, Maeve steadied Edward.

"Bonjour Monsieur and Mademoiselle Perfect Match." A bubbly Pierre stood behind his desk. "How is your ankle today, Monsieur Newell?"

"Excellent. Please thank your staff for the flowers and good wishes." Edward put an arm around Maeve's shoulders. "My lovely lady takes excellent care of me."

Maeve felt the heat rise to her face. She wasn't Edward's "lady," although he did make her feel that way.

"*Tres bon*, monsieur. Carissa will meet you by your fishing boat. Such an exciting day, oui, to fish in our beautiful waters?"

"I don't swim," Maeve reminded him.

"Swimming isn't required," Edward said. "You just need to stand at the railing of the boat and catch a fish."

"How?"

"I'll teach you."

"Your boat is a yacht charter, mademoiselle," Pierre said, "and I assure you it is spacious and stable. Below decks is a shower, toilet, table and a small galley kitchen. Jules Baduoin will be your captain. He founded the original sea company here on the island and you will appreciate his knowledge of Corsica."

"I confess, I'm nervous," Maeve said. "I've never sailed on a fishing boat, or any boat, for that matter."

"Jules is an outstanding captain," Pierre reassured her. "And remember to be back at the hotel in plenty of time because dinner is at—"

"Not tonight." Edward raised a hand. "I'm taking my luv somewhere extraordinary."

My luv. Truly, she needed to say something to stop him from using that term, but the warm feeling in the pit of her stomach told her she wouldn't.

Don't be silly, she told herself, examining and reexamining the meaning of a harmless saying. Brits used the word *luv* all the time.

Pierre riffled through a stack of papers on the reception desk. "Achille asked the chef to add to tonight's menu herb-fed veal cooked with olives, prepared as a stew. And, as always, the champagne of your choice."

Before Maeve could respond, Edward said, "As much as we enjoy the resort's food and Maeve adores her champagne"—he nudged her with his elbow—"I have a special surprise arranged for her."

Pierre leaned forward over the desk. "What is the surprise, monsieur?"

"Good luck trying to drag it out of him," Maeve said. "If the topic is surprises, Edward is as close-mouthed as a clam."

"Now I am even more curious." Pierre couldn't indulge his curiosity, though, as several tourists flooded the lobby, chattering loudly, and Nigel rushed by hauling a cart of heavy luggage.

Leaning to the side to talk to them around the guests rapidly lining up in front of his desk, Pierre gestured to a Bonaparte Resort van idling at the curbside. "Our driver will take you to Porto, a brief twenty minutes from our resort. Enjoy your day."

As they turned to the door, Edward sent Maeve a teasing smile. "You can relax on the sundeck while I fish."

"I thought you said you'd teach me how to fish?"

He clasped her hand and led her outside. "Just say the word and I'll teach you anything you want to learn."

A sunlit day greeted them, and the trees swayed gently in the heady, hot breeze. Spindles of green plants poked through the cracks in the cobblestones.

Promptly, she drew her sunglasses from her bag.

"Your fair skin will burn in minutes with this tropical sun," Edward remarked, putting on his aviators.

"The hat will shade my face." She patted the top of her head. "And I plan to slather on sunscreen."

They arrived at the dock in Porto a short while later. Carissa and a cameraman met them by the fishing boat.

Before Carissa could suggest a pose, Edward pulled Maeve into his arms and gave her a swoon-worthy kiss. "I want to spend every minute with you," he whispered.

"Just think," Carissa said, coming between them. "Next month you two will probably be on the front page of the Perfect Match website as a resounding success story." Her zeal was so contagious they all laughed.

Edward placed an arm around Maeve's shoulders. "I fancy that idea," he said, and she couldn't hide her smile.

"Everything's all set on the boat," Carissa said. "We'll just take one more picture before you get on board. And if you catch a fish today, Jules will let us know. We'll arrange to have your fish cooked in one of our partner restaurants."

After the final photo, Edward stepped away when his cellphone rang. "It's my sister, Karen," he mouthed to Maeve. "I won't be long."

"You're not joining us?" Maeve asked Carissa as she waited for Edward to finish his call.

"No. There are too many tourists visiting the island. August is high season, and I'm booked for the rest of the day." She adjusted her huge dark sunglasses and flipped back her blonde ponytail.

Edward clicked off his phone and rejoined them. As they boarded the boat, Carissa called out, "You two have fun!"

"Sure," Maeve muttered. "She gets to stay on land."

Edward laughed out loud. "And you get to stay with me." Lightly, he kissed her forehead. "Even better, I get to stay with you."

Jules, their captain, greeted them at the helm and introduced himself. His bronzed face and arms were weathered by years in the sun, his hair thin and sun bleached, his hands rough. His smile revealed a few missing teeth, but he had an easy way about him.

"My boat is over thirty feet long, allowing me to easily steer into the coves," he said, his English heavily accented. "Come take a look. I'll be in the wheelhouse once we begin."

As they pulled away from the dock, nearby boats bobbed and then settled as their wake passed. Georges, the deckhand, welcomed them on board. Edward and Maeve stood behind the console while he stored their gear below deck.

Maeve insisted on wearing a life vest. Edward did the same.

Georges set up the fishing equipment on the casting platform and pointed out where the safety gear was located. "We will begin with vertical fishing and drop the decoy to the bottom of the sea." He attached a wriggling squid to a barbed hook and passed the fishing rod to Maeve.

Edward gave her a teasing bump with his hip, then set up his own fishing rod. "May the best fisherman win."

"It's not a contest," she admonished. "And I thought you were going to help me."

"To a man, everything is a competition. I'm here if you need me, though."

"That's a relief, although it sounds more like you're saying, 'Every man for himself.'"

"Are you both amateur fishermen?" Georges asked, then pointed out a blue dolphin on the starboard side.

"So beautiful." Maeve stared at the dolphin in wonderment. "If you count the fact I've never fished in my life, Georges, then I'm a definite 'aye.' I don't know about Edward."

Edward shrugged. "I'm no expert, but I enjoy all sports. Well, most at least. I'm on the fence about golf."

Once Jules got to a sheltered fishing ground and shifted the boat to neutral, Georges went up to the bow and anchored the boat so it stayed in position. Then he guided Edward and Maeve to an open spot on the platform near the railing and they dropped their lines. Above them, buzzards nested in amber rocks, contrasting with the scrublands and wild countryside and sea. A picture-perfect postcard, Maeve thought.

"What types of fish can we expect to catch?" Edward asked, keeping a keen watch on his fishing rod.

"Snapper, tuna, and sea bream live in these waters, as well as barracuda," Jules said as he emerged from the wheelhouse. He grabbed a bottle of water from the cooler and took a swig. "You never know what will emerge at the other end of your line."

"Does that mean I might catch something big?" Maeve leaned her rod against the railing, then let out a shriek when it immediately jiggled.

"You must be fast, mademoiselle!" Jules told her. "Hold tight and start reeling."

"What am I reeling?" She bent over, laughing so hard she couldn't catch her breath. Then she tugged.

Thanks to Edward, she reeled in a snapper weighing eight ounces, and was informed by Jules the fish was not a keeper, because keeper fish were ten ounces or more. He handed her a hook remover. She removed the hook and, grimacing, released the fish back into the water.

"All by myself." She wiped her hands and smiled at Edward.

"You're a born fisherman, luv." He grinned at her and then turned to Jules. "Carissa mentioned on-site restaurants can prepare our catch for lunch. What happens if we don't catch anything?"

"No worries, monsieur. We packed spuntinu, a Corsican sandwich. You may eat at the dinette in the cabin belowdecks."

Edward nodded. "Maeve's an expert sandwich maker. Supply her with two pieces of bread and she's on her way."

She laughed. "Maybe not Corsican sandwiches."

Although she and Edward reeled in five more fish to enthusiastic applause from Jules and Georges, they opted to assemble Corsican sandwiches on deck and stay there to eat, appreciating the view of water and the uninhabited countryside.

After lunch and several bottles of water, Edward sat on the stern's swim platform and dangled his legs in the water. He patted to a spot beside him. "Sit with me, Maeve."

The waves rolled in lazy arcs, foaming as the water broke against a stretch of sugar-sand beach. A school of sunfish swam past. Among the large white-flowered sea lilies growing alongside the rocks, the shore was alive with gulls.

She settled on a beach towel beside him.

"Can I ask you something?" he began.

There wasn't the normal teasing amusement in his voice. "Aye," she said, curious where this was going.

They sat together through a long moment of silence.

"What?" she prompted.

"Why are you still single?" He steepled his hands. "A woman like you is usually engaged or married."

"I don't understand."

His gaze probed hers. "You know, a beautiful, desirable woman who puts everyone before herself. You should've been snatched up long ago."

"As a barefoot, dutiful wife?"

"No. As a woman who should be loved and cherished."

Heat flooded her cheeks. She studied her hands clasped on her lap. "I've been in relationships with men. They never work out."

Memories of the way her last boyfriend, Finbar, had ditched her came to mind. She'd thought he loved her, but it had all been a facade. It was odd how much you could care for someone and feel chock-full of honey and gladness, and then experience only a twinge of a former connection when the name resurfaced.

Edward was watching her, no doubt evaluating her distant stare, her flat tone. He brushed the sweat from his eyebrows and scanned the water. "Care to skinny-dip with me?"

She gave a bark of surprised laughter. He obviously was attempting to draw her out of her apparently upsetting memories with his scandalous suggestion.

"Was it that obvious?" she asked.

"I don't like to see you upset."

"Are you joking about the skinny-dipping?" She added an eyeroll before her gaze darted to Jules and Georges standing in the wheelhouse. Gaily, they both waved.

"Nope." Edward shrugged, mischievously, but an inner beam lit his gaze.

She acknowledged the other men's waves and then glared at Edward. "Neither am I joking. My answer to your question is an absolute no!"

"It was worth a try."

"Don't tell me you actually thought I'd agree."

"No, I didn't. If anything, you're proving to me what kind of woman you are."

"And what kind is that?"

"A woman of integrity. A woman I admire more each day."

Before she could reply, he shrugged off his T-shirt and pulled his phone from the pocket of his trunks, placing them both on a lounge chair. Then he grabbed the pull buoy Georges had supplied, smoothed a kiss on her temple and climbed down the swim ladder.

"I swim like a Spanish mackerel and I'll be right back," he said.

"What kind of fish is a Spanish mackerel?"

"A fast one."

"What about your ankle?"

"The pull buoy will support my legs and I'll use my arms. This isn't a workout. It's purely recreational."

With that, he eased into the crystal-clear depths of the Mediterranean, positioned the pull buoy between his knees, and swam the freestyle stroke. The cool splashes on her feet were a welcome relief from the heat, and someday, she pledged, she'd learn how to swim.

Drawing the line at skinny-dipping, though.

When Edward swam back to the boat, he toweled off, playfully shaking his hair so that drops of water sprayed her.

Perspiration trickled down her arms. The day was hot, the sun was high. Finally, heat won over modesty, and she yanked off her straw hat and coverup. Her bikini—a white scalloped top and flirty black bottom featuring dangling ties—showed off her slim figure. The saleswoman at the gift shop had assured Maeve the bikini was simple and chic.

"Wow." Edward dropped his towel and gave a low whistle. "You're stunning, luv." He hesitated, seeming to grope for words. "Are you aware you're drop-dead gorgeous?"

When she started to protest, he caught his arm around her waist. As he pulled her close, his wet bare skin brushed against hers. He didn't try to kiss her, simply holding her as they stood by the railing. Together they admired the craggy peaks of les Calanche Cliffs breaking against the azure skyline.

"Do you approve of my swimsuit?" Suddenly shy, she couldn't quite meet his gaze.

"I love everything about you. Surely you must know that by now." He smiled at her. This rising heat in his cheeks was more than sunburn, and a smoldering desire darkened his eyes to a deep forest-green.

"I couldn't find a one-piece swimsuit in my size," she said.

He brushed a soft kiss against her lips. "Exceedingly good fortune for me and every other male on this island."

Georges came back out on deck to raise the anchor, and Jules navigated the boat into a cove that offered dappled shade and a waterfall gushing from a mountain. After Georges dropped the anchor again, Jules came out of the wheelhouse and eyed Maeve appreciatively.

"*Tu es belle*, mademoiselle."

"Merci." Her cheeks were most likely scarlet by now, and she caught Edward frowning at Jules.

"Georges and I are grabbing an afternoon snack before we go back to the harbor," Jules said, snagging another bottle of water.

"Take your time," Edward called after them as they made their way below deck. He laid his towel out beside hers. "Finally." He gathered her in his arms and kissed her long and hard. "Privacy."

She wedged a hand between them to create some distance. "You know how I feel about being alone with you. Especially when you look at me with an expression of such … I don't know how to describe it. With such interest."

"Interest is a good start," he said. His breath caressed her cheek, rousing feelings she couldn't define. "Remember you can trust me."

"Aye." She did trust him. But when she was with him, she didn't trust herself.

He bent his head. "Then you realize the affection I feel for you."

She couldn't tell if he was serious or joking, but she was here for several more days, and it seemed senseless not to enjoy her time with him.

Slow and steady, he kissed her again and she couldn't help herself, gliding her hands across the hard contours of his bare chest. She heard his soft gasp as he pulled her closer and gazed into her eyes. She stood on her tiptoes and slipped her arms around his neck. Mouth to mouth, they kissed as if the sun could whirl away and reappear, taking its time before reality revisited.

When the kiss ended, he grinned. "I'm very, very glad I came to Corsica."

"And why are you grinning like a Cheshire cat?"

He grabbed for his phone on the lounge chair and typed a text message. "Because our Wednesday adventure isn't over. I've arranged for us to travel someplace special for dinner this evening."

"Several of the Corsican guidebooks featured restaurants tucked in straw huts near the sea. They sounded divine. Are we going to one of those?"

"Somewhere better."

"Will the resort drive us there?" she persisted. "Several of the restaurants are an hour away."

"We're merely forty-five minutes from our destination." He kissed her again. "And I suggest you dress up for a one-of-a-kind occasion."

She peered at the sun, a ribbon of muted orange as it began its descent. "As if there's enough daylight left after an ideal afternoon like this to do anything better."

"We don't need daylight." He brushed his lips up and down her neck. "And our evening will surpass everything we've done so far."

"Edward," her tone spun over the boyish edge of his, "where on earth are we going?"

At his wide grin, a sizzle of pure attraction coursed through every inch of her.

"We're flying to France." With that announcement, he turned off his phone and set it beside his T-shirt on the lounge chair. "The pilot is fueling my company's private jet to take us to my favorite restaurant along the French Riviera."

8

———

"The French Riviera?" Colleen repeated, when Maeve rang her the following morning. "You flew in his private jet to dine in one of the poshest restaurants on the French Riviera?"

"Aye. Actually, it's his family's private jet."

"Okay, that settles it. Does Edward have any brothers?"

Maeve gave a hoot of laughter. "He has a sister who seems to have an exemplary business sense, and two younger brothers. But what's the craic with Colin? Are you on-again or—"

"Off-again," Colleen completed. "He wasn't my type, anyway. He didn't want to work, but he certainly liked to spend money."

"If he didn't work, where did he get his money?"

"He wanted to get it from me. Thus, I told him to crack on. He was locked half the time anyway."

Drunk.

Maeve rested on her king-sized bed against a pile of fluffy silver pillows. Despite arriving back at La Bonaparte Resort in the early morning hours, she'd hardly slept. Who could sleep after dining in the courtyard of an eighteenth-century French mansion beneath one-hundred-year-old trees, seated across from the most handsome man she'd ever seen, a man who'd never taken his admiring gaze off her?

Cozy and unpretentious, the painted-wood brasserie was tucked down a cobblestoned lane and brimmed with old world Provencal charm.

Edward had been impeccable in sharply pressed black trousers, jacket, and white shirt. His sea-green eyes created a jump in her heartbeat each time she met his stare. His thick black hair was tousled by the ocean breeze, and his strong hands had held hers. The intimate round table had been covered in blue and yellow French linens, a pattern depicting sea and sky, Edward explained. He went on to say that there were close to thirty three-star restaurants in France, and he'd chosen his favorite to share with her.

The menu had featured five courses, and she savored the earthy taste of a beetroot topped with caviar, a delicacy she'd never sampled. Edward preferred the home-baked baguettes and dessert trollies rolling between the cozy tables.

Often, he leaned across the table to brush a kiss along her ear. A full-out laugh had erupted from him as she told a story about her animated, eager-to-please pug. He described a particularly memorable camping trip he'd taken with his lab.

In fact, they talked all evening, hardly pausing to catch a breath.

It was the romantic setting, she decided as she gazed at his face.

But no, it was more, much more. She was seriously falling headfirst in love with him. And it was reckless and divine.

No. She pushed her contemplations back and attempted to regroup. Too many emotions, too quickly. Surely, she was smart enough to keep thoughts of love away.

Her heart, however, didn't want to heed her hesitations.

What was it about this charismatic man? No matter how much time they spent together, they never ran out of conversation. They declined the expensive French wines and Champagnes the waiter suggested, settling on sparkling water. *Sorbet aux framboises*, a mouth-watering raspberry sorbet, had been served between courses to "cleanse the palate and stimulate the appetite."

Edward hadn't brought up his business, or his family, or resuming his London lifestyle.

His life in the real world.

She hadn't spoken of Ireland. She'd begun to wish her days, her nights, her week here in Corsica spent with Edward, would never end. When she was with him, her difficulties slipped to a far corner of her mind.

After dinner, they strolled the perimeter of the restaurant's courtyard, tracing a whiff of honeyed aroma to hollyhocks growing upward against the stone walls.

He'd stood close behind her, his arm around her waist, indicating tiny hilltop villages and ancient paths spiraling to the sea. Lifting her hair, he inhaled a deep breath and nuzzled her neck. "I love the scent of your hair."

"You mean the smell of fish from our boating adventure?" she joked.

"No, I mean your fragrance, like an exotic, sparkling lemon." He kissed her mouth and then murmured, "I like the flavor of your lips too."

"Really? Like beets and caviar?" She still wasn't sure when he was joking or when he was being flirtatious. She only knew she was enchanted by him, and close to losing her heart.

He dotted her face and her lips with soft kisses. His mouth was still moist from their meal, and he tasted of sugar-coated raspberries and sparkling spring water.

Someday, he promised that he'd show her the nearby towns, for he knew the region well. They would take their dogs and wander narrow cobblestone streets flanked by fields of lavender and acres of yellow sunflowers. She could immerse herself in history, and he'd savor the quality of a quintessential French lifestyle—watching old men play lawn games and fishermen hauling in their catch of the day, or buying bread fresh from the bakeries in town.

Lately, he murmured, he'd been longing for a slower pace in order to truly appreciate life.

"I'd like you to see my home near London," he finished.

She hesitated. Save for Corsica and America, she'd never traveled outside her safe little Irish world where brogues were melodic, laughter was frequent and friendly pubs stood on every corner.

Then she looked into his eyes and agreed with a definite, emphatic, "Aye."

They were both reluctant to end the magical night, and lingered over cappuccino and raspberry macarons at an outdoor café. On a side street, the music of an accordionist playing a French melody had drifted down to them. They faced their chairs toward the sea, holding hands, watching the colors of midnight pool on the harbor's waters.

And there she told him everything, her mother's continuous flings with men who lived in a kip, a dump. About her absentee father. About facing up to her worries and fears and even guilt because Owen was sick and she wasn't.

She also revealed her stints in low-budget movie roles as

an extra, the need for time-consuming rehearsals for a scene that lasted only a minute or two, and the constant rejections that came with show business.

"Persevere," he encouraged, tapping her coffee cup with his, and she instantly felt right as rain.

"Can this all be real?" she murmured, half to herself.

"What?"

"The French Riviera, this night ...you."

He flinched, then tipped up her chin and said softly, "Very real, luv."

Why had she told this man, whom she'd only known a few days, so much about herself? Because, she rationalized, of the surreal setting in a romantic new country, along with the emotionally charged days. Or perhaps, although she'd stated on her profile she was a good listener, he was better—asking questions, genuinely relating to what she said and offering to help her in any way he could.

Of course, she had refused his help. She'd learned long ago to stand on her own two feet, to rely on no one else.

Although, with Edward she had no barriers, and he had applauded her milestones as she outlined her university years and how she'd landed her job as purchasing agent for Merrimac.

"I'll teach you another French term," he said, leaning back in his chair.

"What is it?"

For a split-second he said nothing. Then he leaned close, so close his breath touched the strands of her hair. *"Joie de vivre."*

"Which means?"

"The joy of living. The French believe life should be about food and drinks and sharing special occasions with the most important people in your life."

His voice had become oddly rough, and he briefly closed his eyes. She studied him in his moment of vulnerability, trying to decipher all he meant.

And then she struggled to think at all, because poignant tears clogged her throat.

He opened his eyes and she smiled into his searching gaze, realizing the same emotion coming through him had also passed through her.

That connection again. Deeper and more pronounced as the minutes flew.

"Was dinner romantic?" Colleen interrupted Maeve's musings.

"More than you can ever imagine. We sat outside in a courtyard that overlooked a harbor on the Cote d'Azur. Women entertained on their cruisers, wearing cropped trousers and carrying basket bags, very Grace Kelly looking. Edward recognized several socialites and celebrities."

"All glitz and glamor on the French Riviera. What did you wear?"

"My black lace sheath dress and ankle-strap sandals."

"The three-inch stilettos?"

"Aye." Maeve stared out the window wall of her bedroom, which framed the varying landscapes, from the glorious ocean to the rough mountain ranges. "And Edward promised next time we visit the Cote d'Azur, we'll take a drive along the coast and he'll show me his family's resort there. And he said we'll enroll in a cooking class. He doesn't cook, and I'd love to learn how to prepare French cuisine and pair meals with wines and Champagnes."

Edward promised ...

Next time ...

He said ...

There was a pause and Maeve feared the call had been disconnected. "Colleen?"

"I'm here. Look, Maeve, are you certain a guy like him is single?"

"Aye. He told me he's married to his work."

"Then believe him. Regardless of his obvious interest in you, he's off-limits. Even if you wanted to continue seeing him after this week, a long-distance relationship never works. So don't fall too hard, promise? It took you months to get over Finbar."

Maeve rubbed her forehead. "No worries, Colleen. I'm a practical woman and I'll be home soon enough. Who can blame me for appreciating every magical minute?" She rolled to her stomach and studied the morning sunlight, endless pinks and reds spreading across the sky. "Edward and I are exploring more of the island today. There's a strand of beach for sale, and his company might be interested in acquiring the property. If a hotel is on site, Merrimac will want a report on it as well." Maeve came to her feet and cupped the phone to her ear. "See you on Sunday, all right? After I land in Dublin, I'll visit my mom and Owen and then ring you."

"I'll expect every single solitary detail about you and Edward."

"Aye." After assuring Colleen she planned to begin working once she'd viewed the available beach property, Maeve clicked off.

Edward texted her shortly afterward, telling her to enjoy a lazy morning. He was dealing with an unforeseen business problem and needed to talk with Karen, and he would pick her up at one o'clock.

Regardless of her notes from earlier days, Maeve didn't work a smidgen, too busy propping her feet up on the balcony and appreciating the variegated blues of sea and sky.

Several hours later, Edward rapped on her suite door, calling out, "*Bonne après-midi*. Good afternoon, gorgeous." He strode out onto her balcony and leaned down to kiss her.

"*Bonne après-midi*," she agreed.

"Your French is improving every day. Did you miss me this morning?"

She smiled and gazed into his eyes. "Of course."

"Did you think about me?"

"A little." *More than a little.* "Is this a solo interrogation?" She pulled back. "Did you think about me?"

Lazily, he fingered an errant wisp of her hair and wound it around his finger.

"I never *stop* thinking about you, Maeve."

A trill of heat started in her belly and she shivered. "Well, I'm ready."

"Almost." He glanced at her sandals. "I recommend you pack a soft-soled flat shoe and wrap for later."

She poked through her closet and emerged with both. "Later? Why?"

"Another surprise." He unzipped the canvas tote he carried and combined her shoes and pashmina wrap with his loafers and tan sweater. Without further explanation, they headed to the lobby.

In response to Pierre's queries, Edward explained the location of the beachfront acreage his company was interested in purchasing.

"Ah, oui." Solemnly, Pierre parroted the location. "The former owner went bankrupt, and the property is an excellent opportunity."

"My resort may compete with yours once we're up and

running." Edward inclined his head in a half-joking nod. "Can I persuade you to come work for me?"

Pierre straightened even more, if that were possible. "Monsieur, if I am honest, non. No other hotel can compare with this beautiful resort." He swept out his arm toward the grandiose lobby, the ornate chandelier dangling above the broad staircase. "Will I leave all this? Never."

"I appreciate your loyalty, Pierre, but my offer is always open. If not this resort, then any my company owns." With that, he tucked Maeve's hand into the crook of his arm. "Ready for Corsican Adventure Day Four?"

A smile touched her lips, and she pretended she had to think about it. "Perhaps."

In all honesty, she couldn't wait to spend every waking second with him.

As they turned to leave, Pierre enquired, "I trust your dinner last evening on the French Riviera was memorable?"

"How do you know where ..." Maeve interrupted her own question with a head shake. Pierre made a point of knowing the goings-on of all his guests.

"Tonight, we will plan on you both dining on our terrace at eight?" Pierre continued.

"Sorry." Edward held up a hand, a déjà vu of yesterday. "I've made other arrangements for us."

A flutter of anticipation went through her body. Maeve glanced at him uncertainly as she tossed her jute bag over her shoulder. "You're positive I'm dressed appropriately for our mystery date?"

He examined her patterned red silk halter top and tailored capris. On impulse, she'd donned her crystal chandelier earrings, the same pair she'd worn to dinner the night before. As his affectionate gaze returned to her face and lingered, she felt that familiar flush creep up her body.

He wore sandals, striped linen Bermuda shorts, and a kelly-green golf shirt. Utterly impervious to a gaggle of women gawking at him from the bar, he guided Maeve out the lobby's front door.

The hotel van reached the strand of beach in the predicted twenty minutes, and Edward directed the driver to wait for them.

The area proved stunning, the azure sky fringed by dozens of precipitous mountain peaks. Out on the water, sails on colorful fishing boats snapped in the wind, and gleaming steeples atop medieval church towers crowned the nearby hills.

One by one, she and Edward peered inside a row of deserted whitewashed cottages with deep-orange trumpet vines twining up their sides.

Edward took off his sunglasses. Shading his eyes, he gazed at the sea. "What do you think of the property, Maeve?"

As always, the water was as turquoise as a precious jewel, the sand a soft golden brown.

"Ideal for a resort," she said, "though I'm not keen on the notion of spoiling the beach with a high-rise."

"My company will evaluate the target. I'm certain regulations are in place to preserve the natural habitat. Regardless, my intention is to enhance the Corsican character."

"Your intention? What does that mean?"

"It means my assurance. You can count on my word, much as I can count on yours." He gave a firm nod.

She saw the glint in his gaze, the joy of the hunt. This was another side of Edward, the keen-eyed businessman she hadn't glimpsed before.

"And your company?" he was asking. "If the deal went

through for Merrimac, you'd probably receive better bids from your hospitality supplier."

"You mean J and J? Aye, they'd probably offer me competitive pricing on their lighting and seating, but I've never been involved in a project of this size. Granted, I assume Merrimac's intentions are the same as yours." Reflectively, she exhaled. "Still, my vote is to keep this property undisrupted. Once it's gone, it's gone. I'm obviously not a good businessperson, aye?"

"Development is good … sometimes." He gazed at her thoughtfully. "Although I don't want to be the guy who overdevelops this gem of an island any more than it already is."

His phone buzzed, and pensive, he glanced at the text message. His mood changed, and he grinned widely, shoving his phone into his pocket. "Ready for another surprise?"

He grabbed her hand and hailed the Bonaparte van. When they settled into the backseat, he asked the driver to take them to the Bonifacio marina.

"Edward, hold on, where are we going?" Maeve asked. "Your adventures are always special, but this time I want an answer before we arrive."

"We're going to a yacht party."

Rapidly, she blinked, the concept of a yacht party as elusive as traveling to the moon. "What in the world is that?"

"People host a party on their yachts and we're invited."

"Please don't tell me," she ran a hand along her hair, which she'd styled in an elegant low bun, "you own a yacht as well as a private jet."

"No." His smile turned potent. "My friend Bentley, the guy who signed me up for Perfect Match, texted this morning with an invitation and he just confirmed. He's anchored near the harbor. He wants to meet you and said he invited someone."

"Who?"

"Don't know. A surprise, I imagine."

"Is he friendly with any movie stars?" Maeve's eyes widened, and she fidgeted with the edge of her halter top. "I'm not dressed properly. What do I say, how do I act?"

"You act like yourself, Maeve. And if you're unsure, remember you're a professional actress." He gave her hands a reassuring squeeze. "Believe me, just be yourself and you'll charm the entire ship. Now, the first thing you do when you board is to remove your shoes. Or—" He held a finger to her lips before she objected. "You wear the flat shoes you brought."

The van dropped them off at the harbor's tip where a limo tender waited. Timothe, the tender's helmsman, provided a hand onto the boat, pledging to deliver them dry and comfortably. A mega yacht with flashing lights was anchored in the distance.

Overcome with awe at the size of the yacht, she couldn't utter an audible word.

She only knew Edward would stay beside her, soothing her discomfiture. The knowledge made her happy and calmed her nerves.

As the tender sped toward the yacht, they relaxed in its roomy interior with the glass roof open. The wind blew swiftly across her cheeks, snatching wisps of her hair. A filmy mist teased the fringes of the horizon as day eased to dusk. How novel this all was, every hour filled with giddy excitement and heady experiences. With Edward's arm around her, she settled into the saddleback leather seat for the quiet, smooth ride.

When they reached the mother ship, as Edward had named it, he opened his tote, and they switched their shoes.

"Time to charm," he said. He wrapped the pashmina around her shoulders to ward off the sea breeze and steered her onto the limo's stern.

So much of what she'd learned about him was in his little, thoughtful gestures, his constant consideration of her comfort. The way he held doors for her, or took her wrap, or stood respectfully until she was seated. The way he paid attention to her, supportive and encouraging. All these traits were a matter of course for him, because he was a perfect gentleman.

And she recognized that every one of those qualities were the foundations of a true, loving relationship.

She took a deep breath of salt-laced air and squared her shoulders. "Aye. I'm ready."

"Courage, luv. Remember, these people are my friends." He took her hand as they boarded. "I assume my sister Karen will be here. This morning she informed me she'd intended to snag an invitation if it was a go."

As if on cue, a woman in an off-the-shoulder chiffon who had an astonishing resemblance to Edward walked toward them. After embracing his sister with an affectionate hug, Edward introduced Maeve. Then he excused himself to speak with an older man who had shouted "Bonjour!" to them.

"He's one of my father's associates in Nice," Edward explained to Maeve. "I won't be long."

Karen watched her brother walk away, and then turned her crystal-green gaze on Maeve.

"He's very attracted to you," she remarked.

"Who? Edward?" Maeve's mouth opened, but for a second, nothing came out. "Why would you say that?"

"Because he talks about you nonstop."

Maeve felt her cheeks blaze with color. "We've only just met. We were placed together through a dating agency. Neither of us really wanted to be here."

"Well, it's obviously an on-target arrangement for you both. Trust me, he's love-struck. I watched him when you climbed aboard—the way he looks at you, the heat in his gaze—" Karen fanned her face. "My brother and I talk about business every day. Since he arrived in Corsica, he's spent maybe five minutes talking hotels, and then the rest of the time he talks about you."

The women remained in sociable silence for several beats while Maeve mulled this information over. Then she shook her head. "You're wrong, Karen."

"When it comes to matters of the heart, I am right. And you are in love with him."

"How do you know?" Surely, Maeve thought, her feelings for Edward weren't that obvious. Or were they?

"Because I am a woman, so I know you." Karen enhanced her statement with a breezy smile. "And I am his sister, so I know him."

After a brief pause, Maeve said, "The Perfect Match meter is running out."

She tried not to think about it, because thinking caused a sadness she didn't want to face.

Her arm through Maeve's, Karen steered her over to a buffet table ladened with appetizers and scooped up a slice of cantaloupe. "No. Edward will continue to pursue you until he wins you. When he loves, he loves deeply—Our mother, our family ..." Contemplative, she dabbed her lips with a cloth napkin and sighed. "When we lost our mother, our father's grief was so painful to see. Our parents were very much in love, you know. Up till today, Edward hasn't given his heart to any woman. Now he has."

"Sometimes I don't know if he's joking or sincere," Maeve said cautiously.

"Men usually try to hide what they feel most passionate about." Karen shrugged. "He was our family's rock when our mother got sick. After she passed, he closed up and immersed himself in business. I sense you will be good for him." She greeted a passing friend with a French air kiss. "I'm without my husband tonight and enjoying a girl's night out before I divorce him," she explained to Maeve. "When I heard about Bentley's party, I rearranged my schedule so I could be here. I was curious to meet you, and now I am satisfied." She hugged Maeve tightly. "I hope we can become good friends. I'm the only woman in my family, floundering in a sea of males and I need another woman's voice. I hope it's sooner rather than later."

EDWARD HELPED Maeve walk across the huge teak deck and through the midst of chattering partygoers.

"And how did you find my sister this evening? She's a veritable chatterbox."

"She's lovely," Maeve replied, "and very friendly. Did you know she's divorcing her husband?"

"I've heard all about it. And from what she's explained, I can't fault her."

"Edward!" Automatically, Edward looked up and spotted Bentley, their host. He'd noticed Bentley had anchored his yacht just far enough out to sea, so that his guests needed to board another boat to reach it. Typical Bentley and his flair for the dramatic, never to be outdone. Competition was normal between the two men, and Edward acknowledged that he often encouraged it. However, it could go on and on, and truthfully, the money, the bragging rights, meant nothing to him. He much preferred Maeve's warm body pressed to his, her languorous gaze after he'd kissed her, the simple pleasure of hearing her melodic Irish brogue.

"And this must be your Perfect Match," Bentley said. His pale-blue gaze leveled on Maeve, and he didn't bother to hide his curiosity. Without warning he seized her hands, pulled her close, and welcomed her with a triple cheek kiss. "I'm Bentley, Edward's friend from university."

She took a step back. "Hello, Bentley. I'm Maeve."

"Look at this beauty! Edward certainly aced this week with the likes of you, chérie. From the little I got out of him, I knew he was smitten and chose to see you for myself. I'm a twit for entering his name on the Perfect Match website instead of mine. Come with me." Before Maeve could protest, Bentley drew her hand through his arm and started to move away from Edward with her. "Everyone wants to learn all about you."

"Kindly take your hands off my luv," Edward said in a low voice.

Bentley turned back. "Your *luv*?" His blond eyebrows rose in laughing irony. "Point taken, mate. I knew things moved fast in our circle." He scooted back, hands up, palms out, and then clapped a hand on Edward's shoulder. "Sorry you suffered an ankle sprain. The fellows had a jolly laugh —you being an outdoorsman and a lovely, petite Irish-woman coming to your rescue. If it weren't for her, you might still be strung on a high cliff atop Corsica."

Standing close to Maeve, Edward felt himself stiffen at Bentley's jibe. He stiffened further when Bentley took up two flutes brimming with Champagne from a passing waiter. He offered one to Edward and one to Maeve.

"As you well realize, I don't drink," Edward said shortly.

"And the lady?" Bentley demanded.

"While I can't speak for her, I know she is exceedingly fond of Champagne."

Maeve hesitated, a quiet longing in her gaze as she eyed the crystal flutes. "Not tonight. Sparkling water is fine." As she declined, she glanced at Edward.

Bentley caught the glance. "Surely, Maeve, you don't ask this Ivy League bloke for permission?"

"I assure you, Bentley." She slanted Edward an impudent smile and brushed her hand across his. "I can speak for myself."

Edward grinned and wrapped his arm around her. "And I can verify that fact."

"So, Maeve." Bentley gulped down half of one of the glasses of Champagne. "Edward mentioned you're in the hotel business. What's the name of the chain you own?"

She laughed. "I'm merely one of the purchasing agents for the Merrimac Company in Ireland."

"A purchasing agent?" Bentley frowned, and then turned to look over his milling guests.

The well-dressed men and women, in a dazzling display of the moneyed at ease, snickered and chattered, toasting each other with champagne flutes in one hand and plates of shrimp cocktail in the other.

"Follow me, Maeve." Bentley turned on his heels, seemingly assuming Maeve would join him. When she didn't, he looked back at her, frowned again, and started forward anyhow. Over his shoulder, he hollered, "There's plenty of liquor. I'll catch up with you two later."

"Thank you, Bentley, but we don't—" Maeve inclined her head, although Bentley was well past them.

Several nearby guests turned to study her, no doubt wondering who she was, and Edward tightened his hold around her. He felt her push out a breath and set her shoulders straight as she sent the curious group a straightforward smile.

His heart gave an unexpected lurch. She might be taken aback by all this, but she would never cower. Not his Maeve.

Completely unassuming, she was a natural in his often-times unnatural world of excessive abundance. In a world where being seen at all the right places with all the right people was more important than a person's character or deeds, she was the opposite, preferring to carry herself with modest dignity and grace.

"We'll find an open spot by the railing and I'll fix you a plate of food," he said.

"Always the gentleman." She beamed at him. "Even with a hurt ankle that doesn't seem to bother you in the least anymore."

"It still hurts a little, so you can continue to fuss over me." He grinned and was rewarded with her smile in return. "Notwithstanding, I'm a new man because of your judicious care."

"Notwithstanding and judicious in one sentence? You're beginning to sound like Dawson Yates."

He laughed out loud. She looked gorgeous tonight. Her beautiful face and radiant smile brought a surge of longing, crumbling his world weariness. There was an irresistible charm about her, an effortless sparkle that beckoned men closer.

His quick look around confirmed that men were, indeed, staring at her.

Well, he'd make sure each one of them realized that Maeve was his and his alone.

A nagging thought brushed the corners of his mind.

Since when? Hadn't he declared that first night at the hotel that Perfect Match was a game that would end when their allotted week did? Yet when he held her and she snuggled against him, he knew she fancied him. And he fancied her.

Silently, he shook his head.

Fancied was such a trite term.

He wanted her, more than anything or anyone. He wanted to hear her engaging laugh every day of his life, to banter and talk seriously, to fill her days and nights with the same pleasure she gave him.

He wanted her to care for him as much as he cared for her.

Because he loved her.

Love?

The thought swung him impressively back on his heels, so much so that Maeve turned to peer at him.

Love? Absolutely not. No man with a milliliter of sense fell in love with a woman he'd known for less than a week.

But here she was, beautiful and alluring, and he couldn't deny his feelings when his heart skipped a beat every time he looked at her. He was completely and utterly in love with her.

"Edward, are you all right?" Dark with concern, her gaze held his. "Does your ankle hurt, just after you've finished telling me you're okay? I won't be telling you that you should've brought your crutches, although you should have."

"I'm fine, luv."

He couldn't look away from her. Her silk top clung to her

slender curves. Her subtle fragrance of citrus and sunshine perfumed the air. She looked, well, smashing and quite enchanting.

"Honest. I was joking about the fussing." His gaze veered to the buffet and beverage stations situated at strategic points along the deck. Dismissing his ankle with a wave, he asked, "Do you care for stuffed mushrooms or beef Wellington?"

Two hours later, Edward was relieved at a break from the swarm of outwardly good-natured acquaintances who had converged on them. He'd sensed a malevolence toward Maeve from a few women when they learned she *worked* for a company and didn't *own* one. He knew Maeve heard the occasional murmurs of "Gold digger" from the way she gripped her hands together, and he had to refrain from lighting into the insensitive women.

"Ignore them, luv," he whispered at one point as she curled her fingers tightly around his.

"I feel so unsophisticated," she confessed. "Like I'm a silly girl playing dress-up in a world where I don't belong."

"You're perfect. It's them. They don't belong in your world." He sealed his assurance with a solid kiss.

Unlike the women, the men evidently agreed with Edward, showing a decided interest in Maeve. She accepted their over-the-top compliments, their gallant offers to fetch her plates of chocolate-dipped strawberries or a dozen French lemon tartes. With a flattering flush in her cheeks, she conversed with wit and self-assurance.

Now that they were finally alone for a beat, Edward asked if she wanted more sparkling water.

"Aye. Then can we please leave?" She sampled a last bite of strawberry, her mouth enticing, as rosy as her red-patterned blouse.

Her sparkling water forgotten for a minute, he pressed a kiss to her lips. "The problem with a yacht party is we're stranded until the boat heads back to the dock. Since I figured Bentley would try to strand everyone out here until dawn, I hired our tender for the night. We can call for him to come back for us at any time."

Edward circled back with her water a few minutes later, not pleased that Bentley had taken his place next to Maeve. The two of them were looking out at a calm sea. No waves, no white crests. Midnight and moonless, although the ocean mirrored the glitter from the yacht's masthead and sidelights.

"Did you twist an offer of marriage from him yet?" Edward overheard Bentley ask Maeve before taking a gulp of whatever alcohol was in his high ball. Probably vodka.

Maeve kept her head high. "You've known Edward since your university days, so certainly you must realize no one can 'twist' anything out of him."

Edward wedged himself between the two of them, forcing Bentley to step away.

"Back so soon?" Bentley said. "I was just asking Maeve about your relationship."

"And Maeve wasn't naïve enough to presume she had to acknowledge your disrespectful question."

Undeterred, Bentley inquired, "So ... this match arrangement. Do you two share a room?"

"We each have our own suite," Maeve answered. She cloaked a pleading glimpse at Edward, then pointedly stared at the shore. It was high time they got off this yacht, she was silently telling him.

"You're not sleeping together?"

"Maeve and I only met a few days ago," Edward said.

"That's never stopped you before."

Edward's heart pounded a furious beat against his ribs. Weighing his options, he decided not to end the night on a fistfight. With a slight inclination of his head along with a bland smile, he changed the subject. "Before we joined you tonight, Maeve and I discovered a beachfront property for sale."

"Isn't the Newell family wealthy enough? Why purchase another resort for Penelope and Edward?"

"Or for Merrimac," Maeve put in. "My company is also searching for hotel property."

Bentley sniffed his glass. "You'll have little say. You're only a mere purchasing agent."

"Aye," she agreed. "Although J and J Hospitality has saved Merrimac thousands of dollars through the years because of their low bids."

"I've used them on occasion," Bentley said. "They've never allowed my hotels reduced rates."

"Maeve drives a tough bargain for the best price when dealing with suppliers for hotel seating and lighting." With a playful grin, Edward raised her hand to his lips for a fleeting kiss. "She's a skillful buyer."

Bentley slammed back the rest of his drink. "I'm sure Merrimac's accounting department is delighted, although we all like to generate a substantial profit in our businesses."

A limo tender was speeding toward them. Edward wondered if maybe their driver, Timothe, had read Maeve's mind. But it wasn't theirs, so he pulled out his phone to text Timothe to come get them.

Maeve had also noticed the tender. "Are you expecting one more guest, Bentley?" she asked. "If so, he or she has redefined the phrase 'fashionably late.'"

Maeve pulled her pashmina tight around her shoulders, and Edward tucked the ends around her waist. When had the air turned so bitter? he wondered, surveying the sky. All the stars were hidden behind a haze of black clouds. Friday, he remembered, called for showers.

Impatient for Timothe to arrive, he shifted. He was in a hurry to go back to the restful, familiar confines of La Bonaparte Resort, instead of being trapped with Bentley. Somehow, he vowed, he'd make tonight up to Maeve and atone for the behavior of his insolent friends.

"It is a she," Bentley answered Maeve. "And *fashionable* is her middle name."

"Did she travel far?" Maeve asked as the tender pulled up alongside the yacht and a woman stood up. She wasn't the only one watching as the stunning, sensual woman in a form-fitting silver dress boarded the yacht.

Edward keyed in Timothe's number again, willing his phone to connect faster.

"She sailed from Italy, chérie," Bentley answered. "She summers in the Italian Alps and winters in Milan. Her family owns a conglomerate of high-fashion clothing stores, and she is the sole heiress."

Edward swallowed hard, trying to get rid of the odd taste in the back of his throat.

"Italian *Vogue* will undoubtedly discover her, if they haven't already." Maeve watched as the woman glided toward them, waving and calling hello in Italian to various people. "Is she your super-model girlfriend?"

"Edward," the woman called. "I've missed you!"

Edward's head snapped up, and he found himself the center of too many people's attention. Smug Bentley, acquaintances watching avidly, and wary Maeve. And Davinia, her smile as stiff as her tight dress.

"Why haven't you answered when I've texted and

called?" Davinia closed the distance between them. "I thought you fell off the planet this week, Edward."

Stillness reigned, split only by the subtle motor of Timothe's tender finally nearing the yacht.

"Didn't he tell you, Maeve?" Bentley's mocking tone cut through the awkward silence. "Davinia DeVito is Edward's sweetheart. They've dated for years and are practically engaged."

9

Just as the Corsican weather report had predicted, Friday morning brought rain. Maeve peered out the sliding doors leading to her balcony and watched a seabird take flight. Sleek and chilly, the face of the red cliffs looked unfriendly, shadowed by a fierce downpour and framed against an empty bleak sky.

The previous evening, after Edward swiftly boarded the tender behind her, he'd responded to her frosty silence by asking if he could explain himself.

Although she'd felt all the color drain from her face when Bentley had introduced Davinia as Edward's sweetheart, she'd listened to Edward. Still, the shockwave of his betrayal had thumped the breath from her.

She had no reason to feel that way. She had known the entire week was for an online dating promotion. Nonetheless, tears had burned the backs of her eyes, and she'd studiously avoided his gaze.

He'd dated Davinia, he said, although he certainly wasn't engaged to her and didn't plan on ever marrying the Italian heiress.

As the waves vibrated against the speeding limo, Maeve had sunk against the seat and tried to weigh whether or not he was lying. More important, she questioned why his relationship with Davinia mattered so much to her.

Once they reached shore, Edward opened his canvas bag and slipped on his tan sweater, then offered her shoes to change. "Bentley's gone too far with his so-called practical jokes," he muttered. "When we attended university, his pranks were silly. Now they're mean-spirited and hurtful."

"Aye." Her anger had bubbled to the surface, and she let it loose. "Life's a joke to idle men who have more time and money on their hands than they know what to do with.

"Are you referring to me?"

"Perhaps." She heard the Irish temper in her voice and couldn't even it out.

"Is this all because you're jealous of Davinia?"

Bristling at the gleam of satisfaction in his gaze, she didn't answer, chiding herself for refusing to admit the truth, even to herself. She was relieved the tender had reached shore, and gathered her shawl more tightly around herself.

"Well, in any case," Edward said, "I'm jealous of you." Before she could step onto the deck, he planted a firm kiss on her lips. "That's why I kept you within an inch of me all evening."

"You don't trust me?"

"I don't trust other men. They'll all lose their hearts to you, as I have, Maeve."

She'd believed him, his assurances, the slumbering passion in his eyes when he'd kissed her. Hadn't his sister said that Edward was taken with her? Surely Karen, of all people, knew him better than most. Besides, one glance at

Bentley, his thin lips and silver-tongued manner, was all the assurance Maeve needed.

Bentley liked trouble. Some people did, she supposed.

So, the tight clutch in her stomach had dissolved. She'd woken in a good humor, and was perched on a stool in her suite's efficiency kitchen, savoring the breakfast tray that had been delivered to her room. Buttery croissants, fresh melons topped with crushed mint, and café—a shot of espresso in a gleaming patterned cup. Achille had also included a special recipe, a goat cheese omelet compliments of his "Tata Jeanne."

Relishing a bite of the sweet fruit, she glimpsed her sandals, crusted with sand, by the door and her bikini hanging on the back of a living room chair. These were wonderful reminders of her beach holiday with Edward.

Finishing her breakfast with a sigh of contentment, she showered and then dressed for the day in flared woven capris and a white cotton eyelet top. Finally, it was Friday and time for their visit to the Bonaparte Museum—an excursion she'd looked forward to all week. Carissa had planned a tour for after lunch, so she still had a few hours to fill.

Barefoot, she padded to her well-appointed bedroom. She'd already spent several minutes applying eye make-up, something she rarely did. She wanted to look pretty for Edward, especially after seeing the stunning Davinia and the high-powered style of the women who populated his exclusive, wealthy world.

And, she wanted to polish off the bumpy edges of the persistent disbelief in her mind, shake off her feelings of inadequacy in this elite universe she'd scarcely fathomed before this week.

Perched on a generously proportioned armchair, she

picked up a hairbrush. After her shower she'd braided her freshly-shampooed hair to encourage more waves. Now she shook her hair free of the braid and pulled it to her crown in a messy bun.

Her cell phone rang, with Colleen's name and number drifting across the screen.

She'd texted Colleen the night before, summarizing her evening on Bentley's yacht, including her perception of the underhanded way he'd operated, and her encounter with Davinia DeVito.

As the phone rang a second time, Maeve peered at her watch. Midmorning in Ireland. Odd time for Colleen to call because she never rang anyone when she was working.

"Maeve?" Colleen's voice sounded distant when Maeve answered. "This is Colleen from the purchasing department."

Maeve paused. "I know who you are, Colleen."

"Where are you?"

"I'm in Corsica. Why?"

"You need to come home to Ireland immediately."

An icy chill burrowed deep in her bones. "Owen? Is he all right?"

"Owen is fine. Mrs. McShea instructed me to ring you. In fact, she's standing over my shoulder while we speak."

"What's the craic, Colleen?"

"Is Edward Newell in the hotel business?"

"You know the answer." Maeve set down her hairbrush and stood. "Aye."

"Well, the Merrimac Company is being charged with collusion. Did you and Edward visit a beachfront property yesterday?"

"I told you, remember?"

"Aye. And an informant rang Merrimac with the details this morning."

"Who? What details?"

"We're assuming it was Edward or one of his associates who rang. They're demanding J and J Hospitality offer their hotels a better discount on lighting and seating—the same bidding price they extend to Merrimac."

"What's the name of the hotel chain?" Weighted by doubts, she heard the strain in her voice. "Are you certain it's Penelope and Edward?"

"They didn't say. Our accounting department is checking receipts and accounts payable. Maeve," Colleen whispered into the phone, "if J and J raises their prices, Merrimac may no longer be profitable. We could all lose our jobs if the hotel folds."

No. Maeve squeezed her eyes shut. Edward would never undermine her and betray her trust to save money on supplies—although the savings for his business could tally up to hundreds of thousands of dollars.

Still, the suspicions wove a ribbon of confusion through her mind. She kept her eyes closed, trying to recall her conversation with Bentley. If he attempted to discredit her position, why didn't he realize her savings didn't include numerous stocks and bonds and trust funds to fall back on? She lived paycheck to paycheck. Yet she could see him in her mind's eye, smirking, finding her predicament amusing.

"Get on the next flight out of Corsica," Colleen said, "and you'll arrive in Ireland before the work day ends. Hold on." Maeve recognized their boss's high-pitched voice in the background, then Colleen was back. "Mrs. McShea said for you to come directly to the office. She also wants to review all the reports you've compiled this week. She hasn't received anything. Is your internet working?"

Before Maeve could answer, Colleen hung up.

Breathless, she booked a return flight to Ireland at an exorbitant last-minute rate, rang for a taxi, and then packed quickly and charged out the door. A stinging throb pinched her side. She held her hip and ignored the rapid-fire questions Pierre shot at her when she reached the lobby. He gestured to a taxi waiting curbside to bring her to the airport.

"Mademoiselle, does Monsieur Newell know you are leaving?"

"No."

"Forgive my intrusion into your privacy, but shouldn't you notify him? Today is your outing to the Bonaparte Museum."

"Another time, Pierre." Although she knew there would be no other time. "Please tell him I was summoned back to work."

She wasn't lying, really. All sense of right and wrong and proper and inconsiderate was pushed to the back of her mind.

Disconcerted, she flicked a glance around the lobby. When had the hotel become so crowded? And why did every guest seem to hover so close to her?

She breathed in and out. The lobby was too small.

Pierre was typing something into his computer. "You live at 101 Fourth Street in Dublin, oui?"

"Aye."

"You are obviously in a great hurry. I will arrange a taxi for you when you arrive in Dublin."

"Thank you." It was too much effort to explain to Pierre that she was reporting to Merrimac first. She'd tell the taxi driver once she landed.

Somehow, she kept her gaze confident, her expression

neutral. But how could she explain to Amy and Dawson ... to Edward?

Why, oh, why had she been so short-sighted? Prideful of her responsible behavior, she'd lost her head and her heart to a man she'd known for only a few days. And now she and Colleen might lose their positions and their incomes.

And what would happen to the other Merrimac employees if the company closed? Jobs in Ireland were hard to come by.

Her throat tightened around a sob. She'd never belonged here in Corsica, milling with affluent people whose lifestyles were as distant from hers as shooting stars. She hadn't considered the practical, only the impossible. In her dream castle, her life and Edward's could be woven together.

She'd now received the proof that she'd been very, very wrong.

Wheeling her suitcase behind her, she shuffled down the stone steps of the resort. Fortunately, Pierre had abandoned his position behind his desk and hurried after her with an enormous umbrella, saving her from the drenching rain.

"Mademoiselle, is there anything I can do?" he asked as the taxi driver stowed her suitcase in the trunk.

"No, you've been wonderful, really."

"Mr. and Mrs. Yates? Shall I ring them?"

"I'll contact Amy and arrange to reimburse any booking expenses for today and tomorrow, as well as whatever else I might owe."

How she'd repay, she couldn't comprehend, because there was no money in her bank account. The driver opened the back door for her, and she started to step in. Pierre kept the umbrella over her, which left him in the rain. Almost instantly, his tawny-colored hair, lacquered in its familiar side-sweep, was plastered to his head. His shoes, normally gleaming to a fine black polish, were soaked. Funny how she'd never noticed the lines on his thin face before, nor how misplaced he looked outside of his setting behind his desk.

"Come back to our paradise soon?" he said.

She shook her head, sorrow in her farewell smile. "Au revoir, and merci beaucoup, my dear friend."

As she bent down to slide into the taxi, she noticed a stray feather from some seabird lying on the cobblestoned street. She picked it up, knowing she'd never see the exotic island of Corsica again, the wild thyme, the ancient stone ruins, the awe-inspiring coastline.

Or Edward. The man she loved.

And then she cried as the taxi drove away. Silent hot tears. To keep herself from shattering, she focused on the white lace of the Mediterranean crashing to shore.

Edward may have insinuated his way into her emotions, but she was through thinking about him and his trendsetting friends who believed they could manipulate ordinary people.

Well, he and his friends wouldn't be controlling this woman.

Inhaling a sturdy breath, she opened the taxi's window and released the feather into the wind. An updraft carried it for a short while before it plunged to the ground.

As a fat, stubborn tear fell down her cheek, she concentrated on her last view of Corsica—a moss-covered fountain beside a statue of Napoléon, shade-loving vines climbing over trellises, a random scooter skirting past the taxi.

Determinedly, she brushed the tear away. "Good-bye, my

beautiful island, and my Mr. Right. Somewhere in my heart, I knew I could never live in your world."

But she had hoped. And she had dreamed.

What had she expected? An affair of the heart? A story of true love?

She sank her head in her hands and told herself not to cry.

She cried anyway, because she just couldn't govern her feelings anymore.

THE REMAINDER of Friday passed in a blur, but at last Maeve was in her flat and putting the kettle on for tea. She'd been fired from Merrimac, although she'd denied any wrongdoing. Collusion wasn't even part of her vocabulary. Nevertheless, her company was small and couldn't take any chances going up against giant corporations. Besides, Mrs. McShea had pointed out when Maeve had gathered her personal belongings from her cubicle, Maeve had bunked off from work from when she'd landed in Corsica to when she'd returned to Ireland.

Maeve hadn't denied the charge. How could she?

Saturday dawned with the same angry, relentless rain that had saturated Corsica the day before. She drew on a sweater, pulled on a pair of wool socks, and boosted a fire in the hearth. Crinkles sat at her feet, gamely wagging her tail.

"I thank the good Lord every day since I found you at the rescue shelter." She picked up her dog and was rewarded with a light lick on her cheek. What was better than a dog's love—their kind hearts, their devotion for their owner, their companionship?

With Crinkles in her arms, she padded to the window

and gazed out at the somber sky. Then she turned and scanned her tiny living room. Her flat seemed so quiet without her brother.

Despite her mother's questions when she'd stopped in the previous evening, Maeve had been thrilled to see her brother looking healthy and content, and had lifted a prayer of thanks.

To top off her success in avoiding any inquiries concerning Edward, she'd noted that her mother and brother were getting along brilliantly.

Holidays would be lovely this upcoming year with their small family of three. But first came the end of summer, followed by autumn. Even now, she could feel the warm season pushing away, easing into shorter days and gloomy, unfriendly nights.

She crumpled into her comfortable chair by the fireplace and Crinkles cuddled beside her. Tightly, she closed her eyes, but that didn't stop the tears that streamed freely down her face.

By afternoon, the rain had settled to a slow and steady drizzle. Deciding soup would ease the sadness in her chest, she put a chicken on the stove to boil, one she'd bought on her way home the night before. She managed to eat only one bowl, but that left ample servings for her mother and brother.

Feeling revived by the soup, she unpacked her luggage. Routine stabilized her, strengthened her and kept her mind and hands busy.

In the deep quiet of afternoon when the shadows of the day lay long, her doorbell jangled. She glanced at herself in the living room mirror. Her cheeks were streaked with tears, her eyes watery and red. Swiftly, she groped for her handkerchief and dabbed at her face.

"Remember me?" Colleen shouted from the other side of the doorway. "Why haven't you answered my texts?"

Maeve opened the door. "Sorry." Seeing her best friend's questioning gaze, she stuttered, trying to catch her breath. "T-tea?"

"Aye. Are you all right?"

"I'm grand." Her voice cracked, only slightly, but enough for her friend to take hold of her hands.

"Then why were you crying?"

Maeve averted her gaze. "I've excelled in crying ever since I left Corsica."

"That's absurd. I've known you since we were in primary school, and you never cry." Colleen hung her jacket on a kitchen chair and wiped the water drops from her glasses. "The rain is cold and nipping through me like prickles of ice. I'll say aye to that cuppa tea?"

A handful of minutes later, with tea and a plate of biscuits in front of them, Colleen perched across from Maeve in Maeve's cramped kitchen. Crinkles rested beneath the table, crunching a treat Maeve had fetched from the cupboard.

"I'm sorry about your job," Colleen began.

"Fortunately, you're still employed, so a wee bit of fair play there." Maeve chewed on the corner of a biscuit, then drank a mouthful of tea. "Monday will come around soon enough. In the help-wanted section of today's newspaper, one of the shops on Fifth Street is hiring. It's only a block away, so I could easily walk."

"With your experience, you'll find a good job. You're a brilliant purchasing agent."

Was she? Instead of answering, Maeve poured her friend more tea.

"The tea is good and hot." Colleen boosted her sugar intake with another lump. "Maeve …"

"Aye?" Maeve dropped back in her chair and stared at her steaming cup.

"Have you heard from Edward?"

Just the sound of his name sent a beat of pure yearning through her heart and relit a fire she didn't think she could ever extinguish. She missed him so much.

"Aye." She gulped a lungful of air. She couldn't lie, not to Colleen. Desperately, she tried to hide the catch in her voice. "He's left numerous phone messages and texts."

Realization emerged in Colleen's cornflower-blue gaze. "Which, I'm assuming, you haven't answered. And I can see by the look on your face you're in tatters …"

Maeve bent her head to hide the welling tears, but not soon enough for the keen-eyed Colleen.

"You fell in love with him, didn't you?"

"Don't be ridiculous." Chin lifted, Maeve offered Colleen a quivering smile. "I met him a week ago."

"Love isn't measured by time. Why haven't you answered his messages?"

"I can't."

Colleen pushed back her teacup, then clicked her French-manicured fingernails on the table. "Why not?"

"Because I wouldn't know what to say."

Because it would distress her too much to hear his voice.

Maeve flopped back in her chair and gripped the armrests. "If only you knew how he lives. What we imagine to be the lifestyle of the rich and famous doesn't even come close."

"You've told me all week about it, remember?"

"Then you should understand."

"I understand, all right. You're a coward."

"Me?" Annoyed, Maeve flashed her friend a pained stare.

"Oh, don't get your dander up." Colleen threw up her hands and studied a crack in the ceiling. "You're ignoring him because you're upset, although none of this is his fault. We both know it was Bentley."

"Perhaps."

"Perhaps? *Perhaps*?" Colleen jerked from her chair, stalked two paces, then pivoted. "Surely you don't doubt Edward. I did some digging on the internet last night. Bentley's a big front and a slow back. From what I gathered, he's feigning a family wealth that isn't there anymore."

In a deceptively casual tone she hoped would dissuade Colleen, Maeve refuted, "None of this matters anymore."

"I didn't know you were so ridiculous." As if too furious to continue, Colleen went back to her tea, dissolved a handful of sugar cubes in it, and stirred vigorously. "If you want to break it off with Edward, tell him straight on."

Maeve gave a half laugh. "There's nothing to break off."

"Umm, nothing except your starry-eyed week together." Colleen shoved Maeve toward her laptop computer sitting on a narrow kitchen counter. "Tomorrow, book a ferry from Dublin to Holyhead. Then take a train to London."

"Surely you're joking?" Maeve's eyebrows jerked up. Her fingers clenched into small fists. Momentarily irrational, she almost agreed with Colleen before they settled back on their chairs.

"What's the story then, Maeve?"

"Sorry, I just don't know anymore." Maeve rubbed her arms. "Besides, I don't have any money."

"Merrimac gave you two weeks' severance. Use part and go directly to Penelope and Edward's main offices."

"I don't know where they're located." Maeve groped for a

better answer. "Perfect Match didn't disclose any personal information."

"Thank goodness, again, for the internet and your brilliant techie friend." Colleen slipped a paper from her pocket and slid it across the table to Maeve. "Here's the address."

At a loss for words, Maeve frantically considered how to end a conversation that would only lead to more pain if she pursued it.

"Doesn't he have enough, Colleen?" She reached down to pet Crinkles. The dog represented security and everything good in her world. Crinkles nosed her fingers, hoping for another treat. With a heavy sigh, Maeve put her head in her hands. "Shouldn't living an exorbitant lifestyle surrounded by more worldly goods than anyone can comprehend be plenty for one man?"

"He doesn't have you."

"As if that matters to a rugger bugger like him. I'm certainly not showing up on his office doorstep like a pining puppy."

Colleen took a bite of biscuit and washed it down with tea. "I suppose if I was in the middle of a misunderstanding like you are, I'd see things the same way."

"This is more than a misunderstanding."

"Is it?" Colleen held up a hand. "Please, just to stake my argument, let's presume he's in love with you."

Maeve opened her mouth to object, and Colleen stopped her with a sardonic head shake. "From what you told me about all his special surprises, even a cabbage would realize how much he cares."

"No. It's better if I move on and forget him." Maeve surged to her feet and began clearing the table. "Sooner or later, I'd make a right moron of myself and—"

Colleen crossed to her and gave a tight hug. "I doubt

he'd spend all his time, money and energy on a woman he cares little about."

A torrent of clashing emotions swept through Maeve as Colleen determinedly continued. "At least give him the benefit of listening to what he has to say."

"And then what?" Maeve swiveled and busied herself at the sink. She'd tried so hard to numb her emotions, and then here had come Colleen. "He'll give me a little pat on my head and send me on my way? I'll be mortified."

Colleen plunked her hands on her ample hips. "Your pride may need to suffer."

"I can't. I just can't."

"All right, then stay here in Ireland. And when you read about his engagement to Davinia what's-her-name in the Dublin papers, let me know your thoughts then."

"Maybe I'll consider ..." Maeve studied her worn hardwood floor. She needed time to sit somewhere quiet and reflect. Surely Colleen could understand.

She met her friend's gaze. "I'll—I'll wait a while first."

"Which will be even more uncomfortable as the weeks go by." Colleen plucked a slice of chicken from the pot of soup and chewed slowly. Rounding back to Maeve, she poured on a brilliant finale. "Provided, of course, he hasn't wed Davinia in the interim."

10

———

The following morning, Maeve peered out at another wet drizzle streaming down her bedroom window. Her entire flat felt damp. She opened the top drawer of her bureau and sniffed the lavender-scented sachet she'd brought from Corsica to place with her clothes. Tied with a purple satin ribbon, the sachet's fresh, appealing scent reminded her of France.

She closed the drawer, the fragrance too painful a reminder. She'd been a foolish woman who'd chosen to believe fantasy over reality. End of story.

Still, her flat was so forlorn. After showering and getting dressed, she grabbed a history book and sat by the fireplace. Crinkles snored at her feet, easing her loneliness. She'd mindlessly turned several pages of the book before she gave up, realizing she couldn't concentrate on sixteenth-century war tactics.

Save for a cuppa tea, she didn't have the heart for breakfast. For lunch, she'd heat up a bowl of the chicken soup. Perhaps she'd be hungry by then.

As she stared out at the dreary day, her cellphone

pinged. The sound almost sent her to her knees. If it was Edward, should she consider answering his text? These unmanageable feelings for him were so chaotic and powerful.

Uncertainty collided with hope as she picked up the phone to check the screen.

Instead of Edward, an incoming email from Carissa was emblazoned with the title, "Remembrances of a Perfect Match created in Corsica."

Telling herself she should resist the temptation to open the file because her heart couldn't afford to be any more broken, Maeve tried to stop herself and failed.

Slowly, she read and reread Carissa's email.

'Hi Maeve,

Sorry you left our beautiful island so abruptly. We miss you and Pierre says bonjour.

Hope you enjoy these remembrances of Corsica.

Your Perfect Match specialist,

Carissa'

Maeve scrolled through the attached photos, and a sting of longing grew in her chest.

Orange lilies in her hands, the first photo was of her and Edward cuddling at the foot of les Calanches Cliffs. Aye, they'd agreed to act for the cameras.

But had they been acting?

Maeve changed the picture size and zoomed in on Edward. His expression was tender as he gazed down at her, which she hadn't noticed when he'd kissed her.

She rewound the day in her mind, remembering his smile when they'd perched on the rocks with the splendor of Corsica before them.

"*Wouldn't you agree, Maeve?*" he'd said. "*We get along so well. We're never at a lack for words. Perhaps we are made for each other."*

Edward.

She wanted to cry out, to weep. She squeezed her eyes shut, running her fingers across the phone screen to touch his face, willing the tears not to fall.

The second photo was taken in his suite. He'd worn his fleece shorts and Snoopy T-shirt. She was dressed in his chambray shirt, which would have fallen to her knees if she hadn't tucked the edges into her jean shorts. The orchids portrait was propped behind them, and she held a bouquet of Corsican lilies. He was leaning against her, exaggerating his injury. She recalled how the closeness of his hard, toned body had made her feel both faint and lighthearted.

And that feeling had never changed.

She scrolled further to the third photo, taken of them beside the fishing boat. Edward, with his midnight-black hair, startling green eyes, graceful dark eyebrows. He'd surprised her with a passionate kiss, prompting Carissa to exclaim they were the Perfect Match success story.

"I love everything about you," he'd said when there were anchored in a cove. *"Surely you must know that by now."* And then he'd brushed a soft kiss on her lips in that intimate way he had.

A fist squeezed so tightly around her heart she could hardly breathe.

Edward.

She breathed out a shaky sigh. So many remembrances —vaulted stone doorways in ancient towns, the pattern of boat silhouettes and fog on the harbor, their enchanted night on the French Riviera. As they'd sauntered hand in hand, he'd pointed out the trellises decked in climbing vines, and low marble fountains with basin rims broad enough to sit on.

Stop, she scolded herself. Her home was hundreds of miles away from him, from Corsica, from La Bonaparte Resort.

Her Irish lifestyle? Well, that was a million miles away.

Stubbornly, more memories resurfaced.

"Remind me to never quarrel with you."

And she'd assured him she would do anything to avoid a conflict.

But did that mean surrendering, giving up the man she loved?

Her mouth fell open. Her head came up.

With an exclamation, she embraced the fluttering in her chest. Grabbing her cellphone, she rang Colleen.

Maeve kept her tone steady when Colleen picked up. "Will you watch Crinkles for me?" she asked.

"Job-hunting on a Sunday, aye?"

"No, I'm hoping you'll spend the night. I'm off for a wee bit of traveling."

"Really?" Maeve heard Colleen's short intake of breath. "Where?"

"To London."

"You're a fine thing, you know that?" Colleen started whistling the tune from a familiar Irish jig. "I'll be there in twenty minutes."

Decision made, fine or foolish, Maeve bundled her hair up.

She could do this.

She kept her chin up while she organized an overnight bag with her necessities. She was prepared.

Besides, Colleen was right. She couldn't be so spineless as to ignore Edward simply because it upset her to be near him. How could she be so petty? If she admitted the truth, didn't she owe him that same honesty? She'd have a straight conversation with him, then head back to Ireland the following morning.

Still, when Colleen arrived at her flat, Maeve confessed she was panic-stricken and already considering canceling her trip. "Why don't we go into Dublin centre and window-shop instead?" she'd suggested.

Colleen gave her a hard stare. "Finish Perfect Match the way you started, optimistic and determined. Be the woman he fell in love with—the self-assertive woman who always rises in hard times."

MAEVE CALLED a taxi to the Dublin port, where she'd booked a round-trip ferry ticket between Dublin and Holyhead.

Rain was still falling, and she pulled up the hood of her bright-red rain jacket as she walked swiftly into the terminal. A glance at her watch assured there was enough time to collect her ticket and enter the check-in point with maybe five minutes to spare.

She saw the broad-shouldered man immediately, because he was tall among the crowd, striding purposefully across the ferry dock and wheeling a small leather carry-on. In his other hand, he held a bouquet of orange lilies. He paused, questioning a deckhand, then nodded his thanks and passed through the tollbooth.

She tilted back her head, devouring every inch of his handsome face. Steps wide, she ran toward him.

"Edward!"

He looked around. He didn't see her at first. And then he did.

"Maeve!" He found her in an instant, started to reach for her, but then stopped.

"Why are you in Dublin? In the ferry terminal?" Warily, she scanned his face for a sign he'd come on business or for some other reason that had nothing to do with her. Or perhaps he'd come to berate her for not answering his calls and to tell her he never wanted to see her again.

He smiled into her curious gaze. "I just got off the Holyhead ferry."

Holyhead.

"Maeve. Luv." Heartbreakingly handsome, he set down the flowers and held out his arms. She dropped her bag and rushed into his embrace.

"I missed you so much," he murmured against her lips.

"I missed you too." She molded herself closer, fearful that if they came apart, he would disappear; and the painful torment of losing him would become a void she'd never be able to fill.

When their kiss finally ended, his arms tightened possessively, and he rested his chin on her hair. He paused a moment, waiting for their breathing to smooth out.

Slightly, he drew back. "Where are you headed, Maeve?"

"I intended to travel to London. But not anymore." She tossed a rueful glance toward the Holyhead ferry, which was signaling its departure with three horn bellows.

Understanding dawned in Edward's eyes. "For me? You were going to London to see me?"

"Aye."

He lifted her off her feet and whirled her around. He was a man with the power to carry her.

"I was bound for 101 Fourth Street," he said.

Her address.

"Maeve?" He studied her face. "How did you know I'd be here? I didn't tell anyone—"

"A very fortunate coincidence. Call it happenstance, call it fate." She called it the benevolence of a loving God and whispered a prayer of thanks. She and Edward had nearly missed each other.

"Why did you decide to come to me?" His gaze never left hers. "You've ignored all my messages."

She twined her hands around his neck, aching with desire, unconcerned about showing her feelings. "My friend Colleen made me understand that I needed to face my emotions."

"And they are?"

"I love you, Edward, and I won't deny it another second." She lay her cheek against his hard chest, loving the sound of his solid heart beating. "It's crazy, I know, because we've just met and—"

"And I love you." Sincere, honest emotion deepened his words. "Maeve Doherty, I love you very, very much."

She looked up at him and it was all there. His love, his desire for her.

Suddenly awkward, he bent down and handed her the bouquet of orange flowers. "These are for you. I know you loved the lilies in Corsica. They're a bit bent, I'm afraid ... I can get you another ... Maybe roses instead?"

"Lilies are perfect." She took the flowers and breathed in the heady scent of Corsica. "Thank you." Her voice broke. "Thank you."

As a drizzly Dublin day neared to evening, they sat on a bench under an overhang and gazed out onto the harbor. Passengers embarked and disembarked on infinite journeys, leaving behind wet footprints on the docks. Some smartly dressed, some simple and plain.

The lilies were on her lap, their carry-on bags at their feet.

Then, since neither of them had eaten, they took a taxi back into the city to Maeve's favorite coffee shop, The Ground Café. With her bouquet of lilies on the table, they enjoyed lemon scones washed down by the coffee of the day, a rich, strong brew.

"All that separated us was a ferry ride," Edward said. "Why didn't you respond to my thousand and one messages?"

"I was wrong. And I shouldn't have blamed you for the actions of your friend." She lowered her head, twisted her hands together. It was difficult to speak. "I lost my job. Merrimac charged me with collusion and jeopardizing our accounts with J and J Supplies by giving out bidding information. Someone called my company Friday morning to report me. That's why I had to go back immediately." She looked up. "I'm not dishonest, Edward. Merrimac's been fair, and I'd never do anything to damage them."

He took her hands in his, squeezing lightly, offering his loyalty. This persuasive, powerful man was her champion, and the thought made her proud.

"You've done nothing wrong." He paused. "Do you think Bentley ...?"

"Aye. At least I assume."

"I'll find out the truth." He stiffened, a cold, flinty expression crossing his face. Then he nodded, his gaze gentle. "So now you're jobless."

"Aye, although there's a prospect posted in the Dublin paper that I'll reply to tomorrow. The business is a short block from my flat, so I can walk there." She tilted her head. "How did you know my address?"

He looked out the nearest window. "The rain's stopped. How about a walk?"

She agreed, and as they stepped outside, she looked up. Far to the east, a bell tower tolled. Her gaze drifted, resting on the first star of the evening.

He didn't answer and hung an arm around her shoulders. The fierce downpour had stopped. Dusk had turned a dove-gray sky into reddish hues. Low clouds were parting for a clear, bright nightfall.

The same question plagued her and she turned sideways to face him. "Edward, you said you were headed to Fourth Street. How did you know my address?"

He slipped an arm around her waist. "How did you know mine?"

"I didn't. Colleen gave me the address to Penelope and Edward headquarters. I hoped someone would be there on Sunday."

He smiled. "Rest assured, that someone would be me. Karen separated from her husband and flew off to Australia on the family's private jet to spend the weekend with a man she met on Bentley's yacht."

"I wish Karen luck."

He sighed. "At the rate she's going, she'll need it."

Maeve shook her head. Then she stopped walking, forcing him to stop and regarded him frankly. "Edward, how did you know my address?"

"First, I planned to contact the Perfect Match people. The ... the ..." He snapped his fingers.

"Yates. Dawson and Amy Yates."

"Right. But I didn't need to. Pierre gave me your information."

"He'd never agree to give out my personal information. He's much too professional." She raised a dubious eyebrow. "Would he?"

"For love, he couldn't refuse." Edward chuckled. "And ..."

"And?"

"Begging."

"You begged him?"

He shrugged. "I added bribery. I offered him a head concierge position at Penelope and Edward's Nice resort at double his current salary."

"Surely he didn't accept."

"Actually, he did, so his future is ensured." Edward bent his head to capture her mouth in a long, leisurely kiss. "As for your future ... I don't see that you'll be needing to apply for that job. I can offer you a much better one ... Mrs. Newell."

Her heart gave a lurch. He announced his intention so simply, so like him. She understood his core, trustworthy and giving, and she treasured it. Treasured him.

He took her into his arms and gazed into her eyes, which were quickly filling with happiness. "You haven't answered my question," he said quietly. "Will you marry me?"

Her answer began in her spirit as her heart filled with too many sensations to name. In a whisper, and in a perfect French accent, she whispered, "'Quand il me prend dans ses bras, il me parle tout bas, Je vois la vie en rose.'"

Edward held her closer. "Your quote on your dating profile."

"Aye. You remembered. And Pierre taught me how to say it in French."

"So I noticed. Now, will you marry me?"

"Aye. Because I love you very, very much."

"And I love you, Maeve Doherty."

Softly, she recited the English translation of the song lyric. "'When he takes me in his arms, and speaks to me softly, I see the world through rose-colored glasses.'"

This was love, and perfection. And the man who held her in his arms was her Perfect Match.

The End

A NOTE FROM JOSIE

Dear Friend,

Thank you for reading *Maeve,* set on the charming French island of Corsica. I hope you enjoyed it.

If you loved this sweet romance as much as I loved writing it, please help other people find *Maeve* by posting your review.

Maeve is available in ebook, paperback, Large Print Paperback, Hardcover, and Audiobook.

I've always been fascinated with traveling the world and exploring new places. In my spare time, I appreciate "armchair vacations" and watch popular television shows in exotic locales. Several were an inspiration for my story.

You'll find Maeve is a strong Irish heroine. Intelligent and competent, with a beautiful, gentle spirit, she sets out on the adventure of her dreams.

Of course, Edward, the hero, conquers his own challenges.

Despite their differences, and the fact that their economic situations are worlds apart, the characters "clicked," and I enjoyed writing this book.

My Spotify Playlist for Maeve is here.
With sincere appreciation,
Josie Riviera

TATA JEANNE'S CHEESE OMELET RECIPE

Ingredients

- 6 eggs
- 5 oz of fresh ricotta cheese (or goat cheese)
- handful of fresh chives, green onion, or mint
- 1 tsp. grated garlic
- 1 tbsp. olive oil
- salt
- pepper

Instructions

Break the eggs in a bowl and beat. Season with salt and pepper.

In a non-stick pan, heat olive oil. Add grated garlic and fry. Pour eggs over and cook.

Spoon in ricotta or fresh goat cheese. Let ingredients settle until cheese is warmed.

Sprinkle with fresh chopped chives, green onion, or mint.

Enjoy!

USA TODAY BESTSELLING AUTHOR
JOSIE RIVIERA
1·800·IRELAND
A SWEET CONTEMPORARY NOVELLA

1

Why did I decide to do this? I must've been madder than a box of frogs.

Kathleen Kelly nodded politely while listening to Candee, her Realtor, although she scarcely paid attention. While she tried to come up with an animated reply, her mind spun. She hoped she hadn't made the biggest mistake of her life.

I'm in America. I've done it.

Meanwhile, Candee gushed on and on about Roses, their picture-perfect North Carolina town. Voted one of the best places to live by a national magazine, Roses frequently persuaded travelers passing through to sell their homes and relocate there.

Kathleen grinned, because she was one of those travelers. However, she hadn't passed through Roses. Her Dublin hometown was 3600 miles away.

The internet was a marvelous thing, connecting people from all around the world. Finally, after months of preparation, her dream of owning a business had become a reality.

Cause for celebration?

In truth, she'd been full of starry-eyed dreams and didn't know what to expect—this being America with its laid-back style. However, she'd found that professionalism and punctuality were respected here, judging by how efficiently Candee had handled the real estate closing.

She eyed the run-down exterior, the broken-down wooden front door that looked like it had once been painted turquoise. Moss flourished beneath the eaves, and numerous shingles were missing. The brick façade was crumbling in several places.

This wasn't Betty's Diner anymore. From here on in, this was her place: Kathleen's Teahouse.

Critically, she assessed her reflection in the smudged plate-glass front window. She'd swept her red-gold hair up at the crown, and pinned the overly long ends back from her face. Tired lines etched the corners of her dark eyes, and the blush of color she'd applied along her cheekbones had disappeared, leaving her complexion pale. Her lips, which she'd always deemed too full, looked a tad solemn.

Despite the sunny day, she'd dressed in a suede skirt, thick black tights and ankle boots.

Budding leaves on the tulip magnolia trees whispered of spring, and buttery-yellow daffodils had begun to open. So different from Ireland, where hawthorn hedges wouldn't bloom until May.

"So, what do you think of your new business on Pine Cone Lane?" Candee asked.

"Everything is brilliant, absolutely brilliant," Kathleen lied effectively. Sometimes white lies were best to hide her reservations because the place wasn't nearly as brilliant as all that.

In its heyday, the former greasy-spoon diner had served countless meals, the floors and countertops spic and span.

However, it had been boarded up in recent months, which was why she'd snagged the place at a steal before the building went into foreclosure.

With a silent groan, she estimated the number of weeks it would take to sand and repaint, outfit the kitchen and hire staff, and the numerous unexpected details that would surface.

She came up with months, not weeks, although she reassured herself there was no point in olagonin'—whining and complaining—because it only made things more difficult.

However, since she'd arrived in America, being anxious had become her forte.

The long weeks of anticipation and tension had taken their toll and kept her awake at night, and she could think of nothing she'd like better than a tub soak with the lavender soap she'd brought from Ireland. Followed by a lengthy, leisurely nap.

Resignedly, she knew a nap would be out of the question for a long time.

Perhaps forever.

She paused to stand back, surveying the building. If she thought objectively rather than with her emotions, she understood that she wouldn't be able to accomplish everything by herself, especially within a five-week timeline.

She'd scheduled her grand opening on St. Patrick's Day, deeming the date fitting and appropriate.

She envisioned painting the shingles a serene shade of soft-green, overstated by a burgundy-striped canvas awning, much like the awning gracing The Ground Café, her former employer's coffee shop in Dublin. And she wanted outdoor seating on the patio, allowing customers to dine at wrought iron tables beneath vintage-style Edison light bulbs.

Curb appeal. That's what the place needed.

She focused on which project she would dive into first—the interior or the exterior.

She was weighing the pros and cons when Candee asked, "You're not having second thoughts about moving to America, are you? I realize it's a huge undertaking."

"Of course not," Kathleen said. "Ireland was getting a little too small for me."

At thirty-five years old, her mantra had become *pursue my dreams or bust*. Besides, it was too late to check out, things being what they were. Her former coworkers knew she was embarking on a refreshingly different chapter in her life, and it would be disheartening to admit defeat.

Kathleen fidgeted with the gold watch on her wrist, a going-away gift from her employer, Danny Brady. "Also," she continued, "baking and the restaurant trade are second nature to me. I've spent half my life managing a coffee shop."

Candee covered Kathleen's hand. "Sometimes a fresh start is as simple as buying a dilapidated building and getting on an airplane."

"Did I say that?"

"Oh, and much more, because you not only said it, you did it," Candee said. "You've created your dream life."

Kathleen shook her head. "I used to be smart and sensible."

"In the present circumstances, you're even smarter," Candee said. "And you're strong and beautiful. The first time we Skyped, I couldn't get over how put together you were. You'd already composed a business plan."

Kathleen offered a brittle smile. "Don't believe everything on your computer screen."

"Positive thinking, plus action, leads to accomplishment. You're a doer."

"Despite what my so-called friends advised," Kathleen replied.

"Weren't they supportive?"

"Aye, in a polite sort of way. They gave me rock-hard, unsolicited advice." For some reason, her thoughts kept darting back to Ireland, and a sense of isolation rolled through her. "They wanted to protect me from making a mistake."

She longed to tell someone about the successful closing of her new property, the deep-blue sky gracing the warm Carolina days, the way the sweetgum tree branches swayed in the pleasant morning breezes.

But there was no one to tell. Danny and his wife, Clara, were busy with their own lives, with a wee one on the way.

"You'll love Roses, and I predict your teahouse will become a tea emporium," Candee said.

"What in the world is that?"

"An emporium is a retail store selling a variety of goods."

"I plan to serve food—Irish tea and scones, sandwiches and cakes. I'm not a chain of fancy shops."

"Well, you should be. Also sell tea and teapots, because you and Roses are poised for success. I can feel it."

Kathleen smiled. Aye, Roses was enchanting. The once sleepy town was thriving, and the lush green grass packed neatly between the brick sidewalks reminded her a wee bit of Ireland.

Except that it wasn't ...

Remembrances of lyrical brogues brought a poignant yearning to Kathleen's chest that stopped her cold. She hadn't realized she'd be so homesick. With her accent, she'd already found that oftentimes her words got misheard and misunderstood, and she'd had a hard time communicating even though everyone spoke the same language—English.

"This area will get a lot of foot traffic, especially on warm spring and summer evenings," Candee said. "Here in the Carolinas we enjoy a temperate climate, so don't rule out winter or fall, either."

"Unlike Ireland." Kathleen chuckled.

"Does it truly rain buckets?"

"Our term is bucketing down," Kathleen said, repeating the standard Irish joke. "Although the rain is at least warm in the summer."

Candee laughed. "Is it windy?"

"Not much." Kathleen lifted her shoulders in a teasing shrug. "Except small children and pets are sometimes blown clear away to England."

"Believe me, you'll enjoy the weather here," Candee concluded with a laugh. Gently, she urged Kathleen to the diner's doorway.

Kathleen blinked at the dazzling noon sunlight and realized her stomach was growling. She hadn't eaten anything except a slice of her homemade Irish brown bread when she'd woken at six a.m.

"What do you think of your upstairs apartment?" Candee asked. "Internet photos don't do a place justice, but housing above your teahouse is a money saver. You won't have to pay rent nor commute."

"Aye. Although truth be told, it's all in a little worse shape than I expected."

"Manageable, though, I trust?" Candee's puzzled frown swung from the door to Kathleen. "I realize it needs curtains."

"It lacks a lot more than updated curtains," Kathleen said with a laugh. "And it will take an army of crewmen to get everything in working order by St. Patrick's Day."

"My husband, Teddy, is a contractor. He'll get the place

turned around for you in no time." Candee shook back a strand of red hair that had come loose from her braid, exposing a pair of gold cross earrings, the only jewelry she wore except for her wedding rings. Even without an ounce of makeup, the woman was stunning, her green eyes gleaming whenever she discussed her husband and their adopted son, Joseph.

In addition to being a Realtor, Candee had opened an afterschool daycare facility in her home for disadvantaged children in the community. On several occasions, Kathleen wondered how Candee was able to do it all. She'd been inspired to match her stamina and ambition.

"As long as there's running water, a kitchen and a bathroom in my apartment," Kathleen said, "my needs are met."

"Good. Your reference from Danny Brady was excellent, by the way."

"I never missed a day of work."

"And he said your brown bread flew off the shelves whenever it was featured."

"He granted me the option to take my recipe to America, and I ran with it."

"Free and clear?"

"Danny understood I was drained. After countless years as his head assistant, I wanted a change." Kathleen wished the warmth burning her cheeks didn't give her away. Why couldn't she compartmentalize her second thoughts like she did everything else in her life?

Because she was excited.

And mildly terrified.

"I expect he and his wife will come to America and visit me someday," she finished.

Candee studied her. "So, at present, you're alone."

"Aye." Kathleen considered saying more, to explain she

always felt lonely despite her attempts to build relationships.

She kept her lips sealed. Some words were better left unsaid.

In a little over two years, she'd been duped by a man not once, but twice. First, by a moneyed Italian she'd met on the internet who had turned out to be, surprise, surprise, a young boy. And then, Alexander, an American business-man, had played her for a muppet—a fool.

Danny Brady and his bodyguard, Ian, had said Alexander was too talkative. Talkative? Hah! What an understatement! Charmer was more like it, and Alexander was so smooth-talking he could sell ya an eye out of your own head. He'd had her believing he was genuinely inter-ested in her. When she'd fallen for him, his charisma had changed to controlling. He'd quickly become domineering and expected her to be subservient.

As Candee continued to study her, Kathleen offered, "The man I believed I loved was actually two different men. He was fine as long as things went his way and I was passive." She shrugged and tried to act unconcerned. "Although being submissive isn't in my nature. As I advanced in my career, our relationship quickly fell apart."

"You said you wanted a fresh start, and you've created it. Here's to new men and extraordinary opportunities." Candee gestured to the doorway.

"I'll take the opportunities minus the men," Kathleen said. Truly, she was done with con men, eejits—idiots—who expected women to take a back seat to them and their opin-ions. Men who exuded personality while keeping a close watch on their own agendas. Men who fired off derisive comments for no other reason than to feel superior.

She was a woman who had helped Danny Brady's

Ground Café achieve fame. Here and now, with determination and hard work, she'd make her teahouse a noteworthy addition to this quaint little town.

"During our Skype sessions, I mentioned that your teahouse will offset Keiran O'Malley's Irish pub nicely." Candee pointed to a side street. "His building isn't far from here."

"Keiran's cousin, William, first spoke of Roses and recommended you as a Realtor, which is why I messaged you," Kathleen said. "Fortunately, I zoomed in on this town fairly quickly."

"William lives in Dublin, right?"

"He also knows Sean, my coworker from The Ground Café. Both men wanted to date me, and I turned Sean down flat."

"And William?"

"He frequented the café a couple times a week. We dated for a short while after my breakup with Alexander until I realized I wasn't ready for a romantic involvement." Kathleen swallowed, giving herself a breather before continuing. "Sean still texts me now and then. He wishes to come to America to help me with my new business."

"Is that a good thing or a bad thing?"

"I'm not certain. Sean is competent, but I can't imagine he'd actually fancy working for me. He and I were on the same level as managers." She exhaled. "At any rate, William had told me that Keiran loves it in Roses."

"He's married to my sister, Desiree. They are extremely happy."

"I've heard."

Happy. Such an elusive term.

"Keiran said that life called him back to Roses. Maybe the town called you here too."

Kathleen reflected on Candee's words. She'd read about life's calling in self-help books and tuned in to endless podcasts on the subject. Sometimes, it seemed like she'd waited her entire life for a voice to explain which bend in the road led to happiness.

Nevertheless, if one's calling was a voice whispering in her ear, she hadn't heard a sound. Perhaps a calling was the Lord tapping her on the shoulder. Either way, she'd known in her gut that Roses was the ideal spot, and everything had clicked into place.

"In any case, here I am," she replied.

Candee opened her arms, firmly clasping them around Kathleen. "And this is the dawn of the grandest adventure of your life."

Tears welled in Kathleen's eyes—a mix of joy, fear, and reservations. She'd chosen her destiny, following in the footprints of the Irish immigrant.

Don't be an eejit, her inner voice chided. *You're launching a teahouse, not fleeing from a potato famine.*

"And I can't wait to introduce you to everyone," Candee said. "Desiree and Keiran, my husband Teddy, and our son, Joseph—"

"Aye. When the time comes." Now she was sounding standoffish.

She drew a see-through container from her leather shoulder bag. "Before I forget, I baked a loaf of my brown bread for you this morning."

Candee stepped back. "You haven't been here two days and you're already baking bread in your apartment?"

"I ran the oven before I even unpacked." She handed the container to Candee. "This is a thank-you gift for taking care of the million incidentals that came with an international real-estate transaction. And, for fixing up my apartment before I arrived."

"My pleasure. Decorating is my thing, and you advised me on your likes and dislikes. In fact, you were quite decisive."

"I don't have much of a knack for it."

"Oh, but you do."

Kathleen envisioned the packing boxes strewn throughout her flat's hallway, the luggage and clothes piled by her bed. She should have put away her belongings a while ago. Instead, she'd drawn on a ruffled apron, let a batch of dough rise, and baked.

"Take a bite," she urged.

Candee obliged, closing her eyes as she nibbled. "This bread is one of the best baked goods I've ever tasted. And that's saying a lot, because my friend in Miami owns ..."

"I plan to sell Irish brown bread every day," Kathleen said, grinning broadly at the compliment. "Although I'll need to sell more than bread."

"What about pizza?" Candee asked.

"I'll leave pizza to the pizzeria in town. Presently, I'll turn my energy into outfitting the bakery with delicious Irish desserts and an array of tea selections. In Ireland, people aren't in such a hurry. We savor every moment, and I intend to create the same experience in my teahouse."

"Unlike America," Candee said.

"Comfy couches and free Wi-Fi," Kathleen went on. "Brewed tea in a variety of flavors—chamomile, mint, and a host of exotic herbal leaves."

Her ideas overflowed. Were they too ambitious?

"Have you set your hours?" Candee stooped down at the doorway, muttering about the weather stripping not being sufficiently tight to prevent air leaks.

"I'll open at eleven, and close by nine at night."

"You realize you're describing ten-hour work days?"

"Aye." Like a shot, Kathleen's brain worked rapidly. "I'm still on the lookout for locally sourced ingredients so I can serve healthy salads, sandwiches, and wraps. For dinner, stone-baked pita bread topped with goat cheese and caramelized onions will be a nightly special."

Candee linked arms with Kathleen and walked to the side of the building, where rickety exterior stairs led to the second floor. "What you're describing is enough work for twenty people. And that pita bread sounds a lot like pizza."

"It's Irish pizza, so no competition with the local pizzeria." Deciding on her menu options, Kathleen hardly realized Candee had come to a determined stop while saying a man's name twice.

Rob. Rob.

"Who is Rob?" Kathleen asked.

"He's a dear friend and owns a string of popular bakeries." For some reason, Candee's pitch heightened. "His chain is called Rob's Marvelous Muffins and is based in the Miami area where he lives. He's delightful and funny and easy-going—"

"Brilliant, I'm sure." Kathleen went back to the menu choices in her mind. Irish bacon and poached eggs, or a traditional Irish breakfast complete with roasted tomatoes and mushrooms? Perhaps beef burgers and cider glazed salmon for lunch.

No. She reined in her thoughts. This wasn't a full-scale restaurant.

"I'll begin advertising for employees soon and start with a modest staff," she said, "Did I tell you I won't be serving alcohol?"

"Yes, and I applaud your decision."

"Thanks. I've had enough of that in Ireland. People going out on the lash and stumbling home in the wee hours." Kathleen waved a dismissive hand. "I'll leave the drinking to the pubs."

She looked back on the intervention Clara Brady had staged for her alcoholic brother, Seamus. Little good that had done. Once a person was addicted, it was often a long road to wellness.

"What are the requisite number of ovens for a bakery?" Candee asked.

"Certainly a small commercial oven, plus a full-size convection oven is necessary. Also, a deck oven for layer cakes and breads." Kathleen frowned as she considered all the equipment yet to purchase. "Where will I buy a mixer and a—"

"You'll need someone knowledgeable to advise you. Fortunately, Rob has extensive retail bakery experience. He studied at a prestigious culinary school in Florida offering lots of hands-on experience." Candee plucked her cellphone from her purse. The excitement in her voice matched the glow in her eyes. "He was voted Miami's most successful entrepreneur, and he's just the right person to help you."

Whoever this Rob was, he'd be overwhelmed when he saw what needed to be completed in five weeks.

Unless, of course, he was a miracle worker.

"Rob's Marvelous Muffins." Realizing both hands were a sticky mess from rolling out pastry dough, Rob Taylor answered his cell-phone, then balanced the phone against his shoulder. His gaze landed on the commercial mixer on the counter. He switched it on to prepare twenty batches of cupcakes.

Mondays weren't usually hectic, but with Valentine's Day over and the forthcoming St. Patrick's Day holiday, baking green cupcakes galore became the blueprint of the day.

Pushing out a sharp breath, he wiped his hands on the white apron tied around his protruding waist, trying to remember how many cupcakes he'd tasted that morning. One. Well, no, at least two. Okay, three, although the third had lacked his bakery's signature Irish Cream liqueur glaze.

He eyed that same liqueur set near several pounds of unsalted butter by the commercial mixer, ticking off the items on his to-do list. Next, dozens of cupcakes needed frosting.

A diet was in order, but he'd made peace with that long

ago. A man owning a half-dozen bakery shops couldn't resist the smell of mouth-watering chocolate, succulent blueberry, or tart lemon muffins. At least, *he* couldn't. And there was nothing to do except, well, keep tasting.

"Rob, are you there? Hi. It's Candee."

He grinned. "How's my favorite daughter-in-law?"

"Umm, are we all of a sudden related?"

"Your husband is like a son to me." Rob silently motioned one of the bakers to shut off the timer going off on a convection oven. "So if Teddy is my son, then you're my daughter-in-law."

"I've always loved your logic, Rob." Candee chuckled. "How's the muffin business?"

"Busy. Can't complain." He muffled the phone as an employee wearing a company hat and sporting nonslip clogs ran past looking for the espresso. The featured cupcake was a combination of flour, sugar, espresso, and that Irish Cream liqueur.

"How is everyone in Roses?" Rob asked. "Is the weather warm in the Carolinas? The temperature is in the mid-seventies here in Miami."

"We're all well. It's a pleasant, sunny day and quite typical for February. Teddy sends his love." Candee paused. "Can I ask you something?"

"Anything, my lovely daughter-in-law."

"What are your views on helping a damsel in distress?"

"Like in the original silent movies where the villain wearing a top hat ties the woman to the railroad tracks? What was that guy's name again?"

"Snidely Whiplash. And no, I mean a beautiful woman needs your help."

"Wait. Who in Roses ..." Rob stopped in the middle of his sentence. "I assume you're not referring to yourself."

"Correct."

"Okay then. Who? And why me?" He glanced at his wristwatch. The lunch-hour crowd would be flooding into the bakery soon. Mentally, he estimated the hundreds of cupcakes required to refill the soon-to-be-empty display cases.

"Because you're a professional baker," Candee said. "Plus, you're a perfect gentleman."

"I appreciate the compliments, but where are we going with this conversation?"

"Do you remember my telling you about Kathleen, an Irishwoman from Dublin? She managed The Ground Café."

"Actually, I do," Rob said. "That coffee shop chain recently opened in the States."

"At the time, Kathleen was considering relocating to Roses and starting a teahouse. Well, all that talk became a reality."

Vaguely, he recalled the discussion from a few months earlier. "Congratulations. She made it over the pond okay?"

"Yes, and she's enthusiastic and vivacious and—"

"Good. Wish her luck." He paused to bark instructions to David, a new employee plunging a rack of croissants into a roll-in oven. David had been recommended by a friend of a friend, and Rob had hired him on the spot. High employee turnover and a shortage of staff left him no choice. Too bad the kid hardly looked eighteen, his checkered trousers a size too big for his skinny body, a white torque hat overpowering his small head.

According to his application, David was twenty-something.

Either kids were looking younger, Rob mused, or he was getting older.

"Don't take shortcuts," he directed the newbie. "Check the oven temperature again."

"Yes, Mr. Rob," the newbie acknowledged with a slight bow.

"Do I look like the king of England?" Rob held up a hand, palm up. "Check the temperature, or I'll have you clear out the moat around the bakery."

David gave Rob a blank look and scurried away.

Rob eyed the liqueur. He was inclined to grab the bottle and pour himself a large glass.

Clueless. This next generation was absolutely clueless. Surely the kid realized there was no moat.

The clanging of a pan had him cupping the phone to his ear. "Sorry, Candee. I'd like to chitchat, but it's busier than I anticipated today. Can I call you back tonight? Or better yet, in April."

"Things won't be busy in April?"

"I forgot Easter is in April. Maybe May."

"Isn't Mother's Day in May?"

"June. We'll say June." He ran an irritated hand over his bald head and sighed. "June is the month for weddings. Apparently, a baker's job is never done."

"Coincidentally, Rob, she's a baker too."

"Who?"

"Kathleen. The Irishwoman."

"Right. As we've established, so am I. Tell her cheers, or whatever those Irish people say, and to prepare to never sleep."

"She's lovely."

"Bravo."

"She baked me an Irish brown bread," Candee said. "Her special recipe, and it's delicious."

He slanted over the table to snap off the electric mixer

before the over-mixed batter resulted in dense, gummy cupcakes.

"How delicious?" He tried to decide whether he should put the phone on speaker so that he could spoon the batter into tins, or grow a third hand.

"How delicious compared to your cupcakes?" Candee asked.

"Yeah."

"Her bread is the best baked good this side of the Atlantic."

Whoa. Compared to his award-winning cupcakes? Rob frowned and held out a hand to stop an employee from rushing over to him.

"Hold on," he said to Candee. He laid his phone on the counter, yanked off his apron, and stalked to a quiet spot by a window. "Okay, I'm back."

"She is overwhelmed," Candee said. "Relocating to a different country, launching a business from scratch ... I can't imagine how she'll accomplish everything. Do you recall the broken-down diner on Pine Cone Lane? It's been unoccupied for a while."

"The diner is located not far from Keiran's pub, right?"

At his mention of Keiran, Rob rubbed a hand over his eyes. Perhaps he should tell Candee how guilty he felt that he'd been unable to attend the grand re-opening of O'Malley's, the pub Keiran had inherited from his father. Although Keiran and his wife, Desiree, had assured Rob they understood he couldn't leave Miami during the middle of an extensive baking exhibition, he'd missed being in Roses to support them.

"Good memory, Rob," Candee said. "And Kathleen intends to create an old-world teahouse. The problem is the place is screaming for a total remodel. She's experienced, but—"

"What can I do?" Rob conjured up the image of a cherubic, delicate Irishwoman. Slight and fragile, with flaming-red hair and freckles, staring wide-eyed at an undertaking far too large for her.

"You have the expertise and bakery know-how," Candee said.

"Does she need capital and an investor?" Understanding that all new restaurants were under-capitalized, Rob automatically reached for his wallet. A foolish move, he realized, unless cash flew through the phone lines. And even more foolish because he wouldn't see a return on his investment for three to four years.

"She needs advice and support," Candee said. "She's laser-focused on a St. Patrick's Day opening."

"Does she have a business license and sales permit?"

"All set. Fortunately, the diner was already permitted as a restaurant."

"Health and fire department permits?"

"Done."

"Is she making alterations to the building?"

"Major." For the first time, Candee hesitated. "Why?"

He peered out the window. The wrought-iron tables facing his bakery were filled with customers. Between the palm tree border outlining the seating area, low-flowering crepe myrtle trees added pops of vibrant pink blossoms. The effect created a natural arbor, and shade from the bright Florida sun. If customers were comfortable, they tended to stay longer and buy more baked goods.

"She'll need a building permit and possibly a parking permit," he said.

"Good point. I'll check into it."

"Does her business have a name?"

"Kathleen's Teahouse, and the sign is being designed as we speak. She's keeping true to the logo of the old diner. And she's planning to be open ten hours a day and serve breakfast, light lunches, and dinner, as well as tea and baked goods."

"She should add five hours to the beginning and end of her shift for preparation and clean-up," he said. "Tell her to hire a lot of help, which is forever challenging. Bakery employees find the labor exhausting—both mentally and physically."

"Because of those hot ovens, and they're on their feet so much," Candee commiserated. "Anyway, it's my long-winded way of asking you to come to Roses and give her a hand."

He delayed his response, preparing to launch into a thousand reasons why he couldn't leave his bakeries at such a chaotic time.

"Rob," Candee said, "I know how busy you are."

"You read my mind."

"And I wouldn't phone you if she wasn't in such a bind. The woman is beyond desperate and the place is bleeding money."

Frowning, he strode to the counter and took a sip of the liqueur directly from the bottle. There were plenty of other bottles in the storage room, he rationalized.

"She can email me. No charge for free advice," he said.

Silence on the other end of the phone. Oops. Maybe he'd sounded a little too harsh. A second glance at his watch revealed half past noon. The bakery would be overflowing with people.

He pondered. He hadn't been able to attend the opening

of Keiran's pub. However, if he booked a quick trip to Roses, he could be back in Miami by Tuesday.

His bakeries were all closed on Sunday. He'd made the decision since going back to church. It was a religious choice, and a way to honor God.

"You can stay with me and Teddy," Candee pressed. "It will give you an opportunity to see Joseph, the beagles, and Joseph's horse."

The trip made perfect sense. He'd visit with everyone, plus extend his expertise to the Irishwoman. Furthermore, Roses was absolutely delightful in its slow-paced, countrified way. It would be good to get out of Miami's rat race for three days. Lately, he'd felt exhausted both emotionally and physically.

"Maybe you're right," he murmured.

"Fabulous," Candee said. "You'll love Kathleen. She's all Irish wit and charm. Trust me, you'll want to listen to her brogue all day."

For some reason, Rob felt a little toss of excitement.

Why?

This trip was about a hurried getaway, not meeting an Irishwoman with milky-white skin who brewed perfect cups of tea. She couldn't possibly deal with all that owning a bakery, teahouse, and full-fledged restaurant entailed, so he'd set her straight.

If she was the determined type, she'd remain in Roses, although it was more likely she'd high-tail it back to Ireland before the end of March.

"So when did you say you were arriving?" Candee asked.

"Can Teddy pick me up at the Asheville airport?"

"Absolutely."

Rob took another swig of liqueur. "I'll fly out early

Sunday morning, because Saturday is a high-volume day. I'll attend church services on Saturday evening here in Miami."

"Hurray," Candee said with a joyous laugh. "We'll do the same. See you soon."

He started to say more, then stopped, bidding goodbye and clicking off the phone.

How had he been talked into something so quickly?

Truth be told, he was intrigued. This Irishwoman displayed grit by leaving everything behind and coming to America. He guessed she was probably homesick.

He braced a hand on the window sill and stared at the roll-in oven, where smoke was emerging.

"Mr. Rob, do you think the croissants are finished baking?" David, the newbie, asked.

"Did you set the timer?"

"No." David rummaged through a stack of boxes near the oven. "Where is it?

"Do you smell smoke?"

"A little."

"I'd say the entire batch is burned." Rob handed the newbie two oven mitts and snapped a string of instructions. The young man paled and promptly complied, apologizing because it was all his fault.

Rob agreed.

Mitts at the ready, David opened the oven door to a large quantity of burned croissants. He cursed, then swung around. "Are you going to fire me on my first day, Mr. Rob?"

"For cursing?"

"Because ... because the croissants are burned."

"I'll give you another chance because I like you."

With that, Rob pushed open the adjoining door to his bustling bakery. Fortunately, no one realized that under his gruff exterior, he was really a marshmallow.

3

———

The following Sunday, Rob stepped off the plane at the modern Asheville airport. He and Teddy exchanged greetings with a clap on the back.

Now that he'd arrived, Rob checked his phone for messages. Although his bakeries weren't open, he oversaw a skeleton crew as they prepared products and ingredients for Monday.

Freeze the stock we selected before you punch out, Rob texted his associate manager.

Roger, his manager replied.

Roger? Really? Who said that? Wasn't the term used for radio communication?

Teddy chuckled, eyeing Rob's exasperated sigh. "I don't miss those days."

"Of slaving over a hot oven? I wish I could say neither do I, but I'm still baking after all these years. Sometimes I wonder if I should sell everything and move to Hawaii."

"Or the Carolinas," Teddy suggested.

"You're always trying to convince me to relocate here."

"I'm simply fulfilling my role as your best friend, and

friends like to be near each other. For camaraderie. And support."

The men had been chums for years. A decade earlier, they'd met at a men's cooking class. Rob had discovered he loved baking and pursued a culinary arts degree. Upon graduation, he'd opened a prosperous bakery chain. Teddy decided he didn't want to be in charge of all that dough (he'd quoted the pun from Julia Child), and, with Rob's capital, became a real estate professional and flipped homes.

After Rob retrieved his luggage, he and Teddy settled into Teddy's pickup truck. Morning sun lightened the sky, and the beauty of North Carolina—from the majestic waterfalls to an old-fashioned swimming hole—brought a sense of relaxation.

"Beautiful state, isn't it? Candee and I love it here," Teddy said.

"Yeah. I may rent a car for an afternoon trip tomorrow."

"You won't be able to explore everything in a few hours, so file it under your list of reasons to move here."

"I don't have a list of reasons," Rob said.

"You should." A grin flashed across Teddy's features. "The other day, Candee read a travel brochure advertising outdoor dining by a pool of water in Asheville. She also cited many art galleries tucked away in little towns within an hour's car ride of Roses."

"Sightseeing it is, then."

"I'd go with you, but I'm tied up with renovating the teahouse, plus helping Candee with her daycare facility. And, needless to say, seeing to Joseph. I assume you'll go by yourself?" Teddy asked.

"Who else?" Rob laughed gruffly. "I can't remember when I last toured anywhere with a companion." He drew down the mirrored sun visor for a quick glance at his reflection, keenly studying the lines of fatigue around his mouth. He was closing in on fifty years old, and the strained creases were showing.

"Frankly, you seem like you need an extended vacation, my friend."

"Uh-huh. Thanks for the advice." Rob flipped up the visor, then smoothed the wrinkles on his Rob's Marvelous Muffins T-shirt. He'd worn the shirt under a navy sport jacket paired with khaki pants. A white cotton square handkerchief showed from his breast jacket pocket.

"I thought my age looked good on me, although I don't see as well as I used to." He chuckled. "Get it?"

Teddy grinned. "I can always count on you for the one-liners. I'm glad you're here. I wish you looked more rested."

Dismissing his fatigue with a wave, Rob replied to a sequence of text messages.

Teddy flicked on the blinker and merged onto the road leading to Roses. "Mind if I ask you a question?"

"Not at all," Rob replied, still absorbed in his text messaging. "I'm perfectly willing to listen. I won't guarantee an answer, though."

"When have you ever actually relaxed?"

Not in forever. Rob didn't share that fact with Teddy, as he'd probably encourage Rob to extend his stay. Although he might be tempted, his bakeries could never operate without him.

"It's high time you enjoyed life," Teddy said. "Worrying about every minute decision will only magnify your problems."

Rob paused, reflecting how best to answer. He switched on the radio to the Bee Gees singing "How Deep Is Your Love".

"Since when have you become so philosophical?" Rob asked.

"A wonderful woman changes a man." Lightly, Teddy tapped the beat of the song on the steering wheel. "Makes him stop and think about what's truly important."

A ping on his cell-phone drew Rob's attention. His manager asked whether to close an hour later in order to customize a cake for a last-minute wedding.

If you need extra time to get the job done, then sure, Rob texted.

You'll be paying the staff overtime, the manager reminded.

What else is new? With that, Rob snapped his phone shut and jammed it into his pocket. He felt his blood pressure rising. A visit with his physician had confirmed that blood pressure medication would soon be a part of Rob's future. For the time being, he'd refused the brigade of medicines his doctor was all too willing to prescribe.

"That nice-looking Irishwoman might make the ideal companion on your sightseeing excursion," Teddy said. "She hasn't explored the area yet, either."

"Not interested. You and Keiran married the last two good women on the planet."

"There's more than two good women in the world, Rob. And a third is waiting for you to sweep her off her feet."

"Based on the number of my failed dates, a successful match for me is probably somewhere on a remote island in the Pacific. And because I'm not vacationing in the Pacific islands anytime soon, I'd say my dating days are over."

"I don't believe that for a minute." Teddy's expression puckered into a pensive frown, and Rob was reminded of Teddy's older brother, Christian, who had died in a horrific car accident. Teddy had stepped in and gained legal custody of his young nephew, Joseph.

Like his brother, Teddy was dark-eyed and tall, and Rob knew Teddy mourned the loss of his brother every day. Teddy and Candee were exemplary parents, raising a child who had been left frail and devastated after the accident. Fortunately, hours of physical therapy and boundless love had enabled the boy to rebound triumphantly.

"No wonder we never got along," Rob teased. "You're an eternal optimist."

They flew across a bridge, and crushed gravel crackled beneath the truck's tires.

"You'll find your special woman when you least expect it," Teddy said.

Really? Who? He was older now, bald, twenty pounds overweight, and set in his ways. Anyway, bachelor life suited him.

He shifted in his seat. All those long nights in his deluxe Florida condo with a sweeping view of Miami beach had passed in solitude. He filled the void with work, because loneliness only crept up when he had time to think.

He dragged his contemplations away from self-absorption, preferring to stare out the window at the picturesque landscape with a magnificent Blue Ridge mountain backdrop. They traveled past an ancient church, fields of wildflowers, and a garden of violet irises beginning to bloom.

"Candee is preparing a special brunch for us," Teddy said. "Or rather, Keiran is cooking. Desiree hasn't purchased a dining room set yet, so everyone is assembling at my house."

Keiran had met Desiree when he'd been hired to fix up Desiree's Victorian home. They'd married a few months afterward and lived a few doors down from Candee and Teddy.

"Sounds perfect," Rob said. "I'm always up for a delicious meal."

"Be prepared for pandemonium. Our beagle, Kisses, is full grown. Plus, Candee gifted Keiran and Desiree a pup, and the dog goes everywhere with them."

"The more commotion, the better." Rob slanted his head back, viewing a row of shuttered buildings. "What town are we in?"

"We're going through Hollan Farms. It's a few towns over from Roses."

"Interesting little place." Rob noted mediocre shops and an enormous hotel that dominated the main street. "Someone should give it some TLC. Does anyone live here?"

"At last count there were a few inhabitants. A major factory moved out a while ago, leaving a proverbial ghost town. I heard the entire town is for sale, and the asking price is several million dollars."

Not bad for a place with lots of potential, Rob mused. He was, after all, a businessperson.

A businessperson who could barely handle a half-dozen bakeries in Miami, let alone an entire town.

As they passed through, Teddy indicated the rotted wood on a boarded-up ice cream parlor, then focused a conspiratorial smile on Rob. "Don't even speculate about buying this town to renovate. You have enough on your hands, and should be slowing down to enjoy your wealth."

Rob chuckled. His friend was a mind-reader and knew him like the back of his hand.

"I have absolutely no intention of buying anything," Rob defended brusquely. When skeptical amusement crossed Teddy's face, Rob immediately changed the subject. "How is Keiran's pub?"

"The first few weeks were hectic. At present he's settled

in and doing what he loves. Desiree took an extended leave from her law firm to hostess at the pub."

As they entered Roses, Teddy stopped at a crossroads and rounded toward Thompson Lane. The street was lined with trees, large older homes, and plenty of acreage. Window boxes overflowed with velvety purple pansies, ferns, and tulip bulbs, staying true to the traditional origins of the town. Teddy pointed out Keiran and Desiree's Victorian as they drove by.

"Ready to meet Kathleen after brunch?" Teddy eased his truck around the circular driveway and parked in front of his three-story house with its octagonal tower and multi-gabled roof. "Candee has immersed herself in Kathleen's business and vows to make it as popular as Keiran's pub. Too bad the place isn't open yet. Imagine when it is."

"All this Irish charm in one pint-size town," Rob mused. "Sure, I planned on meeting her."

"Excellent." Teddy grinned. "Because she's expecting you."

THAT AFTERNOON, Kathleen stood on her front stoop and watched a well-dressed bald man wearing a navy sport jacket and khaki pants emerge from Teddy's truck.

Her heart thudded with nervousness. The past few days, endless work had muddled the hours. Today she'd been awake before dawn, baking, attending church, and revising her business plan. She made a mental note to ask Candee if there were any local social media sites where she could advertise.

She'd heard so many stories about the legendary Rob and his marvelous muffins that anticipating his arrival had become an exercise in self-discipline. She flattened the collar of her checkered blouse, critically reviewing her navy-print slacks and sensible leather flats. The mint-green cardigan over her shoulders warded off the midafternoon chill.

She'd half-expected Rob to wear a chef jacket and black trousers, while brandishing a wooden mixing spoon. However, the man confidently striding toward her was solid and broad-shouldered, a warm smile crinkling his face and accentuating his electric-blue eyes. Instead of a wooden spoon, he carried a reflective silver wine bag.

"So you're the lovely Irish rose." He came to the doorstep, stopped within a foot of her, and beamed.

"And you're the famous Rob, who owns bakeries all over Florida."

"Only a half dozen, and they're all located in the Miami area." He grinned. "It saves me from driving all across the state."

"Well, I'll leave you two to get acquainted," Teddy called from his truck. "Rob, when you want a lift back to my place, text me."

"Thanks. Probably in a couple hours." Rob's wave to Teddy was quick before he veered to her. "However, I confess I'm at an impasse."

"A confession already? We just met."

"And an impasse."

She lifted an eyebrow. "Impasse?

"Yes, because I may never want to leave." He extended his hand. "I'm Rob."

"I gathered. Why are you staring at me, Rob?"

"Because you're beautiful, and not at all who I expected."

Near the curb, she heard the purring of Teddy's truck engine.

"Who did you expect?" she asked.

"Not someone who makes me flustered because she's so gorgeous. I get tongue-tied around women like you."

"What?"

"Tongue-tied. At a loss for words."

"For a tongue-tied guy, you're speaking quite well, although I appreciate the compliment." She forced herself to stop and think. "*Was* that a compliment?"

"Absolutely. You remind me of Maureen O'Hara from *Miracle on 34th Street.*"

"I love that film. Maureen was originally from Dublin and only twenty-seven years old when she played the role," Kathleen said.

She felt Teddy's gaze on them for another moment before the engine roared and he pulled away from the curb.

"I'm Kathleen, by the way." She accepted Rob's hand. Large and firm, he had the hands of a construction worker with calluses along the base of his fingers. From hours using a rolling pin, she surmised, because she had the same.

"The beautiful Kathleen." He gave a smile, and her heart skipped a beat.

She regarded him, trying to gauge if his words were sincere. She might have given a flippant response, the cool disinterest she employed whenever she suspected men were coming on to her. But wait. Was he—

No, certainly not. Aside from the age difference, he was accomplished and well-educated. She was a country girl who'd grown up in County Galway before moving to Dublin.

He let go of her hand, tugged a bottle out of the bag, and offered it to her. "This is for you. Do you drink Irish liqueur?"

"Tea. I drink tea." She examined the label. "Imported

from Ireland?"

"Yes, although this bottle is from Miami. Consider it a housewarming gift. It's a little reminder of your country in case you were homesick."

How did he know she was homesick? A ripple of sadness brought a sting of tears to her eyes that she quickly blinked away.

His gaze fastened on her. "I use the liqueur as an ingredient for a cupcake glaze."

"Thanks."

"I like it," he said.

"Liqueur? Oh, I'm sure." She stuck the bottle in the bag and set it on the stoop. "Most Irish men love a drink or two." *Or three or four.*

"On special occasions?" Rob asked.

"On any occasion. Many were on the lash."

"Meaning?"

"Irish slang for going out drinking." Ruefully, she laughed. "I've learned to stick with tea, though."

"In that case, so will I." That beam again, flashing charisma, and firing an attraction inside her that took her utterly by surprise.

"And I'll teach you how to create the best buttery glaze on the East Coast," he said.

When, exactly? Candee had told Kathleen that Rob was only in town until Tuesday. He was a wealthy, successful man, setting aside a few days from his busy calendar. Most likely he was overconfident, a tad entitled, and considered his time more valuable than anyone else's.

"Like you, I'm also pressed for any spare hour these days," she said.

"Oh. Sure." He kept his beam. "I understand."

The appeal of his handsome face caused her pulse to

leap, and an awkward heartbeat went by. He waited, apparently, for her to elaborate about the host of things she had yet to do.

She didn't respond, just stared at him as if she'd never seen a man before. She should invite him up to her apartment for tea. However, while she was usually neat as a pin, the living room and bedroom were in dusty disarray and boxes were everywhere.

"However, we have a dilemma," he continued.

So do I, she thought. Aloud, she asked, "Which is?"

"How will I prove who is the better baker if we don't bake together?"

There it was. A not-so-silent gauntlet thrown down between two professional chefs.

Or did he propose more than a bake-off contest?

"We're together now," she pointed out.

"We're not baking. I can show you my cupcake recipe, the one crying out for my celebrated buttery glaze. I presume you store flour and sugar in your apartment's pantry?"

"Of course. I raced to the corner grocer as soon as I arrived in Roses."

"Good." He brought levity to the moment with another smile. "I've heard your Irish brown bread is fabulous."

Aye, they could bake, but she preferred to chat. Here, on her front porch, sitting on the two white wicker rocking chairs Candee had restored, enjoying a cheery afternoon.

Debating, she gazed at the park across the way. February in the South was being pushed to an early spring, and the flower bushes near her entryway displayed the first pink buds. Candee had assured Kathleen that a few more warm days and all the trees would be in bloom.

"Actually, I'm shattered," she said.

His thick eyebrows drew together. They were so close, she saw the threads of gray weaving between the dark hair.

"Exhausted," she explained. "More Irish slang. How about we just chat?"

"I'm up for that." He glanced at his watch, a high-priced brand she instantly recognized. "We can exchange classified information."

"This isn't Scotland Yard," she said. "And my commercial ovens haven't been installed yet, so I've been using the oven in my apartment to bake my breads."

"Will you show me around?"

She felt her cheeks heat. Her apartment? The setting was so intimate.

Aye, that was what he'd asked, and what she'd alluded to. The teahouse seemed the better choice, although kitchen equipment wouldn't begin arriving until Monday. And the large dough mixer was on back order. However, the vendor had assured it would arrive in plenty of time for her grand opening.

She shifted. She was fairly good at thinking on her feet and making quick decisions, but since Rob had arrived, the edges of the afternoon had blurred. Perhaps it was because she enjoyed being with him and hoped to impress him. Woefully, her place was the furthest one got from being impressive.

And he thought *he* was tongue-tied?

She rubbed her hands on her slacks, knowing he stared at her.

"Alright, then. Follow me upstairs," she said. "Before you arrived, I pulled loaves of my Irish breads and batches of scones out of the oven. I'd welcome your truthful opinion on the texture."

Rob seemed the kind of fella a woman could talk to.

Despite his affluence, he seemed approachable. Who else wore a T-shirt advertising his company beneath a sport jacket?

She noticed there was no wedding band on the fourth finger of his left hand. Candee had offhandedly remarked he had never married. So he was alone in life, reminding Kathleen of herself.

"Lead the way, my beautiful Kathleen." He stepped nearer. "Have you ever sung, 'I'll Take You Home Again, Kathleen'? It's an Irish ballad."

"The song isn't Irish, Rob." She picked up the gift bag and ushered him around the building. "It has German-American origins."

"I memorized all the words. I'll sing it to you if you'd like."

Before she could answer, he belted out the melody in a smooth tenor voice, slightly out of tune, warbling lyrics about a wild ocean and a bonnie bride.

She laughed out loud, and it felt good to laugh with a friend, with a man.

Somehow, as they ascended the stairs, she knew she'd always remember this afternoon. The soft, promising breeze on her cheeks, the glint of a dipping sun changing her Carolina world to a silky, golden glow.

And the appealing grin on Rob's features that engaged his entire face. Women could be completely charmed by a man whose emotions were so utterly apparent. He literally wore his sentiments on his sleeve, much like the Irish.

They made their way to the top of the stairs, and he took her free hand as if it were the most natural thing in the world. When they reached the landing, he belted out the second verse, *I'll take you to your home again, Kathleen.*

She joined him, and they sang in unison.

4

When they reached her apartment, they walked directly into her narrow, cozy kitchen as the screen door banged shut behind them. The floorboards creaked as she hung his jacket on a coat rack in the foyer.

The scent of yeast and sugar flavored the air, and Rob sniffed appreciatively. She invited him to sit at a wooden breakfast nook, consisting of corner unit benches and a table polished in a natural white finish and trimmed in yellow.

"Bread lies at the heart of Irish baking," Kathleen said. Efficiently, she sliced Irish soda bread and went to work on a loaf of brown bread. "Before we eat, let's pray a simple thanks to God." She bowed her head, and he did the same. She whispered a blessing, then offered him a portion of each bread.

The brown bread's crust was thick, the texture dense. The soda bread sprinkled with caraway seed tasted like a biscuit. Although hard on the outside, the inside was moist and delectable.

"Wonderful. I like them both." He helped himself to another two slices and washed them down with a bottle of water she'd pulled from the fridge.

"The trade secret is cooked raisins." She slid onto the bench across from him. "Save and freeze any leftover raisin water for a later batch. It will produce a sweeter flavor in the bread."

"I like trade secrets." *And he liked her.*

"Brown bread is a well-known Irish staple, so what I'm telling you isn't classified information. This bread is a treasured family recipe from my auntie Peggy."

Rob chewed and bobbed his head, encouraging her to continue.

"Auntie lived twenty days shy of her one hundredth birthday." Kathleen dashed tears from her eyes. "She was slim, walked everywhere all her life, and was witty and fun to be around."

"Do you miss her?" he asked quietly.

"Aye. She used to say that without a slab of brown bread every morning, no Irish kitchen is complete. In fact, you can't go into any pub or bakery without brown bread being on the menu."

"I've never visited Ireland." *Perhaps they could go together.*

"You'd love it." Wistfully, she sighed, although she didn't extend an invitation. "After drinking pints in a pub, this bread has saved my stomach at midnight on many occasions. Topped with a sliver of sharp cheddar cheese and heated in the broiler, it's delicious and not too heavy."

He carved another good-sized portion of bread for himself, slathered it with butter, and savored. Awe-inspiring. There were no other words for this woman's baked goods.

"I don't drink, and I'm old enough to admit I've learned a lot through the years," she said. "Giving up alcohol and nights at the pub were two of them. I've witnessed too much heartache. It's been estimated that at least half of all Irish drinkers are problem drinkers."

"Why such a large number?"

"The usual reasons." She looked away. "Affordability, ready availability, and heavy marketing."

"Are you referring to anyone in particular?" Gently cupping her chin in his hand, he directed her to face him.

"My employer, Danny Brady." She eased from Rob's grip, stood and surveyed a decorative ceramic platter in a glass cupboard before reaching for it. "Although not him, because he doesn't drink. His wife, Clara, has a brother who struggles with alcoholism." Kathleen's smoky eyes were remarkably expressive, filled with compassion. "Seamus was a dishwasher for a brief while at The Ground Café. He's been in and out of treatment programs since."

"How is he these days?"

She shrugged casually, a bit too casually considering her shoulders tightened. "Last I heard, he's back in treatment. Success rates for rehab are misleading and aren't as high as people expect."

"If you ever fancy a talk about Ireland, about anything, really, I'm a good listener," Rob said quietly.

"Fancy?" She reached beneath the end bench to a hidden storage unit and retrieved two sage-green place mats. "Is that an American term?"

"I'm trying out your Irish slang."

"*Fancy* is British English." She set the place mats on the table. "And I'll keep your offer in mind."

"Good." He broke the somber mood by gesturing to the counter overflowing with scones. Soon, he'd sampled her blueberry and plain scones baked to a golden-brown, proclaiming them exquisite. As Kathleen directed, he smeared a generous amount of butter and homemade strawberry jam on each.

He grinned. He liked taking directions from her.

Lulled by her lyrical Irish brogue, he listened to her jokes about Ireland's rainy weather and ran his hand down the bench's smooth pine finish. She had a discerning eye for design—it showed in her comfy, appealing kitchen. A leafy English ivy plant hung by the window, a cobalt-blue toaster splashed color on the counter, and a hand-woven rug in a creamy blue weave complemented the tile floor with texture.

"I like your sense of style," he said. "You must enjoy interior decorating."

"Hardly. I find decorating one challenge I prefer to leave to professionals." A smile bloomed on her face. "Tea? I'll put the kettle on."

"Sure."

"You're supposed to say *no, thanks*."

"I am? Why?"

"Because that's what is expected in an Irish home. No worries. We'll try again." Squarely, she faced him. "Tea?"

"No, thanks."

"Brilliant." She grinned, waited a beat. "Tea?"

"What's the correct answer? Yes?"

She pressed her lips needle thin.

"Aye?"

"Have you suddenly become Irish?" she asked.

"No?"

"Third time's a charm. Let's try once more." She smiled. "Tea?"

"Yes. That would be lovely." He folded his hands on his lap and watched her uncertainly.

"Very good."

"Whew." Dramatically, he wiped his brow. "I feel like I almost failed an algebra exam. Should I have started with a *cheerio*?"

"*Cheerio* is another British term and means farewell. Are you leaving?"

"I just arrived." His gaze flicked to the platter of brown bread and he grabbed another slice. "I sought the magic word, and the word *cheerio* always comes to mind when I think of you Brits."

With a heavy sigh, she bent to pick a crumb from the floor. "I'm from Dublin, which is part of the Republic of Ireland. We're our own country and not part of the UK. Shall I enlighten you on the differences between Northern Ireland and the Republic of Ireland?"

He steepled his fingers. "Certainly. I'm quite interested."

"That's a refreshing change. In the States, this topic doesn't often come up."

"I told you I'm an excellent listener." *Good. Excellent. Same difference.*

She seemed to digest his words before she spoke. "Let's get back to our tea discussion, shall we? In Ireland, it's customary to answer *no thanks* twice when offered tea. It's impolite to say *yes* until the third ask." She took a breath. "Once more for practice. Ready?"

He gave a thumbs-up, considered including the word *aye*, but didn't.

"Tea?" she asked.

He held up one finger, then two, mouthing the numbers. "I assume I'm safe because this is at least the third try."

"It's actually the first because we were trying again," she said. "I'll let it pass, though."

"Then I'd love a cup of tea, thank you."

"Cuppa."

"Cup of."

She laughed. "Soon you'll get the hang of it. Are you ready for more questions?"

"Sure."

"Do you prefer milk and sugar? Or a squeeze of lemon?"

"My choice is black tea with lots of sugar." His mouth twitched in amusement as she approved. "I see you Irish take your tea quite seriously," he added.

"Aye, which is why I'd like to teach Americans how to serve a proper tea." She put water in a kettle and placed it on the stove. While waiting for the water to boil, she retrieved two china cups, saucers, and a matching creamer and sugar bowl embellished with blue flowers. She poured milk into the creamer, added lumps of sugar to the open jar, and arranged china and linen napkins on the table.

He considered telling her that if she spent that long preparing each customer's cup of tea, she'd never earn a profit. Instead, he wisely opted for keeping silent as she poured the boiling water into the teapot and their two teacups.

"This warms the pot and our cups," she explained. She waited a minute before discarding the water from the pot and cups into the sink. Then she added two tea bags into the teapot and poured in boiling water.

While he encouraged her to talk about her vision for the teahouse, they filled their plates with more bread. She kept an eye on her wristwatch in between nibbles. After three minutes, she removed the tea bags to an extra plate, stirred the tea, and glided onto the bench.

"First draw?" she asked, preparing to pour.

"I prefer a dark tea."

"Me too." Quickly, she added the tea bags back to the pot

for another minute. "A favorite Irish expression is, *strong enough to trot a mouse in* for dark tea."

"Clever. I suggest you not use that expression around your customers, though."

"Mice in the kitchen. The idea would definitely keep patrons away." Her face lightened with wry laughter. "Did you realize the Irish aren't the world's biggest consumer of tea?"

"Who is? England?"

She shook her head. "Turkey, then Ireland, then the UK."

For the next few minutes, he considered voicing his views on buying and selling, and keeping an eye on profit margin. Because he was a competent entrepreneur, he assumed his advice would be welcomed with enthusiasm.

Painstakingly, she poured the tea.

"Thank you." He relished the rich, deep flavor and smiled. They sat silently for a few minutes, savoring their tea.

"If I opened a teahouse," he said, "I'd insert those attention-grabbing tidbits you shared about tea preparation on the menu. Items of interest will enhance your customers' experience and provide them with something to talk about beyond your delectable desserts."

"Maybe." She stared straight ahead while he sipped. Finally, she said, "I'm glad you like tea."

He hadn't said if he liked tea. In fact, he preferred coffee, even over this exquisite brew. But tea was apparently the Irish way, and he sat back on the wooden bench and warmed his fingers around the fragile china cup. Inhaling the fragrant steam, he plated another sliver of brown bread. "Candee was dead-on. Your baked goods are outstanding. And your scones—"

"Thanks. Coming from you, I'm flattered."

"My cupcakes and muffins aren't anywhere near as exciting as your Irish brown bread." He downed the rest of his tea. "I'm thinking about selling fancier pastries in my bakeries. Every one of them needs a face-lift, and foods not normally experienced in standard American shops might benefit sales. Currently, my blueberry muffins are customer favorites. Mind if I pick your brain for innovative European recipes?"

"Certainly. I'm delighted to share what I know." She placed her teacup on her saucer with a clink. "However, if you're turning a grand profit, which I assume you are judging from what Candee has said, why change anything? My ideas aren't any better than yours."

His instinct was to volley her comment back to her while reciting the adage *two heads are better than one*, or some such sage proverb.

However, that wasn't entirely true. The truth was, he wanted to spend time with her, because he could hardly tear his gaze away from her striking face, her delicate smile. She looked utterly gorgeous, her porcelain complexion flushed from a veil of steamy tea.

Mentally, he went over his flight details, suddenly loathe to leave Roses on Tuesday morning. Maybe he'd stay a few extra days, go sightseeing with her, dine with her at the farm-to-table restaurant Candee and Teddy raved about.

"Would you like to see Asheville with me tomorrow afternoon?" he blurted.

"I can't spare the time, although I'm sure Asheville is splendid." Kathleen busied herself with pouring another round of tea. "After March seventeenth, well, perhaps then. Although you don't live here so timing might be difficult."

"I come to Roses often."

"Do you?"

He'd come more now, even if it meant leaving his precious bakeries in the hands of his assistant managers. And to his amazement, he was okay with that.

"By plane, Miami to Asheville is less than a three-hour flight," he said.

"Rob—"

He couldn't gauge her expression beyond that one sharp word. Was she not interested? Preoccupied?

"I'm just saying," he said. "We can exchange phone numbers, alright? In case you need to text me about anything."

"Sure." She gave him her cell-phone number.

He sent her a quick text. *Hi. I'm Rob. 1-800-IRELAND.*

Her smile expanded as she scanned his message. "What does that mean?"

"It means you can call me toll free anytime you need my help and never incur a charge."

She grinned. "I'll remember that. In the meantime—" her voice quieted, seeming to soften her refusal—"I want to stand out with an exceptional product so people will flock to my place. What do you judge to be the best ...?"

So she sought his opinion after all, although she'd adeptly sidestepped any personal conversation. When they focused on shop talk, her eyes lit with enthusiasm.

And while they faced each other in her inviting kitchen, he realized something extraordinary. His heart, cold for so long, was thawing. He loved a woman with enthusiasm, and her obvious excitement about her business ignited her smile. He saw the evidence in her dark, gleaming eyes and the way she sat straighter, gesturing with her hands. Her grin widened, displaying white, even teeth. She was already striking. When she elaborated on her innovative concepts, she was altogether alluring.

In turn, she fanned a spark in him he thought had been extinguished long ago.

"... vegan baked goods using organic products," she was saying. "What do you think, Rob?"

What did he think about what? He'd been too preoccupied with gazing at her.

"Rob, were you listening?"

"Of course."

"What did I say?"

"You were mentioning using ground flax meal in your ... scones."

"Aye, that was ten minutes ago."

"People are opting for a wider variety of choices, so consider customers' lifestyle choices when figuring out your menu." He searched his mind for topics he'd discussed with his managers through the years, and added, "Currently, I'm serving carbohydrates, fats, sugar, and caffeine in my shops, so obviously my menus are on the fattening side."

"It's all a balancing act, isn't it?" she asked.

"Life?"

"I was referring to food, but aye, I suppose life too." Pensively, she regarded him, then fished through a kitchen drawer and came back with two sheets of paper and pencils. "How about we combine taste with nutrition?"

We.

"Don't forget your bottom line," he said. "Otherwise, you'll be out of business within six months."

She seemed not to have heard him, intent on her list-making, mouthing the words as she penned them. "Crave-ability," she wrote with a flourish, then pursed her lips. "Is that a word?"

"It is now. And it's a good one."

"Are you interested in going over my business plan with me step by step?" she asked.

"Can I ask you a question first?"

"Aye."

"Have you begun interviewing applicants?"

"No. I'm running an ad in the local paper soon. If I get stuck, Sean, a coworker in Ireland, has offered to assist me."

"How generous," Rob said sardonically.

"He's a dependable manager, and versed in the restaurant business."

"So he's willing to quit his job in Ireland to fly here to help you?"

"Aye."

"There's plenty of suitable workers here in the US." Rob lifted his pencil off the paper. "Should I start listing my ideas?"

"Aye. Fill up the whole sheet."

A thought struck him. Actually two thoughts.

Without admitting it, she'd concurred that two brains were, in fact, better than one. And any comparing of recipes wouldn't be done that evening. He'd already established that anything baked in her oven came out superb.

He tapped his pencil while she wrote an extensive list in a scholarly penmanship he hadn't seen in ages. Nowadays, everyone typed on their computers.

Soon, her list crammed both sides of the paper.

She nibbled the end of her pencil. "This is too much," she murmured. "I'll never complete all these tasks."

"Have you considered prioritizing?" He skimmed the tasks and numbered them according to importance. "And let's pare down this list. You can do that, right?"

"Aye." She consented, humming a familiar Irish folk

song, "Oh Danny Boy", under her breath, as she crossed out a word and added alternates.

Hours later, when he gazed through her sheer white kitchen curtains, a full, round moon sailed high in the sky. He glanced at his wristwatch in amazement. The hours spent with her had been nothing short of delightful.

She was a stunningly attractive woman. A woman who touched something powerful and unfamiliar inside him.

Lifting his cell-phone from his pocket, he texted Teddy.

Pick me up at ten, Rob typed.

Did your two hours change to six? came Teddy's reply. *Glad U R enjoying your evening. We were wondering what happened.*

Worried about me?

Always.

I'm fine, Rob typed.

More than fine.

Across the table, Kathleen smiled at him, and Rob's heart did a little meltdown.

Because she's remarkable.

Rob finished his message to Teddy and clicked send.

5

<hr>

Although he tried, Rob couldn't convince Kathleen to play hooky and accompany him to Asheville. She refused, and with good reason considering her opening date of March 17. Instead of sightseeing on his own, he shelved the idea until his next visit, assuring her that he was more than happy to assist her.

While she spent Monday morning securing a line of credit and visiting warehouses, Rob followed breakfasting with Candee and Teddy to lunching at O'Malley's pub, where he assumed head waiter relief for a harried Desiree and Keiran. Pleased the pub appeared busy and profitable, Rob walked the short distance to the teahouse.

Although spring hadn't technically arrived on the calendar, pale lavender crocuses burst through the soil in backyard gardens, and a lazy breeze swept across the grass. Rob plunged his hands into the pockets of his gray windbreaker, delighting in the fresh air against his face. Roses' weather made him feel more animated than he'd felt in ages. February and March were transitional months in Miami, heralding a brief spring before the intense summer heat arrived.

Admittedly, the bounce in his step had more to do with a certain Irishwoman than the temperate weather, his comfortable jeans, or tennis shoes.

As he strolled at a brisk pace, Rob mulled Kathleen's comment from the previous evening.

It's all a balancing act, isn't it?

Yes, he thought. You're so wise. For years, he'd sought to appease thousands of patrons—tweaking recipes, solving every complaint, adhering to the adage "the customer is always right". He'd been so focused on developing his business, he'd pushed aside any notion of personal happiness.

Love? Nope, not even a blip on his radar screen.

Armed with painful past experiences, he struggled to recall why love was so important—why poets wrote sonnets, why it made the world go round.

Because love was everything. Because love mattered above all else.

"Ridiculous notion," he whispered. Besides, he was too old for love. And Kathleen ... well, when he calculated their age difference, he came up with fifteen years.

Had it always been so clear, so straightforward, these unspoken rules for dating and romance? Certainly, problematic circumstances occurred, although Candee encouraged his interest in Kathleen. She'd sensed it immediately, sniffed it out like one of her beloved beagles. In fact, he and Candee had discussed Kathleen throughout breakfast while Teddy looked on with amusement.

Before Rob left, Candee suggested that Kathleen join them for an intimate evening get-together at her home.

"Don't forget to tell Kathleen dinner is at six," Candee

reminded as Rob ducked out the door and settled into Teddy's pickup for a ride to town. "And, Rob, a May-December romance is just the thing when two people are so attracted to each other."

He'd given a brief nod, neither agreeing nor disagreeing, although he'd googled age-gap couples on the internet. Studies showed these couples were extremely happy despite social disapproval.

Still, he felt as if his searches let him down, as the findings had encouraged dreams he'd catalogued as unattainable. He wasn't about to fall in love with anyone, including the beautiful Kathleen. Anyone who knew him could recite his unsuccessful dating record. Regardless of his wealth and achievements, women left him flat, and it hurt more than he admitted. No woman chose a man with a retreating hairline (he was being kind to himself—the correct term was bald), and a waistline that increased with every passing year. More important, the sting of heartbreak was too steep an expense for a few weeks of happiness.

When he rounded the last curve to the teahouse, Rob was out of breath from the final rise in the road. Beneath the overhang of the wide front porch, Kathleen paced impatiently, coming to a stop as if she'd sensed his arrival.

"Hi, Rob." She scratched the back of her neck, her shoulders tight. "I'm relieved you're here."

He puffed to a halt. "Anything wrong?"

"I'm waiting for a distributor to ring me about the oven delivery. I admit I'm terribly impatient. And the large dough mixer is still on back order."

"Sometimes things move slower in the South," he said.

"The same holds true for Ireland." She sighed heavily. "I've been known to snap at people if they're late. I don't want a reputation in the States for being rude. Folks in Ireland accused me of bad behavior on more than one occasion, and I was ashamed and apologized."

"You're a person who likes to get things done. I'm the same way."

Her shoulders relaxed. "Thanks for the assurance."

He caught his breath at the sight of her. That smile. Those deep-brown eyes. He knew he'd think about her every minute of his flight back to Florida. Pausing, he remarked favorably on the exterior of the building, the white glossy trim and exposed brick.

"Teddy's crew is painting the interior and exterior," she said. "He provided a generous bid I couldn't refuse. They started this morning and accomplished a lot already."

"What was his bid? Thousands of dollars?"

"He's offering the labor for free. I'm paying for materials."

"Another reason why I always liked him," Rob joked. He chased ideas across his mind. How could he top Teddy's generosity?

"Please, please come in," she said. The screen door groaned on its hinges as she guided him inside. He envisioned how the diner had been situated—the long counter and various booths were still waiting to be removed. The greasy cooktop hadn't been cleaned in years. On the walls were large black square marks where paintings had once hung.

"The place looks ... good," he said. He searched for another word and couldn't find it.

She winced. "Surely, you're joking." She meandered, pointing out wet stains on the ceiling, bemoaning the former owner who had left the windows open, subsequently leading to water damage on the ceiling.

They stepped across the linoleum floor, coated in thick layers of dust.

Amidst the constant pounding of hammers, an Irish band played "When Irish Eyes Are Smiling" on a CD player. Sounding as if the song had been recorded in a pub, the rousing chorus prompted Rob to sing along.

"You recognize this tune?" she asked.

"Doesn't everyone? Irish music is well-known around the world."

She grinned. "I'm proud to be Irish."

"And I'm proud to know you. You're a resourceful entrepreneur."

"You're a grand fella, just like Candee said."

He chuckled.

"Am I turning scarlet this very minute?" she asked. "For complimenting you?"

They stared at each other in comfortable silence. "A little," he admitted.

She burst into laughter. "Well, that's settled then. Crack on."

"Get to work?"

"Aye."

The blue vinyl seating had been torn out and sat in a heap by the back door. Gingerly, they stepped around it.

"I'm baffled about pricing the scones competitively and hope you can brainstorm with me," she said.

"I'll try, but I should warn you. As I grow older, I'm baffled more often than not."

"About scones?"

"About life in general."

She grinned. "Right, well, welcome to my life too."

She had twisted her strawberry-blond hair into a semblance of a bun, securing the hairdo with pins and a shiny green ribbon. The pulled-back style accentuated her high cheekbones and dainty chin. Her wide eyes seemed too large for her refined features, and the swingy striped T-shirt and baggy sweatpants reflected her commitment to hard work, not to being a slave to the latest fashion.

Once at an empty booth, Kathleen plunged into ordering kitchen equipment, leaving little time for chitchat save for her sharp questions. He pulled off his windbreaker, rolled up his sleeves, and sat across from her.

"Tea?" she finally asked.

"Oh no. Will it be an all-day process?"

"Only a few minutes, I promise. And I'll take your answer as an *aye*." She climbed the interior steps to her apartment and came back carrying a tray chock full of stoneware—cups, a teapot filled with steaming tea, sugar and creamer, and scones from the previous evening.

Today she wasn't glamorous. Today she was simply breathtaking. Despite her flushed cheeks, her complexion was bone-white, revealing dark shadows under her eyes. Bound by the invisible strands of a strong work ethic, he'd later look back on the afternoon as the best he'd spent in decades.

In between her visiting with suppliers who stopped in and a meeting with a service rep, he inquired about her years as head assistant for Danny Brady. He even pressed for information about her dating past, to be sure no man waited for her in Ireland.

Her responses were vague, although she revealed she'd dated a couple fellas and discovered both were liars. Actually, she used the word *eejit*.

"These days, I'm embarrassed I was a stook for believing them," she said.

"*Stook* is another Irish word for idiot?"

"Aye." She wove her fingers together and glanced at the floor.

By late afternoon one of the ovens had been delivered, and the last of Teddy's crew packed his tools and left. She stepped over to a rusty sink to wash her hands for the umpteenth time, and Rob came beside her.

"I'm leaving tomorrow," he reminded. "I hope you'll join me for dinner tonight at Candee and Teddy's house."

She wrenched the faucet shut. "Is that an invite?"

"A sincere invite."

"I'm sorry." Her expression became pensive. "I wish, but I'm drowning here."

"I'm wishing too." He wished he could stay in Roses. Another day, another two days. She hadn't encouraged him, although he'd dropped several broad hints.

He decided to take matters into his own hands. He couldn't help himself.

Gently, he brought her to face him. Before she could reply, he bent his head and kissed her, a feather-light touch of his lips to hers.

She tasted of tea and sugar, her fragrance the subtle scent of lavender.

At first, she didn't move. When his hand curved around her back and the kiss deepened, she broke free.

"Obviously," she said, "we're not going to start dating."

"Why?"

"Because you live in Miami. And I live in Ire ... I mean, Roses."

"That's why they invented airplanes. And cell-phones."

She moved backward. "You, of all people, should know I'm not interested, given you've heard my dating history."

"So you dated a few guys who were rogues. Not all of us are like that."

"*Rogue* is a harsh word." Her reddish-brown eyebrows lifted. "Is the term American?"

"I've never used the word before. I assumed it was British, and I was trying to impress you."

"Irish. I'm Irish." She gazed at him and her smile came slow, lighting her heart-shaped face. She was delightful—part cherub and part tigress. His heart beat in double-time.

"My dating track record wouldn't win any awards, either," he said quietly.

She studied him.

Fearful she might feel sorry for him, an old guy, a desperate bachelor, he waved a hand indifferently. "I'm only telling you so we can commiserate."

"About love and romance?"

"About commonality. We both target accomplishment above all else."

"From the sounds of it, we're both workaholics."

The quiet lasted several beats, punctuated only by the drip, drip, drip of a tarnished faucet.

"You know, I could use someone like you in my bakeries," he said. "Someone energetic and organized."

"*Your* bakeries?" Her Irish brogue thickened. "In Miami?"

"Yes. You'd like Miami. It's—" He'd been about to say it was hot and humid before stopping himself. He certainly couldn't illustrate a Miami travel brochure if those were the only adjectives coming to mind.

She plunked her fists on her hips. "As you are certainly aware, I have my own business right here in Roses."

"How could I forget?" He tugged on his windbreaker. "We've dreamt up a million ideas about it all afternoon."

"Don't you understand? I need to do this on my own."

"I understand that you won't allow me to help you."

"By giving everything up? Why would you ask me such a question?"

Because he didn't want to leave her. And he couldn't just abandon his businesses. Hers was just starting up. Perhaps she could sell the diner. Or the teahouse. Or whatever she preferred to call it.

Thankfully, he kept his opinions to himself, for when he rotated, he confronted narrowed eyes and a stormy expression.

"You'd learn a lot," he said, "and I'd promote you to a manager in my flagship Miami bakery."

"Surely, you're joking. *Flagship* was my middle name in Dublin. Been there, done that."

"You won't earn a decent salary here for months, maybe even years."

Definitely the wrong thing to say, judging by the anger flashing from her dark eyes.

"Haven't you heard a word in all the hours we've spent together? My answer is no. Absolutely not." She spun and gathered up the stoneware, placing cups and teapot on the tray.

"What about this evening's invite?" he asked. "Candee and Teddy are expecting us."

"Tell them I'll probably see them tomorrow." She picked up the tray. "You may not live in Roses, Rob, but I do."

"I can stick around a few more hours. Really. I'll text Teddy and—"

"No. We're done here." Resolutely, she shook her head. "Enjoy the flight back to Miami and thanks for your help."

6

———

The following morning, Kathleen was awakened by persistent hammering coming from the floor below her apartment. The sun poured into her bedroom window and she checked the time, knowing she'd overslept.

After a quick shower, she gulped some tea and hastened downstairs.

The five crewmen who greeted her caused her to stop short. All the scene needed was a foreman. As the word came to mind, Teddy appeared. In a lazy southern drawl, he adeptly guided the men to sheetrock, sand and paint. As he joked with them, she could hardly believe he ran such a large construction firm, because he was so laid-back.

Of course, the same held true for Rob. His winning smile was disarming, and he'd been heralded as Miami's most successful entrepreneur.

His dry humor was comfortable, cheerful, and concise. After he'd abruptly left the day before, her reflections continued to revolve around him. Not her business plan, nor her scones, nor a proper cuppa. Just him.

"Good morning, Kathleen." Candee waved from the doorway of the back room. "Teddy and I came to see how your place is progressing."

Kathleen sucked in her bottom lip. "Good as gold, thanks to Teddy."

"It's a virtual circus around here, but a good sign because it means things are moving quickly."

"Aye." Kathleen fidgeted with the skirt of the apron she'd thrown over her jeans and charcoal-gray sweatshirt. She knew she looked a sight and slanted a glance toward the workers. By way of an explanation, she said, "I was experimenting with a new recipe for scones last night, and went to bed later than I planned."

"You're worn out."

"Knackered is the Irish word."

"Have you eaten breakfast?"

"Black tea."

Candee waved several brown bags in the air. "You must eat a decent meal or you'll fade away. Teddy and I brought you a typical southern breakfast, but I won't take credit for the cooking. Grits and eggs, buttermilk biscuits and sausage swimming in creamy white gravy, compliments of Keiran."

"Thank you. I haven't had the chance to meet him yet."

"As you're aware, he has family in Dublin so you'll have lots to chat about." Candee flashed a sunny grin. "C'mon. Let's eat."

"I won't be able to fit into any of my clothes," Kathleen warned, while Candee led her through the back room, littered with debris. By the window facing the yard, they assembled at a three-legged table salvaged from the diner. A chest of drawers Kathleen had brought from Ireland held some of her personal belongings.

Candee brought out warm food wrapped in foil containers, complete with silverware and cloth napkins. For herself, she set carry-out coffee and sugar packets on the table.

"I assume you drink tea," Candee said as she poured three packets of sugar into her coffee and stirred.

"I've had my fill for now." Kathleen pulled a bottled water from the cooler.

She perched at the end of the booth, gestured for Candee to sit across from her, and said a blessing. Although she'd baked, she hadn't prepared a proper meal for herself since she'd arrived.

"I'm sorry you weren't able to join us last night," Candee said over the rim of her coffee cup.

Kathleen helped herself to another forkful of eggs. Candee had bragged about Keiran's cooking with obvious good reason.

"I'm hoping for a raincheck," she said. "I'd love to see your home."

"Rob missed you."

Kathleen felt her cheeks color. "We had a slight disagreement."

"He was unusually quiet at dinner."

Thinking over his offer tugged hard on Kathleen's mood, and she took a deep breath. "He assumed I'd prefer to work for him rather than run my own business."

"He said that?"

"He suggested I become a manager at his bakery in Miami. Why on earth would—?" Kathleen broke off.

"Only one reason."

"Which is?" After studying Candee's determined features, Kathleen sensed the answer. "You think this was his way of us being together?"

"Are you ... together?"

"We met a few days ago. Surely you don't believe we're falling in love."

With a bemused smile, Candee said, "Why do you think people call it falling in love? Love develops quickly and feels like you're losing control. You know—falling, tripping—"

Kathleen dismissed this with a head shake. "I'm not seeking any type of courtship. Too often, I've failed in the dating department. I'm good at business. Strictly business."

She wasn't an obsessed, clingy woman who needed a man.

Nonchalantly, Candee sipped her coffee. "Every person is different. You'll know when the right man comes along."

Like Rob, for instance?

No. Not happening.

Blankly, Kathleen stared at the paneled wall behind Candee. Admittedly, thoughts of Rob consumed her. He made her feel relaxed and encouraged, telling her she could handle the most difficult situation. And he'd made it clear he was available.

She heaved a breath. At this rate, she was focusing more hours and energy on him than her teahouse. How would she ever create a tea emporium if she couldn't even manage to get menus finalized?

"Why don't men ever listen to women?" she asked.

"Because men and women are wired differently," Candee replied. "Knowing Rob, he was only trying to help. He doesn't understand why you should struggle when he can do so much for you."

"He said that?"

"Yes."

"I know he believes in me," Kathleen said. "Now I want him to stand back so I can face the challenges on my own."

"He's a man who looks at a problem and presents a solution. He's practical. Once you learn more about him, you'll understand."

Oh, but she had learned about him. Beneath their light bantering she'd discovered he'd never married and wasn't currently dating. Beneath his laughter, she felt certain he'd been hurt. On their first night, he'd revealed his home life had been filled with rejection. His parents had never responded favorably to his bids for affection and hadn't approved of his profession.

There was more. She knew there was more, although he hadn't spoken of it. Perhaps someday. At present, she wouldn't push, wouldn't pry. Besides, when would she see him again?

Beneath his commanding exterior she sensed an easily bruised sensitivity. And with that insight, she was more attracted to him. Because he was vulnerable, just like her. Sometimes the most prosperous men were the most insecure. Perhaps it was the reason why he was driven to succeed.

She stared out the window. Sunlight exposed floating dust particles. A fluorescent light bulb buzzed overhead, calling attention to the discolored ceiling.

"The thing is," Kathleen said, "Rob is fun to be around. He's well-educated and freely shares his experience."

"When Teddy needed a friend, Rob was there. He's loyal and generous." At Kathleen's inquisitive expression, Candee added, "The next time he comes to Roses, you might see his generosity in action. He's involved in several charitable organizations, including one with Keiran."

"Rob comes to Roses often?"

Candee grinned. "He will now."

Kathleen's heart swelled. When Rob had smiled at her,

kissed her, she'd felt a shiny spin of hope. Perhaps here, in America …

No. She refused to dwell on a future that could never be. If she and Rob dated, she knew the ending. Men left her without a care. Every single time.

She concentrated on the last of her biscuit and white gravy. Some people were meant to live life alone. She was one of them.

"And do you know why?" Candee asked.

"Know why what?" Kathleen glanced up, noting Candee's mischievous grin. "Why Rob will be back? Do you know something I don't?"

"Me?" Candee feigned an expression so innocent, Kathleen burst out laughing. "He talked about you the entire evening and kept looking at his phone," Candee went on. "I think he was hoping you'd reconsidered our invite."

"I couldn't." Kathleen stood and threw open the window to let in some fresh air. "Look around."

"You sent him back to Miami with your rejection." Accusation colored Candee's voice.

Kathleen bristled. "Wasn't he leaving, anyway? He owns a half-dozen bakeries."

"He wanted to stay longer. In fact, he'd been in touch with his Miami assistant manager."

Kathleen knew her cheeks colored. Aye, her refusal had been blunt, but she'd worked for others her entire life. Wasn't sacrificing all those sweat-filled years enough?

"I didn't mean to hurt his feelings, although I doubt he was affected," she said.

"Did you apologize?"

"What?" Kathleen's eyes widened. "He should apologize to me."

Candee settled her elbows on the table and rested her chin on her fists. "Have you heard from him?"

"He texted me last night." Again, Kathleen stared out the window at the post-card perfect sky and shifted on the ripped vinyl seat.

The previous afternoon, she and Rob had tossed designs around. Their conversation had been easy, and she hadn't laughed so hard in years. She'd been impressed with his quick mind, the ease in which he'd presented practical, timely solutions to her questions, writing extensive lists with his bold left-handed scrawl.

"What did he say in his texts?" Candee asked.

"He said he enjoyed his time with me. I wished him a safe flight," Kathleen said.

"Unfortunately, you're both too polite."

Kathleen took note of Candee's set jaw. "Meaning?"

"You didn't discuss what really matters."

"Dating?" Kathleen clenched her hands together. "When I'm drowning in business loan debt?"

"Love is the only thing that matters."

"Maybe in your world. Certainly not in mine. What matters is that I'm starting a brand-new venture and can't concentrate on anything else."

Candee doctored her coffee with another packet of sugar and took a long swallow. "I admit Rob is a little high-handed at times."

"It's because he's skilled and on the ball. And funny and warm-hearted."

Exactly what the other men in her life had lacked. In the short days they'd known each other, Rob had displayed a tenderness she hadn't noticed at first, developing in the course of their hours together. She'd listened as he'd laughingly remarked about his dismal dating history. Although he'd airily portrayed himself as a man who couldn't care less, his admission seemed more heartbreaking than humorous.

"Wow, Kathleen." Candee set down her cup. "You're quick to come to his defense."

"I—" Kathleen rubbed her palms on her sweatshirt.

"I see you're interested in him. It's written all over your face. Admit it."

Kathleen averted her eyes from Candee's attentive gaze. Despite her exhaustion, she hadn't slept well. If she had more time, she might have talked further about Rob, but the sentences wedged in her throat. Unfortunately, time was something she lacked, and life went on.

She dabbed her lips with her napkin. "What interests me is designing this blank space into a charming teahouse in a few short weeks." As she disposed of the containers, Candee wrapped the silverware and napkins.

Through the doorway, Teddy and his crew set up ladders, arranged tools and prepared joint compound.

Kathleen perused the bare walls. She'd never considered interior decorating her strong suit despite Rob's compliments. In any case, he'd only seen her kitchen.

"How can I best utilize every inch of space?" she asked aloud.

"This is where I come in." Candee popped to her feet.

For the next several hours, Candee shared design tips while drawing up a floor plan, adding extra windows and laying out a well-equipped kitchen complete with sinks, a cooler, and oven placement. When Kathleen peered over Candee's shoulder, Candee said, "No worries. I'm keeping in mind the strict health code."

Meanwhile, Kathleen grabbed scrubbing supplies and tackled the shelving.

When they finished, Candee locked arms with Kathleen and yanked her out the front door. "And now, we're going shopping."

"My pantry is stocked with flour and baking soda."

"Good, because we're canvassing all the paint stores for samples. Fun bright colors will look terrific on the interior walls, and I suggest leaving the exposed brick behind the counter. Build a fireplace on the far wall with a wide pine mantel."

"Let's section the rooms to keep them more intimate," Kathleen said. "The smaller room can seat ten to twelve people, the larger up to twenty. I want worn leather couches in the sitting area, a loveseat, and blackboard by the entrance so I can chalk in the soups of the day." A wave of excitement coursed through her as more ideas took hold. "Creamy broccoli or parsnips with apple and curry are favorite soups in Ireland."

"Parsnips?" Candee asked. "What are those?"

"A root vegetable similar to a carrot, only cream-colored."

"When parsnip soup is on your menu, call me," Candee said. "Now, over and above food, let's get back to decorating. Stripping the wood on the sideboards will create an antique feel."

"At some point, I'll need a taste tester for the scones and bread."

Candee paused. "Is that all you think about—food?"

"I own a teahouse, not a bookstore."

Candee gazed at her with an overly satisfied expression. "I know the ideal person for the job."

"Who?"

"Rob."

Kathleen's pulse skipped a beat. The subject, the man

she'd avoided talking about all afternoon, brought a smile she couldn't contain.

"Aye," she agreed.

Did her enthusiasm make her look transparent? The twinkle in Candee's eyes gave Kathleen her answer.

Aye.

7

———

Rob stood in the backyard of Candee and Teddy's Victorian mansion, gazing at the enclosed pasture. Teddy had converted a large shed into a stable and purchased a Haflinger horse, sturdy and energetic with a flaxen mane, for Joseph's therapy.

When Joseph got off the school bus, Rob was propped against the fence admiring the home's gingerbread trim, which Candee had painted burnt-sienna. The shade nicely offset the mustard color exterior.

"Mr. Rob!" Joseph squealed in delight as he charged down the driveway. "I'm so happy you're back in Roses!" Out of breath, he dropped his bookbag on the ground and launched into Rob's arms. "How long will you stay?"

Rob managed a jovial smile. "A few days, maybe more."

Maybe less. It all depended on how a certain beautiful Irishwoman responded when he showed up at her teahouse.

After Candee had phoned him, breathless with the news that Kathleen had spoken favorably about him, she'd used her finest singsong voice and urged him to return to Roses.

That took some planning, but he'd assembled his managers and arranged the necessary details.

"I'm only a phone call away," he'd assured, with the unspoken hope no one rang.

So here he was, a week later, back in Roses. This time, he vowed not to talk shop with Kathleen. At least, not *his* shop. He was here merely to lend a hand.

As the opening drew nearer, she might fly into a panic. Consequently, he was ready and able to offer his support.

"Mr. Rob, what do you think of my horse?" Joseph tipped his head toward the small horse being led out of the stable by the therapist.

"I think your horse is awesomely pint-sized," Rob said.

"His name is Blackjack," Joseph said with an impish smile.

Nearing seven years old, the little boy had quickly emerged from a preschooler to a thriving second grader. The freckles on his cheeks were disappearing and baby teeth had begun to fall out, leaving a gap-toothed grin.

"Yes, I know. Even though Blackjack is chestnut colored and not at all black."

"Blackjack doesn't mind." Joseph's face shone with happiness. "He likes his name."

Rob touched the boy's chin. "I'm sure he does."

Teddy and Candee's love and affection had strengthened the boy's self-esteem, and he bore little resemblance to the broken child Rob remembered from a few years earlier.

"Rob?" Teddy called from the back porch. "Are you ready? Kathleen's expecting you." Thumbs hooked in his front jean pockets, he grinned indulgently. Whenever he spoke to Rob about Kathleen, he smirked. Just like Candee did.

"Be right there," Rob said.

"I've gotta go too, Mr. Rob." With a breeze tangling his fine hair and an eager smile on his face, Joseph scampered away.

A few minutes later, Rob arrived at the teahouse. In several days, the exterior had been transformed from drab to grand. The old-world appearance Kathleen strived for conveyed a welcoming invitation to passersby. Her signage, Kathleen's Teahouse, stained in lavender and blues and exaggerated by pink teacups, had been fixed high above the entrance.

His gaze roamed enthusiastically over the renovated building. Afternoon had settled, and the windows were aglow with lit electric candles.

A very welcoming place indeed. He just hoped the owner's heart held the same welcome.

WATCHING THROUGH LOWERED LASHES, Kathleen stood on her front porch as Rob got out of Teddy's pickup and waved a thanks. The work crew had retired for the day and the house was empty. They began at seven in the morning and clocked out at three thirty, so without the constant rat-a-tat-tat of hammering, the hollowness echoing through the rooms was oppressive.

"Cheers," she greeted Rob as he approached. "It's good to see you."

"A greeting from a beautiful woman is the best form of welcome," he said.

She smiled. "The Irish are known for their hospitality." As much as she tried, she couldn't tamp down the flurry in her chest at seeing him again.

Should they embrace like great friends, erasing their silly squabble? He had texted an apology and she'd done the same. Since then, the subject of her moving to Miami hadn't been broached. Thankfully, that had been settled.

She kept her hands at her sides while considering what to do next.

"It's good to see you again too." His blue eyes were steady and genial, startlingly intense. His tan golf shirt fit his frame perfectly, and he carried himself as a self-assured man, not a young guy who'd disguised his identity on the internet. Rob's tastes were sophisticated, and he was cultured and witty, an enticing combination.

No doubt about it. No matter how she resisted, she was drawn to him.

An expression of unconcealed admiration touched his handsome face. "I came back for you."

"Because of me, or for me?"

"Both."

"Did you assume I needed help, or did you want to see me?"

"Both."

"So you're not here to sightsee or visit friends?"

"I'm here exclusively for you." Warmly, he appraised her. "And you look gorgeous."

"Gorgeous? Hardly." Self-consciously, she patted her hair and offered a fatigued smile. Then she tugged at the pinstriped blouse and dark-washed jeans she'd changed into after a quick shower. Rob had texted saying when he'd arrive, but, as usual, she hadn't allowed enough time for herself and had settled for braiding her hair and applying pink lip gloss.

"Kathleen." He stepped closer. "I missed you. And I want you to know how much."

"You've only been gone a short while."

"The days were long for me."

The heat in her cheeks became a full-blown fire. Her gaze dropped to the flowers he held.

"I missed you too," she said quietly.

Attraction was a funny thing. It made you forget about feigning disinterest, a game suited for years thankfully well past.

"These are for you." He offered the flowers. "I asked the florist in town for something Irish."

"They're lovely." Kathleen accepted the bouquet of fresh-cut green and white button mums and carnations, the perfumed fragrance reminding her of the bushy plants growing wild in County Galway.

Her beloved Ireland. Nostalgia rushed through her, clogging her throat with emotion.

"Thank you," she managed.

"Are you homesick?"

"A little, although it's childish." Her eyes turned liquid, and a tear streaked down her cheek. "This is what I wanted—America and my own business. Fortunately, I've kept myself so busy my mind doesn't have time to wander."

Gently, he brushed the tear away. "I'm here and not going anywhere. Teddy and Candee said I can stay at their house as long as I'd like."

"What about your bakeries?"

"My marvelous muffins are so marvelous they practically bake themselves."

Despite herself, she chuckled.

He took the flowers from her, set them on the porch's wide railing, and gathered her into his arms.

She'd dreamt of this moment ever since they'd parted, and she didn't resist. Instead, she pressed her cheek along the smooth cotton of his shirt. The steady beating of his heart reassured her that he was here, truly here. And all was well.

He'd texted and emailed nightly since her talk with Candee. Which, he'd admitted, had prompted his return.

His emails were humorous and engaging, often describing a nonsensical situation occurring at work—a customer demanding a slice of huckleberry pie, although his bakery clearly sold only muffins and cupcakes and croissants, or an experimental batch of seaweed muffins everyone refused to eat.

We try to sell healthy selections once in a while, he'd joked.

What did you do with all those wholesome muffins? she'd asked.

I gave them to my skinny employees. Along with the remaining seaweed.

Oftentimes, his solutions to her work-related questions were exceptional. And when she uploaded photos of the daily progress to share with him, he replied instantly. Nothing was too unsettling that Rob couldn't solve with a clever, sensible remedy.

Each evening, when she was too exhausted to decide on another scone recipe or the installation of a gas versus a wood-burning fireplace, she looked forward to the end of her workday. She could finally climb the stairs to her apartment, open her laptop, and eagerly read his email.

When worries about money kept her awake at night, Rob would message her as soon as she logged onto her computer, as if he'd waited up for her. Sometimes, his messages were flirtatious. The actuality that he was eight hundred miles away made their exchanges feel safe and risk-free, and she enjoyed the playful bantering.

"The place looks better in person than in your photos," Rob said as she plucked up the bouquet and they stepped inside. He beamed his approval, sniffing the cedar-scented air and indicating the blazing logs in the stone-faced fireplace. "You decided on wood instead of gas after all."

"Aye." She went to the sink, retrieved a crystal vase, and arranged the flowers. "It's more work, but wood-burning is more authentic. And Teddy's hard-working crew deserves the credit, along with Candee's decorating expertise."

"I love these photographs." He stepped to a white-washed wall and surveyed the black and white photos of the old diner.

"I chose to pay homage to the diner's legacy. This place is riddled in history and was originally named Betty's Diner."

She'd set a table in Victorian style, complete with an Irish lace tablecloth, bone china cups, and polished silver. She set the vase of flowers in the center.

"Do you like the ambience?" she asked, following his reaction.

"Very, very much." He lifted back a pale-blue wool Oriental rug. "The wide plank oak floors are gleaming and rustic, which was the effect you were going for, right?"

"Absolutely." She tipped up her chin. "The crystal chandeliers will be hung tomorrow. And the paintings depict Ireland's landscapes. I placed them on the wall opposite the photographs, highlighting the old and the new, and two different cultures." She indicated a particularly poignant watercolor of a stone castle atop a hill, the rugged coastline and sea beyond. "I borrowed this concept from Danny Brady. Irish murals grace the walls in The Ground Café."

Rob came beside her. "Kathleen, you are a treasure." His sincere smile melted her heart. He bent his head and kissed her temple, then brushed a butterfly kiss on her lips. Joy surged through her that had nothing to do with his compliment. She couldn't believe this delightful man was interested in her.

And he was. It showed in his avid gaze, his steady eye contact and how he engaged her in endless chats.

"Would you prefer high tea or afternoon tea?" she asked.

"What's the difference?"

She glanced at her wristwatch. "It's around four, so afternoon tea is better."

"Again, what's the difference?"

"Mostly the seating. Afternoon tea is best experienced on low parlor chairs. If it's a high-backed chair, then it's high tea."

"Easy facts to remember," he said. "So these are low chairs."

"Correct."

"Is there a story behind high and low tea you can place on your menus?"

"I'll give you the abridged edition if you're interested."

"If it concerns you, I'm very interested."

"Well, teatime is a British tradition." She steepled her fingers. "Customarily, tea, scones, cakes and sandwiches were served in the nineteenth century. Teatime filled the gap between lunch and dinner, which was usually eaten around eight o'clock."

"I eat muffins every day at four. Should I call my snacks teatime?"

"If you'd like." She chuckled. "Nowadays, obviously, routines have changed. However, teatime is still observed as a civilized tradition. More important, it brings friends and family together and allows everyone the chance to slow down."

His eyes crinkled into a smile. "I'm more than ready to slow down."

Aye, she reasoned, noting the low crease in his forehead. Despite his smile, he looked as exhausted as she felt.

She whisked a glance at a log dropping in the fireplace. The wood sparked and crackled. Knowing his gaze was on her, she donned her prettiest beam. "So, shall we enjoy afternoon tea?"

"Sure. I think."

She laughed out loud at his wary expression. "You think?"

"Mind briefing me on what afternoon tea entails? I understand the four o'clock part, but is this another no thank you three times discussion?"

"We've done all that." She gestured for him to sit in a flowered parlor chair at the intimate table set for two.

He didn't.

Instead, he pulled out a chair for her before claiming his own. He was a gentleman in numerous ways, opening doors for her, never sitting if she was standing. Always, he was respectful and polite.

She poured the hot tea, which she'd prepared ahead. Gold flatware glinted by the light of tea candles, and metallic gold linen napkins folded in the shape of a crown sat on bone-china plates, the plates so translucent as to be almost see-through. A tiered platter was set with scones, finger sandwiches, clotted cream, and strawberry preserves.

"Is your tea dark enough?" she inquired.

He made a show of examining the brew in his gold-rimmed cup. "Strong enough to trot a mouse in."

"Here, here." She chuckled. "You're learning the Irish sayings quickly."

They bowed their heads and prayed a blessing. When they finished, she presented turkey sandwiches covered in cranberry jelly from the platter.

"I could get used to this," he laughed, taking a bite of a cucumber finger sandwich spread with herbed cream. "How did you make the cream?" he asked.

"It's not difficult. I'll lend you the recipe."

He settled in, slid his teacup closer, and supported his elbows on the table. Tea sloshed over the rim of his cup. "Kathleen, you've made the entire process look easy. You're going to open without a hitch."

The table wobbled, the legs uneven. And with that, the exquisite settings, hot tea, sandwiches, and flower-filled vase clattered to the floor.

Kathleen caught her teacup between her palms, although the brew spilled across her pinstriped blouse, leaving behind a splotchy wet stain. She dabbed at her shirt, her fingertips catching the droplets.

"Aye," she echoed, perching on the edge of her chair. "I'll be opening without a hitch."

8

———

To his customers and everyone in Miami who presumed to know him, Rob's bakeries were the epitome of success. To Rob, his bakeries were fast becoming a weight too heavy to carry on his broad shoulders.

And he was seriously considering selling everything.

More and more, Miami had become a place he sought to escape. He was tired of setting aside his personal life for an ever-elusive joy, no matter the vast amount of wealth and accolades he'd accumulated.

He craved laughter and companionship with people he enjoyed.

With Kathleen.

However, he also wanted to make certain their bond was more than a casual exchange between two businesspeople.

The following afternoon, he sat in the back room of Kathleen's teahouse with his cell-phone on speaker. George, his manager, was working in the Miami office, and he'd asked David, the newbie, to be his messenger and relay the bad news to Rob.

Butter prices had substantially risen and were up by 75 percent.

"Tell George to shop around," Rob told David.

"He has, Mr. Rob," David said. "All the local vendors and bulk supply stores have increased their prices."

"Their timing is perfect for the spring baking season. That is, perfect for them," Rob said sardonically. "I'll recalculate our muffin prices so we can stay within profit margins."

"Not possible, sir, unless you're planning to charge five dollars per muffin," David said. "We're currently selling at two dollars apiece."

"And losing money," Rob pointed out. "Although no customer will buy a five-dollar muffin, no matter how marvelous."

"Correct, sir."

"I'm proud of my products. However, I'm not in business to give them away." Impatience thickened Rob's tone. "Tell him."

"Yes, sir." David muffled the phone, and returned a minute later. "George said he's well aware of that, sir."

Heaving a sigh, Rob tipped his head against the back of the chair.

"Rob?" After a light tap on the door, Kathleen's voice floated through the room. "Oh, sorry." She put a hand to her mouth in apology. "I didn't realize you were still on the phone."

The afternoon sun shone through the window, splashing her cheeks with a hint of color. The past three days, she'd worked nonstop from early morning to late evening. Between Teddy's crew and a constant stream of suppliers, organized commotion heralded each new day.

Rob had appeared each morning at daybreak, rolled up his sleeves, and worked alongside her.

He smiled at her, stood, and held up an index finger to let her know he was finishing the call.

"Text me later with a better update," he said to David. "Or we'll be churning our own butter."

"No worries. We'll need a cow, though, sir."

Rob stared at his cell-phone in stunned disbelief.

Apparently waiting for a response, David stacked on more assurances. "Actually ... we'll probably need two cows, sir."

Frustration reduced Rob's response to a groan. When he did speak, he kept his tone purposefully calm. "Thanks for the helpful tip, David. Goodbye for now." He clicked his phone shut and tossed it across the table.

Kathleen's lips twitched, a twinkle in her sparkling eyes. "You're in the business of buying cows now, are you? I'll take a half dozen. I heard Candee and Teddy own a pasture."

He laughed heartily. With her, every minute was like being in the middle of a splendid dream. She had an aura of exhilaration, a freshness sparking something inside him. Most important, she let him forget his cares, at least for a while.

Strawberry-blond tendrils had worked loose from her high ponytail, which she'd tied back with a teal satin ribbon. She wore a stretchy-knit yellow dress with a pretty V-neckline and tan loafers.

He'd dated beautiful women in his lifetime. No one compared to Kathleen. Perhaps it was her porcelain complexion, or the figure-hugging dress showing off her curves, or her shiny hair glinting in the sunlight. Perhaps it was because, besides being downright striking, she was chic and confident.

And yet she had never married. What was going on in Ireland? Were all the men blind?

Grinning, he placed his hand on his heart. "Kathleen, have I told you you're gorgeous? I liked the jeans you wore yesterday, but the dress—"

"Aye, you have, and often." She laughed. "And I've thanked you for your kindness each and every time."

"You're very welcome." He stepped closer and tucked a silky tendril behind her ear, his fingers brushing across her high cheekbone. "I applaud your conviction to follow your dreams. You're a determined, sharp-witted businessperson."

She rubbed her palm against the door which had been sanded and stained to a satiny oak finish. "Same as you, aye?"

"Yes, and I don't know if that's a good thing or a bad thing."

"What do you mean?"

"When you're focused on victory at all costs, it's easy to forget the important things in life."

A quiet smile, not quite reaching her eyes, lit her fine-boned face.

He was extremely attracted to her and wondered if it was a good idea to work so closely. He was caught up in her. She was caught up in her business.

He knew the feeling. He'd lived that way most of his adult life. And if he continued analyzing their situation, the fifteen-year difference between them would clutter things up even more.

She extended her hands, apparently unaware of his thoughts. "I hope butter hasn't risen significantly in the Carolinas," she said.

He took her small hands in his. "I'll check in the morning." He perused her flawless figure before his gaze slid to her face. "In the meantime, there's something else we can do besides churn butter."

"What?" She didn't seem to notice the telltale huskiness in his tone.

He pulled her near and pressed a kiss on her hair, her temple, her cheeks.

"Rob ..." She gazed up at him and licked her lips. "Maybe we should—"

He swallowed hard. "Kiss?" He framed her face in his hands, stared at her mouth and bent his head.

From the entrance, a crewman's voice called out. The workers were leaving.

Immediately, she stepped back. "I should see them out."

"Why? They can find their way through the front door. They've worked every day since I've been here."

"Aye, but—"

"Kathleen, are you comfortable with us ... with me ..." Wow, did he ever sound desperate. Quickly, he closed his mouth before he revealed something he'd regret.

"Surely you understand I didn't come to America to find a man."

"And surely you understand there's a magnetism drawing us together."

"Your businesses will be calling you back soon enough, so we shouldn't get too attached to each other."

He tried his most charming grin. "Why not?"

"It's like giving biscuits to a bear."

There went her Irish slang, and he had no notion of what she was talking about. "Meaning?"

"Our being together is a waste of time. Look at what I've undertaken. I can't manage anything more."

He got it. He'd take it slow. She had mountains of tasks, and it was too soon for a commitment.

"Will you take a wee peek at the kitchen in my apartment?" she asked, her tone shifting to businesslike. "The crewmen have enough to complete down here, and one of my shelves needs an adjustment."

"I'm not a carpenter."

"It isn't a complicated job." She led him through the rooms, separated by brick archways, and paused by the staircase. "If you fix the shelf, I'll best the deal with a warm bowl of colcannon."

At his puzzled expression, she clarified, "Mashed potatoes mixed with kale, scallions, milk and butter. And I'll fry you a pan of sausages on the side."

"Free labor for free food," he said. "How can I refuse when I'm ravenous?"

He was ravenous all right. He wanted to hold her, glide his fingers through her strawberry-blond hair, spend hours chatting with her. Kissing her.

As he accompanied her up the creaky wooden stairs, she remarked, "My father never owned anything he couldn't fix."

Rob grimaced. Aware he didn't immediately respond, and likewise aware she was waiting, he contemplated telling her the truth. He'd never been handy with tools, and if she evaluated a man by his hammer wielding abilities, he'd fail miserably.

"That's the way with most men, isn't it?" she added.

Real men fix things. He visualized the slogan—resembling a television commercial.

The tension in his shoulders tightened with each ascending step. He hoped she wouldn't judge him for not being able to hang cabinets or install crown molding, because his reply would be *I can't.* His affluent parents had deemed carpentry beneath them, and encouraged Rob to perform well in school and play sports.

So he had, excelling at both.

And his father had continued to beat him. They'd kept it hidden, presenting a fake façade to their community. Despite the proper upbringing in the proper home, there was no love; only disinterest, indifference, and cruelty. However, they'd filled their home with material possessions, and Rob never lacked the latest tech toy.

After his father had broken Rob's nose once, he'd whipped out his checkbook and bought Rob a Camaro for his sixteenth birthday.

"I can fix this," his father had said, as if a new Camaro could fix a broken nose.

It had come as no surprise his parents didn't approve of his baking career. Although he became a prosperous businessperson, they'd dismissed his achievements.

And now they were gone. A few years earlier, they'd died within months of each other, both from lung cancer. Rob was an only child, and had tried to accept the fact he had failed them, but he never did.

Ten minutes later, he found himself crouched beneath a loose corner shelf in Kathleen's kitchen.

"Can you hand me a hammer, Kathleen?" he asked with a nail held between his teeth.

"Aye," she obliged.

He pinched a second nail between his thumb and index finger, lined the nails up and gave them several sharp whacks. Two nails hammered at once seemed more efficient. Thankfully, she seemed blissfully unaware of his many misses as he attempted to drive the nails into the board and kept slamming his thumb instead. He held in his colorful curses and tried again. Finally, on the fifth attempt, he succeeded.

He stood and wiped wood particles from his jeans. "All set."

There it was. The shelf was secure. Now he could swing a hammer like any of the burly men on Teddy's construction crew.

Her gracious smile filled with appreciation. "What would I do without all this help?"

He prayed she'd narrow her selection down to one helpful person: him. She simply couldn't accomplish this project without *him*.

She slipped off her loafers. "I have something special for us!"

"A wee bit of whiskey?" He peered at her bare feet. "Will we be stomping the whiskey like the Italians stomp grapes for wine?"

"I don't drink," she reminded, skipping to a CD player on the counter. "And what I planned is indeed better."

A lively jig sounded through the kitchen, played by the traditional Celtic instruments of a fiddle, flute, and tin whistle.

She held out her hands, positioning him to face her. "Dance with me, Rob."

He was almost as inept a dancer as he was a carpenter, and he primed the argument on his tongue. "Kathleen, I'm a baker."

"You've repeated that a number of times. And so am I, but I also can dance." She dropped her hands to her sides, and he followed her lead.

"You're Irish," he said. "You've probably danced a jig your entire life."

She wasn't listening. "First, assume the stance." She bounced with the beat, shoulders back and head held high.

He tried to imitate her and carry out her instructions—cross your feet, point your right toe, do a hop, hop back, and lead with your left.

"Leave it to you Irish to make your dance as complicated as drinking tea," he groaned.

She laughed. "Execute the reel straightaway." She whirled him around in a circle, sending her knit dress flying up and exposing shapely bare legs.

He pulled a handkerchief from his pocket to wipe the sweat from his forehead. He was dizzy, he was breathless. And he was laughing with an abandonment he hadn't felt since he was little.

She giggled, her deep dimples showing. As the jig ended, she collapsed against him. Tears of laughter streamed down her flushed cheeks. "Not so difficult, aye? You danced grand."

"And you're amazing." He caught her tears with his knuckles. In his arms, she was soft and light and he tightened his grip. He was charmed and totally besotted, and he couldn't recall ever being as in love with a woman.

Whoa. Hold that thought.

"I'll teach you the Irish jig whenever you'd like," she was saying. "There're more steps."

"Uh-huh, I'm sure there's a whole book full. I'll put jigs on a back burner for now, but you're an admirable instructor," he said. "And your cooking—"

"Oh, that reminds me." She tore away. "I'll warm the colcannon. That's part of our deal."

"How about a tour first? I spend most of my life in a kitchen."

She tapped a hand to her forehead. "I forgot you haven't

seen the rest of my apartment." A slow smile came across her face. "Although saying it's crying for a complete overhaul is an understatement. I've been too busy to entertain decorating ideas, and I admit it's not my strength."

Evidenced by her charming kitchen, she was more than capable. She obviously set high standards for herself.

They wandered through the half-empty rooms—bathroom, hallway, and bedroom. The bare walls were devoid of mementos—no pictures, no window treatments save for shades, no framed photographs of loved ones. The carpet was bland and tattered, the white paint peeling from the ceiling. A chipped farmhouse stool stood as a table beside a worn plaid couch, a knitted blue blanket draped over an end chair. In the corner, wind whistled through cracks in the walls.

Where were her personal belongings? He considered asking, but didn't. She'd admitted to missing Ireland. Possibly she was hesitant to set down permanent roots in America.

Suppose she decided to leave? He captured the troublesome thought and kept it in the forefront of his mind.

"Lovely," he crooned politely as they reentered the kitchen.

"You're too kind." She removed the mashed potato mixture from the refrigerator and transferred it to a pan on the stove.

He grabbed plates and silverware and set the table before coming to stand beside her. "And you work too hard."

"Not any harder than you. Besides—"

"Therefore, I declare tomorrow afternoon a sightseeing holiday."

"Rob, I can't possibly take off an afternoon. Anyway, I'll be knackered."

He quirked an eyebrow.

"Tired. I'll be tired," she said.

"You'll be more productive afterward. What's more, this town is the size of a postage stamp."

"We'll stay in town?"

"For the most part."

She frowned, crunching her delicate eyebrows together. "What's that supposed to mean?"

"It means I plan to show you something first. Then we'll eat dinner at a farm-to-table restaurant that's drawing glowing reviews. Aren't you interested in your local competition?"

"I'm running a teahouse."

"They serve food. You'll be serving food. Maybe new recipe ideas will inspire you."

Ever the entrepreneur, her face lit up. "I guess I can quit at four o'clock."

"Make it three. Where we're going will require a few hours of daylight." He glanced down at her smoky eyes, placed a kiss on her lips, and added a wink.

"Ooh. Sounds mysterious. We're not staying in Roses, then?"

He shrugged. "There's a surprise first."

"I don't usually like surprises. Is this a good surprise?"

"It's a fun surprise," he corrected. "And one I'd like your opinion on."

She gave the colcannon a quick stir, then twisted. "Alright, then. Brilliant."

He smiled. The main thing was that they were going to enjoy an afternoon outside of work. And, by doing so, he'd show her why she should settle in Roses for good.

9

———

The following afternoon, Kathleen hummed "Molly Malone", a favorite tune, as Rob pulled up in his candy-red rental car. The afternoon was balmy, foreshadowing the pleasant weather to come.

They'd stopped working at two o'clock after the power had unexpectedly shut off, leaving the crewmen and teahouse in darkness. Fortunately, the electric company had responded and quickly restored power, giving her the opportunity for a hot shower.

She'd taken care with her appearance, dressing in a royal-blue cotton dress with a flared skirt. She paired the dress with brown leather ankle boots and dark tights, topping the outfit with a twill jacket in a light pink print. She'd scrubbed, blow dried, and brushed her long hair until it crackled and shone. Leaving it to lie in loose ringlets around her shoulders, she donned a jaunty straw hat and pinned it in place.

She called out a cheerful greeting as Rob got out of the car. He was at her door before she'd taken a step.

"My beautiful Kathleen." He kissed her warmly on the lips. "Good to see you again."

"You just left my place an hour ago."

He smirked. "And I missed you the entire time." He opened the passenger door for her, and she settled into the plush leather seats.

"Where are we going?" she asked, buckling her seat belt.

He slid into the driver's seat and did the same. "It's a surprise, remember?"

"Rob, I've never liked surprises and—"

"I'll give you two hints." His teasing voice stilled her protests. "It's a town not far from here and it rhymes with toast."

"We're driving to the coast? But we're near the mountains."

Smiling, he pulled to the curb and turned to face her. "I'll give you another hint."

"Alright."

"Boo!"

She jumped, patting her heart. "What on earth? You scared me."

"Sorry." He planted a kiss on her temple, then eased the car back onto the road.

"So now it's presumed I know where we're going?"

He shrugged, an impish expression on his face. "I assumed my clues were useful."

She smiled. "A town rhyming with toast? Boo?" Her smile widened. "Those are clues? Even Sherlock Holmes would have given up."

Their gazes locked—his filled with mischief, hers with a hint of apprehension.

"The surprise is we're driving to Hollan Farms," he said.

"I've never heard of it."

"Teddy and I passed through when we drove from Asheville to Roses." Rob flicked on his blinker and followed a narrow two-lane road, the only traffic a bicycle rider and a lone scooter. "Hollan Farms is a ghost town."

Images of American cowboys and deserted gold rush cities came to mind. "Here? In the Southeast?"

"Technically, a few inhabitants still live there. Sit back and enjoy the ride." He switched on the radio, and James Taylor sang about seeing fire and rain.

They arrived a half hour later, and Rob parked in a graveled car park at the edge of town. Before she could open the door and reach for her straw clutch handbag, he came around and assisted her.

She linked her hand through his arm, their pleasant banter and discerning observations progressing with each step.

"There's a general belief that ghost towns are creepy and haunted," he said. "From my research, this town is none of these."

"Except it looks abandoned." She pointed to a string of empty storefronts. "It doesn't take a genius to realize no one has lived here for a while."

"Yes, there's that."

Her cheeks warmed as he regarded her, his gaze moving to her lips before he took her in his arms and kissed her.

She was with him far too often. He was the picture of who and what she'd intended to avoid—a good-looking man sharing precious, remarkable moments with her.

Risky, risky, risky. If she continued along this path, eventually her heart would be broken.

But this was Rob, and he was different.

Aye. Different all right. He was too appealing, too perceptive, too much of a distraction.

Too much of an *attraction.*

A light breeze caused her straw hat to flap, and she placed one hand on top of her head to steady it. Trees on every street corner blossomed, sending tiny white petals floating through the air.

As they wound through a forsaken alleyway, Rob seemed to take in every element of the buildings—the worn scalloped awning on the supermarket, abandoned café tables outside a bistro, an ornamental stone fountain. She imagined water bursting from the basin, children playing around it, street vendors selling bunches of flowers and delectable coffee and desserts.

"This was a boomtown, a resort boasting a healing hot spring, luxurious spa, and top-rate restaurants," Rob said. "The town went belly up because of the economic downturn a few years ago. Sadly, the anticipated clientele—middle America—could no longer afford spa vacations."

She slowed to peer through a dusty café window. Chairs and tables were arranged in the middle of the floor, menus stacked by the receptionist's booth as if frozen in time.

"And the hot spring?" she inquired.

"What about it?"

"Where is it?"

"It still runs through the center of town."

The sky changed to a dove gray, and the sun disappeared. A minute later, a heavy rain shower caught her sleeves with drops of water.

"Hold on to your hat," Rob joked. He grabbed her hand and led her on a race through the streets.

"This happens in Ireland constantly," she said, winded

and laughing. "One minute it's sunny, the next, rain is bucketing down."

They ducked beneath the canopied entrance of a once impressive hotel, the windows reflecting a marbled tile entryway and carpet at least ten years old.

"It storms and rains on many hot afternoons in Miami too," Rob said.

Water dripped from the brim of her hat, a puddle forming at their feet. "Except Ireland's weather is a wee bit cooler than Miami, to be sure."

"You think?"

"I know for certain." Her hand was still clasped in his warm one. This close, with his warm blue eyes framed by thick brows and his ever-present smile, he exuded self-assurance. Not arrogant the way some men she'd dated carried themselves, more interested in their lives than anything she had to say.

As she gazed up at Rob, she noticed his nose had been broken at least once. Tenderly, she ran her finger across the bridge. "What happened?" she asked softly.

"He liked whiskey and bourbon and cigarettes."

"Who?"

"My father." Rob was silent for several beats. "The combination was frightening when he was angry."

"Your father." She mulled the two words in her mind. Rob rarely spoke about his family or his past. "Did he ... break your nose?"

"Yes."

"So, he beat you?"

"Often."

"Oh, Rob." What could she say? She knew from Clara's brother, Seamus, how alcohol twisted a person's life into a roller-coaster, the ups and downs catching loved ones in a virtual whirlwind of emotions. Inevitably, wreckage and despair followed.

"It happened years ago. Decades, literally." Rob spoke so softly she wasn't sure she heard him. She thought he dabbed at his eyes.

She pictured him as a small boy, chubby, sweet-faced, an infectious beam in his deep-set eyes. "It's alright," she finally said.

"What I remember most is the smell of my father's whiskey and cigarette breath, and the sight of him asleep at the oak desk in his study, an empty liquor bottle lying beside him. I tried to please him, I really did."

The neediness in Rob's voice warmed a secret place in her heart. Perhaps that was why he'd tried so hard all these years to succeed—in his effort to satisfy parents who didn't care. He was a pleaser, thinking of everyone except himself.

"I'm sorry." Something inside prompted her to squeeze his hand and offer reassurance. "The future is what matters."

They stood quiet, the steady rain beating down on the hotel's canopy. He stared at her so long a shiver coursed through her. He trusted her enough to share his heart-breaking memories.

Truly, he cared about her.

And she, in turn, cared about him. Trusted him.

More than cared. More than trusted. She was falling in love with him.

No. Not here. Not now.

Then where, exactly? And when? All she needed to do was gaze at him. The confirmation stood directly in front of her—with his every intention, and devotion shining from his brilliant blue eyes. Somehow, in the madness of two different worlds, they'd found each other.

Knowing her rain-dampened cheeks were a hot pink, she broke the spell and spun to peer through the hotel's grimy window. She tented her hands and read the scrawled sign posted in the lobby. "We are open to patrons during the summer months."

"Wow," Rob said. "Business is booming."

She laughed and pivoted. "For who, exactly?"

"I don't know. It might be an old sign."

"Didn't you say a handful of people still live in Hollan Farms?"

"Yes, but they wouldn't stay at the hotel."

"So, where are they?"

He shrugged. Gently, he wiped rain droplets off her chin. "They're probably in Asheville for the day."

"The entire population?"

"The entire population of ten."

The rain stopped as suddenly as it had started. He kept hold of her hand as they continued their exploration, answering her speculative questions with speculative answers. Eventually, they crossed a rickety wooden bridge.

The famed babbling hot spring nestled beside budding trees and shrubs, and Kathleen caught her breath at the exquisite sight. With mountain views in the distance, the scene could have been a page removed from a travel brochure advertising tranquility.

"Beautiful," she murmured. "Like a fairy-tale reproduction of what real life should be."

"Zen."

At her raised eyebrows, he explained, "Zen is Japanese slang for serenity."

She gazed upward and sighed. White, wispy clouds floated above, drifting leisurely. No rush for the clouds.

Nature was never in a hurry. If only she could harness that same inner peace.

Directly opposite the sun, a muted band of colors formed an arc. "Look, Rob." She pointed. "A rainbow!"

"I'll snap a photo."

"Quick, before it disappears."

He pulled his cell-phone from his pocket, stepped beside her, and snapped a selfie of them framed by the rainbow.

She was too enchanted by this fascinating town to object.

"You're prettier than any rainbow." Rob hung his arm around her shoulders. "But I can delete the photo if—"

"No, of course not." She wanted to relish the growing attraction between them, to spend every precious minute with him. Everything about him was appealing—each shared glance, the feel of his callused hand around hers, his agreeable, mellow nature.

She peered at the sky. Already, the rainbow was fading. A homesickness she hadn't felt in a while enveloped her.

"Are you okay?" he asked.

"I'm fine." She brushed her fingers across her eyes. "Oftentimes, the rainbows in Ireland are brilliant."

"Rainbows are brilliant in America too, Kathleen. And Roses is your new home."

Here. With me.

The words dangled between them.

"Do you desire a soak, my lady?" he asked when they reached the edge of the hot spring. "You know, all those healing powers ..."

"I didn't bring my swimsuit," she joked.

"A pity." He moved behind her and wrapped his hands

around her waist, nuzzling her neck. She turned, considering, then stood on her tiptoes and kissed him.

He drew an inward breath and folded her in his arms. She wrapped her hands around his nape.

This was decisive.

She was done worrying about dating, or relationships, or whether this was the right time. Because here was Rob, a man she trusted. She loved the way his lips were firm, yet tender and enticing. He was so good to her, polite, calm, respectful.

When the kiss ended, he whispered, "You have no idea how often I think about you."

Likewise. He was in her thoughts every minute.

He beckoned her to dip her hands into the water with him.

"I read that famous actors and actresses who visited here often immersed themselves in the healing waters," he said.

Kathleen splashed water on her face. "Whether the spring is healing or not, this town is delightful."

"I agree." He looked around, pensive, deliberating. "And it's for sale."

"What is?" She aimed her gaze across the street. "The hotel?"

"The town."

Playfully, she swatted him. "A town can't be for sale."

"Sure it can."

The whole town was for sale.

And Rob had a gleam in his eyes she instantly recognized. Once an entrepreneur, always an entrepreneur.

"How much?" she asked.

"I've done some investigating. Plus, Candee's a real estate agent, which is helpful."

"How much?" she repeated.

"Several million dollars."

He might as well have stated several trillion dollars; the amount was so removed from her stratosphere.

"Rob, surely you're not thinking of buying a ... town."

He chuckled. "Teddy and Candee voiced the same reservation."

"What about your bakeries?"

"I'm putting them up for sale. I'm retiring."

She touched a hand to her parted lips. "You'd sell Rob's Marvelous Muffins?"

"I'll keep the name and unload the buildings, retail spaces and my condo. I'll start the paperwork when I fly to Miami."

"Is this wise? You've established a wonderful reputation. What about your recipes, your customer base—"

His jaw set. "All too much work."

"Compared to renovating a town?" She couldn't find a coherent sentence to sputter. "Along with the actual price, it'll take several more millions to fix all the buildings."

"True." Lazily, he stroked a stray ringlet falling across her shoulder.

She stepped back. "Isn't that a lot of money?"

"Yes. However, Hollan Farms has one thing Miami lacks."

His words caught, and she looked up at him. The entire afternoon had followed its own course. And in his explanation, she recognized a deep emotion. Commitment.

"Healing spring water?" she half teased.

"Guess again."

"Rob, I ..." She'd forgotten her guesses, anyway. When she was with him, she forgot all her troubles.

She knew he watched her, so she ventured, "The town

offers dilapidated cafés just waiting for your marvelous muffins?"

"Nope."

"What could Hollan Farms possibly offer that isn't in Miami?"

"You." He brought her into his arms, bent his head, and thoroughly kissed her. "I'm planning to move to Roses permanently."

WHEN THEIR TOUR of the town ended, the sun hung low in the sky, the beginnings of a sunset casting vivid purple and orange hues that shadowed the derelict buildings. By the time they arrived at the farm-to-table restaurant, stars blanketed a clear night sky.

Rob's admission that he would sell all he'd built in order to be close to her had successfully breached the last of her defenses. Here she'd assumed the wall barricading her heart had been honed to perfection and nothing could penetrate it. And it had been so, until she'd met this honest, mature gentleman. Until the impossible had occurred.

She'd fallen for him, and there was no turning back.

"Are you hungry?" he inquired.

"I'm starving, actually."

"Next time we go to the hot spring, we'll pack a picnic."

Next time. A promise of shared experiences to come. Celebrations.

Seeing the restaurant's parking lot packed with cars, she remarked, "We may not be eating here tonight."

"I made reservations," he said.

His cell-phone pinged. He darted a glance at the caller ID and scowled. "Sorry, Kathleen, I need to take this. One of my managers—"

She drew in a breath before a sharp retort rolled from her tongue. *Rob,* she wanted to say. *Must your business always come first?*

After a clipped exchange, Rob ended the call.

Scents of smoked bacon and fresh-baked rolls wafted from the doorway as they ascended the restaurant's stairs. Inside, the walls were decorated in cherry-wood paneling. Candlelight and a pianist playing soft background music—well-known Broadway show tunes—completed the understated elegance.

As Rob hung her jacket, Kathleen removed her floppy hat and peered at her outfit, grateful she'd worn a dress.

When they were seated, a black-clad waiter brought menus, explaining the food was fresh and locally sourced, while he poured glasses of sparkling water.

She enjoyed an exquisite meal of a seared chicken breast served on a bed of roasted mushrooms and cherry tomatoes, while Rob opted for the grilled beef tenderloin with spinach and spaghetti squash.

For dessert, she ordered black coffee and a cherry fruit cobbler. She forked a piece of the crust and chewed discerningly.

"How is it?" Rob asked. He'd ordered bread pudding filled with frozen grapes, and raisin rum ice cream on the side.

She placed the fork near her plate and patted her lips with the linen napkin. "Surprisingly mediocre. Yours?"

"The same." He toyed with the pudding, then scooped up a spoonful of ice cream. "Odd, because dinner was delicious. I wonder if they outsource their desserts because I know a certain woman who bakes a heavenly brown bread." A not-so-secret smile appeared on his lips.

Chuckling, she shook her head. "I have enough on my

plate baking bread and scones for my patrons-to-be. What about you?"

"I'm retiring, remember?"

Sure, by buying and restoring a ghost town boasting a hot spring, grocery store, hotel, and who knew what else.

As she sipped her coffee, she felt an unexplainable surge of pride for his tenaciousness. Although he'd told her he didn't have a bit of Irish blood in him—his surname, Taylor, being French and Scottish—he was as sharp-witted as any Irishman.

"What's the finest dessert you've ever tasted?" she asked.

In the softness of candlelight, his face appeared younger. He looked rested and happy. "Your brown bread."

She smiled over the rim of her cup. "No, really."

"There's a mom-and-pop restaurant near Asheville. I dined there with Teddy a while back, and the owners specialize in homemade apple cobblers topped with a flaky crust. I'll take you there some time." He leaned in. "What about you?"

"Ah, well, in Ireland, any coffee shop or café will likely serve desserts prepared in-house."

"I'd like to visit Ireland someday," he said quietly.

Don't go there, she thought. A small part of her demanded she stay on track—launching an up-and-coming teahouse in America. That meant no distractions.

But then, she'd already made her decision. With Rob, her world had changed. They could enjoy America and Ireland together, as a team, as a couple, as two people devoted to each other.

She sat back in the tufted chair, moving in time to the pianist's rendition of the upbeat "I Could Have Danced All Night" from *My Fair Lady*.

She tilted back her head, her smile lighthearted. "It would be an honor to show you my country, Rob."

"I can't wait."

She inhaled, treasuring the moment. She'd made the correct choice coming to Roses, and she wanted Rob in her life.

The way he smiled back at her told her everything. It warmed her weary heart, and there was no mistaking the love in his expression.

"I'll depart for Miami tomorrow," Rob told Kathleen a few days after they'd dined at the farm-to-table restaurant. They stood on the front porch of her teahouse on a brisk day in early March. A sharp breeze ruffled the burgundy striped awning that had recently been installed.

She swallowed and avoided his gaze. "Seven days seems like forever."

"I'm merely a few hours away by plane. In the meantime, I have a gift so you won't forget me." He withdrew a silver-foil-wrapped box from his sport jacket and handed it to her.

Solemnly, he watched her open a black velvet box and snap open the lid. Inside was a Victorian heart-shaped skeleton key locket on a cable chain, plated in twenty-four carat gold.

"Thank you," she said. "It's beautiful."

"For a beautiful woman." He secured the chain around her neck. "My Irish queen, you hold the key to my heart. Always remember that."

She laughed. "Fit for a queen, aye?"

"Yes." He nodded. "Open the locket."

She popped the magnetic closure, and all laughter vanished from her face. She studied the miniature photo tucked inside—the one he'd taken of them at Hollan Farms with the stunning rainbow in the background.

"Turn the locket over," he instructed.

On the back was inscribed: 1-800-IRELAND.

Tears welled in her eyes. "Thank you," she said again.

"I hope you will always think of me when you wear it."

"Every day."

"That's what I like to hear." He embraced her in a loving hold. Against her cheek, his chest was warm and comforting, his heartbeat steady and sure. "I'll return well before your grand opening. I promise, and I never go back on my word."

He was considerate and compassionate, intuitive to her feelings.

She acknowledged his promise, although tears burned. "I'll miss you," she said.

"Not as much as I'll miss you."

She declined his pocket handkerchief that he offered, her thoughts scattering.

When he was near, she felt treasured. Now these crucial hours leading up to March 17 would continue without him.

Well, she'd steel her shoulders and deal with it. He had a business to run. So did she. Furthermore, she was a resourceful entrepreneur. Rob had told her so himself.

He pressed a kiss on her lips. "I'll call as soon as I land in Miami." His gaze flicked to the crewmen busily making adjustments to the wood floor in one of the dining rooms. "Teddy, Candee, Keiran, and Desiree are all around, so you won't be alone."

Despite his assurances, a moment of sadness went

through her, just long enough to cause her chest to ache. She was truly alone now.

Woodenly, she nodded. "Aye."

And with that, the next day he was gone.

As the week passed, she enlisted Teddy's crew as taste testers while she perfected scones and breads. Happily, they obliged.

Candee designed a high-quality menu, and aprons were ordered to match Kathleen's teahouse logo. At the last minute, the crewmen erected a pergola to the outside seating area, where bottled water, tea, and fruit juices would be sold.

Kathleen stationed a NOW HIRING sign near the entrance of the teahouse, and several applicants immediately responded. Interviewing the bright-faced candidates left her invigorated and hopeful.

However, various decisions still loomed. Would customers prefer high tea or a more casual atmosphere? Parsnips in their soup or a traditional creamy broccoli? Spot-on decisions meant enthusiastic regulars, and she counted on Rob's daily answers to her texts.

As the days flew forward, two catastrophes occurred.

First, the large dough mixer wasn't expected to arrive on time after all.

Forcing herself to sound calm and unemotional, she phoned Rob.

"You have countertop hand mixers, right?" he asked.

"Aye, and a dough proofer and all the bakeware."

"Tell the two assistants you hired to use what's available. They're qualified, correct?"

"Which brings me to my second catastrophe." She could hardly voice the words. "One quit before she started because she said the start-up wage is too low. The other is in university and her work days are limited."

"Keep looking."

"I am. There may be a third applicant. Her name is Nancy, and she's enthusiastic and eager."

"How old is she?"

"Twenty-something. She's willing to work alongside me, doesn't mind long hours, and told me that my teahouse is unique and special."

"She's a keeper. People like that are hard to find, so train her well and take any spare minute to invest in her development. And don't forget to phone Keiran too. He's a block away."

"I did. O'Malley's is busier than ever and he can't spare anyone this close to St. Patrick's Day. Teddy has even bussed a few tables there to help Keiran out."

Rob blew out a sigh. "Unfortunately, being short-staffed is typical in this industry."

"Short-staffed is one thing. No staffed is another."

"Part-time employees aren't dependable. I'd refer a couple of mine, but with my stores for sale, everyone is in an upheaval. Many of my steady workers are seeking employment elsewhere."

"Didn't you assure them that their jobs were secure?"

"I tried, although new owners may bring aboard different people."

She paused. "Rob, can I ask you another question?"

"Certainly."

"Should I urge my customers to place their cell-phones in containers when they walk in? You know, to strengthen community, and encourage family conversations."

Through the phone, she heard a man speaking to Rob.

"Sorry Kathleen, it's David," Rob said.

"The cow guy?"

"Yes, and it's apparently urgent. Hang on." Rob muffled the phone. He addressed David's question, then came back on the line. "This place is like a zoo today. What were you saying?"

"Nothing." Kathleen's grip on her phone tightened. "I'll sort it out myself."

"Sorry," he said softly. "Once this place is sold, we'll be together."

When? Selling a huge commercial operation wouldn't be a matter of a few days. It would take weeks, maybe months. Maybe years.

She'd always found herself cheered after talking with Rob. However, her chin quivered as she felt her safeguards being swept aside. She relied on him, but he had enough on his hands without her constant barrage of questions. In the interim, she needed to trust her own business sense.

She inhaled deeply. "Do you remember Sean, my coworker at The Ground Café?"

"The guy who is supposedly interested in quitting his manager job in Ireland to lend you a hand in America?"

"I wouldn't put it that way, Rob," she corrected. "He isn't *supposedly* interested. He is interested and assured he won't accept a salary from me. Plus, he'd work full-time, so there's no dependability issue."

"You've discussed your last-minute problems with him, plus he'll work for free?" She could almost see Rob's eyes narrowing. "Why?"

"Because he's a friend." She bristled. "He's been nothing but supportive. He rang me again last night."

"And now he's phoning you as well as texting?"

"Only twice since you left. He's as experienced as you are."

"Your brogue is thickening, and you sound defensive, which is never a good sign." There was an inexplicable seriousness in Rob's tone, coupled with frustration. "And what did you tell Mr. Sean?"

"I told him I was handling things well on my own, although these days I'm thinking I can use his support. He's ringing me tomorrow morning."

"Sounds like you talk with this guy more than you talk with me."

"Don't be ridiculous. You and I chat every day. It's just that you're ... preoccupied." She couldn't remember the last time her conversation with Rob hadn't been interrupted at least once. And Sean was 100 percent available—and always sympathizing with her.

"Kathleen." Rob allowed the silence between them to go on for twice as long as she expected. "There's a lot involved here in Miami."

"I know." She squeezed her eyes shut. "And I should be more understanding."

He didn't say yes or no. Instead, he continued, "Several of my managers expressed interest in purchasing the entire business. That's heartening, because they've been with me for years and I trust them to maintain the quality. However, bank loan applications are time-consuming. Not to mention, my bakeries are all still running."

She needed him. Now. Didn't he realize that?

She shook her head. She was being selfish.

"I understand," she said quietly, although she heard the edge in her tone.

"Remember our ghost town. Our life together. Remember us."

Us.

The dovelike caress threading his words caused a delicious shiver up her spine.

"I'll remember." She gave a weary smile into the phone.

Hollan Farms. An empty shell of a town. Despite Rob's assurances, she felt similar to that town. Abandoned.

When her cell-phone rang at dawn, she recognized Sean's number on the caller ID. And when he asked if she required back-up relief, she answered with one word.

Aye.

He was capable. He was more than eager. And they'd worked closely before.

ON A RAIN-SOAKED afternoon a couple days afterward, Sean appeared in Roses. His flights from Dublin to Asheville were brilliant, he assured. He'd hired an Uber for the final leg to Roses.

"You quit your job at The Ground Café?" Kathleen inquired as he met her under the front awning. Despite the heavy travel he looked well-rested, his olive-camouflage jacket and black pants washed and pressed.

"Aye. Howya." He placed his luggage on the stoop and grasped her in a fierce hug. "I'm tired of working for someone else."

"You'll work for me now."

He didn't answer. A shadow crossed his hard-lined face.

"Well, travel certainly agrees with you." She pondered her statement as she regarded him. "When I flew the transatlantic flight, it took me several days to recover from jet lag."

"Kathleen, I must confess." His gaze darted. "I landed in Boston last week."

"Boston?" With keen effort, she controlled her temper

while drawing a slow breath. "I assumed you were in Ireland when you rang me."

"I figured I was off to America, anyway. A few days earlier didn't matter."

"And if I didn't accept your bid to help me?"

"Don't know." He waved his hands airily. His hazel eyes darkened. "I may have stayed in Boston, although I knew you'd come round eventually if I kept badgering."

Typical Sean. He'd always hassled big-hearted Danny Brady at The Ground Café, requesting weekends off or extended paid holidays until Danny agreed.

"You're obviously a pro at badgering," she said.

"I suppose I am."

She couldn't keep from staring at him. His medium-length dark hair had been styled into a kinky perm.

"Any comments?" He finger combed the curls. "A man perm is all the rage."

"It's …" She stopped herself before saying *hysterically funny*, assuming he wouldn't appreciate the humor.

"Foxy?" he questioned.

"Aye, especially combined with your dark beard."

"*Go raibh míle maith agat.*"

Thanks a million. The familiar Irish words brought a rush of tears to her eyes.

"Can you recommend a place in town where I can rent a room?" he asked.

"There's a splendid bed-and-breakfast not far from here."

"And a pub with good craic?" He stepped too close, completely disregarding her personal space. "I'm definitely fond of parties."

She moved backward, remembering the times he'd reported to The Ground Cafe after going out on the lash and drinking. Although she'd often smelled alcohol on his breath, it hadn't seemed to affect his performance.

"If you're in search of lively banter," she pointed down the street, "Keiran O'Malley's pub is walking distance from here. Just don't drink on the days you're working here."

"Wouldn't think of it."

"Do you remember Keiran's cousin William?" she asked.

"I do." His gaze leveled on her. "He won your affection and took you away from me."

"We're all just friends, Sean."

"I'd like us to be more than friends, Kathleen. Surely you must know that."

"Sean. No. Although I'm thankful for your support."

"Gotcha. Loud and clear." He raised his hands in feigned surrender. "As soon as I'm a wee bit settled, I'll visit Keiran's pub on my off days." His small hazel eyes left hers to regard the teahouse's green painted shingles. "Your place looks brilliant. The color reminds me of Ireland."

"Do you think so? Decorating isn't my forte, I just wanted an old European touch. Fortunately, my friend Candee guided me. I couldn't even choose curtains until she carried over several fabric swatches and I finally decided on a jewel-tone floral."

"Candee is your real estate agent?"

"Aye. Her husband, Teddy, is my contractor." Kathleen blew out a breath. "I'm trying hard to resist the impulse to text her every time there's a decorating problem."

"Luckily, here I am to solve everything." He picked up his luggage, and they stepped inside, the front bell tinkling to announce their arrival.

"Thanks for coming. You're an asset, Sean."

"It's because our Irish work ethic is first rate."

She grinned, turning her attention to the shelves

teeming with tea. "Today I'm trying to decide how many loose-leaf blends to serve my customers."

"Less is better to keep the quality up."

"Sean, there are over 250 teas to choose from."

"From the looks of it, you've bought them all." He planted his hands on his bony hips. "Stick with a basic selection of twelve."

"I planned a high tea every day at four o'clock. Is that too much?"

"Roses is a little-bitty town," he said. "Compromise and serve high tea on weekends only. You'll end up failing if you overextend yourself."

"You're right," she said.

His boots clicked across the wood floors, and she glided her hand over a lavish tea service she'd polished until the silver gleamed. "I can't believe you flew such a long way for me."

"My pleasure." Lightly, he brushed a curl coming loose from her pony tail in much the same way when they'd worked double shifts together and were exhausted at the end of the day. "You remember I'm the adventurous sort. Like you."

She also remembered he used to point that out a lot. *Spirited go-getters intent on success,* he'd say. Somehow, the words didn't sound as flattering as they once did.

IN THE ENSUING DAYS, Sean inched his way into becoming an integral part of every decision, from improving providers' terms to mounting a decorative box next to each table for cell-phones.

He was shrewd, often voicing her objectives before she did, or latching on to an idea and expanding it. He repeatedly pointed out that her concepts were comparable to The Ground Café's. Therefore, when she described a problem with the teas or scones, he immediately chimed in with eleventh-hour solutions.

Rob phoned numerous times, and she played phone tag with him. She yearned for his quick grin, the sound of his deep voice, his warm-hearted reassurances. However, immersed in a whirlwind of activity, the hours passed all too quickly.

Another snag, Rob texted the evening after Sean's arrival. *I'm coming, but delayed a few more days. I should be in Roses by Friday.*

Understandable, she replied, noting Friday was a week away. *I'll send photos of my new menu.*

Sean watched while she texted Rob and smiled knowingly.

"I'm here for you," was all he said.

The following day, Kathleen went through every nook in her teahouse for elements she might have missed. Lightly, she traced her fingers over the herbal tea baskets, honey dispensers, and a row of clear glass pitchers. Teddy's crew had completed the renovation, and the place was quiet, save for a collection of Irish tunes playing on the CD.

Everything in the teahouse was unique and stylish, a far cry from the greasy, cramped, and gloomy interior she'd first encountered. She knew Rob would be impressed.

Rob.

She'd meant to send him photos of the menu. In the flurry of activity, she'd forgotten, falling into bed at night too weary to think. She'd do it in the morning.

"What will the children drink?" Sean came up behind her and interrupted her thoughts.

"What children?"

"Your customers will bring in their wee ones. You'll want to keep them content and occupied."

"I can serve hot cocoa."

"What about a fun tea experience?" He inclined his head. "Brew decaffeinated tea and give it an unusual name —like cinnamon toast tea served in a cup named Chip."

"A chipped cup?"

"From *Beauty and the Beast*," he prompted.

"Oh, right." She smiled. "Brilliant. Let's include that name on the chalkboard."

LATER THE SAME DAY, a $6000 invoice arrived for the double-deck gas convection oven. It was stamped OVERDUE.

Kathleen scanned the bill and gasped.

Sean peered over her shoulder. "Troubles?"

"How can the supplier expect payment if I'm not even open yet?" She set the invoice on the counter and began mixing dough for wheat bread. For her, baking was therapeutic and gave her something to do with her hands. "Financially, I'm stretched to the max."

"You can't apply for another loan?"

"I'm considered an upstart, and banks don't risk their money. I put up my parent's home in County Galway that was deeded to me upon their death as collateral. After $200,000, I'm tapped out."

He lifted a dark eyebrow, then perused the letter accompanying the invoice. "The company can shut you down if you can't remit."

"Naturally I pay my bills. Just not until the teahouse opens."

"I can help."

She placed the dough into the electric mixer and

switched it on. "Sean, I refuse to accept your money. I know you're not a rich man."

The electricity blew out with a snap. The lights switched off, and the mixer stopped.

"Again?" she groaned. "Teddy said we may have an electrical issue if this keeps up, although the power company blames the problem on the new lines being dug in the area. I hope they're right, because I don't have an extra five thousand—"

"At present, it's an easy fix," Sean assured, finding the breaker box and switching the power back on. Once the mixer started running again, he showed up beside her.

"Kathleen, I have a business proposition for you," he said.

"I already had one."

"From your hotshot Miami boyfriend?"

She winced. She'd confided to Sean about Rob's job proposal. She wished she hadn't. A day hadn't gone by when Sean didn't bring up Rob, and his remarks were never flattering.

"I'm not selling my teahouse and setting back to Ireland with my tail between my legs," she declared, "so don't tell me to give up."

"We Irish have more pride than that."

There it was again. *We versus them.* The Irish versus the Americans, the bankers, even Teddy's crewmen if Sean disagreed with their work. He constantly implied the Irish were underdogs and appealed to her sense of patriotism.

She shut off the mixer, wrested the dough from the bowl, and began kneading. "What are you saying?"

"We share a passion for this type of place." He sidled closer. Instinctively, she moved back a step. "You and I worked under brass-hat Brady and watched him make difficult decisions."

"So?"

"So let's face the truth. You can't run a business. You're too emotionally involved." His tone challenged with a hint of mockery. "And there are numerous details, far too many for one person. You're in over your head, luv. Hey, you can't even make a decision about curtains without help."

Luv. She let the word go by.

She kept her head down while she rolled out the dough, then dusted her flour-stained hands along the edges of her apron. "As you obviously guessed, my specialty isn't interior design."

"This isn't about decorating. This is about realizing your strengths and admitting your weaknesses."

Rather than argue, she agreed, because she knew arguing with him was useless. He was always willing to fight, and she didn't have the energy. Despite the never-ending work hours, her problems continued to mushroom. Somewhere along the way, she'd begun to feel powerless.

Maybe Sean was right. Her corporate sense wasn't strong. Sure, she'd been in positions of management, but that was different from owning a company where every choice meant financial loss and subsequent failure.

She sank onto a high-backed chair. "What are you suggesting?"

"As I said, I'm offering a firm proposition and subsequent solution."

Her eyebrows flicked upward, measuring him. "Which is?"

"I'll buy into your business." He watched her closely as he pulled up a chair. "Your financial worries will end, and you'll be free to bake and serve customers—the services you did best at The Ground Café."

"Your terms ..."

He slid his chair closer, then stretched out his legs. "A 60/40 split. In my favor."

"Absolutely not." Firmly, she shook her head. "I did all the groundwork."

"I'll continue your vision going forward, so don't go flashing those blustery eyes at me." With both hands on his knees, he leaned forward. "I'll take over all business aspects, financial and otherwise, and you can concentrate on a successful opening day."

"Sean, this is a difficult conversation." She rubbed the middle of her forehead and closed her eyes. "Give me time to consider."

"Rest assured I have your best interests at heart. In fact, I'll draw up the necessary papers." He lifted her chin. "It's best for everyone, aye?"

A heaviness invaded her body. Quieting, she gazed down at her rumpled apron, her washed-out jeans, and tried not to twist her hands. She was cornered, and her teahouse deserved no less than the best. She surveyed her supply of china cups and saucers stacked neatly on the shelves, the double-deck gas convection oven. What would happen if she lost her oven because of nonpayment? Her teahouse couldn't survive without the main oven and a large dough mixer, and she'd run out of funds.

"I'll think about it," she replied.

But what about Nancy, the new girl she'd hired, who seemed genuinely interested in learning the tea business?

Kathleen's mind whirled in a thousand different directions.

. . .

Four more days went by. Four more nights she spent staring at the ceiling in her shabby apartment, seeking the serenity of sleep before it vanished, forcing prolonged hours of insomnia and torturous deliberations.

And somewhere along the way, she stopped communicating with Rob altogether.

11

———

On Wednesday of the following week, Rob strode over the tiny white blossoms lacing the front porch of Kathleen's teahouse. He knocked, then opened the wooden door. A tiny bell announced his arrival, though no one acknowledged him.

He'd texted his flight information to Kathleen the night before and she hadn't replied. In fact, he hadn't heard a word from her in several days. A quick query to Candee assured Kathleen was well, albeit "busy beyond words". Still, the silence had prompted him to return to Roses a couple days early.

Despite his focus on Miami and the mountain of paperwork yet to be signed, he congratulated himself. He'd successfully sold his business to a group of managers who'd worked in his bakeries for years. They'd pooled their funds, the bank loans were secured, and the closing was slated in a month.

"Sorry, fella. We're not open until St. Patrick's Day." A pencil-thin man sporting a dark beard and curly hair sat at a round table in the center of the main dining room. He was unmistakably Irish, his dialect quick, his sentences running together. He straightened from his sprawling position and refilled his glass of iced tea. "Come back Saturday for our grand opening."

"I'm aware of when March seventeenth is." Disregarding the man's hostile gaze, Rob strode further into the room.

"You Americans are smarter than people give you credit for."

"Who are you?" Rob demanded.

"Sean."

"Yeah, I figured."

"You?" came Sean's clipped inquiry.

"Rob."

"Aye. Without a doubt." Sean's derisive grin followed his flippant acknowledgement. He lifted his glass. "My only defense against the warm weather. In Ireland, March is a cold, rainy month. Here, the sun shines almost continuously and it's a bit warm for me."

"You'd melt in Miami then," Rob said. "How long have you been in Roses?"

"A few days."

Rob corralled his anger, focusing on the welcoming environment of the teahouse. The stunning renovation was a treasure trove. Orderly shelves displayed simple fruit jellies and preserves, and the counter was stocked with freshly ground coffee and an assortment of loose herbal teas in glass jars. The entire space was airy and bright. On the corner of each table, he noted a container.

Sean followed his gaze. "We added those for cellphones. Kathleen believes in conversation with no interruptions."

Rob grimaced, recalling the number of times his chats

with Kathleen had been cut off by his familiar cell-phone ping.

"Hungry?" Sean raised a silver tray laden with croissants.

"Nope." Rob avoided meeting the man's assessing stare. "Where is she?"

Sunshine eased through the floral curtains, lighting the cozy atmosphere, offset by candles shimmering along an antique sideboard. The cashmere comfort of a welcoming warmth enveloped him. In that instant, Rob saw the realization of Kathleen's remarkable achievement.

Well done, Kathleen.

"She's baking another Keiran O'Malley recipe in her apartment, because she prefers her small oven," Sean was saying. "Keiran has Irish relatives, you see."

"I'm aware."

"He's a decent bloke and has made me feel right at home. His pub is fierce and just the thing after a knackered day in a scorching kitchen."

"And I'm interested in Kathleen, not you." Rob crossed his arms. "I'll wait for her here and you can be on your way."

Since he'd entered, Rob had been struggling with an escalating annoyance, standing by while Sean lazily drank iced tea and tamped up croissant crumbs from his plate with his fingers. He felt like a panhandler waiting to be granted an audience with a queen.

"I'd suggest *you* should be the one on your way." Sean's sharp voice cut through Rob's thoughts. "You're acting like a Holy Joe coming to her rescue, but as you can see, we're ready for our opening and things have gone swimmingly. And we did it all without brainy old you."

"Excuse me?" In three strides, Rob closed the distance

between them. "*We're* ready? *Our* opening? What's going on here?"

"I'll blame your questions on poor hearing because of your age and not poor listening. As you Americans speak frankly, I'll frame this so that you understand. Crack on and leave."

"Don't tell me what to do," Rob warned. "This isn't your place." He yanked out his cell-phone and typed Kathleen a text. *Where are you? I'm standing in your dining room.*

"On the contrary, it *is* my place." Sean examined his well-manicured fingernails. "Kathleen has agreed to make me her business partner. I'm here for the long haul."

For a moment, Rob couldn't trust himself to reply, his brain registering disbelief. His narrowed gaze examined Sean's blasé expression.

"I don't believe it. Kathleen is self-reliant."

Sean shrugged. "She's going in a different direction."

"Indeed?" Rob inquired. "Tell me more."

He'd been gone only a short while and Sean had triumphantly wormed his way back into her life. Slowly, something inside Rob began to crumble. While he was working out details and selling everything for her, she was handing over her business to this pompous Irishman.

He recalled his phone call with Kathleen when she'd sprung to Sean's defense.

"*Do you remember Sean, my coworker at The Ground Café?*" she'd asked.

"*The guy who is supposedly interested in quitting his manager job in Ireland to lend you a hand in America?*"

"*I wouldn't put it that way, Rob. Sean isn't supposedly interested. He is interested and assured he won't accept a salary if he were to come here.*"

Rob scrubbed a hand over his face. He should've

known Sean wouldn't waste a second quitting his job, flying over the Atlantic Ocean and coming to Kathleen's rescue. Nevertheless, she considered Sean a friend, so Rob was willing to endure the rest of the exchange for her sake.

"What are the terms of this offer?" Rob asked. "Because I can make her a better one."

"Can you? Mine is a 60/40 split."

"She'd agree to that?" Rob barked a laugh. "I'm surprised."

"We've always been brilliant together, and I'm her new fella. She's a fine thing, isn't she?"

Rob grappled with a stab of jealousy. "I can afford to give her the world," he said quietly.

"Your wealth doesn't impress me or Kathleen. How dare you flaunt your money around?" Sean enunciated each word in a vicious, thick brogue. "She's thrilled with our recent agreement."

"Oh, am I now, Sean?" Kathleen stormed into the room, her face emanating pure outrage. By the looks of the two steps she'd walked, she'd been in the doorway for some time. The green ribbon tying back her silky hair was askew, and her dark eyes sparked with fury.

Rob's heart thumped in double time, his gaze riveted on her. He trod closer, intending to take her in his embrace. She shrugged him off and marched to within a foot of Sean.

"How are ya, luv?" Sean grinned.

"Luv? Luv? I never decided on any so-called agreement."

"You were earwigging?" Sean shoved his glass aside and rose to his feet. "Eavesdropping on a private chat?"

She stamped her foot. "This is *my* teahouse, not yours."

Her outburst earned her Sean's hangdog expression. "Kathleen, I beg your forgiveness. Just teasing. Obviously, you're a bundle of nerves with St. Paddy's looming. If you'll only—"

"Get out and don't come back."

"What? And go where—" he sputtered.

"Back to Boston, or Ireland. You've ruined it for yourself by your underhandedness." She shook her head and whispered, "I should've realized. Why do I never learn?"

Without so much as picking up his glass or bidding a courteous goodbye, Sean twisted on his heels and blustered through the front door with lengthy, purposeful strides.

"A sound good riddance to him," Rob said as the door slammed. "Now you and I can talk."

Whirling, her glare blasted fury. "As if I'm starving for a chat with you when you're always so preoccupied. I don't need you, and I don't need Sean."

"We've been separated for a while, but now I'm retired. Let's sit down and have a friendly discussion over a cup of tea. Candee mentioned you received an overdue bill for the gas convection oven. I can help by writing out—"

Kathleen's eyes widened, and tears erupted. "How can you be so brilliant and yet think you can buy me? I know what I want, and I can achieve it on my own."

"But I can fix this." He paused. He loathed saying the same words his father had used on him, and it hadn't resolved anything.

Inside his jacket pocket, his cell-phone rang.

She stepped behind a high-backed chair, as if fortifying herself against him. Deliberately, she unclasped the skeleton key locket from her neck and placed it on the chair.

He felt as if his heart was breaking. He rubbed his fist against his chest. His eyes blurred with the effort.

His phone kept ringing.

"Aren't you going to answer?" she asked.

"Later." He came forward and closed his hand over her shoulder. "It's not important."

More tears leaked from her eyes and rolled down her cheeks. He brushed them away, and she flinched.

"Rob, return to Miami where you obviously belong."

They were so close he could see the mix of emotions crossing her face—trembling chin, lips pressed together, the slight freckles dotting her wet cheeks.

"You must know how much I love you," he said.

She drew an inward breath. "Everyone seems to love me these days." Despite her quaking voice, she remained perfectly still.

"I realize you're joking. I know how you Irish love to—"

"This Irishwoman is deadly serious." Her voice rose. "And another thing, which I'm certain will come as a shocking surprise to you: this business is mine, and mine alone."

12

———

At noon a day later, Kathleen sat in a high-backed chair in her teahouse and went through her text messages. Rob hadn't returned since their argument.

Instead, he'd called and left messages, saying he was staying at Candee and Teddy's home if she needed him.

Here's a final idea, he'd texted. *I've partnered with the Roses Chamber of Commerce for a ribbon-cutting ceremony on your official opening day. I know it's late but every bit of advertising helps.*

She hadn't responded.

I've done more market research and can set up a paid advertising media blitz which will coincide with St. Patrick's Day.

No. She'd set up all her online advertising ahead of time. She didn't need to lean on anyone except herself.

Why won't you let me help you? he'd asked again and again. *If you give us half a chance, you will remember how good we r together.*

That dart effectively pierced a nerve, and she'd closed her cell-phone and placed it in her purse.

A soft opening at the teahouse was arranged to begin at four o'clock. This gave her and Nancy, the new employee, a chance to work out the crimps. Although the public was aware the teahouse was launching, Kathleen hadn't actively publicized it. Candee and Teddy sent their regards, as Joseph was participating in a horse show in Asheville and they couldn't attend. Keiran and Desiree were swamped at O'Malley's. And Sean had fled Roses.

Fortunately, another power outage hadn't occurred while customers dined later that evening, although the lock on the women's bathroom door broke.

Kathleen had also teamed up with Keiran and chalked his mushroom stroganoff as a main dinner entrée, quickly learning that serving the dish at five o'clock was too early and nine too late. Patrons preferred their dinner hour at seven, and she'd soon run out of mushroom stroganoff.

By nine p.m., the teahouse had emptied. After Nancy helped clean, she'd scanned a text message on her phone and departed without an explanation, forgetting her house keys in her haste. Because Nancy lived with her parents on the outskirts of Roses, Kathleen assumed she wouldn't need the keys until morning. Just in case, she put them aside near the herbal tea jars.

Kathleen dreaded the silence that enveloped the unoccupied rooms. It allowed her mind to dwell on all she'd lost. No longer could she hide behind work and busyness. She was forced to confront how much she missed Rob.

She slumped in the loveseat near the foyer and picked up her phone. She planned to make notes about the soft opening, tweaking her original vision. Despite her attempts, she couldn't focus, too intent on the honorable, caring man who had stolen her heart.

He'd been justifiably hurt and angry when he'd

returned from Miami to find Sean lounging in her teahouse. And jealous, hiding his emotions by offering her money, hoping it would smooth the rift between them.

Her heart pinched. He'd worked for years to ensure a prosperous business, and desperately wanted her to succeed as well. He was the type of guy who helped people, soft-hearted and obliging. She knew he would never refuse her any favor. Rob was a man she could always count on.

He loved her. He'd told her so.

And what had she done when he'd proclaimed his love?

Why, she'd thrown it in his face.

"You must know how much I love you," he'd said.

"Everyone seems to love me these days," she'd responded coolly.

She read his numerous texts, pleading with her to give them a second chance.

She hadn't replied.

He had inquired about attending her soft opening.

I'd prefer you didn't. Please take my advice and stay in Miami.

And then he'd gone dark and hadn't contacted her since.

Dejectedly, she put her head in her hands and sobbed. Somehow, she'd done it again—succeeded in being involved in a heartbreaking romance with a man.

No. That wasn't true. Rob had given up his life in Miami, his thriving career, *everything* for her. And in the shared hours exploring a ghost town and dancing Irish jigs, amidst toppled tea cups and spilled vases filled with water and flowers, she'd fallen in love with him too.

Restless, she wiped her eyes, stood, and wandered through the vacant, lonely rooms, lighting night light candles and watering the potted green ferns.

Nothing was the same without him. The teahouse wasn't

alive. He'd brought laughter, full of ideas, a ready smile on his face. And now he was gone.

She had driven him away, flatly refusing his help. She'd seen the raw sadness in his blue eyes, the sagging around his mouth, when he'd said goodbye and walked out the door.

She leaned a shoulder on the windowpane and stared out at a cloudless night. Somewhere in the distance, a church bell pealed. When the time neared midnight, she sighted the star-shaped Big Dipper above the northern horizon.

Half-heartedly, she murmured, "Rob, how can you be so quiet after I told you to return to Miami? Did you forget me already?"

With a tattered sigh, she retreated to the back room and burrowed through the chest of drawers. She extracted the skeleton key locket and glided her fingers over the elaborate floral design. He'd confessed she held the key to his heart and requested she wear it always.

"Rainbows are brilliant in America too, Kathleen. And Roses is your new home."

And then the words that had dangled between them.

Here. With me.

She secured the locket, feeling better when it was near her heart, where it belonged.

With trembling hands, she texted him. If he accepted her apology and boarded a plane from Miami in the morning, he might arrive in Roses by midday. There was so much she needed to tell him. She'd been hurt by men countless times in her life and had been afraid to trust again. To love again.

But what was the world without love?

· · ·

A FEW MINUTES after midnight brought a ping to Rob's cellphone. He'd been sitting by the guest bedroom's window in Candee's home, gazing idly outside at the familiar Big Dipper. The house was quiet, as the family was attending a horse show in Asheville.

"It better not be another manager texting me at this hour," he muttered, yanking the phone from his pocket.

Kathleen's caller ID appeared on the screen.

I miss you. Would you consider flying back from Miami?

And then: *1-800-IRELAND.*

He couldn't contain his excitement. He was already on his feet, his heart pounding with joy.

The drive to Kathleen's teahouse, which normally took under ten minutes, he covered in less than five. He didn't know what he'd say, wasn't sure how she'd respond. All that mattered was she had reached out to him and he was able to see her again.

He knocked once, hesitating only a second outside the teahouse's door, feeling the cool nip in the night air against his heated cheeks. Realizing the door was unlocked, he stepped inside. The tinkling bell announced his arrival.

She sat on a velvet loveseat in the foyer, her back to him, peering at a lengthy list. He recognized the business plan they'd drawn up together.

"Nancy?" Kathleen inquired without glancing up. "I put your keys aside for you. You'll see them by the tea jars on the counter."

He longed to rush to her, to pull her into his arms. She looked vulnerable, her red-gold hair shining in the delicate candlelight. Twice, he'd left her alone when he'd flown to Miami.

"Kathleen," he said.

She twisted and flew to her feet. "Rob?" All color drained from her complexion. "You're here? How?"

"I never left Roses."

"I thought you were in Miami."

"I couldn't leave." He strode to a cell-phone container and slipped his phone inside. "Our life together wasn't finished. It hadn't even started."

She moistened her lips, raced to him, and looped her arms around his neck.

He cradled her and guided her to the loveseat. She wore his locket over a starched white shirt and tailored black pants—the uniform she'd decided on for the teahouse. He traced his fingers along her high cheekbones. Her long dark lashes fluttered.

"I wish you'd been here, for the soft opening," she said.

"I wanted to. I'm here now. How did it go?"

"A few tweaks. Actually more than a few." She snuggled nearer his chest. "I learned people in Roses like to eat dinner at seven o'clock and be home early. The place cleared out by nine."

His lips brushed her forehead. "That's what a little bird told me."

She gazed up at him, this beauty he'd almost lost. "Who?" she asked.

"Nancy."

"My new employee?"

"Lovely woman, and absolutely exceptional. Sorry she'll no longer be working for you."

Rapidly, Kathleen blinked. "Excuse me?"

"Nancy will be working for me. Or rather, for us."

"You can't just walk in and steal my best employee."

"*Our* best employee."

"I'm not following." She frowned, her voice uncertain. "I finally ..."

He pressed a finger to her mouth. "I bought another place. A ghost town, actually."

"You bought ..." Incredulous, she stared at him. "You bought Hollan Farms? Now you'll be busier than ever."

"I didn't buy the town for me." He kissed her lips, softly, sweetly. "I bought the town for David to manage. I'm a silent investor."

She grinned, her face lighting with laughter. "The cow guy?"

"The one and only. And Nancy will help him." Rob twirled a lock of Kathleen's silky hair around his fingers. "Those two are young and ambitious. Hey, maybe it's the start of a budding romance. And you and I can oversee their progress once in a while."

"What will you do in the meantime?" she asked.

"I'm retired." He grinned. "But I'll be around, just in case you need my assistance."

"I do." She sat straighter, meeting his gaze with her own. "And I finally realized that accepting help isn't a sign of weakness, but of strength."

"You'll be far more able to reach your goals."

"Aye. So I've learned."

"Since you're so agreeable," he stood, then got down on one knee. "Will you marry an American man like me?"

"This is really happening," she murmured. "And my answer is, aye. Yes."

His smile reached his ears, and he went back to cuddling her on the loveseat. "After St. Patrick's Day, we'll look for a home in Roses," he said.

"I like the mild weather here. In Ireland, the days get dark quickly in the winter, and it's rainy and cold."

"In Miami, it's too hot most of the year."

Her deep brown eyes brimmed with tears. "Then Roses is perfect." She snuggled into his arms as his lips moved over hers.

"I love you more than anyone in the world," he whispered. "When you told me to leave, I vowed to wait however long it might take. I knew we had something extraordinary together."

"I've always wanted to visit Miami."

"I've always wanted to visit Ireland. I even have their toll-free number."

She laughed. "You don't really think that if you punch in 1-800-IRELAND, someone from Ireland will answer?"

With aching tenderness, he said, "I believe she will."

"I love you," she whispered.

"And I love you."

In the container by a table, his cell-phone rang.

She grinned up at him. "Ireland calling?"

"Toll-free."

"Aren't you going to answer it?"

"Nope. She's already answered all my dreams." He gazed around her comfortable teahouse, then at the exquisite woman in his arms. What a magical journey they'd embarked on, a May-December romance.

A forever love.

THE END

RECIPE FOR AUNTIE PEGGY'S IRISH BROWN BREAD

6 cups seedless raisins
  2 cups rain water. Save after cooking the raisins

COVER THE RAISINS WITH WATER. Cook until tender. Drain but SAVE two cups of the liquid after cooking.

DRY

7 cups sifted, all-purpose flour
1 teaspoon allspice
4 teaspoons cinnamon
2 teaspoons nutmeg
4 teaspoons baking soda

WET

1 cup butter, softened/room temperature
3 cups sugar. Quantity is adjustable
6 large eggs, room temperature.

IF YOU WISH, set aside the raisin water that is left and freeze it. Use the next time you cook the raisins. Then, reduce the sugar by a cup. If using fewer than six cups of raisins to start with, reduce the sugar.

ALL INGREDIENTS SHOULD BE at room temperature.
Sift together all the dry ingredients in a large bowl and set aside.

Blend the butter, sugar and eggs. (I like to use the KitchenAid mixer for this step.)

Add the 2 cups of raisin liquid to the wet ingredients and mix well.

Add the wet mixture to the dry mix and blend well.

Stir in the 6 cups of cooked raisins and blend well.

Pour into four greased loaf pans. Bake for 1 to 1.25 hours at 325 degrees.

The top will spring back when touched lightly or a toothpick/case tester works.

A NOTE FROM JOSIE

Dear Friend,

Thank you for reading *1-800-IRELAND*. I hope you enjoyed it. This the third book in my contemporary sweet romance series: *Flipping for You*.

In this story, the 1-800 series continues in the charming town of Roses, North Carolina, and follows 1-800-CUPID, and 1-800-CHRISTMAS.

In 1-800-IRELAND, I gave Kathleen, from Oh Danny Boy, her own story. And, because Rob is a reader favorite from previous 1-800 books, I decided to explore a May/December romance with a guaranteed Happily Ever After.

If you loved this sweet romance as much as I loved writing it, please help other people find *1-800-IRELAND* by posting your review.

1-800-IRELAND is available in ebook, paperback, Large Print paperback, Hardcover, and audiobook.

My Spotify Playlist for 1-800-IRELAND is here.

With sincere appreciation,

Josie Riviera

JOSIE RIVIERA

a Chocolate-Box Irish Wedding

This book is dedicated to all my wonderful readers who have supported me every inch of the way.
THANK YOU!

PRAISE AND AWARDS

USA TODAY bestselling author

1

———

Colum O' Brien didn't believe in Ireland's much-heralded mythology. Aye, he was Irish to the core, but there wasn't a wee bit of truth to mischievous leprechauns guarding pots of gold. Gold buried by fairies, no less. Goaded by skeptical amusement, he shook his head. He didn't put much stock in ancient Irish folklore.

Which led him to another thought: Dreams. Did they mean anything?

In any event, he wasn't looking forward to sleeping in his childhood bedroom tonight. He wondered if he'd have the same dream that had plagued him for months on end.

Over and over, just before waking, he'd gotten lost while driving on a shadowy, winding road, never finding his destination no matter how hard he tried.

Well, that assuredly wouldn't happen on this trip.

With a dismissive smile, he switched on the car radio, humming along to the folksy acoustics of "Wild Mountain Thyme," a Scottish tune.

The weather proved fine and clear for an Irish December afternoon, soon to glow with the dregs of sunset before the sky turned blue black. He opened the car window a crack, inhaling the earthy fragrance of peat smoke mingling with the bracing air of the Irish Sea. He flicked a glance toward the neighboring hills, marveling at the flicker of twinkling white lights in cottage windows—heralding the holiday season—then returned his focus to the zigzag coastal road.

A sign noted the final turnoff to a precarious, narrow two-lane road. Soon, he'd reach his family homestead in Wexford.

Thirty years ago, Colum could have accomplished this drive from his former Dublin ballet studio with one eye closed, but not anymore. His fifty-year-old eyes didn't see as well as they once did.

Unexpectedly, heavy clouds began lowering over the surrounding hay pastures. Rain spattered his windshield.

He slowed his speed. It was as if he'd driven off into a different country with no recognizable landmarks. The sudden storm had even shut off his GPS.

Where was he?

The mist thickened. Road signs became unreadable. He lowered the volume on the radio.

Instinct told him he must be nearing the last tiny village on the outskirts of Wexford. Thankfully, the taillights of another car appeared ahead.

Perhaps a long-lost relative?

Colum's widowed father had insisted on a gathering at his seaside home for his wedding celebration and asked Colum to be the best man. His father was marrying a dear friend and set a December wedding.

At first, Colum had made excuses for not attending; he taught numerous dance classes, plus was helping Sean, a troubled young man in his twenties. Years earlier, he'd met the lad at a volunteer performance in Dublin. A feature story by an American newsman, Patrick Gervez, had spotlighted how Colum's ballet troupe had given back to the city by inviting underprivileged teens to watch free productions. Since then, he'd claimed Sean as his nephew, relocated him to Farthing, and helped whenever possible.

Thus, it was difficult to get away.

This trip was an eleventh-hour decision. Not that Colum didn't love his father—though in truth, he'd been resistant to return to Wexford. The longer time passed, the more he'd lost touch with his hometown. And whenever he drove these roads, his heart remembered Keira, his high school sweetheart.

Now it was her mother who would be his father's bride.

Would Keira be there? Wexford was the last place Colum had seen her several decades earlier. But no, she lived in London now, and his father would have mentioned her attending the wedding.

Perhaps. Perhaps not. He and his father didn't converse much.

The car ahead accelerated around a sharp curve, slid off the main road, then skidded to a stop on a gravel lane.

Colum's heartbeat slowed, his fingers tightened on the steering wheel. He stomped on the brakes and swerved onto the shoulder. Quickly shutting off the engine, he dashed from his car.

As suddenly as it started, the rain quit. The clouds thinned; then slunk away.

He dragged in a breath as the driver stepped out of the car.

A woman. A fair-skinned, willowy woman. And with her came a whisper of a memory: Their shared childhood and his love for her.

"Are you all right?" Anxiety brought a tremor to his voice. Fresh breezes cooled his heated cheeks.

"I'm brilliant." She peered at him with keen blue eyes. Blond hair, threaded with silver, tumbled down her back. The ends were tipped in . . . pink?

"Colum O'Brien. Is that you?" She touched a hand to her full, inviting lips—lips he well remembered.

He froze, his gaze fixed on her. He couldn't reply.

Keira Murphy. Here. He'd never expected to see her again.

"Aye. It's me." He strode closer; a tongue-tied moment.

She offered that same heart-shattering smile he'd thought about for decades.

"I'm delighted to see you, my long-lost friend," she said.

He couldn't stop gazing at her—her vivid blue eyes, sooty-black lashes and lovely slim figure. There were so many things he wanted to say, so many times he'd longed to hear her voice again.

"I'm happy to see you too." He cleared his throat. "You look grand."

More than grand. She looked exquisite.

He took both her hands in his and kissed her, a fleeting, polite brush of his lips on her cheek. Casual, yet intimate.

Her hair smelled like lilies, her skin soft and silky.

She breathed in a slight inhale, then pulled away.

He drew a shaky breath and ordered himself not to question why he'd been reduced to a long-lost friend status when they'd shared so much more.

Without another word, she moved to her car, her motions graceful. He held open the door for her and ensured she was settled. Then he headed back to his car and followed her to Wexford.

2

———————

The following morning, Keira sat in an oversized Adirondack chair on the O'Brien's spacious lawn. Moss grew on the weathered walls of the house, and the thatched roof drooped at the eaves. A string of holiday lights wound around each window, a cheerful reminder of the upcoming festivities. The scent of dew hung in the air, the grass damp from an earlier rain.

She regarded the stone markings at the front of the O'Brien property, the adjacent fields dotted by sheep, the sparkling waters of the Irish Sea.

"Hello, Keira," a deep voice called. Colum came from behind, covered her eyes with his hands, then immediately removed them. "Guess who?"

Her stomach fluttered, and she bit down on her lips to hide her smile. She admired his easy-going walk as he stepped around to face her. He was a man comfortable in his own skin, whereas she considered herself too tall and ungainly.

"That was easy," she teased. "You could've given me another minute to guess."

"I assumed you'd know it was me right away." He grinned. "May I begin our day by complimenting you, because you are gorgeous?"

"Thank you." She'd dressed in jeans and a red wool sweater, and twisted her hair back into a casual bun. She'd fussed with her appearance in anticipation of seeing him. "Were you comfortable sleeping in your childhood bedroom again?" she asked.

"The sea air is a balm. Without fail, I sleep well in Wexford." He dropped into the chair beside her and yanked out a cigarette. "It's a surprise, aye?"

"The fact you're still smoking? You vowed to quit when you were a teen."

"Over three decades later, and I constantly try to quit, although it's obvious I'm unsuccessful." He granted a rueful smile. "You never liked it."

"Still don't."

"I defer to your wishes, then." He slipped the cigarette back into his pocket, then rolled up the sleeves of his jean jacket.

"How can you dance and do that to your lungs?" As he smirked at her response, she studied him. His arms were athletic and muscular, his physique toned and fit in slim-fitting black pants and a grey knit sweater. She remembered when he'd held her at this very spot, on a similar breezy morning—a few days before she'd departed for London—a few days before New Year's Eve.

She shifted her gaze to the water. "So what's a surprise?"

"Your mum is marrying my dad," he said. "A gala event to begin the holidays."

"The best time of the year."

"Christmas?"

"And New Year's," she replied. "In fact, the entire month of December."

"The season isn't special for me . . . although I'm thankful for the adorable children I teach. The look on their faces is priceless because they're so excited."

She gestured to the O'Brien's home. The natural holly wreath hung on the back door. "We used to leave sacks by the fireplace on Christmas Eve, remember?"

"In the hopes the sacks would be filled with toys on Christmas Day." He chuckled. "Then we'd set out milk and bread on the kitchen table."

"In our house, we'd opt for a pint of Guinness and mince pies." She sighed, the memories poignant. "My mum has been alone since my father died."

"Similarly for my dad when my mum passed away."

"I recall that day." Keira had searched for Colum and discovered him sitting by the shore, his arms around his knees, his face wet with tears. At fourteen years old he'd been embarrassed she'd found him crying, for he despised weakness in himself. His shoulders were drooped, and his voice a whisper, but he'd finally relented and invited her to stay. In return, she'd offered consolation and her undying loyalty.

"*Boys don't cry,*" he'd stated.

"*But men do,*" she'd assured. "*Real men aren't ashamed to shed tears and show their emotions.*"

"Our parents have been friends for years," Colum was saying.

"Like us." She folded her lips together. Why had she spoken the words aloud?

Until you left.

Colum hadn't uttered a sound, but, judging from his tightened expression, she could read his thoughts. They'd been inseparable. That's what happened when you were next-door neighbors.

She fingered the sleeves of her sweater. "I realize my departure from Wexford was sudden."

He shrugged.

"You know why." Too edgy to sit still, she shifted. "There were goals I wanted to accomplish before we settled down."

"Shall we give it a name?" he asked.

"What?" She sat straighter. "Me leaving?"

"Let's call it the demise of a friendship."

She flinched, as if his statement was a physical blow, even more so because of the slight catch in his tone. He'd been hurt.

For years, they'd planned to attend the same university in a neighboring town. That had only taken place for one semester. They'd pledged to stay in touch, although the busyness of life had taken hold.

"I said I would wait for you." His voice was quiet and solemn. "However, it was you who declared that we were young and couldn't plan our lives around a final commitment."

"Not once did you demand that I abandon my dreams."

"I wanted you to ride your rising career to the top," he said. "I never would've taken your achievements away."

Why? Did he love her so much that her happiness was more important than his?

She waited for him to say more. When he didn't, she searched his handsome face, although his features were remarkably bland. "You accomplished your dream," she finally said.

"Which dream was that?"

"Dancing professionally. You lifted those ballerinas effortlessly into the air. How many dancers can claim that?"

"All credited to thousands of hours of rehearsals; and workouts." He quirked a silvery-grey eyebrow. "Did you ever attend any of my performances?"

"No, not live, but I discovered YouTube."

He looked pleased. Something stirred in the fathomless depths of his green eyes, and her heart rate doubled.

"You watched clips?" he inquired.

"Aye."

More than clips. She'd watched his full performances.

"And you?" He shoved his hands into his pockets. "Did you find what you were looking for?"

"For a while, until I grew too old to model."

"You're not old."

"High fashion modeling is extremely competitive." The wind pushed her hair back. "When I was awarded a generous contract from an exclusive agency, I couldn't turn it down."

"And off to England you went. You hightailed it out of here before the New Year's bells rang."

She should've felt cornered by his statement—defensive. But this was Colum. She'd known him since they were children. She knew his nature. He was her constant companion, and she'd confided everything to him.

"You're asking me to apologize?" She fixed him with a level gaze. "I did on numerous occasions. How could I start our life in Wexford when London beckoned?"

"True." He watched the sea, and she followed his stare. The water was calm, the salty breeze conjuring images of picnics—wicker hampers stuffed with sausage sandwiches, sliced apples, and spice cake—while herring gulls squawked overhead.

"Fame and fortune, Kiki," he said. "Both are heady sensations."

Kiki. Her cheeks warmed. She'd nearly forgotten his nickname for her.

"I craved more." She swallowed and lifted her chin. "The excitement of a sizable city and glamorous occupation. Wexford is . . ."

He swept out his hands. "Adorable."

"You didn't stick around, either," she pointed out.

"No reason to."

Because of her? She pondered whether she should ask him. She didn't.

"I never congratulated you on your success," he went on. "Or rather, I did, but you didn't respond."

"I'm sorry. I was wrong not to answer your letters." Those precious letters—every word had broken her heart— but she couldn't write back, it would have only broken *his* heart. She'd established a new world—so different from his in only a matter of months. Nonetheless, his letters had slid from her fingers as she'd sat in her tiny London flat and wept. Joy to hear from him, bittersweet longing for leaving him behind, and the injustice of a demanding career that had initiated their separation.

She sighed. "My work was exhausting, and I hardly had a moment to breathe."

He greeted her explanation with a quick nod.

They'd been best friends. No. More than that. They'd been first loves.

"I'm standing up in the wedding." Keira navigated to a safer subject and offered a modest bow. "I'm the matron of honor."

"I'm the best man."

"Your father spoke of your obligations in Farthing," she said. "I wasn't expecting to see you."

Colum's occasional trips to Wexford over the years never had seemed to correspond with hers.

"Sean, a young lad who is like a nephew to me, continually needs my help," Colum replied. "I met him through Patrick Gervez, an American newsman who traveled to Dublin to feature a story on an outreach ballet program. Nowadays, Sean's graphic design business is doing fairly well, and he moved into his own flat. I packed his fridge with food, a matter of great importance to a twenty-something."

Typical Colum, she reflected. Forever helping people whenever possible.

"Is Sean independent?" she asked.

"He's getting there." Colum pulled his hands from his pockets and stared down at them. "I worry for him, though. I want him to be successful."

"I remember how you repeatedly volunteered at the homeless shelter in town and then organized plays for the children. You gave graciously of your expertise and talents."

"I tried."

"Help Sean, but don't give him handouts."

He grinned. "Advice now, Keira?"

"I speak from experience as a mother of two adult daughters who are often headstrong. I continued to indulge them for years, which was a mistake." She ran a hand through her hair. "Do you own a home in Farthing?"

"Renting is better for me," Colum replied. "My savings are stable, although I'm not wealthy."

"I just bought my own place."

"Congratulations! Where?"

"Take a glance to your right."

He turned. "Your mum's grand cottage?"

"She's moving in with your dad after the wedding, so, I

figured, why not? It's my childhood home. Plus, I'm here to care for our parents as they age."

He leaned toward her and gave a heavy nod. "Aging is definitely a fact of everyday life, and it will be a comfort for them to have you next door."

"Their well-being is important, both physical and emotional."

"Aye." He shot a rueful grin. "And convenient when you need a cup of sugar."

"I don't bake." Keira beamed. "I sew."

"Right. How could I forget?" Colum offered a bemused chuckle. "I rang my father about my change of plans—before he requested someone else to be the best man."

"Who would he ask?"

"A cousin, maybe. Can't think of anyone who is suitable, though."

"You work in Farthing?" She'd already asked too many questions. She had at least a dozen more. She was so comfortable, so at ease conversing with him.

"I'm an instructor at Miss Clara's School of Dance," he replied. "Primarily, I teach preschoolers, and I love that age."

"Sweet ages."

"Someday, I fancy directing a public theater for adults and children."

"Underprivileged?"

"Aye, and also open to anyone in the community."

"In Farthing?"

"I haven't decided."

"You never married," she said. "Never had children."

"My longest relationship lasted all of eight months. I wasn't a particularly attentive partner while I concentrated on my career." With a noncommittal nod, he added, "Wexford was abuzz when you wed your agent in London. You were only twenty at the time."

"Henry was several years older."

"By two decades," Colum corrected. "A sophisticated man, I assume?"

Her face heated with the pain of the recollection. "He introduced me to a glittery circle. I thought of you when I met his friends at posh parties. We would've had a laugh at their uppity airs."

He grinned and leaned closer. "And your daughters are now . . ."

"Almost thirty."

"I always wanted children," he said.

"Twin daughters?"

"One would've been fine." His tone softened. "Two are better."

"Yet you never married . . ." Keira stammered with her response. When Colum studied her with those mesmerizing eyes, she forgot all rational thought. "You'll meet my girls. They're flying in from London. They'll miss the ceremony because of work, but will stay for a while afterwards."

"Through Christmas and New Year's?"

"They both have significant others in London, so I doubt it."

"I'm leaving a couple days after the service. I'm teaching several dance classes, then overseeing a holiday recital for the little ones after Christmas. The students have been preparing for months."

"You'll miss Christmas in Wexford, then. I hope to decorate my shop and my new home as soon as our parents are wed." Her brows knitted. "Will you return for New Year's?"

"Perhaps." Assiduously, he avoided her gaze.

"Remember the fun we had on New Year's Eve?"

Gently, he touched her arm. "Our families would visit for nibbles and drinks."

"And beforehand, my mum would clean the house from top to bottom."

"To signify a fresh start for the upcoming year."

"May I confess something?" she asked.

Colum automatically seemed to tense at her question. "Of course."

"On New Year's Eve, I placed a mistletoe under my pillow," she said.

"In the hopes of seeing your future partner in your dreams." He peeked at her left hand. She'd taken her wedding band off years ago. "Is your husband . . .?"

"Henry and I divorced when our daughters finished primary school." Keira rubbed the back of her neck. "We only stayed in a polite agreement that long for the children's sake."

"Was it the right decision?"

"Each couple's choice is personal and involves many factors. From my experience, I should've left him sooner." Her marriage had been a slow deterioration of her self-confidence. As soon as her career had fallen to a standstill, Henry lost interest in her. He'd also worn away her independence and monitored her calories.

Colum glanced up and motioned toward the shore, extending a wave and a smile.

She followed his gaze to their parents. Cheryl and Richard, both in their late seventies, strolled arm and arm by the water's edge. Her mum wore a wide brimmed straw hat and billowy yellow-floral dress. Colum's father was stout and fit, as well as green-eyed, good-humored, and engaging. It gladdened Keira's heart to see their smiles. Love occurred at any age, she supposed. Just not for her.

She'd never been content in her marriage—even before Henry's verbal abuse. Had she been forever seeking the right man? She'd dated after her divorce, but no sparks.

Her chest filled with regret as she met Colum's gaze. He'd been her first love. Had he been her true love?

"Divine weather," he was saying.

"No rain in the forecast." She managed a radiant smile. "Let's hope the sun shines for the wedding."

"It's risky planning an outdoor ceremony in December," Colum noted.

"Wexford is considered the sunny southeast of Ireland. Besides, they're renting a tent with heaters for the reception. They can dash inside if need be."

"Good thing. There is constantly a threat of showers in an Irish forecast."

"Or a downpour," she inserted.

He stood and peered at the blue sky, the stretch of wispy white clouds. "Will you join me for a coffee in town? Just like we used to."

"When we were supposed to be in class."

"We'd have the craic—a good laugh and loads of fun." He chuckled. She remembered that chuckle—rich and pure and inviting. "We were a rascally pair,—ducking out of school early."

She held up a hand. "Speak for yourself."

"Hah! Half the time, you'd initiate our adventures. We'd pool our lunch money, hop on a bus, and eventually land at Michael D's whiling away the afternoon over scones and coffee and homework."

"Homework?"

He smiled. "Once in a while."

"I dine at Michael D's often."

His smile wavered. "I'm trying to get my head around the fact that all this time I assumed you still lived in London."

"I own a dressmaker's shop a few doors down from Michael D's," she explained. "In fact, I designed my mum's wedding dress. Care to take a peek?"

"Isn't it bad luck to see the bride's dress before the wedding?"

"Only if you're the groom." She accepted his extended hand and got to her feet. "Don't take any photos to show your dad."

"You're the one who could never keep a secret. Chatterbox."

She gave his shoulder a playful nudge as they began walking. "And you were quiet."

"So many memories." Conflicting emotions flashed across his well-defined features—his sharp cheekbones that reminded her of a proud Roman warrior. His gaze locked with hers, a silent communication. He knew her so well. She'd never been at a loss for words, and they'd sit for hours. Colum, attentive and encouraging, while she chatted endlessly. She'd become a famous designer, and he'd continue volunteering and open a performing arts school. Perhaps they'd marry in the winter. A Christmas wedding, or New Year's . . .

Their lives had taken such different paths.

But what if . . .

No, no, no. She refused to play the "what if" game.

"What's the name of your shop?" Colum asked.

"Keira's Wexford Boutique."

They stepped onto a stone path, lingering to appreciate the buds of holly and pansies blooming up from the cold ground.

"You loved fashion." Colum paused to pick a bouquet, handing the flowers to her. "You made me a shirt once."

She sniffed, savoring the fragrant scent. He'd frequently slip her a spray of cowslip or clover or shamrocks—depending on the season.

"I sewed the shirt from jersey cotton fabric and a pre-made sewing pattern," she replied. "It was tight on you."

"I wore it often."

"Only so you wouldn't hurt my feelings."

He'd ignored teasing from the other boys and had worn her handmade shirt with pride. He constantly looked out for her. Her protector. He wanted to make her happy.

"*You sewed this for me, Kiki?*" he'd asked with a broad smile when she'd presented it to him. "*It's brilliant.*"

He'd tugged it over his dog-eared t-shirt. He was tanned and muscular by then—on the cusp of adulthood—nearing eighteen.

The shirt hadn't been brilliant—an amateur's attempt at sewing and design—boasting a bold Hawaiian pattern of multicolored birds and leaves. Nevertheless, her interest in fashion, encouraged by Colum, had thrived.

"Is your shop successful?" He stood so close, the warmth of his skin heated her own. She inhaled the crisp scent of the sea. Knowing him, he'd probably gone for a swim at sunup.

He still had the muscular build of his younger self, his profile lithe, yet solid. His eyes were a mossy green—reminding her of the color of the forest after a hard rain. His hair was salt and pepper, raked short and side-swept.

"I'm happy," she acknowledged. "I've come to realize this idyllic wee town is my home. For me, happiness constitutes success."

"Ahh, living in Wexford."

She frowned. "Is there a problem?"

"Little towns are ideal for many chaps." He exhaled. "However, the country character here, coupled with my recollections of the old ways . . ."

"You find fault with our traditions? Our folklore?"

"Some of it. Nevertheless, a large city offers more theater and restaurant choices." He winked. "Plus, no one remembers me as an awkward adolescent."

"You were a pro in every sport. Whereas I—all legs and arms—"

3

"You're exquisitely perfect." Colum blurted the words before he could stop himself. He scanned Keira's delicate profile—the curve of her nose, her flawless complexion with a sprinkling of freckles, and heard the sincerity in her tone. She actually didn't realize how attractive she was.

However, her blue eyes shone with a spirit that hadn't been diminished by hardship.

Her youthful features had matured, fulfilling the certainty of loveliness, enriched with a mellowness that had developed with maturing. Her posture was straight, her figure slender.

His only desire was to touch her, kiss her, cherish the delightful feelings intensifying inside him—the first true emotions he'd felt in decades.

He cupped her cheek. "Numerous points in my life have reminded me of you. I wondered if our mutual memories ever caused you to smile."

He braced himself for her reply. When she finally dragged her gaze to his, she drew a wobbly breath. "I laughed a lot in London whenever I remembered our adventures."

He bent his head and his lips grazed hers. So delicious, so inviting. "You're my precious Kiki," he murmured. "You've been my forever—"

"No." She tugged free. Her complexion was flushed, her eyes wet. "You're leaving in a few days."

"Aye, but there's no reason why I can't return. I've never stopped thinking about you." He brushed the shiny hair from her forehead and grinned at the pink highlighted tips. In her teens she'd been the town nonconformist, experimenting with bizarre fashions. However, the bright makeup and outlandish feather hats had never diminished the beauty of her high cheekbones and expressive eyes. No wonder a London modeling agency had signed her on the spot.

"Words are easy, Colum." He respected the proud grace of her walk as she stepped away. "Circumstances may prevent a person from following through—no matter their intentions."

When they reached her driveway, Keira insisted on driving them to town, vowing to take the curves slowly in light of the previous evening's mishap. She didn't. If anything, she accelerated during the ten-minute drive, while he gripped the edge of the passenger seat. When they arrived at her shop, she rummaged in her handbag for the keys.

He squinted through the wavy glass window of the vacant building next door. The exterior paint flaked at random, the interior was dust-coated, the walls cracked.

"What business was here previously?" Colum asked.

"Nothing for years," she answered. "There was talk of

converting the space into a high-class hotel, but the funds never came through."

She finally found the key, and they stepped inside her shop.

It was tidy and spotless, and scents of cedar and mint lingered in the air. Clothes racks sported fine woolens and tweeds, hand knit scarves and cable stitch cream sweaters tagged to sell.

"Do you employ a staff?" he asked.

"Recently, I hired a mother and her adult daughter. They're smart, efficient, and excellent seamstresses." Keira walked to a back room and brought out a knee-length lace dress in a champagne shade, along with a flowered crown headpiece. She illustrated how she'd sewn each delicate button by hand.

"Tasteful for your mum." He applauded. "May I ask what the daughter of the bride is wearing?"

Keira winked. "It's a surprise."

"In secondary school, I'd ask what you planned to wear the following day, and you'd consistently say—"

"It's a surprise," they chimed in unison.

"Why did you forever ask me the same question, Colum?"

"To prepare myself." He attempted to keep his features straight. "I never knew what newfangled outfit you'd come up with."

"Fashion is fun. An adventure."

He rolled his eyes. "You found enough for both of us." He'd willingly gone anywhere she'd dragged him and felt fortunate just to be with her.

"I wished to dress better than those pretty girls in school who flirted with you," she said.

He chucked her under the chin. "I believe you were jealous."

"Believe whatever suits you."

"Were you . . . jealous?" He drew her near, held her close. He couldn't help himself. His yearning for her slowed his breathing.

As he gazed into her eyes, the seconds paused—becoming the shared remembrances of delightful hours, of days, of years.

He'd sought to deny it, but he'd never been able to resist her. When they were young, they'd fallen into an easy friendship—enjoyable and uncomplicated. By their teens, their relationship had changed. Romance began to bloom—although they'd both resisted the attraction to each other.

For decades afterward, his thoughts had gravitated toward her.

How was she faring in London? Had she forgotten him? Undoubtedly, because she was married.

But now they were reunited, and the seasons apart were a mere moment in time.

"Jealous? Don't be ridiculous. You flatter yourself." Keira fussed with a tweed cape on a hanger, fumbling with the fabric. "The programs you choreographed at the Wexford homeless shelter were fun and uplifting, and you were only in your teens."

"Thank you. I love working with children." He wanted to congratulate her on navigating the subject change so seamlessly.

She turned toward him. "Do you still dance and perform?"

"There aren't many roles for fifty-something males," he replied.

"You were a key dancer with the Dublin ballet."

"Until I reached thirty. Then the younger, ambitious men were happy to replace me."

"Same in my occupation." She went back to fussing with the cape. "Runway models are most successful between the ages of sixteen and twenty-one."

"And afterwards?"

"I did catalogues. And sewing to make ends meet while raising two daughters."

"You're exceptional, Kiki. You lived on your own in London."

Tears welled in her eyes. He didn't expect them.

"My ex-husband, Henry, considered me obsolete when I aged out of working the runway." The cape fell off the hanger. She bent to pick it up. "After our divorce, I continued to question my self-worth."

"Did he abuse you?

"Not physically. His abuse was emotional." She lifted her hands, then let them drop. "I should've divorced him sooner, but I was trapped. Two young daughters and no way to support us."

"Now you're successful and content."

"I am." She laughed, unforced and laid-back. "This tiny slice of the world is my lifeline, and I'm not relocating anytime soon."

Life in a microscopic town was ideal for some people, just not for him. He dismissed the unspoken thought and sought a more manageable topic. Absently, he fingered a velvet hanger, while he relished spending the day with her. Finally, the Keira he recognized was emerging from behind her careful wall. Honestly explaining her hardships, without sugarcoating what he'd imagined had been her opulent London lifestyle.

"Ready to lead the way to Michael D's?" he suggested.

"Considering the coffee shop is a few doors down, it's not difficult."

"Do they still serve tea cakes?"

"Aye. And buttered scones with strawberry jam. Your favorite. The new owner kept the same menu."

He patted his stomach. "Your mum baked superb scones with lemon curd and whipped cream. You brought them to me after my ballet practice, rolled up in foil and topped with a silver bow."

"She still bakes over a turf fire. Batches of soda bread sit on our kitchen counter as I speak."

"Thus a delightful afternoon awaits."

She narrowed her gaze. "Colum O'Brien, you can't sample desserts and bread all day."

"Watch me." He laced his fingers through hers and led her out of the shop.

They passed McKay's jewelers and peered through the display case window. As was customary in many of Ireland's shops, the Claddagh Ring took center stage.

"Love, loyalty, and friendship." Keira admired an array of sterling silver and gold bands.

"Did your mum hand her wedding ring down to you?"

"I married in London, and she didn't attend because my father was sick. He died a year later, and she continued to wear the ring on her right hand. Now that she's marrying your father, she placed it in her bedroom drawer for safe-keeping."

Colum hooked his arm around her shoulders. "Awaiting you."

"I won't marry again."

"Why ever not?" he asked.

"Once was enough. I'm obviously not good at marriage."

Her tone thickened, and she clasped her hands together. "Perhaps one of my daughters will wear it someday."

He swallowed the dull ache in his throat. He could still visualize Keira planning their future all those years ago.

"And after we graduate from university, Colum, we'll marry," she'd declared. Her color was high, her joy bubbling and infectious. *"Won't it be grand?"*

"Aye." He'd cradled her in his arms. *"Grand, indeed."*

4

—————

When they reached the O'Brien's cottage, Keira invited Colum into her home. The comforting scent of buttermilk and raisins and freshly baked Irish soda bread greeted him as they entered the light-filled kitchen. The walls were painted a dove gray, and a bold patterned rug covered the ancient tiled floor. Photographs littered a side bureau. Several were black and white photos of him and Keira. In one, they stood by the shore. He displayed a wiggling fish—their only catch that day—while she beamed, her light-blond hair in a long braid over her shoulder, and proudly held up the fishing pole. They were eight years old.

Keira gestured to the loaves stacked beneath numerous glass containers. "All ready for the reception."

"Your mum shouldn't bake for her own wedding."

"Why not? Baking is therapy."

He lifted a lid. "May I?"

"Sure. I'll slice a loaf and brew a pot of tea."

A few minutes later, she poured two steaming cups of robust breakfast tea and combined loads of milk and sugar into her cup. Once she settled, he seated across from her. The expansive bay window boasted an unobstructed view of the craggy hills and sea beyond.

"Thus, our parents are out and about today," he said.

"They drove to Waterford." Keira set the white porcelain teapot on the table. "My mum wished to speak with the DJ in person."

Colum sat back in joking amazement. "No bagpipes tomorrow?"

"The piper will perform when guests arrive and leave the ceremony." She sipped her tea and gazed at him over the rim of her cup. "At the reception, she insists on traditional Irish folk music."

Colum lifted his teacup in a salute. "She is a wise woman."

"I agree. She allowed me to make my own mistakes." Keira poured more tea. "The rehearsal begins in a couple hours, and the pastor arrives at five o'clock."

"What rehearsal?"

"We'll practice walking in and out, and where we'll stand during the ceremony. Didn't your father mention anything?"

Colum drummed his fingers on the wooden table. "Men don't talk much."

"My mum requested that you and I plan an impromptu party for afterwards."

"Did she now?" he asked. "I could do with more warning."

"Are you busy?"

"Not at all."

"Good." Keira smiled. She was gorgeous when she smiled. Her face was all gentle curves, her silky hair tumbling over her shoulders. "I'll ring a few places in town."

She made quick work of the arrangements, then picked up their tea cups and placed them in the sink. After she finished, she remained silent for a beat.

"When, exactly, do you return to Farthing?" she inquired.

The anticipation of a commitment was unmistakable. The speculation of "what If" he didn't have to leave.

But he did. He'd created another life. He leased a flat and had resided in Farthing for ages.

He traced his fingers along the sides of her face and smoothed back her blond hair. She turned her cheek nearer his palm before she slipped away.

Did his remembrances of their former years—when they'd finished each other's sentences—bring her the same pangs of heartfelt longing? He'd presumed his reminiscences were embellished by the idealism of youth. Now he wasn't so sure.

"My preschoolers await my return," he said.

"Do you enjoy teaching the younger age group?"

"Absolutely. I use distraction and positive feedback. And I heap on the compliments when the children point their toes."

"Do they . . . point their toes?"

"Hardly ever." He grinned as she laughed out loud.

Keira's radiance brightened his mood. When he'd lost his mum, he'd wept, his sorrow unbearable. Keira had been there—quietly consoling, encouraging him to express his grief. She'd put aside her sewing that day, changed her plans. Comrades till the end, they'd vowed. They'd sat tight for hours until the sky darkened.

He was her priority, she'd assured him. As she'd been his.

"My American friends, Patrick and Cora Gervez, have

flown to Ireland for a holiday," Colum continued. "He's the newsman who introduced me to Sean in Dublin. In any case, I want to show him and his wife, Cora, around Farthing. As soon as the recital is over, I'll return to Wexford."

"Is that a promise?"

"A promise and then some." He kissed her temple. "That is, unless you're traveling somewhere for New Year's Eve?"

"Have you forgotten, Colum?" Lightly, she stroked his hand. Or maybe he stroked hers. "I'm not going anywhere."

5

—————

Although rehearsal dinners in Ireland weren't standard, Keira opted for a casual soiree with hors d'oeuvres, oysters, and pints of beer at sunset. They arranged tables and chairs under a canopied pergola on the sandy beach, and Colum and his father built a smoldering bonfire between the sand dunes. The fire whispered hisses, the flames flickering, and the air smelled of smoke and pine.

Bottles of water were plentiful, along with a marble board laden with a wheel of moist blue cheese, sharp cheddar, goat's cheese, soda crackers and crusty baguettes.

Keira reached for a handful of grapes as she admired the blade-leaf potted plants adorning the tables. The men had secured strings of subdued vintage light bulbs to the pergola.

Colum came to stand beside her, his arm brushing hers. He wore slim-fitting swimming trunks and a striped polo shirt, and his smile enhanced his good-looking face.

"May I?" he asked.

"May you what?" Her chest surged with excitement. She

couldn't refute the unmistakable magnetism whenever he neared, as if an electrical arc sizzled between them.

He touched a finger to his bottom lip, a teasing gesture she fondly recalled. "May I have your grapes?"

"There's plenty where these came from, and I can assure they're all the same." She motioned toward the tables. "We requested the caterer bring fresh figs and dried apricots too. Remember?"

"You did most of the arranging."

"Correction. *All* the arranging."

"Right." Her remark earned a chuckle. "Well, I'd prefer your grapes."

"You constantly stole my food when we were young."

He swept an arm around her waist. "Not stealing. I asked first."

With an exaggerated sigh, she handed him the grapes. "Help yourself."

"I'd like nothing better than to help myself . . . to a kiss." His soft breath brushed her cheek. His green eyes smoldered as he bent his head and pressed his lips on hers.

The kiss deepened, and she wound her hands around his shoulders.

Somewhere near the house, her mum called. Colum broke the kiss, and an unexpected loneliness filled Keira's heart. With a sigh, she encouraged herself to yield to reason. Too many years had passed. Was it too late to start their romance again—simply pick up where they left off?

A possibility. But life, she'd discovered, was seldom simple. Twists and turns were encountered around every bend.

She plucked his arm from her waist and turned. "We're coming, mum," she called back.

Colum held her hand as they started toward the house. "I always admired your generous nature," he said.

"As if I had a choice," she joked.

He polished off her entire sprig of grapes and they shared a laugh.

He had laugh lines now. So did she.

As they walked, she reflected on their day. She liked sitting at the kitchen table with him and planning a rehearsal dinner celebration. She liked everything about this charming man with rock solid arms and sturdy shoulders.

"My two favorite young people," her mum declared when Keira and Colum approached. "You make a stunning couple."

"We're hardly a couple," Keira replied. "And we're hardly young."

Colum's father strode over. "Could've fooled me on both counts."

Their smiling approval was so contagious that Keira couldn't curb her grin.

"Your mum and my father are wise." Colum followed his declaration with a throaty laugh. She glanced at him, startled to see the love shining in his eyes, and her heart soared.

After chatting about the wedding and wishing their parents "good night," Colum kept his fingers firmly around Keira's and led her to the waterfront.

Those who chose to swim after the rehearsal had been encouraged to wear their swimsuits, and Keira had arranged a basket of towels on the beach. The full moon rose, a deep silver disc, steady and true, much like the fine-looking man smiling down at her.

Colum gestured with his chin. "Lots of folks are enjoying the water this evening. Are you up for a swim?"

"They're mental. The sea is freezing."

He chuckled. "It'll get even colder in January."

She pointed to the waves slicing across the rocks. "Is your judgement clouded? Have you been drinking?

"I don't drink alcohol."

She knew that about him. He'd never changed.

A sparkle lit his eyes. "We Irish are a hardy people."

"Uh, huh."

"Invariably, I swam faster once we reached our teens."

"Invariably?" She placed her hands on her hips, her legs slightly apart. "Is your fancy word a dare?"

"Absolutely." He shrugged off his shirt. His chest was firm and well-defined. Graceful and compelling. A man who devoted his life striving for beauty and artistry.

"As you may recall," she said, "I'm an exceptional swimmer."

"You should be." Wryly, he grinned. "You live by the sea."

She bumped up against him. "So did you." She untied her white shimmer lace coverup and set it on a chair. Her vivid-purple swimsuit sported a sweetheart neckline and revealed a peek of fair skin.

His admiring stare wasn't lost on her and her cheeks heated.

He grabbed her hand, and they dashed into the frigid water—the spray soaking their faces. Total immersion brought her teeth to chattering within minutes. They splashed each other before Keira admitted defeat and they headed for shore.

Colum snatched several thick towels and wrapped one around her. He arranged another on the sand close to the bonfire and beckoned her to sit.

With a lightness in her limbs, she obliged.

He sat beside her, tucked the towel nearer her shoulders,

and cuddled her. Bits of sand clung to his cheeks, and she brushed it off.

"I would've stayed in the water longer," he declared.

"Uh, huh." She still shivered, but the heat of the fire, the warmth of Colum's body, offered pure pleasure. "Then why are your lips blue?"

"Yours are bluer." A relaxed smile worked across his features. She recalled how his eyes darkened whenever he'd contemplated kissing her after a swim, and her pulse quickened. The scent of salt water and his damp skin brought wants and misgivings.

He bent his head, cupped her face and kissed her with aching tenderness. Oh, the taste of him, the gentleness of an unstoppable kiss. She didn't want it to end—like their youthful declarations. Only her emotions were different now. Deeper and sounder.

She pressed her forehead against his chest, her hands flattened on his shoulders. "I wish you could stay in Wexford permanently," she whispered. "This is your home."

"For many years, but not anymore." He gathered a deep breath. "In all honesty, I can't risk being hurt again."

"You're referring to me?"

"Aye."

She blinked, focusing on his words. "I wouldn't do that." She drew back, attempting to understand the overwhelming emotions he awakened in her. Had she hidden behind outward merriment and animation in London—a vigilant emotional balance that numbed her feelings? She'd clung to that balance for years, thankful for her two cherished daughters to love and care for.

"I realize you wouldn't intentionally." Colum kissed her forehead. "Though, please understand that my heart can only take so much."

She went to stand, and he kept his arm firmly around her. "May I hold you a while longer?"

Why? He'd hedged about continuing their relationship. Maybe he'd never been interested. Still, his affectionate smile melted her insides, and she relaxed. She regarded him and fingered the greying hairs at his temple. His lashes were black and spiky, his features well-defined.

She stirred, and he drew her closer, and the instinctively protective gesture prompted her to smile. He buried his face in her hair, and she leaned back and briefly squeezed her eyes closed. Two people reconnecting on a windswept Irish beach. Two sweethearts. Tonight, she felt wholly at peace with herself, and in seamless accord with the universe.

"There's a family of otters. I saw them earlier when I took a swim. And kingfishers." He pointed toward the water, a sheet of indigo-blue silk. The moon rose higher, reflecting a milky glow across the hills. A chorus of crickets and the sizzling pops of the fire serenaded them, the murmurs of the departing guests fading away. "Do you recall when we'd spend the day intent on spotting an otter?"

"Aye. You'd spin their water frolics into fairy tales." Her throat clogged with tears. She inhaled a deep breath to compose herself.

"Once upon a time," he'd often recited in their youth, *"there was a girl named Kiki, and a guy named Colum."*

A fairytale. A happily ever after.

What happiness had she missed while she'd worn blinders—all to achieve success in a fickle career?

THE FOLLOWING morning dawned pleasant and clear. Keira drew open her lace curtains and gazed out her second-floor bedroom window, smirking as her mum directed the workers on the placement of the large white tent and the cathedral windows on the sidewalls. Colum's father guided other workmen on the location of the portable heaters.

Further down the shore, Colum emerged from the water. His swimming trunks draped low on his hips, his muscular chest glistened with drops of water. The sun glinted behind him, outlining his athletic physique.

He slung a towel around his neck and padded over to their parents.

Watching him, Keira's thoughts emptied of everything except him.

He raised his head, as if he felt her gaze.

"Aren't you chilly?" she teased.

He gave a look of lighthearted superiority. "Not a bit."

"You aren't serious. The temperature of the water is fifty degrees Fahrenheit."

"In truth, I'm frozen."

Her shout of hilarity almost drowned out his next remark.

"Can't wait to see what you'll wear to the wedding, Kiki," he said.

Kiki again.

She ignored the unexpected knot in her chest. Or, at least, she tried. A memory of their mutual years flashed through her mind—holding hands at sunset, shared secrets in the dark. Despite her anticipation of an exciting lifestyle beyond Wexford, she couldn't pretend the flood of emotions whenever he was near didn't exist.

"It'll bring tears to your eyes," she called back.

She assumed she'd moved on with her life. She hadn't. For decades, she'd searched to fill the void in her heart. And she'd fallen in love, once again, with the man she'd left behind.

· · ·

AN HOUR LATER, Keira donned a knee-length, carnation red dress with a polka-dotted sash that she'd fashioned and sewn. The ends of her hair boasted a ruby hue, and she styled her heavy curls to the side with a pearl clip. She opted for braided jute sandals, satisfied that her outfit was tasteful and sensible.

As she gazed at her reflection in her full-length mirror, she recalled the conversation with her mum from the previous evening, after Keira and Colum had parted.

She'd knocked on Keira's bedroom door and entered. "I wanted to speak to you about Colum," she'd begun. "Day in and day out through the years, you looked splendid as a couple, but especially tonight."

"We're great friends."

"So you've made known. Nonetheless, I see the way he looks at you."

"I haven't noticed anything of the sort," Keira had replied.

"He can't stop staring, and you dissolve whenever you meet his gaze."

"He's leaving in mere days."

"Encourage him to stay. You've never gotten over each other. The sooner you both admit the truth, the better."

Her mother had known how difficult it was for Keira to leave him and Wexford all those decades ago. It hadn't been an easy decision.

"He has work and obligations in Farthing," Keira replied.

Even now, she longed for the tenderness of his embrace, the gentle insistence of his kiss. She'd appreciated the precious hours they'd spent in each other's company, and she sensed Colum felt the same. But what would tomorrow evening bring? Or the following? Would they finally celebrate a New Year's side by side again?

All those decades ago, she'd departed the day after Christmas, intent on securing a flat in London before her modeling contract began the first of January.

"*New Year's is symbolic, Kiki,*" Colum had explained. They'd spent every holiday never more than a stone's throw from each other. "*Let's reflect on the past year, then look forward.*"

By the time they were teens, they'd toasted, their sparkling grape juice glasses clinking as they cozied in Colum's living room by a fire in the hearth, while their parents celebrated at the local pub. They'd return well before midnight and switch the television on for a communal countdown.

"*Why do folks insist on coming in the front door, then leaving out the back door?*" Keira had asked him.

"*It's touted to bring good luck.*" His lips had deepened into an exasperated smile. "*Another one of Ireland's traditions.*"

Laughing, she'd refuted, "*Many traditions have a purpose behind them. Rituals are performed for hundreds of years, although few folks can recall why.*"

His look implied a struggle between seriousness and humor. "*Here's a tradition that will last. Come what may, we'll spend New Year's with one another every year.*"

Keira blinked back tears at the remembrance. That was the last New Year's she'd seen him.

"Sometimes the pathway to the person you cherish is a twisty and lengthy road," her mum was saying. Her eyes had misted, although her smile offered encouragement.

Keira snapped up her bouquet, a fragrant mix of snapdragons and sunflowers, then walked to the window.

Laughing and chatting, in a kaleidoscope of vibrant dresses and navy suits, ushers were seating the guests in rows of white chairs facing the sea. The pastor fixed himself at the altar, a classic wooden archway decorated with purple sea asters.

Her veins tingled with excitement at the enthusiasm of the guests. Today was a glorious, sunny day, the rugged landscape dusted with snow on the highest mountain peaks. The stark blue skies promised joyfulness and enchantment.

At noon, the ceremony began with a lone bagpiper playing Mendelssohn's Wedding March. A ripple went through the crowd as Keira and Colum took their places, and the bride walked down the aisle to her groom.

Her mum's champagne lace dress complemented her rosy complexion. The flowered crown headpiece brought a statement of romance to her wavy gray hair. Her closely set blue eyes brimmed with happiness.

Colum's father, dressed in a black notched tuxedo, stood ruddy faced and noble, beaming as his bride approached.

Keira gazed at the two men, father and son. Their resemblance was astounding. The square jawlines and eye color were the same, as were their natures. Attentive and charismatic, both men forever wore a smile.

"You're beautiful," Colum said softly to her. His green eyes glistened with tears.

Her stomach flipped and she smiled—craving all things Colum. The boy he was, and the man he'd become.

Behind him, the sea shimmered—sparkles under the sun. In her teens, she'd imagined the shimmers as magical fairy dust, and that the magic would lead to an enchanted life with him.

After the wedding, they'd sing and dance at the reception. The lively melody of Galway Girl, an Irish tune. Or a romantic waltz, and he'd hold her in his arms.

Her pulse thrummed with the anticipation of another day with him.

She'd suggest he stay a wee bit longer. She wanted him to meet her daughters. She was so proud of them.

"All Those Endearing Young Charms," closed the ceremony. The emotional lyrics about a woman's youth fading away, encouraged the guests to join in.

Dozens offered congratulations, circling the bride and groom as they stepped toward the tent. Traditional Irish pub fare—hearty fish and chips, shepherd's pie, and seafood chowder, would be served buffet-style.

Keira caught up to Colum, who was speaking on his cellphone. His eyebrows crinkled in concern.

"Are you coming?" she asked.

He clicked off the phone. "I can't. I must leave."

"Now?"

"The young man in Farthing I told you about—"

"Sean? You loaded up his refrigerator."

Colum rubbed his jaw. "He hit a rough patch and was thrown out of his flat."

"He recently moved in."

"Correct, but he needs me. Patrick Gervez and his wife, Cora, are also in Farthing. They flew over from America for a visit to Ireland in the wintertime."

"Can't they handle Sean's problems?"

"They're on holiday. They're good friends, but Sean is my responsibility."

"He really isn't."

"He is, though." Colum's tone was strained, his chin high. "I won't shirk my obligation and ask my American friends to shoulder my burdens. I'll extend my congratulatory wishes to our parents and go pack."

What obligation? she thought. You're not even technically related. I need you too.

She respected that Colum always placed the welfare of others before himself, but she wanted him to be a part of her life too.

"Then . . . this is goodbye?" she asked aloud.

"Kiki, I've been thinking. Maybe it's better this way." He strode closer, his gaze locked on hers. "Our friendship has lasted decades, and neither of us can ignore our first love. But we shouldn't complicate our relationship with anything else."

Like romance? Like love? Like kisses under the moonlight?

Her vision blurred, her chest ached. "Aye. Friends till the end." She swiveled. She wouldn't let him see her cry. Keeping her shoulders straight, she quickened her pace to the tent.

She remained out of sight when Colum got into his car a few minutes later. He'd changed into jeans and a button down blue shirt, and shrugged on a jacket. For a moment he waffled, glancing around.

"I'm right here," she was tempted to shout. But she didn't, and the stab of regret pierced deeper as he drove away. She'd never see his lopsided smile, nor hear his easygoing chuckle, again.

HER MUM APPEARED—KEIRA wasn't sure when.

"He left early because someone needed him." Tears clogged Keira's throat. She trembled, despite the sun's warmth.

"He apologized for his hasty departure. He always was the first in line to come to everyone else's aid." She gave Keira's hand a mild squeeze. "You'll see him again."

When? Keira's fingers were cold, but her mum didn't seem to mind.

6

———

Two weeks later, and the day after Christmas, Colum flicked warning glances at his four-year-old ballerina students, but they paid him no heed. They knew he was a marshmallow when it came to disciplining them. Dressed in pink tights and black leotards, their hair tugged back in classic buns, they raced around his studio like it was a preschool gym. They should've been practicing their pitter patter turns by the barre. Instead, they practiced . . . running.

He clapped his hands to bring their attention to him. Alas, no such luck. He hunkered down to tie a tiny ballet slipper, reminded them to work at their dances for the upcoming recital, and then shepherded them to their waiting parents.

After speaking assurances to several anxious mothers, and thanking them for bringing their children for a last-minute practice, he arranged his gear in his locker and leaned his head against the wall. Since resuming his everyday life, he'd grown weary of the town of Farthing—and even his surrogate nephew.

After attending a morning church service the day before, their Christmas dinner had consisted of takeout boxty, potato pancakes stuffed with meat and vegetables. For the remainder of the day, Colum had volunteered at a soup kitchen while his nephew created a custom logo for a local shop.

In addition, Colum's dreams had started again—driving on a shadowy road and being lost.

He grasped a cigarette, then shoved it back into his pocket. He craved a coffee, or tea . . . but he'd have to sit in traffic forever first. In Wexford, everything was a mere ten minutes away.

"*I dine at Michael D's often,*" Keira had declared.

Keira—eternally in his heart, eternally in his mind. He'd assumed he was over her. He'd assumed he'd secured her in a safe, secret place. Returning to Wexford had been bittersweet, but memories of her and their years together had struck him at every turn. He'd even jogged along the beach the morning after his arrival and discovered the oak tree where they'd carved their initials when they were twelve.

But in a forty-eight-hour period, how could he reunite with his teenage sweetheart? He was a bachelor in his fifties and wasn't about to leave everything he'd worked so hard for, to move back to his hometown. Plus, could he truly contemplate settling down?

He blew out a breath. He'd tried to forget her. If anything, his feelings had grown stronger.

With a cheery nod to the straggling parents, he shrugged on his twill jacket and exited the studio.

Restless, he wandered the bustling city streets as people hurried home from work. Bright icicle lights illuminated the shops, and aromatic pine filled the air. Daylight had dwindled, and a purple dusk came earlier than expected. The days, the years, passed too quickly, and each hour was precious.

He paused. So what was he doing in Farthing?

He'd told himself not to care, citing a myriad of reasons, expecting his feelings would fade.

She'd left at eighteen, and he'd been devastated. Nevertheless, he loved her—a love so powerful it exploded within him. Surely, she felt the same.

He needed to take the right path and find his way home. Back to Keira and Wexford.

He drew out his cellphone to contact his father, then Keira's mum.

He hesitated.

Texts were a start. In person was better.

Decision made, he rang Sean, and offered his flat to sublet. Colum had secured a part-time job to enable Sean to get his finances in order and hoped the lad would be responsible. He'd shared his knowledge and been a sounding board. Now was a chance for the young man to transition to independence.

Then Colum enlisted the help of his father and Keira's mum.

Next came a phone call to Patrick Gervez and his wife, Cora, inviting them to visit the southern part of Ireland and Colum's hometown for a special event.

His fourth request was to Clara, his employer and long-time friend. She assured she'd find a suitable teacher replacement, that the recital would go off without a hitch, and encouraged Colum to follow his heart.

His heart. He pressed a hand to his chest.

He hurried to his flat to attend to last-minute details and pack a suitcase.

Then he drove to Wexford as if his life depended on it.

7

Keira wrapped her fingers around a fresh mug of tea, leaned back in the oversized Adirondack chair on the O'Brien's lawn, and gazed at the blue-grey ripples of the water, a reflection of the sky. Today, she wore a one-piece V-neck jumpsuit, a snuggly knit in a bold fuchsia, and draped a thick woolen cape over her shoulders to ward off the chill.

The end of December carried a chilly, overcast day, and the holiday had occurred in a blur. Colum had texted every day—and they'd kept the topics neutral.

After a Christmas church service in town, she'd prepared roast turkey, stuffing, and buttery carrots, and dined with their parents. Colum had phoned, wishing them all a "Merry Christmas." He'd perfected his friendly, amiable tone.

Her eyes burned, but she didn't blame it on the smoke from the turf fires.

She blamed it on the tears she'd shed since he'd departed. All that remained were precious snapshots of their youth that she safeguarded in her mind. Many years ago, he'd unknowingly set the bar high. His likable character, wit, and intelligence had become the standard she'd unwittingly measured every man by since. They were so compatible—pieces of a puzzle fitting in perfect agreement.

"Hello, Kiki, my love," a deep, beloved voice came from behind her.

She gasped. The shattering gentleness of Colum's words sent a jolt through her.

She set her mug on the grass and slowly rose. Now he stood in front of her—his tall frame clad in dark jeans, a flannel shirt, and his familiar twill jacket. She assumed she was still breathing. She couldn't be sure.

"Colum." Her thoughts reeled. His presence was a solid force, mesmeric and undeniable. "Why . . . why are you here?"

"I missed you." His tone was whispered, raw with emotion. "And, I'm here to stay. Do you know any place for rent?"

"In Wexford?" Her gaze lifted to the man who held her heart. "For whatever reason?"

"For you. Only for you." He captured her in his arms. His lips pressed hungrily with an aching desire that would forever remain in her memory.

She molded nearer to him. "I've missed you too." Their breaths mingled. She returned his kiss with all the yearning in her soul.

His hands slid up and down her back. "I came to tell you that I love you. Everything you do—everything you say—everything you represent."

The taste of his lips brought unbearable happiness. She didn't want him to stop, fearful he might disappear.

"My precious Kiki, you're goodness, decency, and all that's true in the world," he said. "You're the treasure of my life."

She pressed a trembling finger to his mouth. "And you're the treasure of mine." Heat radiated through her body. Her heartbeat raced so loud, surely he heard it.

Tears glistened at the corner of his eyes as he kept her firmly in his embrace. "I was fearful of having my heart broken anew and ordered myself not to love you."

She wiped away his tears. "And?"

"It didn't work." He cradled her face in his hands. "When we were apart, I realized we'd missed out on love once, and I won't allow it to happen again."

"I can't believe you're here. I'm speechless."

"All I need is a single word." He pulled a small black velvet box from his pocket and handed it to her.

She opened the box, which revealed a sterling Claddagh ring. "When did you—?"

"The ring is your mum's. She's a grand woman."

Keira ran her palm along the gleaming silver. The crown symbolized loyalty, friendship, and the heart represented love. Tenderness pulsed through her. He'd returned, determined to recover the love they'd begun decades earlier.

"Do you like it?" In his eagerness, his features appeared almost boyish.

"Nothing can ever mean more."

"If you don't . . . I'll buy you a new ring, although it's bad luck."

"You don't believe in Irish folklore."

"I'm changing my mind about many beliefs, especially if it ensures your happiness."

His response made her throat ache. Her Colum, ever wanting to please her.

"The ring is perfect," she said.

"Keira Moira Murphy." Colum brushed his lips over her forehead, her cheeks, her mouth. "Will you marry me?"

"I can't wait to be your wife." She looped her fingers around his nape. Her lips parted for his lengthy, loving kiss. "Aye. Aye. Aye."

"Let's plan a New Year's Eve wedding, if you agree."

"New Year's is only a few days from now."

"That'll do."

"Our engagement will last less than a week?"

"Our engagement has survived decades." He glanced at her cottage. "We'll make our home there."

"You'll be living with me?"

"When we're married. Aye. A place next door to our parents is ideal, as we can care for them as they grow older. We have a responsibility to ensure they are secure, protected, and we're providing the help they may require."

"It's more than a responsibility. I consider it a privilege."

"Well stated. Plus, it's convenient whenever your recipes call for a cup of sugar." He winked.

"I don't bake. I sew."

"So we'll dine at Michael D's a lot."

She smiled. "A definite improvement over my cooking."

"I remember you were never much of a cook."

"What else do you remember?"

"I recall you always fired my heart into a tailspin." He tossed her one of his lopsided smiles. "And, I remembered the vacant building in town. I located the owner, and I've secured a lease on the place adjacent to your shop. This little town needs more culture and a community theater is an excellent beginning."

"You mentioned you preferred bigger cities."

He quirked an eyebrow. "Can a man adjust his opinions, or is that a woman's prerogative?"

"Both." She laughed. "Colum O'Brien, you've made me so happy."

"Kiki, I've only just begun."

EPILOGUE

New Year's Eve day brought a brisk breeze and threat of showers. Outside, a huge white tent had been erected near the Irish Sea, and both the ceremony and reception would be held inside. Large propane portable heaters had been set up to take away the bite in the air.

Keira gave a last glance at herself in the mirror at her light-peach lace wedding dress, pleased with her appearance. The ivory netting veil with a feather and tulle flower; accented the feminine, flowing lines. She'd dipped the ends of her hair in a subtle shade of dusty yellow.

At two o'clock, the ceremony opened with the swell of keyboard music, and a hush went through the crowd. The tent glowed with candlelight, perfumed with rich bouquets of shamrock and crimson roses, tied with red satin ribbons. She savored every second, giving a special nod to her two beautiful daughters and her new friends, Patrick and Cora Gervez.

Colum had introduced her to them when they'd arrived from Farthing for the wedding, and they'd immediately invited her and Colum to America—enthusiastically chatting about their colleagues and family in Bloomingfield, California.

"You'll enjoy Julie Rossi's restaurant, The Pasta Junction, because she makes her own homemade pasta every day," Cora had gushed, as she tucked a dark-brown curl behind her ear. "Her husband, Lorenzo, is the local weatherman."

'We work together at the television studio." Patrick's blue eyes gleamed with pride as he beamed down at his wife.

Keira and Colum assured they'd love to see America.

"Perhaps for our honeymoon?" Colum asked her. "January weather in California is mild and has it all—beaches, mountains, and, from what Patrick has described—Bloomingfield Candy Shop—the finest chocolate shop in the world."

"Aye, it sounds grand," she'd replied.

As Keira started down the aisle, she carried a photo in her mind of this day—her true wedding day, exquisite and with the promise of a lifetime of love.

When she approached the altar, she grinned at her mum, her matron of honor, and Colum's father, the best man.

Then her gaze locked with her tall, handsome groom, resplendent in a dove-gray suit and emerald-green tie that matched his eyes.

Colum gazed at her with quiet joy. "Hello, my love," he whispered.

She recalled everything they'd been through, their decades apart. Love had emerged from friendship and taken hold. In harmony, their journey had led them back to exactly where they'd begun, and truly, this was the happiest of New Year's. Welcoming the future and letting go of the past, in the company of her loved ones.

With her hands laced with his, she repeated her wedding vows with him. They commenced the ceremony by reciting a traditional Irish blessing, an ancient Celtic prayer:

"May the road rise up to meet you.

May the wind be always at your back.

May the sun shine warm upon your face; the rains fall soft upon your fields and until we meet again, may God hold you in the palm of His hand."

And then she silently added to herself:

Once upon a time, there was a girl named Kiki, and a guy named Colum.

A fairytale. A happily ever after.

THE END

RECIPE FOR CHERYL'S IRISH SODA BREAD

Ingredients:

2 1/2 cups all-purpose flour

3 tablespoons sugar

2 teaspoons baking powder

1 teaspoon baking soda

1/2 teaspoon salt

1/3 cup cold butter, cut into chunks

1 1/4 cups buttermilk

1/2 cup currants or raisins

Substitute 4 teaspoons vinegar or lemon juice plus enough milk to equal 1 1/4 cups. Let stand 5 minutes.

Preparation:

STEP 1

Heat oven to 375°F. Line baking sheet with parchment paper; set aside.

STEP 2

Combine all ingredients except buttermilk and currants in bowl; cut in butter until mixture resembles coarse crumbs. Stir in buttermilk and currants just until moistened.

STEP 3

Turn dough onto lightly floured surface; knead gently 10 times. Shape into a ball. Place onto the prepared baking sheet. Pat into 6-inch circle. Cut 1/2 inch deep "X" in top of dough with sharp knife.

STEP 4

Bake 30-35 minutes or until golden brown. Serve warm.

A NOTE FROM JOSIE

Dear Reader,

Thank you for reading *A Chocolate-Box Irish Wedding.*

I wanted to write another story loosely connected to the "Chocolate-Box" series, and located the story to Ireland during the holidays and New Year's. I chose Colum, a character from Oh Danny Boy, and also brought two characters from A Chocolate-Box Christmas Wish—Cora and Patrick—to share a winter romance with you.

If you loved this sweet romance as much as I loved writing it, please help other people find *A Chocolate-Box Irish Wedding* by posting your review.

A Chocolate-Box Irish Wedding is available in ebook, paperback, Large Print paperback, audiobook, and Hardcover.

My Spotify Play List for A Chocolate-Box Irish Wedding is here.

With sincere appreciation,
Josie Riviera

Love sweet romance holiday stories?
Be sure to check out my book bundles:
Holiday Hearts Volume One
Holiday Hearts Volume Two
Holiday Hearts Book Bundle Volume Three
Holiday Hearts Book Bundle Volume Four

Love the Chocolate-Box sweet romances?
Be sure to check out the other books in this series:
Click here.

ABOUT THE AUTHOR

Josie Riviera is a *USA TODAY* bestselling author of contemporary, inspirational, and historical sweet romances that read like Hallmark movies. She lives in the Charlotte, NC, area with her wonderfully supportive husband. They share their home with an adorable shih tzu, who constantly needs grooming, and live in an old house forever needing renovations.

To receive my Newsletter and your free sweet romance novella ebook as a thank you gift, sign up <u>HERE.</u>

Become a member of my
Read and Review VIP Facebook
group for exclusive giveaways and FREE ARC's.

josieriviera.com/
josieriviera1@gmail.com

A CHOCOLATE-BOX SUMMER BREEZE
(EXCERPT)

CHAPTER ONE

At seven o'clock on a Thursday evening, Emily Varon sat alone in a corner booth in Olive's Diner. She swallowed some black coffee, pushed the cup aside and checked her watch.

Joe Vertucci was ten minutes late. Odd, because he was always punctual when he phoned her.

Emily bit her bottom lip, drew back the diner's thick tan-colored curtains, and peered out the window at a sultry California evening. The parking lot was empty except for the few cars that belonged to the customers who were dining inside.

She grabbed her cellphone from her leather handbag and read the last words Joe had texted.

After all these months, I'm looking forward to seeing you in person again, Emily.

Her stomach fluttered as she imagined their reunion. She was looking forward to seeing him too and told him as much. He'd responded with a thumbs-up, which had prompted her to smile. She'd attempted to explain different emojis to him, he didn't always have to use a thumbs-up. However, he couldn't seem to get the hang of new technology.

Of course, emoji stickers weren't new, and he'd beamed on their video chat when she'd assured that she'd teach him how to use them.

Their only disagreement had taken place when Joe had insisted on paying for their meal. Eventually, she'd conceded and offered to leave the tip.

He'd concluded their conversation with a quip. "That's why I'm crazy about you, Emily. You don't take advantage of me."

Frequently, he'd referred to himself as a blue-color, working-class guy, and she'd heard a trace of disparagement in his voice, as if he was putting himself down. Although people took pride in referring to themselves in that way, she repeatedly wondered if he genuinely believed in himself.

He should. He was a thoughtful, good-natured man.

Again, her gazed flitted to the window. He could have been delayed by rough weather, or unexpected traffic delays. Hazards on the road occurred in seconds, and driver fatigue often caused serious accidents.

Or, perhaps ... Joe wasn't interested in her after all.

She rubbed her cheek with the back of her hand, attempting to pry herself free from the anxious speculations. She hadn't dated in years, and her nerves wavered as if she were a schoolgirl.

This isn't a date, she reminded herself, nor a naïve teenage crush.

She opened the menu and scanned the dinner selections. The special featured grilled chicken, and a baked potato, which suited her nicely. However, the diner's delicious coconut cake would surely ruin her diet.

It was her proper upbringing, she supposed, that kept her focused on the latest fashion trends. Often, though, she pondered if there was a reason to stay trim anymore. The only people she encountered besides the diners were her son and his family, the weekly grocer, her hair stylist, and Sunday morning churchgoers.

A Moonglow Chocolatiers truck pulled into the lot, and Emily's heart leaped. A short man with silver-white hair emerged from the driver's side. Several patrons whispered Emily's name, like the murmurings of a breeze rushing through a forest. Somehow, they knew Joe was here to see Emily.

"I haven't seen Joe in a long time." Oliver, the owner of the diner, stepped over to her booth. He held a steaming pot of coffee.

Emily jumped. She was so focused on Joe's arrival that she hadn't realized Oliver had approached.

"You're eating dinner later than usual." Oliver grinned and gestured toward the window. "Are you waiting for Joe?"

"Yes." Hastily, she jammed her cellphone into her purse. "He's overnighting near here for a couple days."

Oliver refilled her cup. "How did you know Joe was in the area?"

"Why are you asking?" She sat straighter and adjusted her flawlessly creased white slacks. Through all her months at the diner, she'd kept her personal life private. "Sometimes, people need to eat dinner with someone else, rather than all alone."

At the swift, questioning look he shot her, she grimaced. Her response had a breathless, edgy quality. "Sorry."

"No worries, Emily, and you're one hundred percent right. I shouldn't pry." Oliver patted her hand. "I can't help being an old-fashioned Cupid, and I detect a romance is brewing."

"Hardly." She dismissed any further inquiries Oliver poised on his lips with a wave. "Joe and I regularly talk on the phone."

"Ever since you met him here in my diner?"

"Yes," she acknowledged. For an instant, she closed her eyes and relived that stormy February night.

After panicking because she'd never been in a situation like that before—stranded in a diner—her nerves had settled, and she'd enjoyed several hours conversing with Joe. The narratives about his over-the-road travels had made her laugh. It felt good to laugh, especially after she had visited with her son the previous weekend. He, his wife, and her grandchild had been cordial, but their life was hectic and Emily had felt useless and in the way.

She knew they loved her, but they didn't need her.

"May I call you?" Joe had politely inquired that evening,

after the road had been cleared and the customers could safely leave the diner.

His request had wrung a reluctant chuckle from Emily, but the sight of his incredible smile had done odd quivery things to her pulse.

She'd agreed and wrote her number on a napkin before handing it to him.

Following an exchange of "safe travels", she'd driven back to her large, empty home in town, and hadn't felt quite so lonely.

"I remember you two got along well." Oliver grabbed a cup and paper placemat from an adjacent table and set them across from Emily. "You never mentioned that your relationship with Joe had blossomed. You eat dinner here nightly."

"Your food is delicious."

"Thanks. I might use your testimonial as advertising." He paused. "However, you're not answering."

"Is this a question or a statement?"

"Both, considering I'm an old-fashioned Cupid," he reminded.

"Joe and I are too timeworn for a romantic relationship." She tasted the coffee, which was always perfect, then dabbed her lips with a napkin. "Even though I gave him my phone number, I didn't expect him to call me."

"Why not? You're an attractive, classy lady."

She shook her head. She wasn't. She'd continually considered herself plump and the opposite of model-thin, but she wasn't about to introduce a lengthy psychological discussion. Plus, she'd been obsessed with tanning salons, believing a tan made her look younger. However, she'd finally recognized that tanning aged her, and had given that up after she'd met Joe.

One didn't need any more wrinkles at her age.

*** End of Excerpt *A Chocolate-Box Summer Breeze* by Josie Riviera ***

Continue reading on Amazon.

FREE on Kindle Unlimited!

ALSO BY JOSIE RIVIERA

Seeking Patience

Seeking Catherine (always Free!)

Seeking Fortune

Seeking Charity

Seeking Rachel

The Seeking Series

Oh Danny Boy

I Love You More

A Snowy White Christmas

A Portuguese Christmas

Holiday Hearts Book Bundle Volume One

Holiday Hearts Book Bundle Volume Two

Holiday Hearts Book Bundle Volume Three

Holiday Hearts Book Bundle Volume Four

Candleglow and Mistletoe

Maeve (Perfect Match)

A Love Song To Cherish

A Christmas To Cherish

A Valentine To Cherish

A Christmas Puppy To Cherish

A Homecoming To Cherish

A Summer To Cherish

Romance Stories To Cherish

Romance Stories To Cherish Volume Two

Cherished Hearts Six Book Volume

Aloha To Love

Sweet Peppermint Kisses

Valentine Hearts Boxed Set

1-800-CUPID

1-800-CHRISTMAS

1-800-IRELAND

1-800-SUMMER

1-800-NEW YEAR

The 1-800-Series Sweet Contemporary Romance Bundle

Irish Hearts Sweet Romance Bundle

Holly's Gift

A Chocolate-Box Christmas

A Chocolate-Box New Years

A Chocolate-Box Valentine

A Chocolate-Box Summer Breeze

A Chocolate-Box Christmas Wish

A Chocolate-Box Irish Wedding

Chocolate-Box Hearts

Chocolate-Box Hearts Volume Two

Chocolate-Box Double Hearts

Recipes From The Heart

Leading Hearts

New Year Hearts

SENIOR HEARTS

Summer Hearts

Christmas in the Air (1-800-Book)

A Very Christian Christmas

The 1-800-Series Volume Two

The 1-800-Series Complete

Christmas Tails of the Heart

Most books are available in ebook, audiobook, paperback, Large Print paperback and Hardcover.

Many are FREE on Kindle Unlimited!